**Praise for the Retrievers novels of**

# laura anne gilman

*DISCARD*

### Staying Dead

"An entertaining, fast-paced thriller set in a world where cell phones and computers exist uneasily with magic and a couple of engaging and highly talented rogues solve crimes while trying not to commit too many of their own."
—*Locus*

"An exciting…unpredictable story that never lets up until the very end…I highly recommend this book to fans of urban fantasy, especially [the works of] Jim Butcher, Charlaine Harris, Kim Harrison or Laurell K. Hamilton."
—*SF Site*

### Curse the Dark

"Gilman has managed the nearly impossible here: a cleverly written and well-balanced fantasy with a strong romantic element that doesn't overpower the main plot."
—*Romantic Times BOOKreviews* [4½ stars]

"With an atmosphere reminiscent of Dan Brown's *The Da Vinci Code* and Umberto Eco's *The Name of the Rose* by way of Sam Spade, Gilman's second Wren Valere adventure…features fast-paced action, wisecracking dialog and a pair of strong, appealing heroes."
—*Library Journal*

### Bring It On

"Fans of Charlaine Harris, Kelley Armstrong and Kim Harrison will find *Bring It On* a very special treat. The author is an expert worldbuilder and creates characters that are easy to care about."
—*Affaire de Coeur* [5 stars]

# curse the dark

## laura anne gilman

LUNA™
www.LUNA-Books.com

LUNA™

Recycling programs
for this product may
not exist in your area.

CURSE THE DARK

ISBN-13: 978-0-373-80295-1
ISBN-10:      0-373-80295-1

Copyright © 2005 by Laura Anne Gilman

First mass market printing: March 2009

First trade printing: July 2005

Author photo copyright © by Peter R. Liverakos

www.LUNA-Books.com

**Printed in U.S.A.**

Dear Reader,

Welcome, or welcome back, to the world of the *Cosa Nostradamus,* where the person walking next to you on the sidewalk may not be…entirely human, and magic not only didn't fade away in the modern age, it got *stronger.*

In *Curse the Dark,* a lot changes for Wren and Sergei as they take on a job for the mysterious—but well-paying—Silence. Decisions are made, surprises are sprung and consequences are dealt out, both tragic and joyful. Life isn't always easy, it's rarely ever fair. But when Wren's around, you know it's always going to be an adventure!

And don't miss Wren's other adventures in *Staying Dead, Bring It On, Burning Bridges* and *Free Fall,* available now, and *Blood from Stone,* coming in May 2009.

Enjoy!

Laura Anne Gilman

For Amy and Sue.
Even if they did want to trade me in for a puppy.

## Acknowledgments

The past year was probably the toughest ever
in my life, and a number of people were
much-needed, much-appreciated lifelines.

Keith R. A. DeCandido
Jenn Saint-John
James A. Hartley
Lesley McBain
Lisa Sullivan
Jennifer Jackson
Susan Shwartz
Peter Liverakos
Howard Shaw

And in the memory of Kath Lawrence,
who reminded me to take those lifelines
and hold on tight.

# curse the
# dark

Secure yourself to heaven.
Hold on tight, the night has come.
Fasten up your earthly burdens,
You have just begun.
— Indigo Girls, "Secure Yourself"

# Chapter One

"Next time," Sergei muttered out of the corner of his mouth, not taking his eyes off the security guard leaning against a wall several paces ahead of them, "we're taking a boat."

"Sorry, okay?" Wren said, doing her best not to snap at him. "I'm trying. I really am." And she was. It just wasn't helping.

Her partner's deep sigh was the only response she got. They'd had variations of this conversation ever since she threw her bag into the cab outside her apartment that morning, and things had only slid downhill since getting to the airport. If they could have gotten through all this quickly, and not given her so much time to think about it… But, well, that wasn't going to happen. And the weird feeling of being stared at, even though there wasn't anyone paying any attention to her, was just making things worse.

The line shuffled in place, people shifting bags and checking watches. Sergei took a small case out of his suit coat pocket, opened it and removed a slender brown cigarette, then put the case away. He rolled the cigarette between his thumb and forefinger, then started rotating it end to end, as though practicing for a coin trick he already knew how to do.

Another person made it through the metal detector and escaped into the depths of the airport. There was only one line feeding along roped-off lanes into seven different metal detectors, three of which were currently out of service, with technicians standing around them looking puzzled and not a little annoyed. One of the techs did something to a touch pad, and shrugged helplessly.

*I hate airports,* Wren thought. As though overhearing her thought, Sergei flicked a glance sideways at her, one dark brown eyebrow raised in inquiry over paler brown eyes. After ten years of working together, he didn't have to say anything; the message came through loud and clear. *Get it done.*

"Right." It wasn't that he wasn't sympathetic. He was. She knew that. But it was her problem and she was the one who had to deal with it. And sympathy didn't actually help. Adjusting her sweaty grip on her brand-new carry-on (finest you could buy on sale on two days' notice), Wren closed her eyes and refocused her attention inward, to where the tendrils of current coiled and flickered within her like snakes in a pit.

She wasn't a good flyer even under the best of circumstances. No, call a spade a spade and admit that she was a *terrible* flyer. She avoided traveling by air whenever possible. Sometimes, though, it wasn't possible. Sometimes, you just had to suck up the phobia and get on with it.

Unfortunately, the only thing worse than a phobic Talent under stress was a phobic Talent under stress near a lot of electronics. Such as, oh, the one found when going through departure security at a major airport just outside of New York City.

*We shouldn't be here. We shouldn't have taken this job. Don't think about it, Valere. Focus. Stay calm. Or everything's going to get ugly.*

"The usual mess," a man behind her grumbled to his companion. "And what do you want to bet once we get on the plane we'll be stuck on the tarmac for another hour anyway?"

Oh, God. So much for calm and serenity. Just the thought of that was enough to make her nerves—and the current inside her—roil. The "snakes" hissed sparks of current, seething in her own agitation. *Damn, damn and—*

There was another *snap-ping!* noise, and the lights on one of the still-working metal detectors went out, then came back on. The security guard swore under his breath and said something into his walkie-talkie. The seven people in front of Wren and Sergei on the security check line groaned. Wren felt a twinge of helpless guilt, opening her eyes and looking at the chaos she was, however unwillingly, creating. Admittedly, one of the machines had been out of commission by the time they got on line. She was pretty sure she wasn't to blame for that one. But the other two had died in a rather spectacular array of sparks not thirty seconds after they arrived. That was in addition to the meter of the cab that dropped them off, the check-in desk computer that decided to crash in the middle of confirming their seats, and the cell phone of the guy next to them on the escalator.

All those old stories about magic being wiped out by technology so had it wrong. Magic didn't hate tech. It *loved* it. So much so that a Talent instinctively wanted to reach out and drag all the lovely bits of power floating through the wires and tubes and chips of modern society into his or herself. Especially if she was, even subconsciously, preparing for a worst-case scenario in which she might need all the power she could grab.

Sergei had suggested a sedative when she started to hyperventilate in traffic this morning, but Wren was terrified of what she might do if she were *too* relaxed when the inevitable panic hit.

"Last time I got stuck in security I missed my connection and had to wait three hours for another flight," Wren heard the woman ahead of them say to her companion, more resigned than annoyed.

*Oh, God.* A muffled whimper escaped her, and sparks danced on the backs of her hands until she shoved them into the pocket of her pale blue linen jacket, bought new for this trip and already stained under the arms with sweat. "I hate airports," Wren muttered. "They're full of *planes.*" She could hear the panic in her voice and hated herself for it.

"Hang in there." Sergei shoved the cigarette back into its case and shuffled in line, moving bags and his laptop case until he stood just behind her, a little closer than the crush of people demanded. At six-two he was almost a foot taller than she, and broad-shouldered into the bargain, creating a comfortable barrier at her back. The defense might have been mostly psychological, but it worked. She welcomed the closeness, breathing deeply of the scent of warm spice and musk that was so perfectly and only her partner. She could almost ground herself into it the way she would into rock or soil; emotionally, anyway, if not magically. Not that she thought she was going to do anything stupid, but…

Well, they called them phobias because they were irrational, after all.

"I'm here, *Zhenchenka*," he said. "I'm here, and everything's okay. Just focus. Keep it under control…" It was equal amounts order and a gentle reminder. Sergei might have finally given up that "senior partner" thing he'd been carrying for the past decade, but old habits died hard.

Fortunately, this was one directive she was willing to follow.

She took a deep breath, released it, nodded, and then closed her eyes again, shutting out everything around her: the white noise of the busy airport, the palpable irritation of the people around her, the smell of her own nervous sweat. Last to go was her physical awareness of Sergei, standing guard over her. Narrowing down further, shutting the mental chute until all that existed was her awareness of her own awareness, and the enticing, invigorating current. Black silk covered with static electricity, jumbled fireworks of a thousand colors. It was beautiful, and tempting, and only with a severe force of will did she keep herself from falling into those fireworks, narrowing even further until all that existed was the current within herself, the natural core that was inside every human Talent.

She had described it to Sergei once as being dropped into a tank of virtual snakes, sinuous electric beasts, bright blue and red and orange and green and silver, like some cyberpunk wet dream. The core of what she was, what she could do. You couldn't ever show fear as they curled around you, hissing in a reflection of her own unreasonable panic about flying, because if you ever lost control current would destroy you.

Dangerous. At the same time, they were beautiful. And *hers.* She moved closer, soothing the snakes, gathering them in. There was no fear, no loss of control. They were part of her, and would do as she willed them, damn it—

"Miss?"

Wren started as someone touched her shoulder. She could sense Sergei swinging into action even as she gasped, putting his well-tailored bulk between her and the intruder.

Wren wasn't used to being noticed—she normally cultivated her slight, innocuous appearance into invisibility. She must be screaming tension in her body language. Not good. The last thing she needed was attention from security making her even more nervous.

"Yes?" she said, moving around her overprotective partner and shoving the current-snakes down even more firmly. *Everyone stay cool,* she thought, not sure if it was directed at herself, the current, or Sergei. Or all of the above.

The guard took a hard look at her, glanced at the passport held out to him and then reached out one hand, palm up and fingers flat, as though calming a nervous horse. His hand was covered with fine lines, a webbing of creases run amok, and there was a callus on the pad of his index finger. Wren thought that someone who read palms could have a blast with him. "Are you all right, Ms. Valere?"

Sergei started to answer him, but Wren shook her head at him in warning. *Let me handle this.* "Yes, thank you."

She shifted her carry-on, and took Sergei's hand in her own. The cool, firm skin of his hand was like a lifeline, and she squeezed it once, gently, feeling him return the pressure. *It's okay,* that squeeze said.

Rather than restraining the current any further, Wren focused it instead, turning her full attention to the guard. Seeing the suspiciously twitchy passenger relax under his gaze, the guard—a baby-faced blonde in his mid-twenties, if that, probably just out of training on how to use the gun in his holster—began to relax. His watery blue eyes were kind, at odds with the weary boredom on his face. *You're feeling sorry for me,* she thought, her brain taking on an intensely dreamy but sharp-edged feel of a working fugue stage. *You think I look terrified of flying—true—and it's a shame I have to be put through all of this.*

The "Push" was one of her strongest gifts. It was also the one she hated to use the most, for purely embarrassingly moral reasons—more than any other skill, it had the potential to be abused. The problem was, it was so damn useful. Coupled with her ordinary looks and slight frame, it was enough to get her into the most closely guarded places without being seen. But sometimes you wanted to draw someone's attention to you, not away…and once you had it, you could move it to other places…other thoughts. And they would never know, if you were careful, how they had been coerced. *Get me through this… get me past these machines so I don't have a screaming fit and set off every single security measure you have….*

"Bad flyer, huh?" the guard asked conversationally.

"Bad doesn't even begin to cover it," Wren admitted, squelching her self-disgust into a tight box and locking the lid. Her mother would have a fit if she knew how badly her only daughter was messing with some poor guy's mind. But when needs must, as her own mother forever said—if about other, way more ordinary things— you did what you had to do….

Sergei Didier watched his partner wind the security guard around her little finger, and stifled a smile of relief. With luck, having something to focus on other than her fear of flying would keep anything…dramatic from happening. He'd been intentionally not thinking of all the ways a panicked Talent could create chaos in an airport, especially one as tightly wound as Newark, as though that blankness in his mind would prevent anything from happening. Talismanic magic, the ancient kind Wren scoffed at.

His feeling was, don't knock anything that might work.

He glanced at the decadently expensive and self-indulgent wind-up gold watch on his wrist and made a bet with himself that it would take her less than three minutes to "push" the guard into hand-walking them through security. There was much less risk in her being wanded off to the side than walking through one of their damned machines, in the state she was in. If she managed that, it would be the first thing that had gone right since they'd taken this damned job.

No, scratch that. The first thing to go right since May. Since that damned Frants case, since that damned Council—since *everything* had changed.

He rested his gaze on his Wren, currently being ushered out of the line by the solicitous guard, and smiled again. Not that everything that had happened in May was so bad.

She looked back, making sure that he was okay with her being taken out, alone, and he made a small go-ahead gesture. It wasn't as though they were joined at the hip. She'd catch up with him on the other side of the security gate. Once she was out of the way, things were bound to go more smoothly.

Picking up his bag, Sergei shuffled forward with the rest of the line to fill the space Wren had left. Yes, things would go more smoothly without her there. But he missed her presence already.

Since May…although he wondered again how much

had actually changed, and how much was just finally being dragged out into the light of day.

*Two days earlier…*

"Why the hell don't you get an air conditioner?"

Wren looked at her partner as though that was the stupidest thing she had ever heard. He flushed slightly, the color rising over his damnably fine cheekbones, although that might have been the heat. It was seven o'clock in the evening, and the temperature was still hovering in the low nineties. Summer in Manhattan. God, how Wren hated it.

They were sitting on the hardwood floor of the largest room in her apartment, not that large meant much in the city. The space was empty save for the stereo system against one wall and an overstuffed armchair at the perfect midway point between speakers. All the windows in the apartment were open, on the off-chance of catching a breeze to supplement the low-tech floor fans that were pretty much just redistributing the warm air. But at least they were low-risk, compared to running an air conditioner. She wasn't going to be the Talent who shorted out the entire city because she couldn't stand a little heat.

She could, she supposed, have drawn the oppressive heat off her body magically. But even thinking about it made her exhausted. Actually doing something was beyond her ability right now.

Sergei, who didn't have that option, looked as exhausted as she felt. Still dressed in the grey summer-weight wool slacks and long-sleeved cotton shirt he had worn during the day, he was sprawled on his back, a clear plastic cup on the floor near his hand, the dregs of a squeezed lemon and the last drops of iced tea at the bottom of the cup. His collar was undone, and his sleeves had been unbuttoned and then left, as though it were too much effort to roll up the cuffs. He wouldn't be caught dead in anything more casual, not when he needed to be "Sergei Didier, owner and proprietor of Didier Gallery, home of overpriced artwork," anyway. Sergei, her partner in we-don't-call-it-crime, it's-Retrieval-thank-you-muchly, could dress down as needed. Although she could probably count on two hands the number of times she'd seen him in jeans. Pity, that. For thirty-nine-ish, her partner's ass was worthy of well-fitting jeans. Not that slacks weren't a good look on him, too….

She shook her mind away from those thoughts with an effort, aware he was waiting for a response.

"You could have gone back to your own place, you know," she said. He had central air. And tile flooring, which was much nicer to lie on when it was really hot outside. Not that she'd done that…more than once or twice. Two weeks of ninety-degree-plus temperatures. It wasn't fair.

"God." He shuddered like a tired horse as though he'd been following along with her thoughts. "The idea of getting on the subway tonight…" His voice was a low growl, unlike his usual precise newscaster enunciation. "Too many sweaty people, all unhappy. If we all weren't so tired the murder rate would be skyrocketing. Besides, we need to talk, and you've been avoiding me."

"Have not." She had been, of course. And lying to her partner was supposed to be reserved for times of real need, not just because she was a candy-coated wuss.

She'd been avoiding everything, lately. Not good. Trust him to call her on it.

"Genevieve…" Another growl. God, as much as she hated her given name, she loved the sound of him saying it. It made her feel like her spine was melting. Even when he was scolding her, the way he was now.

"No calls, huh?" Stupid question. If there had been, he would have told her.

"None," he confirmed anyway. "And it's starting to show."

She knew that. It just all added to the avoidance factor. Bad enough to be in this miserable heat wave. Adding a dry spell to it was the proverbial insult to injury. She hadn't gotten a single job since June. Three months, and Sergei hadn't fielded a single solitary badly-paying inquiry.

She might be the best Retriever in the business, but being the best didn't mean anything if you weren't getting the jobs.

"Everyone scrams from the city in August," she offered, fanning herself halfheartedly with a paper fan made out of a folded take-out menu. Someone told her once that the action used more energy than it cooled her down, but Wren didn't care. It *felt* good.

"Wren." He sighed, rolling over on his side to look at her. "Face it. You know what's going on."

Unable to meet his steady brown gaze any longer, Wren stared instead at the can of Diet Sprite waiting by her feet. The polish on her big toe was starting to flake off, and she rubbed at it idly with her free hand, thinking that she was long overdue for a pedicure. Knowing didn't mean wanting to admit. Because admitting would mean also admitting that maybe she'd really messed things up.

And worse, that she'd messed up by doing the right thing. A simple job—Retrieve a stolen chunk of concrete, spell intact, and return it to the rightful owner—that turned out to have politics and underhanded dealings and paybacks written all over it. And a ghost with trouble staying dead. And murder. Never forget the murder part of it.

A fifty-year-old murder she had tried to avenge. She might even have succeeded, although it probably would be a few more decades before she'd know for sure.

Along the way, she had also managed to piss off the Mage Council, the self-proclaimed hall monitors of the Talent world, by letting it be known the part they had played in that murder. Not that they had anything against snuffing out a life or two, especially if the victim was a Null, a nonmagic user. But they hadn't exactly played by their own rules, and that was supposed to be a no-no.

That disclosure had led them to the dilemma under discussion. At least partially—mostly—because of that job, the Mage Council had put Wren on their Most Annoying list.

Well, big whoop, she had thought at the time. The Council and lonejacks, the unaffiliated Talents, had been sparring for generations. As a lonejack, Wren always figured she came under the general Council evaluation of "shiftless, undisciplined, and not worthy to polish our expensive shoes." Apparently not. Instead, they were looking closely at her. Way too closely. And plotting… something. Wren didn't see what it was about her specifically that made the Council so particularly nervous. But whatever it was, it did. And a nervous Council was a nasty Council.

"They've started a whisper campaign," she said finally, reluctantly. "Tree-taller—Lee—told me when he and Miriam stopped by for drinks last week." The lonejack artist and his wife had made a point since all this started of dropping in regularly, as much a "bite me" to the Council as anything else. Although the fact that Miriam, like Sergei, was a Null, a non-Talent, and maybe—Wren bit that thought back before it could go anywhere. Now was not the time to be worrying at what anyone else thought of her romantic relationship (or present lack thereof) with her partner. Another thing she was avoiding.

"The Council, that is. Whisper something in one ear, whisper something else in another. Nothing obvious, nothing anyone can pinpoint, but—"

"And you're just now getting around to telling me this?" Sergei was pissed. You could tell by the way his face went totally stone, except that little twitch at the corner of his left eye.

Well, yes. Because, as he pointed out, she had been avoiding him. For any number of really uncomfortable reasons. "I was hoping…I don't know. That maybe Lee was overstating the case? That it wouldn't work? That the weather would break and we could have this discussion without it disintegrating into a snit-fight?"

"I don't take snits."

Sergei sounded wounded, and even under these conditions she had to grin. "Partner, you are the King of Snits. And it's too damn hot to deal with that, okay?"

Ten years of working together allowed her to interpret the heavy sigh that came out of him this time. He was letting it go. "You still should have told me."

"I'm telling you now. And it's not like you could have done anything, anyway. My rep's too good for them to actually say I'm incompetent, or anything. Whatever they say, it's harmless until you actually try to counter it." She hoped. "But if you do protest, then people start to wonder if there's something to make you deny it…. Only I guess they're saying more than that, if the jobs are drying up that fast." She hadn't honestly expected it to get this bad this quick. Which was why she wasn't supposed to be handling the business end of things. Sergei was.

"Probably not saying much at all, actually. Just enough to make people wonder if maybe hiring this particular lonejack is such a good idea after all," he said now. "Especially if they're not anxious to get any scent of publicity about their situation." Which was pretty much the point of hiring a Retriever rather than one of the more traditional and legal forms of getting back missing property. A thief who used magic to get the job done was a thief much less likely to come under official attention, at least in the Null world, and was the only type of thief you'd want to consider if the situation had even a whiff of magic about it. The fact that Wren, rather than depending solely on her Talent, combined it and general more everyday illegal Talents to perform her jobs, made her able to move effectively against any kind of surveillance or countermeasures, and made her very popular for "normal" world jobs as well.

She was good, she was smart, and she had been very, very lucky. Until now.

"Yeah. I'm guessing that's the plan." She frowned at the thought, and twirled the end of her shoulder-length braid between two fingers as she thought. "Most of the *Cosa*—" *the Cosa Nostradamus*, the magical community made up of human Talents and the nonhuman fatae "—knows it's bullshit. At least from what Lee says. But they're going to lay low anyway, until whatever's going on is gone."

"The *Cosa* are not the ones who usually hire us," her partner said. He was the one who handled the offers, so he knew that for a fact. A lot of their commissions came from Nulls, those who had no ability to work current, the stuff of modern magic. Most, in fact, knew nothing about *how* the Retriever known as The Wren did her work, only that she was the best available for the job.

Whatever the job might be. Hell, most of them thought that *Sergei* was The Wren. Which was how both Wren and Sergei liked it.

But the Council had its hooks set in flesh outside the *Cosa* as well, and was proving they had no hesitation about using that influence. And they knew damn well who she was.

Wren put down the fan and finished off what was left of her now warm, now flat soda. "At least they're not trying to kill me anymore," she said, trying for cheerful.

Sergei only grunted, shaking the plastic glass as though more iced tea would suddenly appear in it. "I'd almost rather they were."

Wren slanted a dirty look at him, but didn't ask him to elaborate on that comment.

"No," he went on, oblivious, "you were right. Any overt move by the Council would only set the lonejacks even more in opposition, and maybe even force a direct revolt against perceived Council interference. They don't want that.

"But they don't want you in any position to be a focal point of unrest, either. Shutting you down reduces your influence, and sends a message to the rest of the lonejack community as well. Time-honored tactics."

"Jesus wept. The Council being subtle. Now *that's* scary." She scraped up the few tendrils of coca-brown hair that were plastered against her neck and tried without much hope of success to shove them back into her braid. "They don't need to shut me down! I don't *want* to be a focal point! Why does everyone think I want

to be any kind of leader?" The whole point of being unaffiliated, a lonejack, was to not have to worry about anyone but yourself. And your partner, yeah.

Sergei shifted with another grunt, the back of his shirt
plastered to him with sweat. "It's not what you want
that matters to them, Wren. It's the perception. You've
told them to take a leap before."

Wren winced at the reminder of a more youthful and
astonishingly stupid incident in her life. That was the
problem with working with someone for so long, especially if they had a good memory.

Her partner, he of the most excellent memory, was
relentless in ticking off more reasons. "You hang out
with lonejacks and Nulls and fatae equally, which we
already knew made them nervous. Especially the fatae."
Nonhumans, the fantasticals. "And then, adding injury
to insult, you—we—faced them down over the Frants
deal this spring. And won. People know that. Gossip
spreads. And that's what they're afraid of."

Wren looked at him through narrowed eyes. He could
be such a plainspoken bastard sometimes, for all that he
made his living making nice in order to close the deal.
Although his suit jacket had been dropped on the back
of a kitchen chair with no regard for how much it had
cost, and the well-polished oxblood loafers had been
kicked off the moment he got inside the apartment, he
still looked far too trendy-normal to be lying on the
floor of an East Village apartment trying to figure the politics of a world most of humanity had no clue existed.

You could see him easily in the center of his art gallery.

Or going nose-to-nose with the Council in a war of words, like he did during the Frants job. Not so easy to recognize the guy who pulled a gun to get her out of a job gone bad, last winter. But they were both in there. Plus the guy who held her when she was too sore and scared to move, while she slept, but refused to do her laundry.

Wren gave up on trying to catch any sort of breeze sitting up and lay facedown on the floor, spreading her body so as to get the maximum amount of coolness from the hardwood. She turned her face so that she could look at her partner but still feel the wood under her cheek, and whimpered pitifully, her feelings about the heat, the Council, and her current lack of available funds all rolled into one convenient sound.

He smiled at that, his narrow, expressive lips begging for her hand to reach up and touch them. Even now, she was always astonished that the skin there was so soft.

"Things're bad, huh?" she said instead, curling her fingers in against her palm to keep them still.

He sighed again. "Not so bad, but not good, either. You have cash in the retirement fund, of course—" she actually had an IRA, plus a separate savings account from which to buy the apartment when and if it went co-op, being a practical bird "—but in the short term it's probably going to get a little tight, unless you've been saving even more than you've told me."

"Not much more, no. Rent to pay. Groceries to buy. P.B. to feed."

"You should make that little fur-covered mutant get a job." But despite Sergei's long-standing xenophobia, it was said without heat. The two of them, demon and human, had come to some sort of…she hesitated to call it an agreement, but a cease-fire, since she was injured by a sniper's bullet during the Frants situation. Through his own choice or Sergei's suggestion, the demon had become Wren's semiconstant companion, not leaving her side until he judged her able to defend herself physically again. Sweet. And totally unexpected. She had spotted him more than once since then, out of the corner of her eye, lurking within running-to-help distance. It was tough to miss a four-foot-tall white-furred, white-fanged, red-eyed demon, after all. Despite the fact that three quarters of the city managed it on a regular basis.

*The fatae, the nonhumans, the magical ones, are always with us,* she could hear her mentor saying, years now in the past. *But it takes looking with an open mind as well as open eyes. Most people don't bother.*

"Their loss," she said quietly. "Their loss."

"What?"

She looked at her partner and gave in to the impulse, running one finger along his lower lip until he nipped at the offending fingertip, then propped himself up on one elbow and heaved himself to his feet, surprisingly agile for a man his size.

"You hungry?" he asked, his body language pretty clearly moving them on from that moment of physical contact like metal shutters coming down. "I could go for some Thai tonight."

*Story of our lives,* she thought as she reached up one arm and let him help her up off the floor. *Give us busi-*

*ness, give us danger and mayhem, and we're good to go. Personal stuff…not so good. Hence, avoidance.*

It had been four months since the combination of a seriously crazy ghost, a Council sniper, and the opening of Sergei's Deep Dark Secrets Closet had forced them to admit that there was more to their partnership than, well, partnership. And here they were, still at the hand-holding and awkward kissing stages. Not that Wren particularly wanted to go leaping into bed…well, okay, there were days when that was *all* she wanted. But this geeky awkwardness was so…embarrassing. They could talk about everything and anything else. Why was this so different?

"Y'know," she said, suddenly unable to face another night of pretending everything was okay, that they were intentionally taking things slow and casual. "I'm really not hungry. You go on. I think I'm just going to make it an early night."

She pretended not to see the disappointed expression on his face, reaching up to give him a quick kiss at the door. But her hands found themselves threading into his hair almost without meaning to, and the quick kiss turned into something a little longer than that. God, his lips were soft. And warm. And the way he nipped at her mouth, just like that…

But just when she was starting to reconsider the whole "sending him away" thing, Sergei dropped his hands from her shoulder and was out the door before she could react.

"Damn," she said, leaning her back against the closed and locked door. "And, well, damn." And she really didn't understand why she was crying. Maybe it was the heat finally getting to her.

"I need to get away," she said to herself. "Away from the city. Away from Sergei. Away from this damned heat, and my own damned brain."

In short, she needed a job.

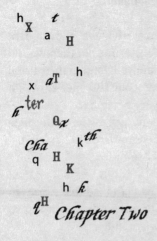

*Chapter Two*

Wren wasn't sure how long she had been leaning against the door staring blankly down her apartment's short hallway like the answer to her problems was going to appear in front of her. Might have been five minutes, might have been fifteen. So when she heard the heavy footsteps coming up the stairwell outside, she thought that maybe Sergei had changed his mind, turned around outside and come back. But that mixed hope/fear died quickly. That wasn't her partner's tread. And the usual weird but familiar desire to brew a mug of tea that always preceded his arrival was missing, although it might have gotten confused, since he had just been there.

The footsteps stopped on her tiny landing, which made sense since the next-floor apartment was currently vacant, the nudist with the craving for curry having moved out last month. Whoever this was hadn't had to ring to be let in, which could mean it was a fellow tenant from the lower floors—unlikely, as most of them would have leaned out the window and yelled up in their usual way of communicating—or someone had once again left the front door ajar for a delivery person.

"So glad we paid all that money to have the new security intercom put in," Wren muttered to herself just as the rarely used door buzzer sounded.

"Oh, now you'll ring, huh?" Still, it was hotter than hell out there, and someone had climbed five stories to ring her doorbell. If it was a burglar or wannabe rapist, the heat alone would take care of him.

"Ms. Valere? Are you there?"

Wren closed her eyes and leaned more heavily against the hollow metal security door; excellent for keeping fires out, not so good with the soundproofing. She would rather have dealt with a burglar.

The bell rang again.

Avoidance. Not a good thing. Even when it seemed like a really good thing. Besides, if she knew anything about her visitor, it was that he wasn't going to just go away. He'd stand out there all night if he had to. Politely. Apologetically. But he'd be there.

"Right." She swung around and started undoing the locks she had just done up in Sergei's wake.

"Andre. So *not* a pleasure to see you again."

Andre Felhim. Serpent in an Armani suit. Handler— middle management spymaster, according to Sergei—for the Silence, an organization that was prime offender in her partner's Deep Dark Secrets Closet. Fanatic do-gooders with boatloads of money and very specific ideas of who defined what was good and who got helped. The organization that had grudgingly offered salvation when the Council tried to take her down in various lethal ways—but only after Sergei negotiated out some of the nastier bits of their contract.

The organization whose monthly retainer fee was all that presently stood between her and total unemployment. Right. Damn. The fiscally responsible part of her brain kicked in and opened her mouth for a second take.

"Andre. Such a pleasure. Why don't you come in?"

His grin at the second greeting, said in the same tone as the first, was appreciatively sardonic, and for a moment Wren could believe that this dapper, oh-so-controlled figure was the man who had allegedly trained her partner in all ways sneaky and manipulative.

Not that Sergei ever tried to manipulate her. Much. Consciously. Anymore.

Andre walked across the doorway, and Wren, channeling her mother for a terrifying moment, panicked. The thing about her apartment was that there was nowhere to invite someone in to sit for polite conversation. She just didn't have that kind of a life.

*Kitchen,* she decided, escorting her guest into the small room. There were seats here, and a table she could lean on, to put between them. At least he hadn't brought his junior associate, whatsisname, Jorgunsomethingorother, along this time. So they could skip the physical threats portion of the discussion. Probably.

"You just missed Sergei." She barely paused before going on, "I'm thinking that's intentional?"

Andre settled himself into one of her battered kitchen chairs, not reacting at all to her comment, as far as she could tell. Instead, he put his best avuncular expression on and said "It's time for you to earn that retainer we pay you."

He might have preferred subtle and sneaky and all those other serpent words, but he'd learned that polite chitchat wasn't her thing when they had met during her last job. Which also happened to be when everything in her life started to go to hell. Coincidence? She thought probably not.

"We have an assignment that suits your skills," he went on, "and—"

Or maybe he hadn't quite learned. Once a serpent… "And nothing." Wren really didn't feel up to playing games. It was too damn hot, and she was too frustrated. Professionally *and* sexually, thank you very much.

"You know the deal. Sergei handles the arrangements, I do the job. Talk to him about the details. You're no different than any other client."

"We're rather different," Andre corrected her. "And at the moment, you have no other clients, if I'm not mistaken."

*Smarmy bastard.* But he was right, no matter how he'd gotten the information; they couldn't afford to piss the Silence off. Not yet, anyway. Sergei could loan her cash, sure, but it wasn't like his art gallery did more than pay for the lifestyle he had to maintain in order to keep the gallery making money. And be damned if she was going to dip into her retirement fund. That was for *then*. She had to worry about the now, now.

Damn it, she hated not having options. A good lonejack *always* had options. Always had an escape route. Never had to take a job that smelled of brimstone, either literally or figuratively, if they didn't want to.

*Damn it, Sergei, where are you?*

"All right. Talk. But whatever you say is going directly to Sergei and he'll get back in touch with you with our terms. You got both of us in this deal, remember?"

That was a directed dig. They had really only wanted her; whatever relationship they'd had with him ten years ago, now Sergei was merely the means to an end, the former troublesome employee who led them to the new employee. Yeah, well. Not even the Silence got exactly what they wanted all the time.

Whatever else the Didier-Valere relationship might or might not be morphing into, they were partners, first, last and always.

"We have a situation that needs…a particular touch."

God, she so hated dealing with negotiations. *Sergei, damn it, why'd you have to go and run off just 'cause I told you to?* "Something's gone missing, you need it retrieved. I get that. What's the deal?"

Andre looked nonplused for about a millisecond, then buried it down under the veneer of smooth he always wore. "A manuscript. Circa tenth century. Italian. Handwritten, one sheet of vellum, quite valuable. It has disappeared, and we require it returned. A simple enough job."

Wren snorted. *Old manuscripts. Riiiight. Give me a*

*fricking break*. Anything that old, handwritten, and gone missing equated Big Trouble. Especially if they had to hire a Talent to retrieve it. What, they thought she was stupid? Probably.

She turned her back on Andre, filling the teakettle and putting it on the stovetop, then reaching into the cabinet for a pair of mugs, the nice matched set her mother had bought her at Crate & Barrel last summer, in despair at the mismatched assortment of mugs that Wren normally used.

"And?" she asked, turning back to him, arms crossed in front of her.

"And?" Andre parroted, one eyebrow raised politely.

"Stop yanking my chain, it's getting old. And what's the story? Who stole it, why, what's the time frame…. Come on, pal. I may be Talented but I'm not godlike. I need information to work on. Who, where, why, and how fast, to start." She smiled at him, making sure to show all her small, even, very white, teeth.

Sergei Didier prided himself on his business acumen. His negotiation skills. An ability to read the client. And the physical conditioning that allowed his six-foot-plus frame to jog up five flights in a dimly lit stairwell in truly disgusting heat without passing out.

He had intended to go home. To his nice, cool, air-conditioned-without-fear-of-magically-shorting-out-because-Wren-got-careless apartment. Where he fully intended to make himself a brutal martini and take a cold shower. Probably, although not necessarily, in that order.

That was before the hairs on the back of his neck prickled in a way that had nothing to do with the sweat running under his collar and everything to do with intuition and a finely honed sense of danger nearby, two skills he'd tried his best for ten years to ignore, to bury under the facade of a desk-bound businessman of mostly legal endeavors.

It wasn't anything magical—he wasn't a Talent—just animal instinct. But he trusted it as much as he did his partner's ability to channel current, the magic that was her genetic inheritance. And it led him unerringly back to Wren's door.

Which was closed, but unlocked.

*Don't assume. She was upset, probably—definitely—and maybe she just forgot to lock the door after you left.*

That thought was discarded as soon as it formed. He clearly remembered hearing the bolt slide home as he stood on the other side, trying to get a grip on himself. The overriding desire to wrap her around him, skin and sweat and the sweet-salty mint chocolate of her mouth, was driving him moderately insane. And he didn't trust that in himself, not at all, and especially not with Wren.

Not if exploring those tantalizing lures she kept casting and then pulling back risked damaging the relationship they already had. The partnership—the friendship—that was all that kept him afloat, some days. He knew his weaknesses, too well. He hadn't wanted her to become another one. But you can't always get what you want, as Jagger once said.

If everything was okay, she'd yell at him for fussing. And he'd take it, gratefully. Only let everything be okay....

He pushed open the door gently, wishing feverishly that he had his gun with him. It had once been as much a part of his wardrobe as his shoes or tie, back when he worked full-time for the Silence. Wren hated it; she had just enough psychometry to be able to tell there was blood on it, and just having it around disturbed her. So for the past ten years he had carried it only when he knew—or strongly suspected—there would be trouble. But recent events were making him think that there was always going to be trouble.

Trouble that historically came in the pocket of the man whose voice was currently coming from Wren's kitchen.

Sergei ran a hand through his hair, shoving the thick strands back off his face. He settled his breathing, then walked the four steps into the apartment, down the hallway, and into the long alcove his partner insisted was an eat-in kitchen.

Wren turned away from the counter and looked at him, then looked down at the mug of tea in her hand as though surprised to see it there. Her eyes narrowed, finely curved eyebrows communicating dismay, amusement, and a little bit of disgust before she shook her head, and those lips he spent far too much time thinking about curved in a smile. She handed him his tea, and turned back to the counter to pick up the other mug still steeping.

"Andre was just telling me all about our new assignment."

Was Andre, indeed? Sergei didn't like the tone in her voice. It was light, cheerful, almost perky, and boded not well for anyone who pushed her even one inch farther.

The temptation to let Andre hang himself was great, but odds were he'd regret it. Not right away, but eventually.

"A situation?" he asked, turning to face his former boss. Andre was seated on one of the chairs at the narrow kitchen table, his suit as impeccably tailored as always. Andre Felhim. A dapper black man somewhere in his well-kept sixties, clearly out of place in the homey disaster of Wren's apartment, but seemingly unaware of the fact. And if he was dismayed to see Sergei appear when Andre had obviously hoped to avoid him, none of that showed on the older man's face.

Then Sergei looked closer, and took a sip of his tea, suddenly thoughtful. No, Andre wasn't unaware. There was a look in those hawk's eyes that wasn't as in control as he wanted to portray. Interesting. Worrisome. When Andre got worried, it was time for his agents to get *very* worried.

All his instincts were telling him to shove Andre out the door, possibly without bothering to open it first. But he couldn't, for the same reason that had probably led Wren to let him into the apartment in the first place. The retainer he, Sergei, had negotiated for her. The retainer that allowed the Silence to call on them for occasional jobs. Jobs, he knew from experience, that the Silence could and would pay handsomely for. And Wren needed that money. Damn it.

Andre had them by the short hairs, and everyone in the room knew it. All Sergei could control now, even a little bit, was how they played it.

"The deal was you'd work through me," he said, just to make sure all the protocols were followed, then leaned against the counter next to Wren, their elbows almost but not quite touching. "So talk to me."

Wren wasn't sure if she was annoyed that Sergei had come barging in when she'd finally gotten control of the situation, pleased to see him, or disgusted at the wave of relief she'd felt when she heard him come through the door. And there was *absolute* disgust at the fact that she'd made two mugs of tea without clicking onto what it meant. She was slipping, totally slipping.

"It's a simple enough Retrieval," Andre was telling her partner. "A monastery outside of Siena, in Italy, has requested our help in reclaiming a parchment that was taken from them last month."

"Taken, as in…?" Sergei really had the most wonderful poker face, Wren thought, watching him watching Andre. The lightly sun-reddened skin stretched nicely over cheekbones that were just enough to envy but not enough to make him look male model-ish, and his chin could get so damnably stubborn…like right there, the way he shoved it forward just a hint. Uh-oh.

"Walked off on its own, from what Andre's been able to not tell me," she said, heading off a potential testosterone fit.

"We—and the monks—are unsure of what happened

to it," Andre admitted. "It is possible that someone stole it. Or…" He shrugged, a subtle gesture meant to imply that anything under God's hand was possible.

"Or?"

"Or there may have been an unknown magical element involved, considering the nature of the manuscript."

Oh-ho. Wren really wished she could do the one-eyebrow-raised thing. That was new in the telling. She knew, damn it, she *knew* old manuscripts always meant trouble. And if it was that old, and maybe magic, she'd lay heavy odds with any bookie in town that it was old-style magic, too. The kind that wasn't supposed to exist anymore but everyone except the most obsessive, tech-happy Mage knew did. Same power, different channels. Unpredictable channels. If you did A with current, you got B. Consistent, quantifiable. Mostly. Wish up folk-style magics—hedgewitchery, voudon, faith-healing—and you never knew what might come out.

Bad stuff, sometimes. The older the magics, the less human-friendly they were. She'd never dealt with any of that herself. There were stories, though. Even the *Cosa* had bogeymen.

"So, what's this unknown, maybe-magical bit of paper do?" she asked, focusing herself on the problem at hand. *Don't worry about the long-term stuff, Valere. You're not in this to save the world. You're not even in this to save the innocents and uninformed, the way the Silence claimed to be. You're in it for the paycheck, and the smug satisfaction of a job decently done.*

"It's a parchment. And we don't know," Andre said,

finally looking back at her. Guy didn't look like he wanted to give them that particular bit of information, either, but she wasn't sure if it was because he was worried about Silence secrecy, or he just didn't want to tell them anything on principle. Probably both. Sergei had warned her, and warned her, and then warned her again that the Silence liked to play things close.

"It's a difficult situation, as all we know is that a number of people have disappeared after coming in contact with it. With no other available information, save that the monks were most insistent that it be returned to them, we have to assume there's danger."

"So you're acting as agent for them, not taking this on your own?" Sergei, wheelin' the deal.

"In this instance, yes. Although we would have taken steps of our own, had they not contacted us."

"If you'd heard about it," Wren said, her tone intentionally doubting.

"We would have."

Andre was solid, confident. Wren had her doubts, but it wasn't really important here and now.

Sergei exhaled, a sharp, loud breath of air that recaptured Andre's attention, his head turning as though he were watching a slow-motion tennis game. "You said that people disappeared after coming in contact with the manuscript? As in, they put it down and walked away, or…?"

The older man hedged uncomfortably, and Wren took malicious and unashamed pleasure in it, after that little omission of information, earlier.

"We're not sure," he said, finally.

"Where did it go?" Sergei asked with marked patience.

"We don't know."

"Okay, so what's written on this parchment?"

"We don't know. Everyone who has read it has disappeared."

Sergei exchanged a glance with Wren, who made a "what do you want from me?" gesture back at him. He was the guy who got the details, she was the one who acted on them.

Sergei's mouth set in a really tight line. "So, basically, you're sending us in after an unknown factor in an unknown location with an unknown threat vector."

"Yes."

She couldn't help it; she'd swear it on a stack of bibles, the words just came out. "And you people wonder why you can't keep help…."

She might as well not have said anything, the way the two of them were still staring at each other, cobra to mongoose.

"We have arranged for you to take a flight out from Newark airport tomorrow evening. When you arrive in Milan—"

"Monday."

That stopped Andre, who was clearly not expecting to be interrupted at this point, and certainly not by her. "Beg pardon?"

"Monday," Wren repeated firmly. "No way I can just up and leave the country in twenty-four hours. Nuh-uh. Forget about it. I need two days, at least." Leave the country? That meant flying. She didn't want to fly. Anywhere. "A week would be better. I don't even know where my passport is—hell, I don't even know if it's still valid!"

"We can and will take care of that," Andre said, trying to be reassuring.

Wren was already running off a checklist in her mind. "Yeah, today's what, Wednesday? Saturday, earliest. I have to let my mom know, and—how long do you think I'll be gone? I need…luggage. Sergei, can I steal a suitcase? Borrow. I meant borrow. You must have something I can use. And I'll need to stop my mail. And pay bills. And—"

"Wren. Be still." Sergei didn't use that tone of voice very often. Not in years, she thought. But the ice-sharp tones worked. She stopped cold, the panic that was threatening to take over her brain subsiding to somewhat more manageable levels. Negotiations. Let him handle it. Right.

"Two tickets. For Friday," Sergei said to Andre in that same tone of voice. It didn't work quite so well on his former boss.

"Ah. Actually." Andre tapped his fingers on the kitchen table, and the sound immediately pulled Wren out of her own internal nosedive and put her on alert. That was the *tap-tap-tap* of doom. She shot a sideways glance at Sergei, and was not reassured by what she saw. His shoulders were broad to begin with, but now the way his head had lifted, and he was looking at Andre, she swore he'd gained another couple of inches across, all of it annoyed.

Andre didn't seem to notice the storm brewing. "We had hoped that, while Ms. Valere was otherwise oc-

cupied with this situation, you would be available to
work on another project back—"

"Two tickets." The faint rose flush over his cheekbones was subsiding, but the jaw and neck muscles were
still corded. "Two, or none."

There was a brief testosterone-fueled staring match
that broke when Andre looked away. Wren suddenly remembered to breathe again. *Score one for the home team.*
But the thought was a little shaky.

"Wren doesn't speak Italian," Sergei said. It was almost
as though, Wren thought, he were apologizing for winning.

Maybe he was. She still so didn't get their relationship,
her partner and Andre. Yes, she knew they'd been
coworkers, back in Sergei's We Don't Discuss It days
with the Silence. And that Andre had been the one to
train him. But other than that, a big blank nothingness
of information. A mistake, letting that go on. She
counted on her partner to get her the necessary details
so she could do her job, damn it. And if the two of them
were going to have Dramatic and Meaningful pauses in
the conversation, she needed to know *why*.

She hated being out of the loop in her own life. And
she already hated this job.

"I do hope you're not going to insist on business
class," Andre said, finally, dryly.

"Wouldn't dream of it," Sergei said in return. She was
relieved to see that he'd dropped the menacing body
language, not that he wasn't a tall bastard to begin with,
at least by her standards. Kitchen wasn't large enough for
all the egos in here.

"Fine, fine, details settled. One last really important question Sergei seems to have forgotten to ask." When the two men looked at her she put on her very best, guaranteed-annoying chipper and chirpy inquisitive face, this time smiling *without* showing teeth. "How much—in addition to the stipend—are we getting paid for this?"

*Chapter Three*

"Andre Felhim. Code 28-J8-199-6."

"Good afternoon, sir." A chime followed the almost-human-sounding voice, and the door of the restricted elevator opened with a soft hum, giving him access to the inner building where the Silence had its unmarked, unremarked world headquarters, on a side street in a side corner of Manhattan.

Andre put his keycard back into his pocket, touched the display pad on the wall, and rode in silence up to the seventh floor. It was quiet, now; most of the activity on seven occurred in the morning, when new reports were compiled and distributed. Friday afternoon was a time to catch up, to cover all your bases and plot strategy for the next week. Or, for managers like himself, for the weekend. The Silence slept, but not for long. There was a review meeting scheduled for Saturday morning, and he still had to look over the agenda.

"Ho, the glamorous life," he said wryly, walking down the hall toward his office, a plain square of space carved out of the floor plan by three walls and a window. He still wasn't quite sure how he rated one of those rare windows, but the first lesson you learned was take what you can get and never let anyone think it might have been a mistake.

While he'd been out of the office this morning, meeting with an extremely particular and paranoid new client, someone had dumped a dozen or so files into his in-box, threatening to topple the stack that was already there. A series of salmon-pink "while you were away" slips were taped to the back of his chair, fluttering slightly under the flow of air from the vent overhead. Andre pulled them off the fabric, flicking through them while he checked to see if his message light was on.

It was.

"It never stops," he muttered, more amused than annoyed. Far worse if it were to stop. Information was the lifeblood of the Silence. And the more information you had, the more essential you were. If anyone thought, however rightly or wrongly, that you didn't have access to new information…

The only thing equal in sin was not to bring money into the coffers, to pay for the less lucrative situations they had been founded to deal with. Endowments, even impressive ones, only went so far when you had the entire world to save.

Well. For the moment, anyway, he didn't have to worry about either of those sins. Bringing The Wren—

and Sergei—onto the Silence's roster had been a coup he could rest on for a while longer yet, information-wise. Especially with this new client, who thought that the island estate she had just inherited might be infested with something unworldly. It was probably nuclear-irradiated cockroaches, considering where she lived, but the Silence would earn a pretty penny checking it out and cleaning it up, whatever the cause.

He almost hoped it *was* glow-in-the-dark cockroaches. They were still collecting royalties on the movie that got filmed after the last one of those Man-meets-Nature, Screws-it-up situations.

But that sort of project was a sideline. The supernatural screwing with the natural was their raison d'être; specifically, the Italian situation was where his focus needed to be, right now. Matthias would be annoyed not to have Sergei's help on his current project, but Andre was not entirely unhappy that his former protégé had dug in his heels about letting the girl work alone.

He'd refrained from giving them anything more than the official, filed details of the situation, as per policy, but this felt… wrong. Bad, in his gut. And not only because they had so little information on the missing manuscript itself. Something about this had put his hackles up, and only the knowledge that these two really *were* the very best he could put on it made him sign off on the assignment.

That, and the fact that "I have a bad feeling about this" was not an acceptable reason within these hallways.

"You're back."

"You're a master of the obvious." He regretted his

tone the moment he saw his assistant's expression. "I'm sorry. It's been a hellish twenty-four hours, and I'm a proper bastard for taking it out on you."

"Make it two boxes of truffles at Christmas this year and you're forgiven. As always." Bren was office manager and dogsbody to three managers, Andre included, and they all ran her ragged. Chocolate once or twice a year seemed to him the least he could do.

"Anyway, you can see that disaster has once again struck while you were off-premises."

She twiddled two red-nailed fingers in the direction of his desk, and Andre sighed dramatically. "Indeed. Any actual corpses?"

"None you have to dispose of. Coffee?"

He considered the offer briefly, then shook his head. "Thank you, but no. I'm irritable enough already without adding that swill to the mix this late in the day."

"True, too true. Just yell if you change your mind."

Andre paused a moment to enjoy the view of Bren's backside as she strode down the hallway to her desk. He had an acknowledged weakness for tall, leggy blondes. Pity she'd prefer him to be Andr*ea*.

With a chuckle at his own foolishness—the first even faint laugh he'd had since being handed the Italian project three days ago—he moved to the door and closed it against the external office distractions. And in that time his brief good humor fell away as though it had never existed.

Magic. This entire situation smelled of magic. Stank of it, actually.

Andre had been among the first, years ago, to endorse the use of Talents within the Silence. He knew their value, in an organization that dealt with the results of magic in more than three-quarters of their situations. But magic itself—the basic, unpredictable power—still made him uneasy, despite or maybe because of his continued exposure to it. For all their talk of current and channeling, it wasn't the same as building a generator, and then flipping a switch. It was random, unpredictable—untrustworthy. Uncontrollable. Almost as uncontrollable as this unaffiliated Talent, his best (former) student at the reins or no. It was a pity he was becoming so fond of the girl. That might become a problem, eventually.

Sitting down at the glass-and-brass table he used for a desk, Andre spread the message slips out in front of him, scanning the names and sorting them into order of importance.

"Damn, damn, and damn." It was the strongest expression of displeasure he would allow himself in the office. Andre leaned forward and stared at the blank wall opposite him. Two of the messages were from Alejandro, wanting to know with increasing levels of impatience what was happening with the Italian situation.

Alejandro wasn't his superior…technically they were both on the same management level, and Andre in fact had seniority in years. But he was the person with oversight in that area of the world, and so despite having to come to Andre for aid, he still kept the upper hand. Levels and negotiations. The Silence was a masterpiece of levels, and every level you went up there were more appearing above you.

There were levels of trustworthiness, as well. His—what was the term? His lonejack didn't trust him at all. Her handler trusted him just so far. How much did he trust them?

And how much of what they trusted him with could he in turn place in trust with others?

Last night, Sergei had called him. At home, not ten minutes after walking through the door, which meant the Handler had been waiting for him since Andre kept no set routine. When Andre tried to trace the call back, he discovered that the call had been routed through two different pay phones, ending up with one of those prepaid mobiles that was bought for cash. It was a level of paranoia the other man had never shown, even when he was in the thick of situations a decade ago, and normally Andre would have been amused by it, but for what his operative told him.

Not that Sergei's cause of concern—a whisper campaign to discredit one of their operatives—was anything to worry about, not when the whispering wasn't about the Silence itself. If anything, the Council's attempts to discredit Wren worked to the Silence's benefit, binding her more closely to them, if only fiscally.

But part of their deal with Sergei had been that they would protect Wren in the case of attack by the Council, and the means of attack had not, in their agreement, been specified as purely physical.

And it bothered Andre a great deal that no one in

the organization had heard about this "whisper campaign" earlier. Information wasn't the name of the game, it *was* the game.

Picking up the phone, he ignored the glowing message light and dialed a three-digit number. You didn't keep Logan waiting.

"You got my report?" Andre asked.

The answer was affirmative, followed by an interrogative.

Andre picked up a rough-edged chunk of marble from his desk and rolled it in his right hand as he spoke. "I don't know. It could be nothing, it could be good for us— or it could be potentially very ugly."

The baritone on the other end of the phone got louder, just a shade too vehement for it to have been a polite comment. You didn't hedge in front of Logan, either.

"We don't know enough about what the Council knows. Truthfully, we don't know anything, really. If our sources were compromised, then everything in the file is suspect." He didn't think that had happened, but it was a contingency they had to cover. That was the real reason the upper levels of the Silence needed Wren working for them; she was their conduit into the *Cosa Nostradamus* and the gossip therein. Gossip about the magical world that was so often the cause of the situations the Silence existed to clean up.

Although her admittedly extraordinary ability as a Retriever was a very useful thing to have in the toolbox, indeed. And the P.R. value of letting it be known—selectively, oh so selectively—that she was on their roster, that could not be overlooked or undervalued, either.

"We didn't hear anything because we're not the ears they're whispering into, no…and none of our clients have reported anything in their nets. It's not likely… Sir, yes… Yes, sir. Yes, I would say that it is entirely possible that our involvement is being whispered as well."

A pause, and he reached for the bottle of antacid sitting on his desk, shaking out three pills but not taking them just yet. Bad form to chew while getting chewed out by your boss.

"Yes, sir. We're already on it."

Andre hung up the phone and exhaled sharply through pursed lips. That hadn't been as bad as it might have been. Logan was a bastard, even for the Silence, but a decent Division manager despite that. Or perhaps because of it; he knew that praise and beatings had to be carefully balanced for maximum result. Being reamed by a senior administrator the way Andre just had was always a learning experience.

And the only thing to do with experiences like that was to learn from them.

Andre mentally sorted through the list of people available to him, and jabbed a button on the phone.

"Darcy. Pronto."

While he waited for his researcher to arrive, Andre went through the list of "while you were aways" and dropped almost half into the shredder placed discreetly beneath his desk. The rest could wait until he had a spare moment to deal with them.

"You rang, oh mighty one?"

When Darcy Cross was born, office gossip claimed,

the presiding doctor had asked her mother if she wanted to file a complaint, since clearly not everything had been delivered. The ensuing years hadn't done anything to refute the doctor's comment: now in her mid-thirties, Darcy could claim four foot five inches if she wore heels, and her bone structure was so frail it reminded one, inevitably, of a baby chick. People always stepped carefully around her, as though she might shatter from a sharp word. But the mind in that delicate body was first-rate, and the Silence paid very well for the use of it.

"Two of our ops are getting pressured from an external source, creating doubt as to their effectiveness, their veracity. Subvert, nothing concrete, nothing provable." He pulled a three-inch-thick folder from the pile to his left and handed it to her. Everything was on disk, of course, but the surest way to keep something secure these days was to keep it offline.

"You want me to find the source?" The remote expression in Darcy's hazel-blue eyes made it clear that she thought she was being undertasked.

"Not exactly." His headshake made her perk up, more interested. She perched on the edge of the sole guest chair and waited to hear more.

"We know who is doing it, and why—more or less. The current situation is to our benefit, but only so long as it remains...imprecise." So long as his players remained off balance and uncertain, but not irreparably damaged in mind or reputation. Logan had been quite emphatic about that. "We need to know exactly what is being said, and to whom, on an ongoing basis. Monitor the flow. And if the pressure is ramped up in any way, or you feel that there is any cause for alarm—"

"Insert counterpressure in such a way that it would appear to issue from the same source as the original pressure to confuse the issue and weaken the first source." Skin that sunlight rarely saw had its own glow as she processed the intricacies of the assignment. "Will I have support on this?"

"No." The fewer people who knew anything other than "we're looking into it" the better, just in case. "But you're hereby released from anything below a St. George-level priority." He'd catch hell for that, but Logan would have to cover for him.

"Most excellent." She weighed the folder in her hand, as though that could tell her anything. Who knew, maybe it could. She wasn't a Talent, but her mind was nonetheless impressive. And not a little terrifying, if she looked at you the wrong way. Santa Claus might know if you were naughty or nice, but Darcy could give you details about what, with whom, when and how much you paid for it.

He was quite reasonably glad that she and he worked for the same side.

"Go on, then. Shoo." He made a "go away" motion at her. "Go be dangerously brilliant elsewhere. I know for a fact that your office is larger than mine."

"Because you're never actually in your office," she said in return, then stood to leave, folder in hand. But as she turned to go she hesitated, as though something in her brain had clicked over unexpectedly.

"Yes?" He leaned back in his chair, watching as whatever it was she was processing worked its way to the front.

"I was just remembering—it may be nothing…but I was working on another situation, and part of that involved interviewing a couple of FocAs, and one of them said something… okay, Cross, what did he say?"

FocAs was slang for Focused Actives, field agents who were also Talents. There weren't many, and none of them were overly gifted—until Wren Valere—but still useful enough to warrant their own category.

"Right." She snapped her fingers, making Andre blink. "He said that there'd been rumblings back home…. They were talking to each other, actually, so I was only half-listening, and yeah, 'my dad says there's a schism in the community, something coming big and ugly.'" She broke off, her voice rising back to her normal tones. "Think it's related?"

"No, it's not—wait."

This might not be related to the specific item he had set her on, but from what he knew of the political structure among human Talents—and damn Sergei for the tight-lipped bastard he was—the relationship between the Mage's Council and the rest of the Talent community was a fault line just waiting to rupture. As he understood the gist of Sergei's reports, the Council wanted to be the sole arbiter of what all Talents did or didn't do within their community. Lonejacks, the freelancers to the Council's union, if you would, were the largest, loudest—if totally disorganized—voice in opposition to those plans.

Wren Valere was a lonejack—and one already in the Council's crosshairs. Any trouble would certainly impact her. And now, by association, the Silence. That was reason enough to follow up on any gossip, no matter how vague.

"Sir?"

He held up one finger, to indicate that she should allow him a moment longer to process.

Even if this newest information were completely un-related—unlikely but possible—the information could still be useful, long-term. While all Talents were considered part of what they referred to slightly tongue-in-cheek as the *Cosa Nostradamus,* not all of the *Cosa* were lonejacks *or* Council members. None of the Talents successfully recruited by the Silence Handlers, for example, had affiliations to either group; few of them knew much about the *Cosa* other than the fact that it existed. Like any large family, Andre thought without amusement, there were always branches that hadn't spoken in generations.

That was the main reason why the Silence knew a little about the *Cosa,* but until Sergei had met up with his Wren, nothing at all about the Council. *Cosa* members were gossips, and the *Cosa* creed was inclusionary. The Council was neither.

While they might have been able to pry details from their FocAs, Handlers were instructed never to place their active's personal obligations against the Silence's interests, to the point where Andre had taken people off situations entirely if it was deemed a conflict of interest.

It had nothing to do with compassion and everything to do with practicality. The Silence needed their people to be one hundred percent on the job, and conflict impaired judgment. And that was even more emphasized with FocAs. They were too few, too valuable to risk.

Not to mention, Andre thought mordantly, that having even a low-level Talent gunning for you could make life in this electronic age…uncomfortable.

"So…?" Darcy was still standing in his doorway, waiting while his thoughts chased each other to a decision.

"Get him in here, *without* his Handler," Andre said. It was a risk, but since the boy had already had contact with Darcy, less of one than sending someone else might have been. "Quickly, but quietly. And—no, wait. Send him directly to me." That *was* a risk, but knowledge was power. And this might be—or become—something it would be wiser to keep for himself, rather than sharing.

After she left, he picked up the phone once again and dialed an outside number.

"Poul. I have an assignment for you."

It was going to be a longer afternoon than he had planned.

"You think P.B.'s going to be okay while we're gone?"

Sergei finished putting their carry-on luggage in the overhead bin and looked down at his partner.

"Yeah. I think the obnoxious little walking blanket will be fine." He shifted to let another passenger drag his luggage by, and then closed the bin, unlacing and removing his shoes and placing them in their fabric carry bag, then storing them under the seat in front of their row. Wren had already kicked off her own shoes, practical and comfortable leather skimmers, and curled up on her own seat. The only good thing about being short, she thought, was that she got to be sort of comfortable in airplane seats.

"And Andre's check cleared?"

"Cleared before I let you start packing."

She knew all this. She just liked hearing Sergei say it again. His voice was deep and raspy, like a lion's purr. It made her feel better. He could probably be reciting the back ads in the *Village Voice* and it would still make her feel better. *You're so astonishingly easy, Valere.*

"Passport?"

"In my pocket with all our other papers." He was fighting back a smile behind that stern expression, she could tell. In any other situation it would annoy the hell out of her. But not right now. Now she was out of the airport, with all the worried-looking people and loudspeaker announcements and hurry-hurry-wait-wait and all those windows looking out at all those…planes.

The fact that she was currently sitting in one of those planes hadn't escaped her attention. But somehow being in one was better than looking at and planning on getting in one.

Wren knew it didn't make any sense. And thinking about it just emphasized the fact that she *was* in a plane rather than a weirdly shaped train, or something. And if she thought in that direction too long, bad things would start to happen again.

"Emergency rations?"

"Are in your bag, next to the newspaper. And yes, I packed those disgusting maple nut things." He sat down next to her, raising the armrest between them to put his arm around her more comfortably. "Wren. Hush. It's going to be okay."

Easy for him to say, she thought a little resentfully. He didn't feel this beast singing beneath him, all filled with electronic devices practically begging to be drained. What happened if they ran into trouble, and she panicked, and tried to reach for current? What if—

"You're thinking too much," he said.

Guilty as charged, Officer. But he was right. If she just stopped thinking about it, her instinct for self-preservation—incredibly strong, as she knew from previous close calls—would kick in and keep her from doing anything suicidal in her panic. Probably. So. Change the subject.

"Do you think that Andre wasn't telling us everything?"

Sergei snorted at that. "Andre never tells anyone everything. But no, I think that he was as up-front as he's capable of being on Silence business."

Oh, *that* was reassuring. She felt totally reassured. Really.

"Did I mention that I'm hating this job already? Even without the being on this thing I'm not thinking about being on?"

"I don't like it either, woman. If you've any better ideas, I would love to hear them."

"Bet Noodles would hire me."

"Yes, I can see you spending your life as a Chinese

short-order cook. Or a bicycle delivery girl. If you could Translocate better, maybe."

"All right, that was low." Her recent attempts at Translocation had been done under only extreme duress, once to save their own lives during a job gone bad, and once to keep a client from getting killed. But she'd gotten the job done, hadn't she? So what was a little vomiting and current-spillover between friends?

"It will all be fine. Just another job." Sergei took out the newspaper and checked to make sure that the business section was intact, then put it away and pulled a burgundy folder from his bag and extracted a sheaf of typewritten pages from it.

"See? All the information we need, hand-delivered by Andre's little messenger boy this morning, including names, dates, places, and driving directions. Why don't you try to sleep, okay? It's a long flight, and we're going to have to hit the ground running when we get there."

She rested her head against his shoulder, feeling the comforting familiarity of him. None of the awkwardness or uncomfortableness of recent months, just…Sergei. The thought almost made her cry. *You don't know what you've got till it's gone…only it's not gone. Still here. Still Sergei.* He was right. P.B. was a big—well, okay, full-grown demon, he could take care of himself. And if he did run into trouble, Tree-taller was around, had promised to keep an eye out. The other Talent had no beef with the fatae, the nonhuman members of the *Cosa Nostradamus*, and would listen if P.B. came to him. And anything Andre hadn't told them in that packet, they'd figure out on their own. Wasn't like they needed the Silence, the Silence needed *them.*

"Wren?"

They'd probably only be gone a couple-five days, anyway. A week, tops.

"Yeah. Sleep. Right. Okay. I'll try."

Twenty minutes later, the plane pulled away from the gate. Sergei looked up from the papers he was reading as the safety instructions tape began to play, then down at his companion. She was still leaning against his shoulder, strands of chestnut hair falling into her eyes, and he could hear the faintest completely unladylike snore coming from her half-open mouth.

"Rest well, Wrenlet," he whispered. "Tough job ahead."

# Chapter Four

"Oh God, there's fur on my teeth."

Sergei winced. "That's a lovely image, thank you so much for sharing."

"You're oh-so-welcome. Bleah." Wren twisted her mouth up in disgust. "I need my toothbrush. Or some sandpaper."

"Wait until we're through customs, okay?"

"If I breathe on a customs inspector they're not going to let us into the country."

"Wren, I've smelled your morning breath. It's not that bad. It's not good, but it's not that bad."

"This is worse. This is overnight-in-an-airplane morning breath."

They were walking through the Malpensa airport, having just picked up their bags from the luggage carousel. It was seven o'clock Saturday morning local time, but her body was claiming it was one o'clock in the morning, and since she had only managed to sleep the first hour of the flight, every cell in her body was clamoring for a shower, a nap, and a king-size candy bar. In exactly that order.

"Where is everyone, anyway?" A stark contrast to the chaos of Newark airport, there seemed to be only a dozen or so people walking with them toward customs, and only one very bored-looking security guard leaning against the wall farther down near the doors. The wheels on her luggage stuck and she stopped, swearing slightly, to get them straightened out. She really wanted to take her jacket off, but that would be one more thing to somehow carry, and it just wasn't worth it. Besides, her T-shirt was probably a mess of wrinkles. And not the fashionably acceptable kind, either. Her partner, on the other hand, looked as pressed and proper as he had when he got on the damn plane the night before. It ought to be illegal. It was probably some as-of-yet-unknown skill set of Talent, and he'd been holding out on her all these years.

Sergei shrugged, pausing to let her catch up. "Not a very busy airport, I guess. Mostly businesspeople. Tourists all fly into Rome, probably."

"Why couldn't we have flown into Rome?" Not that Wren cared much, one way or the other—all flights were hellish, no matter where you ended up.

"I didn't make the flight arrangements, Genevieve."

His voice sounded brittle, suddenly, and Wren backed off. He hadn't slept much either, and Sergei without sleep was a total bear. She ran her tongue over her teeth again and grimaced. She felt so disgusting, it was barely human. She knew there was a travel bottle of mouthwash in her kit, if she could just convince him to stop for a minute so she could duck into the bathroom…

Not that there were any bathrooms to be seen. Stifling a sigh, she picked up her carry-on and yanked the handle of her wheeled case, following after her partner. The moment they were through customs, she was rinsing her entire body out.

*"Signore? Signorina? Vieni con me, per favore."* They had reached the end of the hallway, and the guard—a middle-aged woman who looked bored behind belief—was pointing them toward a group of people standing patiently in several different queues.

Sergei tugged Wren's arm gently, and led her into one of the lines. She blinked at him, then grinned, her pique forgotten. "They're speaking Italian!"

"Welcome to Italy." He took her passport out of her hand, checked over the documents, and then put them with his. She barely even noticed.

"No, I know, but…it's so neat!" All right, so yes she had understood they were going to a foreign country. And that they spoke a different language. She grew up just outside of Manhattan, so people speaking foreign languages were no big deal. But an entire country that wasn't the same….

She had a sudden thought, and reached out gently with the inner sense that made her a Talent to tap at the wiring running through the place. Gently, carefully, just in case.

"Huh."

Sergei looked at her sharply, and she realized she must have said that out loud. "What?"

"Nothing. I just thought…I guess I thought the current would feel different. But it doesn't." She shrugged, suddenly annoyed at herself. "I mean, it does, yeah; different voltages, different flow, like a stream versus a creek versus a…whatever. But I thought…"

"It would have an accent?"

She looked up at him accusingly. Sure enough, he was smiling at her in that annoyingly amused way.

"Yeah. Okay? I thought it would have an accent."

He did laugh then, and she thought briefly about kicking him. "Too much effort to beat you the way you deserve," she grumbled.

"I'm sorry. Honestly. I am." But he kept chuckling.

Wren didn't mind, really. Smiling Sergei was always better than grumpy Sergei, especially when they were being gestured at by pissed-off looking guys in uniforms.

*"Signore?"*

"I think we're being summoned," she said, poking her partner in the ribs and jerking her chin in the direction of the customs counter.

"Right." He grabbed his bags and moved forward, Wren close on his heels. *"Buon giorno."*

*"Buon giorno. I passaporti?"*

Sergei handed over their passports and entry paperwork, and the official gave them a cursory once-over. *"Vieni in Italia per affari commerciale o come turista?"*

*"Affari."*

Wren's attention wandered. Having touched the current in this place, she was now overly aware of it. And of the fact that dipping into it would be almost as good as a shower.

Then she caught a glimpse of an armed guard standing just beyond the security gate, clearly ready and able for trouble, and her exhausted-into-quiet nerves pinged again.

*Maybe not. Somewhere not quite so…stressed.* This airport didn't have the same tension as back home, but it was still an airport, and screwing up in airports was still very much not a good idea. Especially since she didn't know any of the *Cosa* in town, assuming there even were any. Oh. That was a twist she hadn't thought of. Not that it mattered so much here, but when they got to where they were going she would have to check things out, see if she could meet up with someone, maybe get the lay of the land. It would be rude to be in town and not even try to say hello, right?

And then Sergei was nudging her, indicating that they were done, moving her through the doors and into the terminal itself. Here was the noise and bustle Wren had been expecting, although it was still relatively empty.

"Coffee!" She started forward, then stopped. "ATM first. Then coffee. Then…wasn't someone supposed to meet us?"

Sergei looked around. "Yes." He reached into his carry-on and pulled out the burgundy folder again. "One Marina Fabrizio. She's supposed to be our contact person here."

"Fine. You look for her. I'm gonna hit an ATM and then get some coffee. You want anything?"

"A double espresso, please. And bring back a couple of sugar packets."

"A double?" She gave him a dubious look. Sergei was a tea drinker—he drank coffee reluctantly, and without any real enjoyment.

"It's a long drive to where we're going," he reminded her. "I need to stay awake."

"Right. One double, extra sugar. Oh boy."

Sergei watched Wren head off into the terminal, slipping past the few travelers like a ghost. His partner was statistically ordinary with a capital O—five-four, well built but not in any way that would draw undue attention, brown hair and brown eyes and skin the color of…of pure vanilla ice cream. Tasty, yes, but unless you knew that, decidedly ordinary. And when you added in her ability to warp current into a sort of no-see-me force field…

Many years ago, she had told him that when she tapped into current she could dye herself blue, wrap herself in bells, and waltz naked through Grand Central Terminal at rush hour without anyone noticing her. He had believed it then. He knew it for a fact now. Not that she had ever actually done that particular—at least, he didn't *think* she had.

Sergei also suspected that, despite knowing perhaps five words in Italian, his partner would have no trouble at all finding an ATM, buying coffee, and possibly finding their missing contact while she was at it. Invisible to the casual eye did not mean incapable. Far from it. He had told Andre that he was along because he was the one with the language skills. The truth was…

Sergei raked one hand through his hair, impatient with himself. The truth was that their…relationship, for lack of a more accurate word, was far too fragile for her to be out of his sight for very long. Or him, hers.

Not that he had any real worries about her being wooed and pursued by the stereotypical dashing Italian loverboy, but he still wasn't about to let her go haring off on her own. Not until they'd actually gotten past this damned push-me-pull-you thing they'd fallen into. The past few months had been hellish. First her getting shot, and recovering—it had been okay then; taking it slow, discovering the sweetness of her mouth, the pleasure in just being able to hold her while she rested. But the moment she was back on her feet, everything went sour.

His fault. He knew that. He'd spent so many years in stasis, emotionally. Intentionally. Trying to avoid repeating the one impossible mistake that had driven him from the Silence. And still she'd managed to get under his skin. Into his heart in a way that couldn't be safely packaged up by "friend," or even "partner."

*Time for denial is over, old man. Over, gone, kaput.*

He was hoping that this trip, away from the preexisting patterns their partnership fell into, they would be able to stop overthinking everything and just *feel.* For good or ill, but the fiddling about was going to kill him. And he didn't think she was doing much better.

Feeling his shoulders start to tense up he forced them down, extending and flexing his fingers toward the ground, trying to remember the basic grounding exercises Wren had taught him back in the earliest days of their working relationship. Grounding was essential to a Talent, who routinely drew the magical essence from electricity and sent it back out again through their bodies. For him, it was a way to destress, forcing the anxiety out of his pores the way Wren said she handled current.

And thank God she'd been able to handle it on the plane, he thought, not for the first time. In the airport, he'd only been worried that they would be delayed if something blew up spectacularly, or if she sent the airport into a blackout. In a plane…

But he had kept his fears tightly to himself, and she'd managed admirably. Although he suspected that the entertainment system going on the blink two-thirds of the way through the movie had been her fault.

He'd seen the film before, anyway.

"Where are you, Ms. Fabrizio?" he asked the airport at large. "I don't like it when things go wrong this early in the plan." A good Handler prepared his agents for all probabilities. The information Andre had given them was far sketchier than he had let on to Wren, and not up to the old man's standards, as Sergei remembered them. So it was time for him to stop being Sergei the businessman, or even Sergei the Retriever's partner, and become the Handler. Keep control. Maintain confidence in the active agent.

Checking his watch only informed him that he'd forgotten to change it when they got on the plane. Unfastening the slender gold timepiece from his wrist, he moved the hands forward, all the while looking around to see if there was anyone who looked like they might be looking for them. Or, better yet, holding up a sign that said Silence Operatives, Report Here.

He didn't think they were going to get that lucky.

By the time Wren returned, balancing two small paper cups and a handful of sugar packets, he knew they weren't going to be lucky at all.

"Did we get stood up?"

"Looks that way." He took the smaller cup from her, took off the lid and dumped four packets in without tasting it first. Wren, more cautious, sipped hers delicately, then reached over and snagged two unopened packets out of his hand.

"That'll put hair on your everything," she said, stirring the sugar granules until they dissolved and then trying it again. "Oh yeah. Way better. So?"

"So?" Maybe he was more jet-lagged than he thought, but he'd lost track of what she was talking about. Perhaps he should have gotten two coffees.

She gave him a wide-eyed look of impatience. "So how late is our alleged contact?"

Oh. Right. Sergei checked his watch again, needlessly since the hands had only moved five minutes since the last time he'd checked. "Two hours from the time we landed, minus the time it took us to actually make it through customs, including the time I've been waiting for you to get back—"

"Yeah, I stopped in the bathroom, okay?" She bared her teeth at him. "No more fur. Anyway. I'm voting this chick isn't going to show. Ya think?"

He thought so as well, but was hesitant to agree too quickly. It wouldn't do to blow off their Silence contact on their very first assignment. Wren was cheerfully, aggressively able to ignore anything that wasn't in the process of attacking her. But he was supposed to be the business guy, and part of business was dealing with the political aspects of it all. *Maintain confidence in the active agent.* But be cautious. "There might have been a delay…."

"Two hours' worth? And she couldn't delegate someone else to meet us, or maybe, y'know, call us about the delay?" He flinched, and reached for the mobile clipped to his belt. No, it was turned on, and still working. Good. Carrying a cell phone in close proximity to Wren was always a risky thing, but staying in touch was more important. And she was pretty good about warning him before a major current pull so he could turn it off in time. Mostly.

"Sergei, is there anything she could tell us that they couldn't have given us beforehand, or called in? Or, maybe, have waiting for us at our hotel?"

He shook his head. "Unlikely, no. I mean, it's unlikely that they, or rather she—" He gave it up as a bad job and took another gulp of the coffee, finishing it off. The brew was heavy and bitter, and even the sugar didn't make it easy to drink, but he could practically feel it slapping his neurons into firing properly.

"Then screw this, and screw her." Wren said, crumpling her coffee cup and looking around for a convenient trash bin. "Let's go."

It galled him to abandon a meet, even if the other person had flaked on them, but she was right; the contact was probably only a courtesy. And they had waited. The important thing now was to get to the monastery where the manuscript had disappeared from, and start their search. Anything the Silence needed to tell them—well, the Milan office had made the damn hotel reservation, too, so they could pick up a phone and call the hotel, or send a fax. Although it would probably be a good idea to find an Internet café somewhere if he could and check e-mail, even before they got to the hotel.

He took the cup from her, and threw it out with his own, then looked around to take his bearings.

"This way," he said finally, leading her to the elevator, down two floors and then through a covered walkway to where the car rental offices were. "Stay put," he told her, depositing her in the corner with their luggage. "If I remember anything about Italian bureaucracies, this will take forever."

However, his expectations were unfulfilled, and the registration went smoothly enough. He collected Wren and the luggage, and they found their way without too many problems to the car assigned to them. He unlocked the doors, then did a double-take. "Damn. I had forgotten about that."

"Forgotten about what?" Wren dropped her carry-on

into the back seat of the battered, dark blue sedan and looked at him. "BMW. Sweet."

"They're like Chevrolet over here, don't get too excited. And I haven't driven overseas in so long I forgot to request an automatic transmission."

Wren's brow creased, and she reached up to tug at the short braid she'd gathered her hair into at some point. "I can't drive stick," she admitted.

"I can. But it's been…a while."

"Oh boy," was his partner's only comment as she got into the passenger seat and strapped the safety belt on. "Oh boy."

*Chapter Five*

The drive from Malpensa to the monastery in the hills just north of Siena took five hours, most of it on an endless winding highway where driving under one hundred and sixty kilometers per hour got you flashed lights and eloquent hand gestures as they zoomed past. Finally Sergei had gotten the hang of changing gears, and they'd moved up to speed themselves.

"So how does the Silence end up with this gig, anyway?" Wren asked, more out of idle curiosity than anything else. "Do they hand out flyers on street corners? 'Lose something magical? Call us!' Hey, there's an idea. Maybe—"

"Nothing quite so crassly commercial," Sergei said, cutting that bad idea off at the knees while shifting to pass a double-axle truck going one hundred kph. "The Silence is a watchdog organization, for the most part. Think of it as analogous to the United Nations."

"Yeah, so you've said before. 'Always on the lookout for things gone wrong to set right,' like the Marines meet *Quantum Leap.*"

"I never said that."

"Close enough. But what you never said was how the Marines got called."

"Networking, mostly. 'Someone knew someone who was helped in that sort of situation, let me put in a call' kind of thing. And then they parcel out the assignments, based on who has the best skills to handle it."

"And how many of those someones are actually Silence employees?"

"Cynical woman. Not as many as you would think. The Silence *does* do good work. The fact that the rest of the world hasn't imploded yet, from means magical and otherwise, is proof of that."

Privately, Wren thought her partner was still showing signs of Silence brainwashing. But saying that would probably be poking the bear with the grumpy stick. Fun, sure, but ultimately a bad idea.

"So. Where are we going, anyway?" she asked, in order to move the conversation on.

"A small town in Umbria called…something or another in Italian. The monastery where the object was kept is there. We'll take a look around, see what you can pick up, and go from there. Okay?"

He was making plans without her. Normally that would lead to some harsh words—she was the Retriever, not him, and she knew what needed to be done—but the need for a nap was winning over the planning portion of her brain, and the yawn she could feel coming on overruled anything else. For now.

"Yeah. Okay."

The rest of the trip was a blur, to her, of speeding cars, rolling green and yellow hills, and Sergei's muttered curses forming a melody that finally sent her off into dreamland.

"We're here."

Wren opened her eyes to afternoon sunlight bathing her vision with a soft golden tinge. She got out of the car and stretched, then looked around. "Sorry, didn't mean to sleep all the way." She paused. "Where are we?" The car was parked on a small patch of gravel surrounded on three sides by tall, narrow trees. It all looked the part of a scenic destination, but the low stone building on the rise of hill behind them didn't look like any hotel she'd ever stayed at before. She sniffed the air. It was fresh, clean, filled with allergens, and…off, somehow. She sniffed again. No, just your ordinary fresh air. Then why was there this weird trickle of unease down her spine? *Jet lag. Italian coffee. Could be anything. Where the hell are we?* "Sergei…"

He reached into the back seat for his jacket, but didn't put it on right away. The expression on his face was one she knew all too well: him about to try and talk her into a job that he knew she wasn't going to like. Except that they were already *on* a job she didn't like. "I thought it might be a good idea to stop in and let the monks know that we're here."

Wren thought of a few particularly good comebacks,

but settled for an unhappy grunt. She had fallen asleep and left the driving to him. That put him in the decision-making seat, and his instincts were pretty damn good about stuff like this. Even if she was still in dire need of that shower and a candy bar.

"Besides…" He looked down at the view, but his attention was clearly elsewhere. The breeze ruffled his hair slightly, and made her wish she were wearing a long-sleeved shirt for the first time in weeks.

"Besides?" she prompted him.

"It's nothing. I just wanted to get started, is all."

"You sure they're going to want drop-in visitors?" she asked mildly. "I mean, monastery, monks, isolation, etcetera, right?"

"We're hardly unexpected. And I don't think it's a cloistered monastery in the way you're thinking—according to the sign we passed on the way up, they have a gift shop."

"Oooookay…." For some reason, Wren had the sudden visual of pasta in the shape of the Crucifixion, with red sauce, and shook her head violently until the image was gone. She was already probably going to Hell, but why make it even worse? "But monks and prayers and bell-tolling, right?"

"Indeed. And we even wear robes occasionally." They both spun around to see a middle-aged man in a pale grey robe that should have looked silly but didn't, standing in the grass to the side of the parking area, smiling at them. "Forgive me. I heard the car coming up the hill and came down to see who it could be. I am Brother

Teodosio. And you, obviously, are our visitors from the States."

"Sergei Didier," Sergei's hand was engulfed in the other man's. They were about the same height, but Teodosio had at least fifty pounds on him, and very little of it was muscle. His face was round, but not jolly, and Wren didn't think many people challenged him twice.

"Wren Valere," she said, and had her own hand swallowed in turn. His skin was warm, and a little moist, but nothing unpleasant. His eyes were surprisingly blue, under the black hair peppering into grey, and Wren noted that he didn't have a tonsure like she'd always thought was required style for monks.

*And he's wearing jeans under that robe. And sneakers. Another fine myth shot to…okay, maybe not hell, for a monk.*

"I hope that your drive down was a pleasant one. Welcome to the Sienese, and specifically to *I Monaci delle Sante Parole*—better known to some as the House of Legend."

"House of…?" Sergei's ears practically perked up, probably hoping it had something to do with artwork he could cart back home and make a nice chunk of change on the side.

"Legend." Teodosio's attention went back to Sergei, promptly dismissing—forgetting about—Wren. That was a side effect of her particular blend of skills, and part of what made her so effective. And why her mentor, Neezer, had nicknamed her Jenny-wren. Because nobody ever saw the small brown bird—but she saw them.

"Indeed," the monk continued, "as with any building

over a century or two old, there are stories attached to it. And the House is quite old, indeed. It is our heritage, our reason for being here. And, indeed, the reason for your being here as well, sadly."

"As to that—my information said that you would be able to fill us in on the specifics?"

"You were not told?" The monk seemed taken aback by that, then shrugged as though asking why the works of man should be any less obscure than the works of God.

"To understand, you must first understand who we are, and what we do here. The story is—" and he made a gesture to indicate that they should walk with him along the path Wren now saw leading through the field and up the rise to the building she had noted earlier "—that in the early years of the thirteenth century, four monks came north, fleeing the aftermath of one or another of the endless squabbles between the city-states and the papacy."

Sergei fell easily into step beside their guide, leaving Wren to take up position behind them on the path.

"Their abbey had been destroyed?" Sergei was in smooth mode, she noted. She kept her ears open and took mental notes, in case anything seemed relevant—or might become so, later on.

"They kept no records of where they came from—we don't even know their names, as they simply referred to themselves as, how would it translate?" He shook his head as though searching for something inside. "As 'the brothers of the gathering word'? Close enough. And that is the assumption, yes. Destroyed, or taken as spoils of victory by whichever princeling had control of that town on that particular month."

Sergei was nodding, drawing the monk on to tell the rest of the story.

"With them, so the story goes, they had little money, no supplies, and two chests filled with manuscripts they had taken from their abbey when they fled. That, we assume, is why they took the name they did, referring to the gathering of the manuscripts into a library of sorts. They arrived here, and with the permission of the local Ghibelline nobility and the local bishop, built the House first, not for their own protection, but for the books they carried with them. And so it has been ever since; we are the caretakers of learning, of the wisdom established by those who have come before us."

"Librarians, you mean."

Rather than looking offended, Teodosio smiled and nodded. "Exactly."

Somehow Wren doubted that it had been anywhere near as simple or neatly tied up as that. From what little she knew of history, the rivalries he mentioned had been pretty nasty, and making an alliance with the wrong person could be deadly. So what had those four monks offered the local bishop that he gave them—homeless, with no money or military strength—permission to build their own independent housing on what looked like some seriously prime property? Sergei's notes said, for all they were Catholic monks in name, there wasn't any direct control of the order from Rome. She was just a nice lapsed Protestant girl, but that seemed really odd to her. Wasn't there a whole chain of command thing, orders of obedience, ad extreme nauseum?

She made a mental note to follow up on that particular question, when she had time. It might be nothing—or it could be everything. You never knew.

They came around a bend in the path, and were on a cliff overlooking a valley town that could have come out of a tourist's guide.

"Wow," Wren said, taking a step closer to the edge. Absolutely prime property, yeah. You could see for miles, the horizon a smudge of sun-yellowed fields intersected by the occasional ribbon of black road and dotted by random buildings that were probably either barns or farmhouses.

"Indeed. It reminds one of the glory around us, every morning, when I come out here."

Not to mention being totally defensible, Wren thought, casting a look over her shoulder to where the low stone building was revealed to be a more elaborate structure than it had first appeared. Yeah, red stone fortresslike building put on the top of a hill, near a cliff, sure they'd just hand that view over to a couple of rabbiting monks, no questions asked, out of the goodness and charity in their hearts.

Wren didn't much believe in the goodness of anyone's heart. Not without references.

"You speak excellent English," Sergei said finally.

Teodosio laughed. "I went to university in Boston," he said. "M.I.T. I thought I was going to be a mathematician, but God had other plans for my curiosity." Wren looked away from the view at that, but his face seemed as serenely unlined as before.

"Come, you'll want to visit the room where the manuscript was taken from, and see what you may see, yes?"

"Yes, please," Sergei said, shooting Wren a warning glance. She returned it with a look of wide-eyed innocence. They had played out variations of this scenario before. The big, well-dressed man would take the lead, asking the questions and hogging the attention. After a few more carefully smart but not too imaginative questions, Wren would start to fade from their awareness, leaving her free to do the real looking around. Not that there was much to see.

"The building to your left is our dormitory." It looked like a traditional rustic farmhouse; three stories high with wide windows framed by wooden shutters, two grey chimneys, one on either end; and faced entirely of the same brick used in the larger building. But something about it said modern construction, without being obvious about it. A carefully tended garden ran the entire length of the left side, filled with tall green leafy things and splashes of red and yellow that Wren couldn't identify. Vegetables came from the supermarket, usually wrapped in plastic. She didn't think about it much beyond that. It was surprisingly quiet, just the sounds of birds and wind, and the occasional low thump and murmur, like someone moving something somewhere else. Her skin prickled uneasily.

Two men came out of the front door, talking in low

voices to each other. They were dressed in plain brown trousers and button-down shirts rather than Theo's robe, but their postures were more hunched over, more defensive. They caught sight of the newcomers, and froze.

"Ah, just who I wanted to see," Teodosio said. If he wanted to see them, they clearly had not wanted to see Teodosio. Although it might have been the Americans they were reacting to, the way the duo scuttled around to the other side as they approached.

"Brothers Alain and Frederich. This is Signor Didier, from the States, and his associate, Signorina Valere. They work with Signor Mattenni and are here representing the *signor's* interests."

Wren kept a straight face, and managed not to shoot her partner a glance. She supposed that name would have come up in the briefing their no-show contact would have given them, because there had been no Mattenni mentioned anywhere in the quickie briefing they got before leaving, including all the paperwork Sergei was hauling around.

Or maybe they hadn't planned on giving them that particular info at all.

*Gee, Silence information not up-to-date or fully accessible. The shock. Sergei was right, their motto really is know all, tell nothing. Even to their own people.*

"Alain, if you would inform Jacob that our guests are here?" Brother Alain made a hunched-forward gesture that looked like it started out as a bow, and ran back into the farmhouse. "Frederich, come with me, please."

Frederich looked even less happy than before, but

obediently fell into step with them as they continued toward the larger building.

Now that she was on a level with it, the structure looked even more like a fortress than before—a rectangular shape, two stories high, with narrowly arched windows at odds with the larger, square openings of the farmhouse-dormitory. The facade was arched, and the double-door opening could have taken a full-size Cadillac and not scratched the chrome on either side. In the afternoon sunlight, it glowed against the summer-blue sky, like something out of one of those paintings, the ones where it always looked as though it were about to thunder. Hudson Valley school, right. She had retrieved one back in, what, '97?

Teodosio led them right up to the doors and unlocked the left-hand door with an old-fashioned metal key. "Any time you wish to enter the House, either I or Frederich must be with you. We have many treasures within these walls, you must understand, and we are the entrusted caretakers of them."

"Of course," Sergei said politely. Personally, Wren figured the lock would take her about seven seconds to tumble, even without using current. And there didn't seem to be any other kind of security, no alarms or tripwires or—

The doors closed behind them, and Wren felt herself shiver not from the sudden dark, or the echoing quiet, but from the fact that she knew, instantly, that she was inside a building with absolutely no electrical wiring at all. The walls were thick brick and mortar, and insulated to a fare-thee-well. Current could not find her there.

She could not find current here.

The uneasy prickle turned into full-fledged worry, just one small step down from panic, and she touched the magic inside her, warming suddenly-cold nerves on the responsive flickers deep in her core.

"Wren?" Sergei cast a concerned look sideways, obviously having sensed her reaction.

"I'm fine." She wasn't, not by a long shot, but couldn't let it throw her. What she was going to do now was seriously low-power anyway; even as tired as she was, it would barely disturb her natural level of current. And if anything happened, well, she'd been told there were ways to get current from stone, if you needed it badly enough. And there was a lot of stone around her that had likely never been tapped, if the building was as old as it looked. As old as Brother whatsisname, Teodosio, said it was.

"If you will come with me, please." Teodosio turned a knob on the wall, and the gas lamps placed along the main hallway flared brighter. "I apologize for our old-fashioned ways of doing things. We try to remain true to our traditions. And besides—" a brief smile flashed on his basset hound face "—the money is not there to upgrade."

He was lying. Wren didn't know how she knew that, but he was. Which meant they had a reason for not having electricity available. Old-fashioned? Or cutting a Talent off from an easy source of energy? *Don't get paranoid, Valere. Not yet. Not while you're still gathering information.*

They went up a shallow stone staircase, ten steps, then a landing, then turned and another ten steps to the second floor. The torches seemed brighter up here, or somehow more light was getting through the narrow windows, because Wren could see more details around her. The walls had been plastered over with a slightly rough-textured white coating, and the wooden beams of the ceiling were blackened with age, creating a pleasing contrast. At intervals along the walls there were alcoves holding wooden carvings of figures—saints, she supposed—in various benevolent poses. Wren, with her lapsed Protestant background, didn't have a clue who any of them were. Her mother might have. Sergei probably did.

There were five doorways on either side of the hallway, each arched in a smaller echo of the main entrance. Passing by several of them, Wren caught a glimpse of glass-fronted cases and heavy cabinets. It wasn't so much a library, she thought, as a book prison....

"In here, please."

They were ushered through a doorway on the left, into a room that seemed incandescent compared to the gloom of the hallway. Light came in through the windows, split into prisms by the leaded glass. There were a number of the heavy cabinets here as well, plus thick glass-topped desks with obviously old manuscripts displayed underneath. One of them was conspicuously empty, the faded green backing noticeably darker where something had been removed.

"It was there?" Sergei asked, pointing to the empty space.

"What? Oh, no, no. That is an illuminated manuscript we've out on loan to a brother organization. The

Nescanni parchment, that was never left on display, no. No, never that." Teodosio was flustered, far beyond what the question would seem to merit, until Wren remembered what Andre had said. *Everyone who has read it has disappeared. Right. Displaying it where anyone could lean over and take a looksee…not such a good idea, no. Although the way he's reacting, I bet that's exactly what they did once. Wonder who went and disappeared? And how long ago?*

"How did you even know it was gone?" Wren spoke without thinking, earning her a sharp glance from everyone, Sergei because she wasn't supposed to be talking, the two monks because they had almost forgotten she was there. *In for a penny…* "If nobody ever read it, how did you know it was gone?"

"Ah. The parchment was bound between two sheets of slate, like a sandwich. We would check the edges every six months, to ensure that there was no water or spore damage to it, as we do all of our charges. At the most recent check three weeks ago, the young brother whose assignment it was sensed something wrong and opened the slate perhaps a bit more than was wise. Fortunately for him, the paper that had been left in the manuscript's place did not have the same effect on him as the original would have."

"He's still around, then?"

"Oh, yes. You will wish to speak with him?"

"Please." Seemingly taking back control of the situation, Sergei turned to Wren with the air of someone used to delegating. "Stay here, look around, learn whatever you can. I will meet with the young man and see what he has to say." Wren—recognizing the voice he used with Lowell, his gallery associate when the well-bred wonder got a shade too uppity—had to make an effort to keep a straight face as she nodded her understanding of her assignment. An assignment that was exactly what she had planned to do, anyway, had she been scouting the scene on her own.

Teodosio and Sergei exited, leaving Wren alone with Frederich, who looked as though he'd still rather be anywhere else, although that expression had been softened a little by boredom.

*What had boyo been expecting? Clearly they were told we would be coming, but what exactly were they told they'd be* getting? That was a valid question—Teodosio had not specified the Silence, and Sergei told her that more often than not their operatives worked totally detached from the main organization, so you could be working for them through a series of—what had Sergei called them? Cutouts, that was it. You could be working through cutouts and never know who was actually footing the bill. If that was the case here, then this Mattenni might not have said anything more than "two Americans coming, give them assistance." Or he might have told them exactly what she was, and what she did.

Not knowing limited her options considerably. They had agreed, on the flight over, to keep Wren's status as low-profile as possible. Especially since the Catholic Church—Rome just down the block, as it were—was still a little hinky about the whole magic thing. The Holy See could be awfully touchy about anyone using current on their turf, sans dispensation. Without knowing if this particular little subsect was *Cosa* friendly or not, she'd have to be totally closeted.

Moving over to the cabinet where Teodosio said the missing manuscript had been stored, Wren looked over at Frederich for permission, then slid the drawer open. It was shallow, maybe two or three inches deep, and the wood had been polished until it gleamed with the patina only really old, well-used furniture got. She took a deep breath, feeling for the stone around her. Normally she preferred to ground on wood or earth, more familiar, human-friendly bases, but she was focusing on something made of wood, so that wouldn't work as well.

*Cool, firm, solid…. Standing in place, forever and yesterday….*

She had been right, there was a faint trickle of current in the stones, but it was deep and buried and sleeping. She left it alone. Satisfied that her body was settled, Wren reached down into her core, pushing a mental hand down and coaxing up one vivid blue tendril. It climbed up into her arm, pulsing with raw possibility.

This was the tricky part, to engage but remain passive, receptive instead of proactive.

*And three and two and one and…* She felt herself fall into the familiar working fugue state, where the entire world was narrowed down to what was exactly in front of her, the familiar hazy sharpness kicking her Talent into gear.

Opening her palm over the surface of the drawer, Wren let the current flow gently out of her like a sprinkling of multicolored confetti falling in slow motion.

Watching the current-confetti, she directed it to show her the item which had been there before, the shape and outline and concept of it, but not the details, not yet.

Normally this worked better with words to shape the intention, but she didn't want to tip her hand in front of her already unhappy observer, not when she was supposed to be in the closet, as it were.

The current swirled, as though confused by her instructions, then seemed to catch on, flowing and co-alescing into a rectangular shape. It seemed as though it were taking hours, but she didn't dare look away to see what Frederich was doing.

Wren blinked at what was forming under her hand, and had to hold on to her temper for fear of disrupting the current. A blank surface…that couldn't be right. Oh. Duh. *Show me the shape of what was* in between *the slate,* she amended her direction, annoyed beyond belief at her own stupidity. Hadn't Teodosio just told them about it being stored in an envelope of sorts, to protect it?

She committed the image that appeared before her to memory, and slowly released the current, allowing the now-useless particles to dissipate.

Pulling her hand back, she cast a quick look at Frederich. He had only moved a few paces, and from his still-bored expression she figured that only a minute or two had passed. Closing the drawer carefully, she pulled up another spark of current and fed it the memory she had in her mind of the parchment and its covering. Shaping the current into a bloodhound, she set it on the trail of the missing item. Where had it been? Where was it moved to? The spark flitted back and forth as though confused. Either the tracks were too old for it to follow, or it had been moved too often, to too many places in the room for it to settle on any one trail.

Neither of those options made sense. Teodosio had told them that the parchment was checked every six months like clockwork, no less and no more, and that it was never taken out of its slate envelope, the implication being that it shouldn't have moved very far from the drawer except on the occasion of it being stolen.

Normally, on something like this, she would be looking for elementals to question. They were mindless bits of electrical fluff, but they were occasionally useful, if you could get them focused long enough. But elementals were lazy things that preferred to gather where there was already a source of current for them to rest in. A building without electrical wiring was not going to appeal to them.

Appeal…current…elementals…slate covers… Something about that—

Suddenly she was back in the tiny office off the bio lab in her old high school. John Ebeneezer perched on his usual stool, lecturing her about what she needed to know, to control her Talent, to be an effective conductor of current…

Wren unconsciously pulled more current up out of her core, molding it in her hand like clay as she tried to remember. It was an old habit, from back when Neezer was on her constantly to think of current as an extension of her own body.

Think, Valere, *think*. Slate was graphite, at least partially. Graphite conducted electricity. But slate was the least conductive form of the natural graphites, which is why it was okay for roofing... Why had they used slate to protect the parchment? Were they trying to keep current out? Or bring it in? Something was wrong. Something didn't fit.

*"Ehi! Che cosa fai?"*

The sudden noise startled her, and she lost control of the strand of current. It leaped from her hand, hitting the ceiling and bouncing back at her, expanding onto a sparkling, sparking jellyfish shape as it stretched out like a living thing, visible to anyone, Talent or Null.

Frederich screamed, and Wren swore, trying to recapture the current before it did damage to any of the furnishings. Frederich could take care of his own damn self and whatever happened he deserved, spooking her like that when she was working!

"Damn, damn, damn, damn," she singsonged. *Calm, damn it, be calm!* She reached out, coaxing it back into her hand. As each bit touched her skin, she took it back down through her epidermis, through the muscle tissue, and down into her core. She was too tired, too suddenly hyped on adrenaline, to be as thorough as she should, and it fought her, sparking and burning wherever it could.

*"Diavolo! Strega!"* Frederich was screaming at her now, but she couldn't focus on what he was saying, even if she'd been able to understand it. He was waving his arms and making faces. She hoped, with whatever atten-

tion she had to spare, that he wasn't having an epileptic fit or anything.

"Wren!"

Sergei burst into the room, followed hard on by Teodosio and two other men. She assumed they were monks. She didn't particularly care, at that point. The last of the current sank below her skin and disappeared with a sharp, stinging slap on her flesh. Sinking to her haunches, she curled her arms around herself and tried to force the current all the way down, down to where it couldn't do any harm, couldn't give her away.

"Wren?" And then Sergei was there, his arms around her, and she felt herself fall apart. "I'm sorry," she thought she whispered, but didn't know quite what she was apologizing for.

"What do you mean, mellow out? She's never been out of the country before, you know." P.B. bit back a growl, feeling his ears go flat against his head in agitation. The water fountain against the far wall made a metallic plinking noise as drops fell, turning wheels and gears that powered the ceiling fan circling lazily overhead. Through the one window the sounds of midday traffic came through, sounding farther away than it actually was.

"I mean, relax, okay? Genevieve's a big girl. She knows how to take care of herself. And anyway, she went to Vancouver last year."

P.B. waved a clawed paw in dismissal. "Vancouver. *Pffhah.* Canada. That's not a real border. And they speak

English there. Mostly. They do, don't they? Yeah, 'cause they filmed *X-Files* there. And *Forever Knight*. And *SG-1*."

"You watch way too much TV."

"Oh yeah, 'cause there's so much else in my life that needs to be doing. Gimme a break. Cable is all that makes Western civilization worthwhile."

The demon was pacing back and forth in the open area of Lee's studio, tapping his claws together in a way that Wren had once told Lee indicated extreme emotional agitation. So far, the lanky artist had been forced to redirect P.B. at least once, when his pacing path came too close to the work in progress, a surprisingly delicate apple tree, four feet high and made entirely of copper and pewter. Sergei had promised him a show if he could come up with works smaller than his usual garden installments of bronze and steel, and Lee rather thought this piece was the start of that show. Be damned if he'd let some hyper-tense fatae screw it up by waving an arm in the wrong place.

"What's really bothering you? The fact that she's out of the country—or the fact that Didier's with her?"

P.B. stopped, turned, and stared at Lee. While the human was glad that he'd gotten the demon's attention, having those dark red eyes stare at him was…unnerving. He mentally ratcheted his opinion of their mutual friend up from "brave but crazy" to "brave but insane" for describing the fatae in front of him as "adorable." Even if she had added "like a rabid mongoose" to that.

"You think—that I—I could…" He finally spluttered

down, and returned to glaring at the Talent. "It's not that I don't like the guy, okay? 'Cause, well, I don't. Much. Okay, he's okay for a human. And Wren loves him, even if she's way too freaked by the whole concept of a relationship to admit it—"

Lee did a mild second take at that bit of information. He had noticed that things seemed a little more tense around the partners than before, but hadn't realized they were heading in that direction. Suddenly, a few things made a little more sense. He made a mental note to discuss that turn of events with his wife, once he got rid of his surprise guest.

"No, the fact that her fataephobic partner is with her is…actually reassuring. In that if I'm not there to look out for her he will, as much as his wussy human reflexes allow him to. If the Council comes gunning for her, 'cause you know they will, they've got their people everywhere. But, see, I could do it better. But did they ask me? No! All I get is 'P.B., gotta go, watch the apartment, willya?' Like I was some kind of plant-watering petsitter."

"Oh for…" Suddenly Lee had had it with the demon's self-pity party. The bastard was lonely—which explained why he'd made this unexpected drop-in to the human's studio only a day after the two had left—and he just had to get the hell over it. "That's not what they asked you to do at all."

P.B. threw his compact body onto the only other chair in the room, a brown leather recliner that must have seen better decades, and was in the studio as a stopping point on its way to the dump. A disconsolate snarl rose from his throat, and Lee's skin prickled. Then the noise stopped, as though P.B. had suddenly realized it was coming from him, and the demon sighed instead, a remarkably human sound. "Yeah, I know. But it felt like that. They get to go off and do exciting things, and I'm stuck behind. Ignoring the whole 'how the hell could you get on a plane' thing 'cause yeah, know that, live that. It sucks living in a human world, you know that?"

Demons, unlike any of the other known fatae races, were created—according to one story, somewhere back in the mists of magic, a mad Talent had manipulated several races into creating what he had thought would be an interesting subspecies of servant. Over the generations since then the bloodline had gone in several different directions as the parent genes reasserted themselves, but they were all immediately recognizable by their blood-red eyes. The *Cosa* referred to them all collectively as "demon," with all the implicit emotional and psychological baggage attached.

"I know." Being a Talent was no picnic either, even if he only used current to weld his sculptures. The fact that he had married outside of the *Cosa* was a constant source of amazement to all concerned; it was rare to find a Null that you could *tell* about magic, much less admit that you used it on a regular basis.

Maybe that was why Wren and Sergei felt, once he got over the shock, like such an obvious idea. They already knew each other's secrets, after all. After Wren, even the most fascinating socialite on the Manhattan art scene was probably a bit…tame.

"Look, P.B., the truth is I know for a fact that Wren asked you to do something really important, because she asked me to be your backup. So take that for what it's worth—you're point person, and I'm office support. How's that supposed to make me feel?"

P.B. made a rude, wet noise through his nose. "Relieved?"

Lee laughed at that. Point, made and well taken. His reputation for noninvolvement in *Cosa* affairs was widely known. He heard more gossip that way. And nobody expected him to actually act on any of it. Which meant he could—when he chose to.

"So, what have you heard?" P.B. leaned forward, his chin resting on the pads of his hands—claws now semi-sheathed—and looking unnervingly like a petite, white-fur-covered version of Rodin's "The Thinker."

Lee leaned back in his own chair, legs the length of P.B.'s entire body stretched out in front of him. "The gossip mills have been churning," he admitted. "It's mostly low-level stuff, no more boneheaded moves like they did last spring, locking down anyone who bucked them, Mage or not. But I don't think they've backed off. That's not Council style, much as those bastards have any.

"Stuff that might affect us directly? I've already told Wren most of it, the stuff the Council's spreading about her. But that's personal, not…" Lee picked up a scrap of iron and smoothed it with his hands, almost absently

softening the edges until the metal flowed into gentle un-
dulations. "I've heard some talk, though. Not even
rumors, but hints and whispers of rumors. That the
Council's gearing up for another push against unaffiliates—" lonejacks, he meant. "A push that's going to be
ugly."

"It ain't never been anything but," P.B. said strongly.
"Not when it comes to the Council. Just you guys, or all
the fatae who ain't them? And any idea if Wren's going
to be the primary target again, like this spring, or…?"

"Not a clue. I think, though, they're going to go for
less… alerted targets." He grimaced. "Christ, listen to
me. I sound like a bad made-for-TV war movie."

For the first time, Lee was able to discern a distinct
and recognizable emotion on the demon's flat, furred
face. Unhappiness. "It *is* a war," he said sadly, his claws
flexing again. "Or if not yet, soon. Really, really soon.
And we're gonna be right in the middle of it."

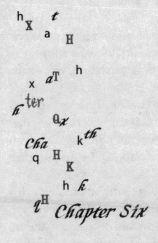

*Chapter Six*

Despite the optimistic words of the forecasters that morning, the heat was, if anything, worse when Andre finally left the unmarked, unremarkable building that housed the Silence at seven o'clock on Saturday evening. There was still a stack of work on his desk, but all the reachable fires had been put out, the recalcitrant cats herded into a corner, and only one last item of business to deal with before he could collapse with a brandy and the book he had been trying to finish now for almost a month.

The asphalt was soft underfoot, and he winced as he stepped onto it, mentally tabulating the cost to get the marks off his shoes. God how he hated summers in the city.

A plane roared overhead, and he looked up instinctively. His two reluctant operatives must be on the job in Italy by now, hopefully with the bit firmly between their teeth. Giving them a tip of his nonexistent hat, he continued across the street and on to his meeting.

His assistant was waiting in a far booth, out of the busy flow of traffic.

"Sorry I'm late." He put his briefcase down on the seat next to him, between himself and the wall in an instinctive New Yorker's paranoia that had nothing to do with the actual contents of the briefcase. "Did your task turn up anything?"

Jorgunmunder nodded in greeting, then shook his head in a negative response. "His apartment was clean. If he keeps any notes, which I'm starting to doubt, they're on him at all times. His computer was password-protected. I managed to crack it, but there was nothing there but details from his little business front."

"Damn. He's probably got everything locked down in a secured PDA kept in his pocket at all times, knowing Sergei. The man does protect his privacy. No," Andre reconsidered, "not a PDA, considering his associate." Working with Talents was hell on personal electronics. More likely he had gone back to the old-fashioned notebook in an off-site safe deposit box. Low-tech was best when you had close contact with magic. Or…

"Damn," Andre said again. "Of course. The gallery. There is already a very nice security system there, I've no doubt, and he would think we'd think it too obvious to search." He was amused again at how proud he was of the boy. "Well, we have time to look there now, as they'll be out of the country for several days at least."

His associate shifted in his seat, clearly uncomfortable

in the role of sneak-thief he had been forced into. Poul had such an outdated notion of honor and dignity. It was delightfully retro and somewhat appealing to observe. Just so long as it didn't keep him from doing the job.

They were meeting in the coffee shop two blocks down from the Silence building; less for privacy and more to ensure that the coffee was drinkable. For a multinational, extraordinarily well-funded organization, they had the most astonishingly disgusting coffee in every single kitchenette. A coworker had once run an experiment, bringing in a different kind of high-quality bean every week. And each time, the pot came out borderline undrinkable.

They drank it anyway. You had to, to get through the day. But they didn't enjoy it. The diner, while decorated in a distinctly nauseating pale green color and chrome scheme, had excellent coffee.

"Why are you so certain he has anything, anyway? He caved to us, remember?" Jorgunmunder had met Sergei only once, when Andre was sent to bring the agent back into the fold, but they had formed an instant mutual antipathy in that meeting.

"Sergei came to terms because we were useful to him, specifically in protecting our shared mutual interest, Ms. Valere." Wren had told him off in their second meeting about using her personal name without permission, and he adhered to that formality now even when she wasn't around to hear. "That is not 'caving,' and I would advise you to not let that perception in any way color your expectations or conclusions about what Sergei may or may not ever do."

Jorgunmunder didn't take the rebuke well, but Andre cared only that he took it. Remembered it. Sergei might not have been the best Handler he had ever trained, but he was one of the most independent-thinking. That had made him flexible, and remarkably successful. Of course, it was also likely what had driven him from the Silence in the first place. And while that had ended well, there were lessons to be learned about not repeating the mistakes. You didn't survive in the Silence if you made the same mistake twice. Or even once, all too often.

And that meant not repeating certain other mistakes with his current trainee, either.

"You did well, Poul. Thank you. And now get the hell out of here. It's Saturday night, don't you have someone to take to the movies?"

Jorgunmunder blushed, the color startling under his flame-red hair. "Yessir. I will see you on Monday, sir."

The waitress came and cleared away the other man's debris, and refilled Andre's mug without asking. He sipped at it, in no great hurry to go out into the heat again, when he had the sudden feeling that he was being watched. Not that this was so unusual—he wasn't a bad-looking man if he did say so himself—but it didn't feel like the normal kind of once-over New Yorkers gave each other in social settings.

Sure enough, three or four minutes after Jorgun-munder left, which made it long enough to seem accidental, and yet soon enough to let him know it wasn't—another man slid into the recently vacated seat, the fabric of his hand-tailored suit moving smoothly against the vinyl upholstery. Andre was pretty sure that it was coincidental that the new coffee suddenly smelled of sulfur and smoke.

"You're a busy one this week. Sending people hither and yon and hither yet again…."

"That *is* my job." A cold sweat started to trickle down the back of Andre's neck that had nothing to do with the air-conditioning vent behind him. Duncan. What the hell was going on?

"And mine is to know the whys and wherefores of all my operatives' actions. Yours I am not so sure of."

Andre looked directly at the other man then, knowing that it was more dangerous right now not to meet his gaze. "My goals are the same as they have ever been."

"To serve the Silence to the utmost of your abilities?" Duncan's voice was dry, mocking. His eyes were hidden behind dark glasses, and his narrow, aesthetic-looking face gave nothing away. He never gave anything away.

"That, and to survive—to the utmost of my abilities."

*That* surprised a harsh laugh out of the bastard. "Very good. Very good. But be careful as you go, Felhim. There are traps laid even for the most wary."

"Sir." A warning, or a threat?

Only after the other man had gone did Andre allow himself to shudder. It didn't matter what had been meant by that cryptic statement. Duncan never gave anything away, to anyone. You always had to pay.

What the hell did the über-high head of Ops suspect, to be dropping hints in such a cryptic fashion? Nobody could say anything, with any certainty, about Duncan.

Not even how high he actually ranked within the Silence. Some said he *was* the Silence. Andre had never met anyone who claimed to be equal, much less higher in the food chain. So what did it mean that he'd left his dark upper-floor lair in order to have this little tête-à-tête in public? Why was the bastard watching *him* so closely?

And what in bloody hell was it going to take to get him looking anywhere else?

## Chapter Seven

The pillow was too flat. She shoved a hand into it, trying to force more fluff into the feathers. It was too hard, too. Hard, flat…not her pillows.

That processed, Wren let consciousness slip over her a little more. Not her pillow. Not her self-indulgent three hundred-count Egyptian cotton sheets. Not her bed.

Right. Memory filtered back; the light, the monastery, Frederich screaming at her, making what looked like rude gestures as she tried to control the current struggling under her skin, Sergei yelling, then half-carrying her down the stairs, out to the car, Teodosio apologetic at the edges of her awareness.

It had hurt, pulling the current in like that. It shouldn't have hurt that much. It shouldn't have hurt at all. Something about that place, that room…

She opened her eyes, suddenly and painfully wide-awake, in the really bad, monster-in-the-closet way. Her heart sounded loudly in her ears, loud enough for her instinctive duck-and-cover Retrievers' instinct to try and take over, and she fought it down with an effort, slowing her breathing and forcing muscles physical and Talented to slowly relax. Whatever the danger, it wasn't here.

She rolled over under the starch-scratchy sheet and saw Sergei slumped in a straight-backed chair pulled close to the bed. For a moment she had a flashback to the spring, when she'd spent far too long in bed recovering from current outlay, with Sergei sitting guard in a very similar pose. Only sometimes then he'd be on the bed with her, his arm around her shoulders. Not so much lately, though. Weird, and bad, how quickly things could get messed up.

Maybe being away from everything, away from home, they'd be able to find time to talk things over, figure out what they wanted, where it started getting weird.

But not today. Not until they had a handle on the job. Something was totally wonky. Things just didn't add up. But she didn't even know what they were supposed to be *counting*, much less what was missing from the total.

*Goddamned Silence. And Andre and the alleged white horse he rode in on, too. Sergei warned me. He did warn me.* Warned her that the Silence had their own agendas, their own reasons. And that she would be at their mercy, if she had him negotiate the contract. *But what other choice did we have? Even he agreed to that.* The Silence stood between her and the Council, for as long as she was useful to them. And while the two organizations might not fear each other—might, in fact, know damn little about each other and weren't we all thankful for that?—they knew enough to know that it wasn't a good idea to make the other their enemy. Not over so small an item as one lonejack called The Wren.

So here they were. Sergei had changed out of the outfit from the plane, and was wearing what she thought of as a Retriever-y outfit—softly pleated khakis and a faded blue button-down shirt. Something that could pass for business casual or dressed-up trash, depending on how he played it. But his hair was a mess, and blue shadows rested under his eyes and along the line of his chin.

*Five o'clock stubble. Moment he wakes up he's going to be scraping his face. What time is it, anyway?*

Time to use the bathroom, according to her bladder. Moving slowly, alert to the return of pain anywhere, she got out of the bed and looked around for the bathroom.

It was your basic hotel room, apparently the same worldwide. Narrow bed, check. Sturdy-looking wood-textured laminate writing desk and chair, the latter currently occupied by Sergei, check. Small dresser with four drawers of the same laminate, check. Carpeting of a slightly disturbing color, check. Insipid painting bolted to the wall, check. Two white-painted doors, check. Odds were the one without the lock on it was the bathroom.

*Yay me, deductive scientist.*

The bathroom was as basic as the bedroom, but about one eighth the size. Still, it was clean, and there was a mildew-free shower curtain around the skinny-people-only shower stall. Shower soon, she promised herself. She closed the door behind her, which created enough room for her to sit down on the toilet.

The flush seemed unusually loud, and she flinched at the noise as it echoed against the tile. The tingling of a headache started on the edges of her skull as she turned to wash up. Warm water splashed on her face made the tingling recede a little bit. Cold water might work better to wake her up, but the thought alone made her flinch. Bracing herself on the white ceramic sink, she raised her head and looked into the mirror.

Sergei must have unbraided her hair when he stripped her down to her plain white T-shirt and panties, not that she remembered any of it. Her hair was tangled, but better than the scalp-soreness that usually came from sleeping with the braid in.

Taking closer inventory, Wren wasn't too displeased with what she saw. Her eyes were a little bloodshot, but the shadows underneath weren't too bad. This might have been the most consecutive sleep she'd gotten in weeks, between the heat back home, the stress, and then the overnight plane trip. Skin was a little blotchy, a little puffy, but a good hot shower should take care of that. Overall, she looked somewhere between mildly hungover and human, which was pretty much how she felt.

Her toiletries kit was on the narrow ledge above the sink and she rummaged through it until she found her toothbrush and toothpaste.

"Hey."

"Murmph," she said around a mouthful of paste, waggling her fingers in greeting at her partner's reflection in the mirror. "Murhmizit?"

"Around seven," he said, interpreting her without too much difficulty. "Sunday morning," for further clarification. "You slept almost twelve hours."

Well, that explained the lack of jet lag. She wondered how much if any of that he'd slept as well, but knew better than to ask. She rinsed and spat, and put the brush into the glass on the ledge to dry.

"Hungry?"

And suddenly, she was.

"Shower first, though. You should have one too, you're starting to get a little ripe. Um, you *do* have a room, right?" Not that she'd mind sharing with him, but the bed was way too small for two people, even if he'd been a foot shorter.

"Yes, next over. Meet you in about twenty?"

Wren cast a look at the shower. Probably not going to be a luxury experience, no. "Yeah, twenty should do it."

She reached in past the curtain to turn the water on, and pulled off her T-shirt, only afterward realizing that Sergei was still standing there. Not that he hadn't seen her naked before, but…it was different, now. Now she'd be nude, not naked. Nude was a lot more…naked.

"Out, Didier."

He blinked, as though not sure what she was talking about, then grinned like a little kid caught with a handful of cookies, and was gone. She heard the door close and lock behind him as she stepped into the shower. *Hot water. Bliss, oh bliss….*

She ended up waiting for him, despite taking her time in the shower after all. Getting dressed hadn't taken much thought or effort, pulling the nearest thing out of the suitcase Sergei had brought in for her. She'd simply braided her hair into two short plaits that tucked behind her ears, intentionally playing up how young that made her look. Her hands had moved automatically, weaving the damp strands, while her mind moved over the pieces they'd gathered so far, shifting them like a puzzle cube, not really trying to make anything of them yet, but looking-not-looking for a pattern to surprise her.

This was the part of the job that was the most difficult. Out of the planning stage (not that they'd had any of that, and damn she hated subcontracting!) but not yet really into the meat of the Retrieval. It was all thinking. She was a lot better at acting, and reacting, than thinking. And while being on a Retrieval usually meant there was a crystalline sharpness added to her brain, for some reason that organ seemed even duller than usual, this morning.

She needed coffee. Badly.

The lobby was as bare-bones as the rooms, comprising a wood and marble registration desk with mail cubbies behind it that looked like it had been lifted off a movie set, and a pair of straight-backed chairs and small glass table that could have fit into any small-town dentist's waiting room. Overall, it felt as though the place had been built around 1950 and then abandoned in that decade. In her jeans and button down shirt, this one a dark blue, she felt oddly out of place, as though she should be wearing a sundress and heels instead. Well, her sandals were suitably ladylike, she supposed, even if they didn't have a significant heel. You never knew when you'd have to run.

The only grace note to break up the monochrome feel was the long fish tank on a metal stand against the far wall. She had wandered down the hallway that connected the two floors of rooms to the lobby to take a look at it, fascinated by the flick-and-turn of the brightly colored tropical fish inside.

"You're late," she said to the familiar footfalls on the linoleum behind her.

"Sorry. Picked up e-mail before my shower, took longer than I expected."

She turned to look at him. Same clothing, but freshly shaved and bathed. Fine lines around his narrow-lipped mouth that indicated he was worrying at something. "Stuff?"

"Mmmm. P.B. checking in, mainly. Do I even want to know where he's logging in from?"

"There's an Internet café in the Village that doesn't blink at anyone who comes in, any hour." She saw Sergei's look of disbelief. "No, I didn't give him my password. He's a friend, but he's still a freelancer. He'd sell everything I had to the highest bidder and feel no guilt whatsoever."

He had slicked his wet hair back in his usual styling, but a strand was curling over his forehead unnoticed. He must have forgotten to pack the hair gel. She resisted the urge to smooth it back into place.

"You two have the strangest friendship."

"Yeah well, that's what he says about us, too. So what's up back home?"

"We've been gone for all of forty-eight hours. What could have happened?"

She opened her mouth to give him a probable list, and he shook his head. "No, please don't answer that. Don't worry, I think he just wanted reassurances. Oh, and that he and your friend Lee are quote 'pooling their gossip resources,' unquote. Does that fill you with as much fear as it does me?"

Wren snickered. "Hah, good for them. Bet they have all the *Cosa* gossip from Baltimore to Montreal tied up in a cute red bow by now. If they take it professional, we had damn well better get discounted rates for introducing them."

Sergei now looked a little worried, but Wren was cool with it. Not that P.B. couldn't make a disaster out of a church picnic, if he wanted to, but everything was totally under control, so long as Lee was involved. Tree-taller was the steady sort—if P.B. got too wound up, he'd sit on the demon until things mellowed again.

"So what's the plan?"

"There's a café in town that the guy at the desk said was rather good. We can walk there, then come back and get the car."

"We're in town?" Damn. Maybe it was the lack of information, or the jet lag showing up another way, or maybe it was just Sergei's relatively unusual presence on the job, but she wasn't feeling sharp at all. Coffee. Fast.

"You were rather out of it when we got here last night.

Yes." He escorted her out the lobby door and into the same golden-clear sunlight as yesterday. She raised her face to the blue sky and couldn't help but smile. Her natural Talent-fueled preference was for thunderclouds and heavy ozone, but this was nice, too.

They were, in fact, in a very pretty little town—the one she had seen from the cliff yesterday, Wren suspected. The hotel—more of a motel, really—was set off on a side street, with a small parking lot to the side. They strolled to the corner and turned onto what was obviously the main drag, a two-way street lined with small businesses and shops, none of which were open this early.

"I'm having the sudden urge to go shopping" she said wistfully as they passed a window with colorful watercolors displayed.

Sergei took a quick look and sniffed. "Junk. You want souvenirs, we'll find the real thing."

"I can't afford the real thing," Wren said. "Hell, I can't even really afford the fake stuff, either. But it's fun to look." And if something were to happen to fall into her pocket…it's not as though she'd be taking anything really expensive. Probably. Just to keep her hand in, as it were. The thought seemed to add an important tingle to her musings about the job, and she coaxed it a little closer.

She had talked, once and long ago, to a cop her mom was dating about the mental makeup of professional criminals. Especially thieves. There were all sorts of theories, he'd told her, and nobody could agree on anything, but the one thing he'd seen over the years was that a really good thief—the ones he knew about but could never catch—were professionals; not junkies, not kids on a crime spree lark, not someone out for a high-profile smash-and-grab. Solid, reliable workmen. That's who made a living out of crime.

Wren suspected she was more of a kleptomaniac, at least at first. She'd started stealing because it was a way she could calm the anxiety and loneliness her Talent made her feel, isolated from everyone else, even her mother. But those feelings had gone away once Neezer came into her life, and all that remained was the satisfaction of planning, the intensity of the Retrieval, the emotional crash afterward, and overall the sense that this was what she was good at, in life.

So why wasn't that rush, that sense of apprehensive pleasure, coming, here?

"Earth to Wren, come in, Wren…."

"Sorry." She smiled up at her partner. "Just trying to think. Not good results. Will stop now."

"You need caffeine," he said.

Yeah. That was it. Coffee would set everything back on track.

At the café they stood with a couple of old men at a long polished brass bar and ordered coffee and fruit-filled pastries from the woman behind the counter, and then took them to a small table off to the side of the shop, away from where all the old men in town apparently gathered to argue over whatever was in the newspapers.

"There was also, as expected, a message from our

contact waiting at the hotel," Sergei said, once they were settled with their coffee and breakfast. Wren, most of her attention focused on figuring out what kind of fruit was inside her pastry, just nodded to keep him talking.

"Or rather, there was a message from her office. Apparently Senora Fabrizio was in a car accident on her way to the airport yesterday morning."

That got Wren's attention, one hundred percent sharp and shiny. "Bad?"

"She's in the hospital. The message was worded in such a way, however, as to make me believe that they did not expect positive news."

"Accident?" Wren believed wholeheartedly in accidents over coincidence, but this seemed a bit of a stretch.

Sergei made a "who knows" gesture that seemed to fit particularly well in their surroundings. Very Italian, from the little she had seen so far. Lots of arms and hands getting flung around. "The way people drive around here? Probably. Not certainly. Coincidence isn't always another word for plot."

"Lovely. Was there anything they needed to tell us we should have known before we went to the site?"

"Yes." He paused. "To be careful."

"Oh. Well that was damned helpful now, wasn't it?" Because she hadn't already figured that part out. *Goddamned Silence living up to their name again.*

Silence. Stillness. She frowned, digging mentally into her memory, to no avail. There was something there, something in the puzzle pieces she hadn't quite remembered yet. But you couldn't force that stuff; the hindbrain worked in its own slow and mysterious way. Especially when you'd gotten it zapped twelve hours before.

She finished the pastry and decided it had been some weird but tasty blend of apricot and strawberry. The cappuccino was also divine, with just the right balance of bitterness to the gentler influence of the milk, and a hint of something spicy on the top. She could almost feel the sharpness beginning to take over her thoughts, making it easier to function.

"So. Want to tell me about what happened up there yesterday?" That was the thing about Sergei that freaked most people out, how he went from kid gloves to brass knuckles without a flicker of hesitation or any other sign of warning.

"Not really." She stopped with the mug halfway back up to her mouth, hearing the way that sounded even as she was saying it. "Sorry. Wasn't trying to be flip. But…"

*Oh.*

She put the mug down, watching his hands as they tore strips from his pastry and then placed them back on the plate in neat rows, not really processing what she was seeing.

*Stillness. Silence. Lack of electricity. Secrets. Silence.*

All the bits, flickering on parade through her brain. *Don't jump just because you're frustrated, Valere. Talk it out. Use Sergei's reactions as a sounding board. Make sure your ducks are in order before you start shooting.* "I'm really not sure what happened. It might just have been that I was tired. Or that I'm so not used to working in dark spaces—"

"Dark?"

"Um." Wren tried to figure out how to verbalize it when she'd only just that moment really figured it out. "Not dark as in unlit, although that place was that, too. Cut off from current. You know." She looked up and saw an all too familiar expression on his face. A little amusement, and a little frustration. "Sorry. I forget sometimes you don't know. Weird, isn't it? I mean, I know you're mostly Null but sometimes you're not, and I think—"

"Wren?" The frustration was overwhelming the amusement.

"Right." Her pulse sped up slightly, the current coiled in her core just awake enough to hiss and seethe slightly. To remind her of who and what she was. And what she knew.

"You know there are places where current sort of gathers, right? Ley lines, magnetic points, power plants…" When he nodded, impatient, she went on. "Well, a dark space is just the opposite, somewhere that, for whatever reason, rejects current. Or is somehow cut off from it. This whadayacallit, the House of Legend, is cut off, totally. There's some current in there, same as with just about anything natural, but it's so faint, I bet I couldn't call it up even if I tried. And I wouldn't want to try, with all that going on around it." She shuddered involuntarily, thinking of how close she had come to even worse disaster. "I thought it was just that they don't have any electrical wiring, but I think maybe the reason they don't have wiring is because they're so cut off. I bet they could lay cables from here until the next millennium and they still wouldn't have stable electricity."

"Is that common?"

"Nuh-uh." She shook her head emphatically. "Totally rare. So much so, like I said, that even we forget there are places like that, 'cause you'll run into them maybe once in your lifetime. More likely never. And they're almost always natural formations. Finding a man-made structure that's dark—"

"It was built that way?" His hands stilled on the pastry for a moment.

"Can't imagine anyone accidentally building something that size out of dark materials, so…yeah. Probably was."

"And the reason for that would be…what?"

"To prevent current from getting at whatever was stored in there, probably." She nodded, fitting the available pieces together finally into a pattern that made sense. Her unease, the weird way she had woken up, the way the monks treated the building… "Using current… it's tricky, when you've got the dark space sucking at you. And back before they figured current-science it was even worse, 'cause you didn't know *why* what had worked perfectly well before suddenly didn't near this tree or that rock or those mountains. And back then was when, according to Brother Teo, the building was put up. A Talent would be pretty much blind. If they weren't trained in more ordinary practices as well, they'd never be able to get in and out."

"Like you."

Wren acknowledge the fact. "Like me." When she

and Sergei had first begun their partnership, she had only the basic shoplifting skills bored suburban teenagers pick up, and even those had been rusty with disuse, thanks to Neezer's disapproval of her "hobby." Once Sergei approached her with his proposal, however, she had decided that using current where none was needed was wasteful. Finding herself a number of dubiously legitimate teachers over the years, Wren had learned a little lock picking, a little B and E, a little this and a little that of whatever might come in handy, including the ability to read blueprints and electrical wiring plans. Jane of all trades, Mistress of one.

"So this House of Legend really *is* a house of legend," Sergei said now. "Makes you wonder about those four monks arriving out of nowhere, doesn't it?"

Wren cradled her cup in her hands and stared down into it. "Makes me want not to wonder. I'm thinking maybe those are the kind of things it's healthier not to know about, probably." She looked up, and saw that his hands were moving again. "Oh for…Didier, are you going to eat that or weave it?"

Sergei looked down at the plate of pastry strips as though seeing it for the first time. "Oh. Sorry. You want?"

"Not after you've played with it, no. I do want some more coffee, though."

She pushed the mug over to him, and he looked at the white ceramic cup with surprise. "So go get yourself some. You have money, right?"

"No *habla* Italian, remember?"

"Improvise."

Wren gave him her best glare, but he merely went back to picking apart his pastry. With a put-upon sigh, Wren took back her cup and went up to the counter. Once again, he was acting like the senior partner, telling her what she should do. And she was *letting* him.

The woman who had helped them before was gone, and in her place was a very large old man, with white hair standing up in tufts all over his head. "Ah…*scusi? Un cappuccino, per favore?*"

"Of course," he said in clear, if accented English, taking her cup back from her and reaching down to pull a clean one down from a rack. "That will be two-twenty, *grazie.*"

Wren felt her jaw drop, then swung around to glare at the back of her partner's now neatly groomed head. "Bastard," she muttered under her breath, reaching into her wallet to take out the required euros. All right, he was one up on her. She would not give him the satisfaction of a reaction. She would *not.*

"Bastard," she said as she sat down with her coffee.

"It was a long-shot bet that anyone working a café would speak some English, even out here," he said mildly, but she knew better. *You're so going to pay for that,* she promised him with a glare. *Some day.*

"On the topic of languages, what was Frederich going on and on about yesterday, anyway? Speaking of annoying."

"Oh." Sergei had to stop and think about it for a moment. "He was calling you a witch, actually."

Wren rolled her eyes. "Great. So much for low-profile. Is that going to be a problem?" She was speaking both politically and practically, and from the way her partner pursed his lips and thought for a moment, he was taking both under consideration.

"If it is, it's their problem, not yours. The worst they could do without admitting to the world that they've been robbed—which they clearly don't want to do, otherwise Rome would be involved in this—is hang over our shoulder breathing fire, assuming the Silence was even allowed near this place, which I doubt. And that's assuming Frederich can even get anyone here to believe what he saw while you were working."

"Not that he saw much," Wren agreed. "Although…I was assuming that he was Null, because working there on a regular basis if you weren't… Drive you nuts. But if you were a Talent, and knew about it, and could adapt…"

"Wouldn't you have done the mage-dar thing, if—?"

"Yeah." She hated that phrase, but it was a pretty good way of describing how her instinct sort of whispered at her around other Talents. "Yeah, I was close enough to him to know. And he would have reacted differently to what happened, unless he was totally untrained, which would mean he wouldn't be able to handle the dark space, so never mind. How did Brother Theo react?"

"Teodosio," he corrected. "I just told him that you'd had a blood sugar crash coupled with jet lag, and that we would be back after you were more rested. He seemed quite concerned about your delicacy."

Wren made a rude noise and finished off the coffee while he skimmed a newspaper lifted from the now-empty table next to them. Deciding that any more caffeine would probably just make her way too jumpy, she put the cup down and pushed back her chair. "Think the monks are awake?"

"Bells, prayers. Etcetera," he said, quoting her back to herself. "I bet they're awake and already hard at work. I need to make a phone call. Be back in a minute."

She watched, idly curious, as he left the café and went to stand out on the sidewalk, speaking into his mobile phone. He could use it around her—she could even use it, carefully. But it was better, if he could, to get some distance between himself and a Talent before pulling out the electronics.

She wondered who he was calling, and why, then shrugged. He did have another business to run, besides her. Maybe he was trying to set up a viewing of some local artist, make this trip a legal tax deduction.


"You set us up! You sent us in with incomplete files, no follow-through, faulty data—"

"Our data—"

"Sucked."

Andre could hear the flat tone, even through the trans-Atlantic static on the line. A flat tone that indicated his Operative had reached a breaking point.

"Ms. Valere is all right?" That was the most obvious thing that would send Didier into a rage, if his partner had been harmed or threatened. Since that was how he had convinced them to work for the Silence, in a roundabout fashion, Andre had faced that anger before.

"She's all right. Barely. There wouldn't have been a problem if you'd told us about this House of Legend, and what was in it—and what it was. I can buy these monks being clueless, but Douglas's people are better than that. Much better."

Sergei was right. Douglas's people knew things nobody else did. They knew things, and they put everything into their reports for operatives to work from. That was their sole reason for existing. The fact that he had kept Darcy from them, despite her skills, was due merely to the fact that she had a whim to stay.

If Sergei was right, and odds were ugly that he was, intel was missing from their base files, because Andre had no idea what Sergei was talking about. *Intentionally* missing intel, withheld from the main office as well as his operative.

Layers within layers inside shadows. Someone was pulling very delicate strings. Hell, someone was *always* pulling strings. The important question wasn't who; that would come out in the wash. The important question wasn't even why. The question was how much damage had been done to Andre—and by extension his people—by it.

"Nothing was withheld from you." The lie rolled smoother than truth off his tongue. "You have our full support, and the support of all our resources. You know that. Our entire philosophy is about solving problems, not causing them."

"Right." Nobody could pack so much cynicism into one word as a Russian. All right, Russian-American. He still nailed it, and Andre could feel amusement slipping through the fog of anger at being left out of the loop.

"Go deal with your situation, Sergei Kassianovich. I will cover your backs here."

"Damn well better." A click, silence, and then dial tone.

"Damn, damn, damn." Andre stared at the phone, then jabbed a finger down on the intercom button. "Bren! Now. And page Jorgunmunder, too." He wanted to say more, but tamped the urge down. Anyone could be listening. Anyone probably was.

First things first. Get the intel Sergei needed. *Then* strike back.

Sergei looked peeved when he came back from his call, but shook off her question, so she backed off. They walked to the car in silence, the only thawing in his mood coming when she let her hand slip into his. He squeezed once, then let go. It was enough.

Through the rolled-down car windows they could hear the echoes of church bells coming from behind them, as one town after another called the faithful to morning services. But none of the bells, surprisingly, came from their destination. Wren was going to comment on that, then shrugged. Sergei was probably right, monks probably got up at three in the morning to say their prayers before going out to do…whatever it was they did. Maybe bells would be a distraction, now. She'd gotten the feeling yesterday they weren't exactly the most religious order in the confession booth, anyway.

It was a relatively quick drive from the village to the monastery, despite the steepness of the hills. As the car chugged steadily up a narrow, winding road, Wren really wished she were in a better mood, to enjoy the scenery. But the closer they got to the House, the more on edge she felt. *A dark space. Dear God.* Neezer had told her about them, but even he'd never encountered one. Nobody she knew had, or at least if they had they'd never mentioned it. And wasn't that the kind of thing you'd talk about?

Wren recalled the sense of isolation and coldness she had gotten when she first walked into the building, and shivered despite the early morning warmth. Maybe it wasn't.

"You okay with this?"

It was unnerving, sometimes, how well her partner could pick up on her moods.

"Not really. But the job's got to get done. And the sooner we're out of here and done with it, the better." He grunted what she took as an assent, and she reached over and put her hand over his where it rested on the shift. "Just stick with me this time, okay? No running off to interview any monks?"

"Agreed." His hand shifted a little so he could curl his fingers up around hers in a comforting touch. "He was a waste of time, anyway. My Italian is fine for ordering dinner and navigating customs. Interrogation? That I don't have the vocabulary for. So everything had to be funneled through Brother Teodosio."

"You think Teo was holding out on us? Or not telling you everything the kid said?"

"I think he has his own agenda," he said. "Yes, they want the manuscript found, but—"

"But all his openness and sharing makes you think there's a lot he's not letting us see."

"Exactly."

"Today's just going to be a blast, isn't it?" She could feel the adrenaline starting to build in her system and from the tight grin Sergei shot her, he was having the same experience. It wasn't like actually executing a Retrieval—nothing could beat the rush she got from that—but it was the start. Anything was possible. And in their job, typically anything that was possible was probable as well. You had to stay alert, stay loose, stay focused, not let anything distract you....

"Witch!" In English, this time, shouted out the window in the dormitory's upper floor. Somebody had clearly hit the books overnight, to learn the proper word.

Teodosio looked deeply apologetic about his monk's behavior. Again. This time, however, Wren was entirely conscious and capable of taking care of herself, leaving Sergei time to watch their host's expression more closely. And he was pretty sure the look was a put-on, surface deep at most. There was something about Teo's eyes that was at odds with everything else. Not that Teodosio wasn't sorry for the fuss, but more because it annoyed him personally than because it possibly distressed Wren.

Interesting. Not that Sergei expected more of men of the cloth than he did of anyone else, which was to say, not much at all.

"I am sorry," the monk was saying in reaction to the shouted commentary. "I had been informed that you had…certain abilities which would aid in the location of the Nescanni Parchment, but I chose to keep this information from others here, as I was not sure they would understand…."

"Oh, I'd say they understand quite well." Sergei held on to his temper, even though he wanted nothing more than to strangle the whelp screaming invectives at his partner. At his side, he could feel Wren shaking, and he resisted the need to draw her in close to him. No weakness. They couldn't afford to show weakness.

The stream of insults had begun the moment they walked up from the parking lot to the main landing, Frederich clearly having been on the lookout for them that morning, waiting by the path. Sergei had seen antiabortion activists behave the same way, lurking like a bird-dog until a target appeared, and then springing forward.

Teodosio had intercepted them before anything physical could happen—as though Nulls could stop Wren if she got seriously pissed off—and on his command two other brown-garbed men had come out and hustled the rabid monk from sight the moment he began ranting, but they didn't seem inclined to muzzle him once he was inside the house. Sergei suspected more than one of the monks shared Freddie's views, but weren't foolish enough to express it so clearly. Or at least not in English, so she would be certain to understand.

And how many monks were there here, anyway? The size of the house and the garden suggested that there couldn't be very many living here. Twelve, maybe twenty, unless they slept strung up in hammocks like old-time sailors. Damn it, they needed information. He would never have let Wren walk into this, if he'd been the one putting the file together.

He realized that he was sizing up the situation as though it were a hostile zone, and wished he hadn't thought that particular thought. Especially since he hadn't been able to take his handgun with him. Maybe someone in the Milan office would be able to get him one.

"Blasphemer! Monster! Devil's whelp!"

That one got Wren's attention, and she started forward. Sergei reached out and grabbed her by the arm, ignoring the nasty jolt he got from her. She tried to shake him off by more mundane means, but he held firm.

"Wren…"

"Let. Go."

"Ignore him, Wren."

"He's—"

"He's a nasty little close-minded shit who should not be allowed to see he's getting to you."

She didn't turn away, but he could feel the tension in her body start to fade. Teodosio looked from one to the other, now all but visibly wringing his hands. Sergei really wanted to tell him to not try so damn hard. He looked less like the jolly monk stereotype now and more like the Dean of Students on a really bad day. Which, Sergei supposed, he was. Well, they were *not* his students. It was time to take control of this situation, and—

"All right," Wren said. "All right."

He let his hand drop from her arm as she turned to face Teodosio. With those two words, their roles had changed; she was back in the leadership role. And, to be truthful, he preferred it that way. They each had their strengths, and hers was best utilized in the field.

"I want to see every piece of paper you have that refers to the...what did you call it? The Nescanni Parchment. Any invoice or Post-it, any letters, records...anything." Without waiting for a response she walked off toward the House, her shoulders back, head up. In her jeans and braids she should have looked as intimidating as a kitten. But the monks between her and the doorway fell back as though she had been an angel bearing a flaming sword.

Or, given the filth still coming from the second-story window of the other building, a devil with pitchfork and tail.

"There will be no interfering with Ms. Valere's work," he said to Teodosio in his best "That's the final price of our services" voice. "Or we'll walk, and you'll have to explain to your patron why and how you did not cooperate with the investigation he is paying for." A wild guess, that Teodosio had not been the one to contact the Silence. Probably the unknown Signore Mattenni. Was he a Papal representative, distancing this place from the Church proper? Wouldn't be the first time, certainly, although they did prefer to clean up their own messes. Or was it a secular authority watching over, some previously unseen third or fourth player on the scene? No matter right now. Let Andre cover their backs on that, too.

They were here to handle a Retrieval. That was all.

Teodosio looked as though he might protest, then blue eyes met brown, and the monk nodded and fell back, presumably to round up the material Wren had asked for. *God, I hope she knows what she's doing....*

He caught up with her on the stairs.

"Do you know what you're doing?"

"Haven't a clue."

"Oh."

She laughed then, and it wasn't a pretty sound.

Wren saw the expression on Sergei's face. She knew that look. Checking inside, she felt her current-core seething like fresh-molten lava, despite the dampening effect of her surroundings. Yeah, she was still angry. *Tamp it down, Valere. Control. Control.* "No, I have a plan," she said to him. "Or the beginning of one. It all depends on if my theory is right."

"And that theory is…?"

They were on the second floor now, almost to the door.

"Think about the pieces, Sergei. Four monks, come out of nowhere, carrying not money or holy relics or whathaveyou, but manuscripts. Books. Papers. And before they even put up a shack for themselves, they build this building. The House of Legend."

"And it's a dark space."

"Exactly. I bet you even money the original four weren't monks, either. Assuming the current crop here are."

"Talents? But—"

"No. Not this generation, anyway. The dark space would have taken care of that; forget what I said earlier, no Talent would survive close contact for long, not without wizzing, probably. But they're not men of God, either."

Sergei put his hand to the door. "What was it Teodosio said they called themselves? The 'brothers of gathering.' I assumed they meant gathering together, like any sort of monastery or chapel. But if they didn't—"

She loved working with this man. "They were gathering the things they carried, binding them. They were maybe even the binding itself; if you're dedicated enough, you can do that, tie yourself into your spell, feed it off you. A dark space might have been a relief, after that. That's why the local powers that be let them build here, in this nice fortressy spot, with this nice fortressy magically Null building. Not to keep the magic out...but to keep it *in*."

"*Svyataya deva.*"

"Uh-huh." She didn't know *quite* what he had just said, but she got the gist. "And not just one manuscript, either. The building is chock-full of them, all probably signed and sealed in the same way. And, natch, not a word from anyone about the effect a dark space would have on Talents, not from anyone. Either we got played, partner, or there's a lack of cluefulness here that's criminal. This entire place, everything inside, is like a powder keg of current, I bet. And I almost set it off yesterday. That's why it hurt so much, because the building was trying to shut me down the way it would something that got loose. Everything overreacted, because it was assuming worst-case scenario."

"You're talking about this place like it's alive."

She shrugged, flipping her braids back over her shoulder in annoyance. One braid really was so much easier. Maybe she'd cut it all off when they got home. "Maybe it is. I mean, we use current all the time, but nobody's ever really been able to figure out what it is. And elementals are alive, if really really stupid…. Maybe energy's just another life form. I don't worry about it too much. Philosophy's not really my thing."

She could practically see Sergei filing the conversation away for later. She might not find the implications fascinating, but he clearly did.

"So, if you can't use magic, what are you going to do?"

She shot him an exasperated glance. "I never said I couldn't use current. I said that the building reacted to it."

Sergei blinked, and his mouth opened to say something as he processed that.

*No time. Do it now, before you lose your nerve.*

"You might want to brace yourself," she advised, moving into the room. Behind her she heard him mutter something else in Russian that, if this place hadn't been so dark, she suspected would have sparked the air around him blue. He had a way with swearing, her Sergei did.

Drawing in a deep breath, she reached into the stone floor again, finding the wooden beams, the red clay bricks, and moving even farther down to the soil below, the rock below the soil. Bedrock. Mother Earth at her most stripped down basic. Wren could have gone farther, but her awareness of herself was starting to fade, and that wasn't good, either. She would have to assume she was grounded enough.

And that she was good enough.

Reaching deep into her core, she grabbed it with two mental hands, and *ripped*.

Sergei Didier wasn't quite sure what he had been expecting when Wren stepped into the middle of the room and went into the strange stillness he had learned to recognize as her working trance state, what she called a fugue. For a long moment he didn't think anything was happening, but then the hair on his arms started to prickle, and he got the strange sense of *something*. He was a Null—according to Wren, mostly-but-not-entirely Null—so he couldn't see the current moving around the room the way a Talent could. But he could *feel* it. Like an undertow at your ankles, or wind at your back, pushing and pulling and trying to force you to where it wanted you to go....

Acting purely on instinct, he stepped forward and wrapped his arms around her waist, resting his cheek against the top of her head. She could ground in him, if she needed extra support. They'd done this before, but only at her direction. It was a risk, yes...

Her body was vibrating slightly with tension, but he could feel her lean into him and relax, just the faintest touch.

And with that contact, suddenly he could almost see the ghosts of what she was seeing, like glass outlines of things that in her world had substance and form and color. Shimmer-snakes of translucent light went into drawers, under cabinets, through walls, chased by something more substantial, less…familiar. Directed-current, he realized. Hers first, followed by the antimagic built into this place. Like cats chasing mice, except that the mice didn't seem to be trying to escape, but find one more piece of cheese before they became cat-food.

"What are you doing, *Zhenchenka*?"

*Tasting*…came the whisper of her thought.

Then the "cats" suddenly swelled, gained shading and form. Shadows became teeth, and he *felt* them in his skin, tearing and rending with poisoned fangs that were impossible, impossible, *impossible!*

Even in his agony, Sergei felt her writhe under his hold, twisting and gasping as she fought to regain control of her current, even under attack.

"No, Wrenlet. I've got you. I've got your back." If she could ground into him, release some of the excess, deflect the attack, she could get it back under control. She had to get it under control, otherwise he suspected that what happened the day before would look like a love tap.

She heard him, he knew she did, but instead of using him, she cut the current-ties with an audible and painful *snick*. He felt her sag into his embrace at the same moment his vision went completely black and the world disappeared in a wave of red pain.

A

h X t a H

x aT h
h ter
Q x
Cha k th
q H K
h k

q H *Chapter Eight*

"You back with us, partner?"

His eyes fluttered, but there was no other response. For all that the reassurances of the monastery's resident doctor, a tiny little stick of a man whose name she wasn't given, Sergei still didn't look too good. Her fault, entirely her fault. God, why did he always seem to get hurt when they worked together?

Wren pushed a curl of hair away from Sergei's too-pale face and continued to beat herself up. She should know better than to try and ground in him. Yeah, he felt amazingly solid and grounded and *safe* when she was in fugue state; that was part of his appeal from the very beginning, that solidity. But he was a Null, damn it, or as near as made no nevermind, and he couldn't handle current surges like that! And then to panic, and cut ties so abruptly—was she a total newbie again, pulling a stunt like that?

"Stop it."

"What?"

"Whatever emotional flagellation you're doing." His eyes were open, and staring directly at her. "I'm okay. And you got what you needed?"

Wren nodded, still feeling shaky deep inside all the way out to her skin. She'd almost killed him. Had underestimated the aggression of the dark space itself, and almost killed him....

*Enough. Job, then nervous breakdown. Later.*

"Yeah, I got it."

"Then it's all good." He tried to sit up, and flinched. "Good, but sore. I feel like I've gone several rounds with a cattle prod."

"That would be me, yeah." The emotions seethed like current inside her, self-hatred warring it out with anger at his utter stupidity in even being in the same room with her. And in a dark space! But she was able to joke about it now, watching him slowly roll to a sitting position on the bed Teodosio had gotten him to after she'd managed to drag his unconscious bulk out of the House.

She had no idea how she had gotten them both down those stairs—it was all pretty much a blur. But she suspected that two scenes like that in twenty-four hours wasn't going to get them invited back to the chapter house for dinner. Which was fine with her. They'd rushed into this damn job on Andre's say-so, without doing their usual thorough job of researching. Their contact had landed in the hospital, and there was no way she thought that was coincidental, now, before passing along any information or warning. And now these…idiot monks and their dangerous little collection had almost gotten both her and her partner killed in less than twenty-four hours for lack of a little goddamned communication. There would be some serious wordage with Andre on that subject. Never again were they taking a job, no matter how damned urgent, without proper prep time. She wasn't going to risk her life—her reputation!—on the Silence's word.

She was a lonejack, damn it. She didn't play other peoples' games.

The sooner they were out of this place the better. For everyone. Even this building, complete with electricity humming under the plastered walls, was making her jumpy. It might just be nerves, the aftereffect of feeling and then seeing her partner crumple like a tissue, but she didn't think so. It was this place. It wanted her gone.

Wren hated animate objects. Living things were living things, fine. Not-living things were not supposed to… live. It was unnatural.

"He's awake?" Teodosio appeared behind her, carrying a glass of water in one hand. She took it from him and handed it to Sergei, watching intently as he drank it all down.

"I'm fine, thank you. Although another glass of water would be helpful, please?"

Teodosio looked at Wren, who nodded curtly, still too angry to speak to him. He went off to fetch more water.

"You scared the hell out of me," she said, helping Sergei sit up and swing his feet to the floor.

"Payback's a bitch, no?"

"Bastard." She rested her hand on the top of his head, petting his hair almost absently. It was crisp and a little coarse under her fingers, and she found herself threading her fingers through it without meaning to. Easy habit to fall into. He sighed a little, and rested his cheek against her shoulder.

And then Teodosio was back, and Sergei was standing up, drinking the water and testing his legs as he paced.

"So, what is the situation?" he asked, turning to her.

Wren shot a glance at Teodosio who showed no intention of leaving the room again, and shrugged. He wanted to get all involved now, fine. Some things she wanted to ask him, anyway.

"The situation is that these boyos have got some seriously righteous mojo tucked away in your cabinets. Did you know that?" The last was directed at the monk, and at his blank look, she rephrased it slightly. "The manuscripts and stuff you're guardians for? Powerful. Very, very powerful."

"Are they dangerous?" Teodosio looked startled, as though that idea had never occurred to him before.

Wren bit down her first, immediate response, which would have been to call him an idiot. Out loud, this time. And then slap him.

"Anything powerful is dangerous." She took the glass from Sergei and took a sip of water. Her mouth seemed to be awfully dry, all of a sudden. Rage repression. That's what it was. Nothing to do with fear, not at all. "That's why your House of Legend is built the way it is, out of native materials that are decidedly magic-unfriendly, and no wiring, or anything that could be used to bring current into contact with the items. It would have been a lot easier if you had just told us about that, by the way."

Teodosio looked startled again. "I didn't know."

Bing-fucking-o. Wren pursed her mouth in disgust. "You didn't know they were dangerous? You didn't know they were chock-full of power? Did you know anything about what you're guarding?" Okay, so much for repression.

Teodosio stared at her blankly, both the cheerful guide and the stern administrator replaced by a confused and uncomfortable human. She liked this version much better. Which wasn't to say she liked him at all.

"How dare you speak so! I was trained... The Holy Fathers...our history..."

Wren waited, staring at him.

"We do not..." he tried again, then seemed to deflate totally. "No. Whatever the founders may or may not have been, it was not passed down. Obedience was emphasized. Not questions. Not doubt or hesitation—those were not to be allowed."

"Jesus wept." She was really cursing too much. Maybe it was being so close to so much religion. "See, that's the problem with legacies and hereditary burdens and whatever. They never come with a user's manual. Or in this case: a do-not-use manual."

"On track, please, Wren." Sergei had taken possession of the only other chair in the Spartan bedroom, a ladder-back chair that looked only slightly more comfortable than the padded footstool she was perched on. "Established, that they were woefully unprepared to do anything other than dust off their exhibits. That's why they came to us, the Silence, rather than running down the street to Rome."

From the way Teo reddened, Sergei was right on the mark.

"You said that everything in the House is magic?"

Wren shrugged. "Probably. No, not everything. You've got stuff out and on show, I suppose the stuff on the first floor's about as safe as anything that needed to be stored here can be. And probably over the years you've gotten your hands on stuff that just looked neat?"

"I…yes," Teodosio said. "Although we've not added to the collection since my tenure began."

"Right. So not everything, probably. But enough. Overloading the House, too, I bet," Wren muttered. You could only fit so much in before the seams started to crack. Cracks that allowed the aroma of heavy-duty, old-style current to waft out…and nasty-minded people to come looking for it. *Idiots*.

"Which isn't our concern," Sergei said, cutting into her rebuilding rage. No problem, she'd get back to that later. "How was the parchment removed?"

Wren took a deep breath, held it, let it out, repeated the process. "Not through magic, that's for certain. There's no way it could have been. Not with the way the room reacted to even inert current, like I was using yesterday. The thief who took it might have been Talent… but I doubt it."

"Why?" Teodosio had been standing between the two of them, staring off into space as he listened, but now he looked directly at Wren. She had to give him credit, he recovered fast. From the look in his eye, the next generation of robed ones might get an earful about their charges. Good.

"Because my reaction to the dark space—where current can't go—is not unique. And if you didn't know about it, odds are decent-okay that nobody outside this place knew either. Which means nobody could have prepared him or her, which means—"

"That they would have lost control of the current as well, the way you did."

"I didn't lose control," Wren came back swiftly. "I was just…"

"Noted. Any Talent who entered the House would have been similarly discomforted."

"And unable to finish the job, at least within the time it would take to get in and out without being noticed, without using Talent, yeah. Especially once they hit the slate."

Now both men were looking at her with confused expressions on their faces.

"Oh, right. The slate. That's what started me thinking, this morning." She tapped a finger against her mouth, trying to figure out where to begin. Sergei could pick it up from shorthand, but Teodosio would require more explanation.

"The slate confused me, at first. See," and this was directed toward Teodosio, "some things conduct current, the same way they conduct electricity. They're symbiotic, sort of. Where one is, the other generally is, too. Which is why, obviously, we call it current. Or they call electricity—right. Keep on track. The slate confused me because it's a moderate conductor. Not great, sort of like trying to run your fingers through thick mud. But if your original monks had meant to keep magic out, then why put the parchment between slate sleeves? And same thing if they were trying to keep something *in*."

"They wouldn't," Sergei said. "Not if they were as savvy as this place would suggest. But to keep something *around*…?"

Wren nodded, smiling at her partner. "Yeah. Exactly."

Teodosio looked blank.

"One of your founders was either a Talent—otherwise known as a warlock or witch, or something in those days—or he hired one who was. All things considered I'm betting on the former, and more, that all four of them were Talents. And that for a couple of generations after so were their students, until they started to forget the real story and just took in the ones who had a flair for secrecy and ritual. Sorry. That stuff you have in slate? The mineral's holding current wrapped around things they must have felt were particularly not healthy to have out and about."

"A binding." He finally got it. "The Brothers of Binding, not Gathering."

"Give the monk a cookie." She only partially meant to be sarcastic. "And while we're sharing all this lovely and useful information—finally—you might want to play up Brother Prejudice's rantings. Throw a few witch-burning pep rallies." When Teodosio looked at her as though she'd grown another head, she shrugged. "I told you, that building's a magic-damper on a major scale. What you have in there should not be advertised. Get someone to plug up the holes—official Church magisters or local *Cosa*, I don't care, just get it done. Also? Keeping unwary Talents out of here, not such a bad idea. You might be saving their lives, if they don't have a partner who keeps cool under fire."

She wasn't certain, because the light was iffy, but she was pretty sure the tips of Sergei's ears had turned pink. And there was definitely a faint flush across his neck, a sure sign she'd embarrassed him. Yay her.

"So who was the thief? That is the question which must be answered, yes?"

"Yes," Sergei said, leaning forward before obviously remembering that he was still sore from current overload. She winced in sympathy. If you weren't built for it, current could do some heavy-duty bruising. If he was lucky, it missed the kidneys this time. "If Wren is correct about the level of protections put around this manuscript, then the warnings we got about its dangerousness may have been severely underrated."

Okay, that was a really ugly thought. But he was right, and it wasn't anything that hadn't been in her lizard brain since she realized it was being kept in a dark space. Wren found herself chewing on the end of one braid nervously, and spat it out in disgust.

*If a human took it, we can take it back.*

"Someone took it…to use as a weapon?" Teo seemed

awestruck by the very idea. Was he so totally wrapped in cotton up here? He must have been the most innocent postgrad to ever walk out of Harvard Square. Or maybe they wiped all evil impulses out of him when they got him here. Pity, if so, they hadn't done the same with Brother Freddie.

"We have to consider that a high probability, yes," Sergei was saying. "This was not simply a dangerous document, Teodosio. It was a dangerous document taken from a room of potentially dangerous documents. *Why?*"

"Two choices," Wren said, coming back to the conversation with a crispness she didn't feel. "Either it was a professional hit—that someone, presumably un-Talented, was hired to take it—or a chance removal. Me, I'd vote for opportunity. This place isn't exactly on the beaten path, and generally speaking the only ones who would come near this stuff would be Talent, and we've already pretty much ruled them out because of the dark space issue. And I can't see the Council—on any continent—hiring a Null to do anything this delicate for them."

"No, it would be too lowering to their collective ego," Sergei agreed. "But it's still something to check out. Especially for any mad archivists dying for the latest in major mojo documents with which to blow up their rivals and impress their heirs. I'll pass word along to Andre, let his people do some work for a change."

"Oh goody. I always wanted to have staff." Wren then shook her head. "Okay, but if I'm right, that leaves us with an opportunistic grab. Someone smelled it, magic-wise, had the chance, took it. Which would be a somewhat better scenario—want, take, have. Bad idea, because bad things happen when you're pig-ignorant." Teodosio ignored her dig, and she continued, "so who's been here, had access to that room, in the six months before your youngster noticed it was missing?"

The monk looked skyward, as though asking God for an answer. "I would have to look at the records...."

"So? We're waiting for what, exactly?"

"Yes. I will be right back." Teodosio paused at the doorway. "You might wish to, ah—"

"Stay here, out of sight of Brother Freddie. Got it."

He was back in a little over half an hour, just as Wren was starting to wonder if playing "hangman" with Sergei wasn't one of her Worst Ever ideas. So far he was up 78 to 24. It was depressing, really. And was doing nothing for the knowledge that they had only solved half the problem— and the unimportant half, at that—by closing down the barn after the potentially rabid bull's been set loose. She needed to be on the job; needed to be on the Retrieval.

"There were three scholars here during that time." He handed the slip of paper to Sergei, despite Wren's hand being outstretched for it. She bit back another comment and sat back to hear what else he had to say.

"One of them was interviewing our brothers for an article on monastic life today. He had no access to the House, and in fact never went near it, much less inside." Teodosio shook his head, his jovial monk mask firmly in place again and positively exuding bemused indulgence. "I am not sure what he thought to find for his article. I am afraid we disappointed him."

"And the other two?

"One was a researcher from the Vatican." Teodosio paused. "A secretive fellow, but he worked primarily with the newer artifacts in the main room. I don't believe that he ever went down the hall to where the Nescanni Parchment was kept."

"But you can't be certain of that," Sergei said. "A Vatican scholar, I bet he wasn't kept on leash every minute of every day."

Teodosio's face creased with humor. "You might be surprised."

Actually, she wouldn't. Within his sphere, Teo probably did a pretty good job of keeping this place in line. They'd just thrown him a pretty mighty curve.

"The third?" Sergei asked.

"A British academic here at the same time, working on a comparison survey of—well, it was a fascinating project, but I'm afraid that we weren't able to help him very much, as his access was limited to the basement room. Oh yes, as you suspected, there's another room below; purely historical documents we've accumulated over the years, available to any scholar who might be interested."

"And you never thought about the differences between the stuff you had upstairs, and the ones anyone could look through?" Wren didn't want to pick on the guy any more than already required, but honestly, did he have no independent thought or curiosity at all?

"We follow the directives of our order, Signorina Valere."

He shrugged, that Italian thing again. "I told you, obedience, not questions. In that, we are the child of Rome."

Right. That answered that question. "Number three is probably our boy."

"He was in the basement," Sergei pointed out.

"Yeah, but they probably thought he was harmless. All it would take is one inattentive monk…"

"And he would know of it, or where it was—how?"

"He might not have done it intentionally. Some things, they decide when it's time to get up and go, and no amount of binding can stop them." She was thinking specifically of Old Sally, a stuffed warhorse/portent of doom she had been chasing for three years now. Sally went where and when she would, and all you could do was pick up the pieces.

"You think that this thing is self-aware?"

Wren shrugged. She seemed to be doing a lot of that these days, too, without the excuse of being Italian. Frustration had replaced the anger in her veins; the need to be up and *doing* weighted down by the lack of a place to start. Or rather, to start again.

"I think it's powerful, and very old, and very missing. Not going to rule out the possibility that, instead of an outside snatch-and-grab, it took up on this guy's frustration and made use of it."

What she thought was more likely, however, was that the guy took a whole bunch of stuff, in retribution for being shunted aside while the Vatican guy got whatever he wanted. They'd probably catch up with him and he'd have it all shoved under his bed, not a clue what he'd done. *Nice thought, Valere. Keep it for a teddy bear.*

"Okay. You have all the contact info on these guys here?" and she indicated the papers Sergei still held in his hand.

"Yes."

"Great." She turned to their host. "Been a blast, unfortunately literally, but I really don't want to hang around your House any longer and your people would be just as happy to see us go. Besides, we have the real job to do now, which is getting back what you stupidly let go. So thanks for all your help, and we'll be going now."

Wren hopped off the stool and stood, her body practically straining for the door. Sergei stood up more slowly, although nowhere near as gingerly as before, and started speaking in Italian to Teodosio, who had been pretty much taken aback by Wren's sudden rush. She was sorry for that, really she was, but a wave of ickiness had gone from throat to tailbone just then, and it said *leave.*

She'd watched enough horror movies as a kid. When something told you to git, you got.

They were getting gone, if she had to drag her partner by the belt all the way down to the car, and then strap him in and drive the damn thing herself.

"You okay?"

"Yeah."

It was the first words they'd exchanged since leaving the monastery—Sergei had been tempted to stop at the little gift shop that was indeed at the bottom of the hill and buy a replica of the House of Holding, but he didn't think Wren's nerves could handle it. And his muscles were sore enough from the incident earlier without having a "that's not funny, Didier" glare thrown his way, too.

They were both more than a little on edge, he supposed. This was a strange sort of job; normally they did the research needed, and then Wren went in to deal with whatever it was. Bass ackward, that's how they were going on this one: jump in and then try to figure out what's going on. Damn the Silence anyway, for getting them into this. And damn the Council twice, for making the Silence an acceptable alternative. And damn him, for letting her talk him into negotiating that contract.

There was silence again until he pulled the car into the hotel parking lot. He cut the engine, and stared ahead, not sure what they would do next.

"You want to go get something to eat?" she asked, finally.

From Wren, that was a flag of truce. Her mother, a woman of some considerable temper herself when riled, had laid down a very strict rule of no battles at the dinner table. So if Wren was angry, she just didn't eat.

"Yeah." It was only midafternoon, but the breakfast he hadn't actually eaten seemed days ago. "With luck, someplace is still serving. They run to late and long lunches in Europe, traditionally."

They got out of the car and walked in companionable silence back toward the little piazza where they had eaten before. All the stores were closed again, this time for lunch, and he wondered briefly if he would ever get a chance to actually see anything open.

"We've spent too much time sorting out the monks' problems," Wren said, not looking at him. "I don't think there's anything more they can tell us—and their security problems aren't ours."

"If anything else, any of those things you talked about gets out, or the cracks widen…"

"Tell the Silence. That's their grand reason for existing, right? Write 'em a memo." She'd clearly had it with doing other peoples' jobs for them. Time to do her own. Fair enough. Wasn't that, after all, what he was always telling her? Get the job done. Let the Silence worry about saving the world.

"God, now I'm starved. That place smells good," Wren said, taking his hand and tugging him over to a small restaurant. There was a white paper menu tacked to the wall, and he skimmed it quickly. "Looks like your average trattoria. Do you want to—"

"'*Scusi.* You are, ah, the Wren?"

The few times someone approached them cold, the client always assumed that Sergei was the one they wanted. So it took them both a moment to realize that the man who was speaking was addressing *her.*

Sergei took that moment to check out the speakers. Theoretically nobody should know anything more about them than the fact that they were a pair of American tourists off the usual track. And asking about Wren using her formal "working" nickname, since he had checked them both in at the hotel under his credit card, meant that either they had done some suspicious research, or they had insider information. Either way, it put him on alert.

The speaker was tall and skinny, nerdy in a way Sergei hadn't thought Italian men could do. His companion, on the other hand... Sergei fought down the instinctive need to shove Wren behind him, away from this stranger. Knowing that she would kick him until he went down and then step on him where it hurt helped kill that impulse.

"Who's asking?" Then Wren blinked, and studied the two of them more carefully. "Yeah, I'm Wren. My partner, Sergei." She took his hand, pulling them together in a way that didn't leave much room for interpreting "partner." *Bless you, Zhenchenka,* he thought, seeing the disappointed look on both the strangers' faces. Although not strangers, he amended. By her reaction, or lack thereof, the local *Cosa* members had found them.

"I am named Anastagio," the nerdy one said, "and this is Pietro. May we..." He was searching for the words. "May we buy you lunch?"

Wren looked at Sergei, who merely raised an eyebrow in reply. If they were Talented, then he was just along for the ride, and to smooth over any translation problems that might arise. *Pity there wasn't any vocabulary list in Italian for magic-related phrases. Might have come in handy right about now. Maybe I should add that to my to-do list.*

"We'd be delighted," Wren said. "Please, lead the way."

The two men—boys, really, Sergei realized, relaxing his guard a little more—took them away from the trattoria Wren had found, choosing instead a plain storefront. The door was hung with the beaded curtain they saw everywhere, and there was no menu posted outside. Inside, worn wooden paneling that looked as though it had been stolen out of some American basement in the 1970s lined the walls, and the overwhelming smell of something fabulous that made his stomach rumble in anticipation.

Pietro flashed them both a grin. "Nonna, she cooks the best."

*"Mangiamo molto bene e ci godiamo."* In a business negotiation, he would have kept his abilities undercover. But social situations required that you be aboveboard. Mostly.

Pietro and Anastagio both looked surprised at his fluency, then embarrassed by their surprise. Out of politeness to Wren, who was giving all three of them a dirty look, he switched back to English. "I'm sure we'll enjoy it a great deal. It's always best to eat where the locals choose to eat, after all."

They were seated by an old man wearing black dress slacks and a plain white T-shirt. There were no menus. A woman who looked to be in her early sixties—nonna, Sergei guessed—came over and rattled off the choice of three first courses, or primi. He translated quietly for Wren, and they both chose the asparagus risotto.

"Don't fill up," he warned her. "There will be another course."

She nodded, reaching for a breadstick while Sergei

poured everyone a glass of red wine from the carafe placed in the middle of the table even before he could ask for it.

"You guys in apprenticeship? You have mentors?" Wren didn't waste any time with small chitchat, but when the boys took it in stride, Sergei supposed that, for the *Cosa*, that *was* chitchat.

He listened in unashamedly. Wren spoke very little about her own apprenticeship; it had ended early, and badly, when her mentor had wizzed—gone insane from the current, in lonejack parlance—only a few years later. Sergei had met her more than a year afterward, when the wounds had begun to heal over, and he did not dare pick at those scars.

"Ah, *si*, yes," Pietro said, nodding his head. "Six years now, both."

"Nice start." Sergei could hear just a tinge of envy in his partner's voice. She hadn't found her mentor until she was almost their age, he did know that much.

"It is…they do not teach us fast enough. You are not so much older than we, but you are on your own, not held in by teacher."

"Mmmm." Wren was being deeply noncommittal. He knew that *mmmm*. It meant that she didn't want to get involved in whatever they were complaining about. It also meant that she suspected they were Council, not lonejack. Assuming they made a distinction here: lonejacks had seemed to be a mostly New World phenomena, in his experience.

She sipped at her wine, then narrowed her eyes at the

boys as though channeling some seedy cop in an interrogation scene. It didn't quite go with the breadstick in her other hand, but Sergei knew better than to point that out.

"Nice place. Good bread. So. You didn't come by and drag us to lunch just to say hi and welcome to Italy, I'm betting."

Anastagio looked at Pietro, who looked at Sergei, almost as though…asking for permission? He nodded slightly, curious, and took a sip of the wine. Young, fruity, and much better than he had been expecting.

"'Stagio and I…there are not many of the *Nostradami* here, you understand." Pietro's English was thickly accented but understandable. "But we hear… Stories, they are told. About the Talent who says to her Council where to get off?"

"I did not! And they're not *my* Council!"

Sergei shook his head, trying very hard not to laugh and spill any of his wine as he took another sip. "You're famous, Wrenlet."

She put her head down in her hands, to the boys' obvious dismay. "Why me? Lord, why me?"

"Makes for a better story this way." He wanted to be sympathetic, but the thought of Wren, her entire life spent in the shadows, suddenly destined for pinup status among the younger, more restless members of the *Cosa*…

Suddenly, it didn't seem so funny. Then he looked at Wren again, moaning, and he started to chuckle again. All right, so there were a lot of drawbacks to her sudden fame. But the *Cosa* could be trusted not to let things get too out of control among their own people—especially since her friendships with Nulls like himself and fatae like P.B. made her a little on the suspect side to begin with.

Odds were, it wasn't anything to worry about. Each Talented community was its own self-contained pool, from what he'd learned over the years, no matter their politics. Maybe it was only here, where the younger set obviously didn't have too much to do with their days…

Pietro took a deep breath, a deeper sip of his wine, and then blurted: "Might we… May we have your autograph?"

And Sergei lost it, right as the primi was being delivered. The waitress looked at him with an expression of such pity that his laughter became a howl, and Wren and the boys all glared at him with varying expressions of disgust.

"Sorry, Wren. Truly. But the look on your face…and the looks on theirs…"

"I hate all of you," she announced, but signed their napkins with a flourish anyway.

By the time they had finished their first course, and started on the second carafe of the excellent house wine, even Wren had begun to see the humor of the situation, recovering, ever-so-slightly, from the emotional and physical roller coaster of the past twenty-four hours.

"You have worked together long, you and Signore Sergei?" Pietro, his earnest face flushed with wine and laughter.

"Since I was just a little older than you, actually," Wren told him, forking another mouthful of pasta into her mouth.

In years, maybe. Emotionally, Sergei suspected that she had been born older. His mother had said once that girls mature at twelve, boys at thirty-two. So far, he hadn't seen anything, including his own life, to prove her wrong.

She looked up in time to see him smiling at the thought, and stuck her tongue out at him. When he would have poured her another glass from the third carafe, however, she put her hand over the glass and shook her head.

"And you two should slow down, too," she said to the boys. They made scoffing noises, and Pietro swung his hands out as though to show how much alcohol he could handle. Wren looked at them with a calculating eye, and then shrugged. She called the waitress over and asked for water, using a mixture of English, Italian, and hand gestures. The waitress seemed to understand, because she went away and came back with a bottle of carbonated water and a clean-ish tumbler.

The woman looked at the boys, their glasses already half-empty again, then gave Wren a knowing smile and a nod and went away without a word.

"What?" Sergei had the sense that something had just happened there, but be damned if he knew what it was.

"No, it's okay. Kids gotta find their own way, same as ever. You never learn from listening."

He had absolutely no idea what she meant by that, either. But if it wasn't bothering her, he wasn't going to let it bother him. Besides, his *bistecca* had just arrived, and the peppery smell of the meat was making his mouth water.

"Here, try some," he said, cutting a piece off and forking it up to Wren's mouth. She took the morsel off the fork, her teeth barely touching the tines, and Sergei felt an interesting response from his groin.

Well. That answered one question he'd asked himself, anyway. They'd not worked together since actually acting on several years of pent-up sexual tension, and he'd been worried. But there hadn't been a single twinge while they were working. Put the situation away for half an hour, and it's all back front and center again.

He took another bite of his *bistecca,* and closed his eyes in gastronomic satisfaction. Another sip of the chianti should be just the thing…. He opened his eyes to reach for the carafe, and was startled to see that it was levitating several inches off the table.

"Ah…"

The boys were trying to pour themselves each another glass without using their hands. Sergei looked around the restaurant hurriedly, but there was only one table still occupied, and that was two old men in the back, so deep in conversation he doubted they would notice anything shy of the roof coming down over their heads. Nonna and the man who had seated them were up front, their backs pointedly turned away.

Wren shook her head ruefully, her eyes literally sparking with mischief as she leaned forward and, with a finger, beckoned him into private conversation range. "Did you ever wonder why I only ever have a few glasses of wine with a meal back home?" she asked him quietly.

He shook his head. He hadn't, actually. He was starting

to think that maybe this had been a significant failure of observation on his part.

"Way back when…okay, not so far back, but about a couple-four hundred years ago, one of the ways they used to find witches was to get 'em drunk."

"Really?"

"Mmm-hmm." The wine poured safely into the boys' glasses, the carafe then levitated over to Sergei. He took it with some trepidation. When it seemed perfectly normal in his hand, he refilled his own glass and placed it firmly back down on the table.

Wren leaned back, and nodded. "Not quite as splashy as dunking them," and he winced at the pun she didn't seem to notice she had made, "but really really effective. And don't worry about anyone watching. I think this is the local *Cosa* joint. At least Nonna is."

"Oh. That's good." He thought. It was surprising that the boys had been their first contact, if there were enough Talent here to actually need a local joint. But then again, if he had unknowns walking into his neighborhood, maybe passing through, maybe planning something, he'd check them out, too. And if he had someone sort of innocent-looking, or better yet actually innocent of any sort of guile beyond hero-worship, yeah, he'd probably use them too.

Innocent #2, 'Stagio, was now trying to cut his meal without using his hands. He wasn't quite as agile with current as he was with his fork, however, and a piece of chicken went skittering off his plate and into Pietro's lap. The other teen howled, flicking the chicken back up onto the plate without using his hands.

"I take it that wine affects Talents?" he said, going back to the conversation.

"Not so much more than anyone," Wren said. "But there do tend to be more interesting results than just a hangover. So," she said, turning to address the teens. "Have you two been studying *The Intangibles,* or does your mentor prefer another source?"

"*The Intangibles,*" 'Stagio said with a sigh, giving up and using his hands to manipulate his fork and knife. "It is, how to say, boring."

"It's a history of Talent," she said to Sergei. "Boring is too kind a word for it. You'd think we'd make for a more interesting history, wouldn't you?"

"I suspect the really good stories got left out," he said, pouring himself another glass of wine. No reason it should go to waste, and it wasn't as though he was going to be driving anywhere any time soon.

She laughed at that. "Yeah, probably. It's mostly do-gooders and upright moral characters. You can imagine how well that goes over, when you're a teenager."

Pietro, meanwhile, had decided that he would show his friend how it should be done. His chicken cut more evenly, but he was having some difficulty keeping it on his fork.

"Be careful, there," Wren warned him, half-turning to watch the cutlet wobble, splattering sauce all over his shirtfront. "The thing is," she said to Sergei, but clearly speaking for the entire table's benefit, "using current's more than just having the ability to channel. It's all about self-control. You've got to be able to control yourself all the time, so nothing gets loose."

"You've got that, in spades," he muttered, then winced when he realized he had said it out loud. He stared at the glass in his hand, then put it down. The boys weren't the only ones who might have had too much to drink. And he was probably still jet-lagged, to boot. Wren gave him a look he wasn't quite sure how to read, but went on, a little more loudly. "Historically—which if the boys have been reading *The Intangibles* they should know, as that's one of the few nonboring parts—inquisitors would get their suspected witch—or warlock—drunk, and see what black magic was done."

'Stagio was trying to keep his attention on what she was saying, but Pietro's actions were clearly more fascinating.

"And?" Sergei said, prompting her to continue.

"And a lot of witches got burned. Literally. Although the inquisitors were more fond of drowning or pressing, historically. Burning just looks better on the screen."

There was a loud *snap* that made everyone at the table jump, and Pietro's chair went over backward into the wall, Pietro in it. 'Stagio began giggling madly, and the silverware started doing their best impersonation of tin soldiers, marching along the edge of the table.

"Right. We might want to get out of here," Wren said, wiping her mouth with a napkin and standing up, ignoring both teens, who were now waving their hands madly, shouting at each other in Italian.

"But…"

"Now, Sergei. Trust me." Grabbing his hand, she yanked him out of his chair and they were halfway to the door when another, much louder *crack!* echoed through the now-empty restaurant, and what felt like a sonic boom pushed them the rest of the way out the door. He looked back to see Nonna's companion beating out flames with what looked like a filthy apron, and Nonna dragging one of the boys—he thought it was Pietro—forward by one ear, yelling in rather inspired language something about idiots and…just deserts?

Clearly, the older woman had things well in hand. He put on a burst of speed and caught up with Wren, who was bent over, laughing hard enough he wasn't sure how she was still breathing. A trio of old women, sitting outside one storefront and knitting, stared at them as they staggered past, and that only made Wren laugh harder. The sound had the faint edge, to his ear, of hysterics, and his own amusement disappeared.

"Wren! Genevieve! Calm down!"

He caught her by the arm and swung her around. She staggered into him, chortling, and then looked up. Tears were streaming down her face, she had been laughing so much.

"Alcohol," she managed to choke out, gasping for breath. "It's a tradition, I swear. But the two of them, oh, such *idiots*!"

He gathered, as she went off into gales of laughter again, that alcohol and current mingled badly but not fatally at least once in every Talent's life.

"They wanted to impress you," he said mildly, relieved that she seemed to be a little more under control now.

"Oh, they did," she agreed. "They absolutely did. I bet they were so nervous beforehand they didn't eat anything, and were drinking way faster than they're used to. It's a good thing they didn't blow up the entire restaurant."

"Um. Was that likely?"

"It's possible." She shrugged, wiping the tears away, still grinning. "The more pure your Talent, the more current you can channel, the more likely alcohol's going to screw with you."

"And they let these kids drink? *Bozhya mat.*" Sergei was starting to feel the faintest tinglings of unease. Lord knows he wasn't the foremost authority on raising kids, Talent or otherwise, but that seemed…careless, to say the least.

"Why not? Sergei, it's a rite of passage. An occasionally spectacularly stupid thing you can brag about for years after."

"That's insane. Someone could have gotten killed!"

"Nah." Wren didn't mean to sound quite so blasé, but she didn't see why he was freaking so much over this. He'd faced wizzarts, for Christ's sake. A couple of tipsy teenage boys, watched over by their nonna, wasn't anything compared to that. "Besides, it's not like they *know* it's going to happen, exactly."

"I can't believe that they don't know, by the time they're old enough—"

"Know how? Not if their mentors don't tell them, and most don't bother. It's not like there's a guidebook, Serg. You know that, you've threatened to write one often enough."

"*The Care and Feeding of Lonejack Talent,* yeah. I just can't—in all the generations of Talents, there hasn't been any underground gossip, no secrets passed on in the schoolyard?"

"This isn't Hogwarts, Didier." She hated those books. "No secret school, no set coursework, no exams. And no external interference with how, or what, each mentor chooses to pass on. No PTA or academic review."

"So a bad mentor?"

"Screws you royally. Yeah. But you're judged by your students as much as your own work. So them as choose to mentor generally do a decent enough job. 'Stagio and Pietro's mentors were keeping an eye on them, I bet. Maybe through Nonna.

"But even if they weren't, nobody would interfere. Nobody asks. It's like sex-ed in a conservative world— one source of information, and one source only. Even among the most hog-tied, march-in-line Council members, that sort of independence is still sacrosanct."

"That's insane." He was obviously thinking about her own situation, left half-trained and in mourning when Neezer wizzed and disappeared, rather than put her at risk from his madness.

"It's the way it is, Sergei." All traces of her laughter were gone, now. "Sergei, there are reasons for the mentoring system. Good reasons. And you aren't in a position to understand them."

"Are we about to have a fight?" he asked.

"Not yet. When I start yelling, and you storm off, and I spit sparks onto your belongings, that's a fight." But she was starting to smile again. "This is just an exchange of strong opinions."

"You're all insane."

"Look, Mister Joins A Secret Society That Wants to

Reorder the World Without Getting Credit or Pay, don't talk to me about insane."

True. At least the *Cosa* was up front about being self-ishly oriented. It was easier to trust someone who was blatant about their motives.

"Ah hell, Genevieve. Sometimes your world scares the hell out of me. Those two kids…"

"Were kids. Innocents, in their own way. That's why the training is one-on-one, Sergei. Okay, one reason. Another being that we none of us play well together. And we're all deeply paranoid. And cranky even without wizzing."

She felt his hand slide into hers, and curled her fingers into his, twining them. A silent, two-sided apology.

Behind them, the square was quiet again, the fire contained, the boys carted away, doubtless by their ears, the old women gone back to their sewing and gossip. Ahead of them, down the street, the hotel seemed to glow with an inviting light in the windows.

It seemed to call to her. Not the electricity itself, that was nominal; the entire town, she had the awareness to realize now, was extremely low-draw, even for a remote town in a relatively low-tech area. Effect of the dark place, probably.

No, the appeal was something more. An awareness of aching exhaustion. Of being jerked around from pillar to post, the conflicting demands of *Cosa* loyalty, the need to "finish the job" no matter what, and a growing, seeping sensation of her own self disappearing under all that.

The lights promised a respite from that, if only for a little while. Clean sheets. Soft pillows. All that was lacking was the safety of a warm body against hers to snuggle against. Not that she *needed* that, but…

*But admit it, Valere. You want it. You want him in your bed. Against your skin. And whatever else might follow.*

*It's not a bad thing. It's not a sin. It's not going to make everything fall down and go boom.*

They had reached the hotel door now, Sergei letting go of her hand long enough to unlock the door and usher her inside.

"It was good to laugh," she said. "We haven't done that in a while, have we?"

"No. We haven't." He put his arm around her, risked dropping a kiss onto the top of her head. She not only didn't pull away, he was pretty sure that she snuggled closer. And when they walked down the hallway, and stopped by her door, she didn't untangle herself from his hold.

Instead, she looked up at him with eyes that were perfectly clear and serious, her mouth open just the slightest bit, trying to decide if she should say anything.

"Wren?" Almost as though he were afraid to say anything more, for fear of scaring her away. Or scaring himself away, maybe.

Placing her hand on his own, she slid it from where it rested on her shoulder, bringing the back of it to her mouth, and pressing a soft, dry kiss on his knuckles. One, two, three, four…

"Wren…" She almost didn't recognize his voice this time. It was soft, hoarse, and totally raw.

They stared at each other over his hand for an impossible instant, then she reached backward and did something to the door so that it opened. Backing up, never letting go of his hand, she pulled him gently into her room.

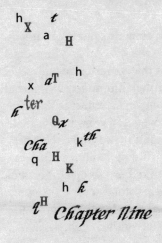

## Chapter Nine

She could feel her heart pounding so hard it was about to become a cliché and burst out of her rib cage. Sergei, on the other hand, looked as though his heart had stopped in midbeat.

"Are you sure about this?"

She pressed her hand to his mouth, letting her fingers linger on the smooth dry texture of the skin. "Don't talk. If we talk, we'll think and if we think we're right back where we've been and I might as well just have let Jamie kill me back in June."

Jamie Koogler. The long-dead architect who had wanted so badly to live, and been denied his chance. Pietro and 'Stagio were idiots, but they were idiots having *fun*. When was the last time she'd had fun? Real fun, not work-fun, as fun as that could sometimes be? The fact that neither of them could remember the last time life hadn't been all worry and work wasn't just scary, it was depressing as hell.

She wanted Sergei. It was that simple. She had been terrified of damaging the partnership, so terrified she'd overlooked one very basic, simple, incontrovertible fact.

They had already been lovers for years before their first kiss. Not physically, no. But their minds, their personalities, had been doing the flirtation thing without realizing it. Every job they worked, every meal they ate, every argument they had and absolutely every truce they made. The way she needed to touch him, she who didn't casually touch anyone else. The way he watched her, like no one else was in the room.

There wasn't anything to be afraid of. Not with Sergei. Never with Sergei.

"Do you want me?" It was stupid, but she had to ask. Was terrified to ask.

Wren had never believed that old cliché about someone's eyes darkening with passion. But his did. Passion, and hunger and a need that made her spine feel as though it were melting. She could almost smell his arousal, an intensification of the scent she categorized as "Sergei," and a sound that was almost a whimper collected in the back of her throat.

Before she knew quite what was happening, he had spun her around, pushing her up against the wall; her hands trapped in one of his and held over her head. Warm fingers moved against the skin of her neck, sliding under the weight of her hair to stroke the nape, fingers threading into her hair, pulling her head back. She shivered, leaning instinctively into that rough caress. His weight pressed against her, sandwiching her between him and the wall.

"What should I tell you?" he asked. "That I want to taste you?" She could feel the warmth of his breath as he spoke, and his mouth settled briefly on her neck, first nipping and then soothing the bite with his tongue. "That I want to feel you?" His free hand was wrapped around her waist, pulling her more tightly into his body. She felt a shudder rising through her, and tilted her head so that she could lean against his chest. "That I want to be inside you, feel you around me? Yes, damn it. I want that. I want *you.*"

He tugged on her earlobe with gentle teeth, and Wren heard herself moan. She thought it was her, anyway. Her body wasn't quite responding to her control. Flashes of something kept running along her veins, tickle-prickles that were familiar, but not. That had never happened before. Strange.

She tried to turn around, to face him on a more equal basis, but he wouldn't let her move. His mouth moved from her ear in a line down her neck and then back up again, tongue dipping into her ear in a way that should not have been sexy and was almost unbearably so. "Damn it, Sergei..." He laughed, the sound rumbling through both of them.

She finally freed her hands and reached back, grabbing his hips to pull him tighter against her ass. *Knew he dressed to the left.... Jesus, this is...they were actually... Stop thinking, Wren. Right now. Thinking bad.*

He turned her around again, more gently this time, and his hands went to her shoulders, holding her steady as he slanted his mouth a little, catching her lower lip between his teeth, and she felt her knees weaken suddenly, completely, like someone had kicked them out from under her. *Right. No thoughts.* Not *a problem.*

Now, with him so close, she could feel the heat that rose off his body, the smell of warm skin making her dizzy. Or maybe it was the feel of his hands that was doing that. Hands that were holding, stroking, caressing her back until her shoulder-blades felt like melted wax.

She shivered, and he stopped, pulling away slightly.

"Are you—"

"Bastard," she practically moaned. "Don't stop…"

She felt more than saw his smile and raised her own hands tracing the line of his jaw, drawing his head down to her for another kiss. Not a peck, not a smooch, nothing like what they'd been playing at before, back home, in those few awkward moments before one or the other or both of them ran away….

Wren knew she was a decent enough kisser; careful of the teeth on delicate flesh, just enough nip and play. But her confidence level rose another notch when she heard him moan deep in his throat as her tongue swept the inside of his mouth, tasting the toothpaste he had used that morning, not quite hidden by the tannic flavor of the wine from lunch.

"Love, bed."

It was both an order and a plea, and Wren grinned despite the shivers that were racking her body. Pulling away, she slid her hand down his arm, ending when their fingers were laced together. With a gentle tug she led him to the too-narrow bed. She stopped, eyed it warily over her shoulder, then looked back at him.

"This might get tricky," she warned. "Are you sure…"

"Unless you want to be slammed up against the wall…."

*Ooooo….* "Maybe next time," she decided. His gaze locked on hers, and she smiled up at him. "After we figure out all the…logistics." *Overtall bastard.*

That surprised a laugh out of him. "Let me undress you?" he asked, his voice rubbing against her nerves like soft sandpaper and making the shivers intensify for a second. She nodded, and he stepped forward to lift one hand to the top button of her blouse. His fingers shook a little at the first, but then seemed to remember how to do what he was telling them to do, and before she knew it her shirt was hanging open, and he was pushing it off her shoulders.

"Hang on, hang on…" She held up the cuffs for inspection, and he unbuttoned those swiftly, stripping the blouse off her and dropping it on the floor.

The look in his eyes was almost enough to make her blush.

"You've seen breasts before."

"Not yours. It makes all the difference." He reached out to run his fingers across the tops of her breasts the way a blind man might read Braille. His fingers slid down, reaching the metal snap of her jeans, and jerked his hand away with a faint yelp.

"Um. Sorry?" Wren looked up at him, mortified, and was relieved to see that he was grinning even as he put his fingers in his mouth to soothe the burn.

"Control that current of yours, woman. I've no desire to fry anything off tonight, thank you very much."

"Right." Gathering a little control over herself, Wren reached down inside and quieted the roiling sparks. "Take it as a compliment," she said, looking up in time to see him draw his fingers out of his mouth slowly. The power of speech suddenly deserted her totally. "Undressed. Now."

She had never understood the beauty of how fast a man could get naked before. And then there was a tangle of arms and legs, her jeans still down around her knees, shoes kicked off somewhere across the room, the two of them half on and half off the bed trying to get as much skin-to-skin contact as they could manage.

"You're so…mmmm…" and his words were muffled as he put his mouth to her breasts, his hands stroking everything available. Wren hooked one leg over his hip, luxuriating at the feel of his hardness against her. *Hardness. Jesus, Genevieve. Oh well, at least you're not calling it a ram—mmmm….* Her thoughts sort of fluttered off somewhere when his hands moved to her thighs.

"Why—why did we wait so damn long?"

"We're idiots." He managed to get her jeans off her, and they fell to the carpet with a heavy thump. She still wore her panties; skimpy floral things that she suspected were going to join her jeans very soon.

Wren squirmed, trying to get the pillow underneath her head, and instead found herself swung on top of her partner, knees on each side of his hips, her body perched over his midsection. His eyes glittered up at her, a lock of hair plastered to his forehead with sweat.

"Hi," she said, suddenly shy again.

"Hello."

He let his hands fall to his sides. She understood immediately what he was telling her. She was on top, literally. She got to call the shots. Logistics aside, it was a remarkably…romantic thing to do, she decided.

Even though she knew his body—had seen it in swim trunks, in workout gear—it was as though this was a totally new body. A different person. He had a light scattering of hair on his chest. His shoulders were nice; firm and you could see the muscles when he moved, but not bulky obvious. His stomach wasn't washboard flat either. A little rounded, soft and smooth to the touch. Not perfect, no. Sergei. She could feel his heart beating underneath her questing fingers, and the power of that made her heady. *I'm doing that. I make him react that way.*

She flexed her fingers, letting her blunt nails draw down across that skin, and was rewarded by an involuntary buck of the body beneath her.

Her gaze flicked up to meet his. Those darkened brown eyes met hers steadily. They were a little amused, a little pained…and a lot hungry.

Sliding her hands back up his chest, she leaned down to capture his mouth with her own. There was a moment of that damned awkwardness, then they found the right fit again, mouths open, their tongues flickering and tasting and teasing each other. His hands reached to her hips, pulling down sharply even as he rose to grind into her.

Wren broke off the kiss with a gasp, arching backwards, her hands bracing against his shoulders. "Mmmm…." She could practically hear herself purr. She knew this feeling, the friction and pulse of fabric scraping on fabric. Then his hands were on her backside, on her thighs, slipping underneath her panties to find the dampness there, and the purr deepened. Then those fingers were underneath the fabric, the awkward angle hampering him slightly.

With a frustrated grunt, he flipped her over, moving with swiftness that always surprised her, even now, from such a big guy. Flat on her back, she instinctively brought her knees up, allowing him better access. The times they had worked together on jobs, moving in silence through someone else's property, made words superfluous.

Her underwear was off before she had time to be aware of it sliding down her legs. The cool air hit her overheated skin, and she shivered, then his fingers returned to their explorations, and she was shivering for a different reason, her fingers digging into the bed beneath them. Then he slid a second finger inside her, turning his hand so that his thumb rested against her sensitized skin, and the thought—*you have the most incredible hands*—only emerged as a whimper.

He understood her anyway. One thrust, then a second, and a third, all so slow and deliciously teasing, Wren thought she was going to have to start beating on him to satisfy the urges that were building inside her.

"Serg…"

"Shhhh…let it go. Let go, *Zhenchenka*. Ah, Genevieve…" and his other hand stroked the hair away from her forehead, sliding down to caress one breast.

*Mmmm, nice…Oh!* as he tweaked one nipple, the pain a sudden and surprising turn-on. Her body twitched and hummed under his ministrations, and her attention focused inward, spiraling down the same way she did to reach current. Then he scraped and pushed with his thumb at the same time, somehow, and her body jerked forward, her legs practically spasming up.

And it was gone. Wherever she had been heading too, whatever was coming…wasn't. *Damn.*

But he only sat back, wiping his fingers slowly along the inside of her thigh, and smiled the smile that the canary probably saw just before feathers flew. She propped herself up on the pillow, and got her first un-obstructed view. *Oh…niiice.* "Wow."

He flushed a little then, taken off guard and totally adorable. "I'm hoping that's a compliment?"

"Yeah. Compliment. Totally."

She sat up on the edge of the bed, reaching one hand out to touch him. Velvety. Smooth. It invited you to stroke along its length, slide your fingers up, rub your thumb across the tip….

She smiled in accomplishment as this time he jerked under her touch, and uttered a soft, almost pained moan.

"Genevieve…stop."

"You don't like?

"I…like…very much. But it's been a while since anyone but I did that and…I'm not eighteen anymore. Hell, I'm almost forty. If you make me come now, we may as well stop for dinner."

"Oh." Her hand faltered, then let go, moving a little to allow him to sit beside her on the bed. Part of her mind threatened to giggle at the visual of the two of them sitting there bare-assed naked. But her body was in no mood to laugh.

As though sensing her mood, Sergei lay back down on the bed, stretching his full length on his back. He crooked his fingers at her in a "come here" gesture, then tugged her forward, positioning her so that she once again straddled him. Her legs clasped the sides of his torso.

"Good. That's right." His hand stroked the side of her face, lingering on the edges of her smile. "Enjoy yourself…"

She settled in, adjusting her weight. His hand traced the skin of her hip idly, then reaching down to tangle his fingers in her pubic hair. She squirmed a little, uncomfortable with the fact that she was so wet that each hair practically glistened, but he seemed to enjoy the feel of it.

His hands were cupping her now, curving around each buttock, then stroking up slowly along her spine. Wren felt a shiver run through her, just ahead of his touch. Like someone had walked over her grave, only…not.

He reached over the bed, making her whimper at the seeming abandonment, and rummaged for his slacks, pulling out first his wallet and then extracting something from it. *Oh. Right. Bet he was a Boy Scout.*

"So…" she picked the packet out of his hand and looked at it. "Is it flavored?"

His laughter made his body move against her in ways that almost made her lose her train of thought. "Sorry, no. I will make sure to buy something better next time—"

"God, just shut up, Didier."

Ripping the packaging open with her teeth, she carefully extracted the sheath. And then his hands were around hers, guiding her as she rose up onto her knees and reached back to slide the condom down his length, slowly and carefully unrolling it as they went. It might have been easier, if she had gotten off him entirely, but…

*But nothing. Your legs wouldn't be able to hold you, anyway.*

He hissed once, sharply, and she stopped, afraid she had done something wrong. First time nerves, all over the place.

"No. Go on. Just…a little more slowly."

"Right." Biting her lower lip in concentration, she rolled the condom the rest of the way down, feeling his cock jump gently under their hands.

Task completed, she shifted her weight again, kneeling over him, with her hands braced against his chest.

"Relax, my Wren. I've got you."

And he did, his hands sliding back up her spine, coaxing a stuttering purr from her throat even as she felt every goose bump on her body rise to attention. *Now? Now. Oh, now…*

Almost without conscious thought, she lowered her

body down, feeling one of his hands move down as well, holding himself, guiding it into her, cool from the latex, but still warm, somehow, and then he was fully inside her, filling every available sliver of space. Oh that felt good. Achey, but warm at the same time. Wet and sticky and thrilling, all at once. And then he shifted, pulling her away and then bringing himself home again with a gentle thrust.

*Oh. Jesus wept.*

"Do that again!" she demanded.

He laughed, and obliged, his hands holding her steady as she braced herself, hands flat against the pillows.

The sensations…there were so many, it was difficult to break them down into any kind of order. The ache of her legs and knees, the burn in her arms as she supported her own weight. The cold shivering down her back, whenever his hands stopped touching her. The heaviness of her breasts, teased into hard-tipped peaks by his tongue and teeth. The faint pain, where his fingers were gripping the flesh of her hip hard enough to leave bruises. And, overriding everything else, the slick friction of him sliding within, building her back into that spiral of tingling sensation, as though every nerve ending in her entire body had somehow migrated into her vagina. She had the sensation of being on an amusement park ride, spiraling up in absolute darkness, feeling the tension build heavy in her belly—and lower—until she needed to scream with the weight of it.

Day-am. So this was what the big deal was about. Not one-two-three in the back of someone's car back in high school, not a drunken fumble in a dorm room somewhere or a casual overnighter with some guy she didn't remember a year later. But this, the adoration she could feel in his touch, the fire sparking between them, the mutual music they were creating in the slow strokes of their bodies, and frantic squeaks of the bed frame.

She forced her eyes open enough to look into his eyes. They were wide open, the pupils dilated so much she felt as though she were falling into them. He grinned, for once showing all his teeth in a gesture that was as much a growl as a smile, and the fear that shivered through her was a completely pleasurable, completely feminine one. He saw that, must have seen in her face that the spiral was reaching its pinnacle, and changed his angle slightly.

"Oh! Yesssss, like that, there…right there…"

Apparently, those were the right words to say.

Her head went back, exposing her throat, and Sergei rose to meet her, fastening his mouth to the pale flesh there. His teeth clamped down at the same time he thrust once more, hard enough to fracture something, and the spiral up turned into zero-g, and the sensation of dropping straight down off an endless cliff into a fiery pit of hissing, sparking sizzling current.

"Um, wow?"

They were sprawled together on the bed, the pillows on the floor, and the covers askew. She had been afraid to move, after that initial collapse, but he had shifted, making room for her to curve into the sweat-slicked warmth of his body, his arms closing securely around her. Even the stickiness between her legs wasn't incentive enough to move. Although the thought of a hot shower was an appealing one….

"I don't suppose you packed any Bactrian?" he asked lazily.

Wren sat up abruptly, the sheet sliding off their bodies. "Oh God. Oh God!" she said again, seeing what he was talking about. Thin white welts covered his body from knee to chest, and down his arms.

"Wren, shhhh, Wren, it's okay. They don't hurt."

"You're sure?" She was horrified. "That's never happened before. Not ever!"

He looked way too smug for someone with current-burns over seventy percent of his body. "I could have hurt you! I mean, worse!"

He sat up next to her, grabbing her hands in one of his and holding the tip of her chin with his other, forcing her to look at him. "You didn't. You wouldn't. I don't think you could. Wren… Genevieve, that was…incredible. Truly. For a moment I could almost *see* what you've talked about, the core…current all around us…."

"We need to be careful," she said, distressed not only at what happened but by the fact that he wasn't taking it seriously. She had seen what current could do—hell, he had seen it, too! "I don't know why it happened—"

"Don't you?" He nuzzled her shoulder and she sighed a little, feeling her body respond even as her mind was racing with the causes and problems of her, well, sparkage. "Wren. My Wren. I love you."

Her heart stopped, stuttered, resumed an almost

normal beat. Her eyes closed, she lifted his hands to her mouth and kissed the knuckles tenderly. Somehow, it sounded…more than it had the other times he'd said it. More real. More solid.

"I didn't even know why I wasn't looking; it's because I had already found it. It was just waiting until I had enough guts to realize it. And then, when I did…"

Oh God. They were going to get sappy. She wasn't sure she could handle that. Not now, with the sex-high still burning up her veins. She'd say something stupid, some-thing totally stupid, and then *fuggedaboutit,* as Lee liked to say. But he was looking at her like he expected some-thing in return.

"Neither of us are very good with relationships. Romantic ones, I mean. Lasting stuff. I…" She paused. "I should warn you about that. Relationshipy-wise. Didn't have the greatest examples when I was growing up, I guess. My mom…she wouldn't ever tell me anything about my dad. We didn't even have any photos. And the guys she dated were…well, they didn't hang around either."

"I'm not going to be scared off, Wrenlet. I think that's a safe conclusion."

"No but…" Sex-high was starting to turn into panic-low.

He stopped her with a kiss. It started out hard, a si-lencing kiss, but gentled into something more playful, nipping and tasting until she squeaked, a noise he had never heard out of her before.

"Don't. That tickles."

Pulling her back into his arms, they curled together

on the bed, Sergei having to spoon around her to keep from falling off. "Damn European beds," he muttered, and she snorted in laughter.

"God. Long day. Long, long day. Hrmmmm. I feel sort of almost guilty for booking out of that restaurant so fast. You think Pietro and 'Sta—"

"They're fine. Other than probably getting strips torn out of them for being such idiots. And terminal mortification for blowing their chance to impress their heroine, the great American Retriever—"

"I hate you." But her giggles mitigated whatever heat she put into the words.

It was only…she opened one eye and looked at the cheap clock on the nightstand table—yeah, it was barely six o'clock. But it had been a long, long day. She felt a yawn coming and indulged in it. "Too much wine," she said. Sergei murmured an assent, his face resting between her shoulder blades, and she grinned. Her partner was the pass-out-afterward type, apparently. Still, if she'd had a long day, he'd had an even longer one. Had it really only been yesterday afternoon they had gotten off the plane? Yeah, it had been.

*Okay, I'm comfortable, but there's no way he is.*

"Come on," she said, rolling out of his hold and pulling the sheets with her.

"Huh?"

She tugged the sheet until it came off the bed, and snagged her pillow. "This is silly. Get down here. She put the sheet down, then grabbed the blanket where it lay folded at the foot of the bed and dropped it on top of the sheet, laying down and adjusting the pillow under her head. "Get over here, Sergei."

He grinned, and followed orders.

"Much better," she murmured, wrapped in his arms again. "Much, much better."

Lee's wife—P.B. could never remember her name, just that she was a Null—opened the door. If she was taken aback to see a short, white-furred demon standing on her doorstep at eleven in the evening, she managed not to show it.

"Lee's in the studio," she said. She had a lovely alto, totally at odds with her ugly-even-for-a-human face. Long and skinny, like a carriage horse's, and bad, rose-pocked skin. But her dark blue eyes were kind, if too small for her nose. "Up the stairs, first door on the left. You going to need coffee?"

"Will you marry me?"

Her laugh was as lovely as her voice, and a welcome note in what had been, until now, a really shitty evening. "I'll take it that means yes. Go on, I'll bring it up."

P.B. took the stairs as best he could, clinging on to the banister. Old apartment buildings all seemed to have the same narrow, deep staircases that were almost impossible for his much shorter legs and claws to handle. He loved Wren's building, with its easy-access fire escape. Much easier to go up and down that without looking like a malformed idiot.

He found the door, knocked, and pushed it open when Lee's voice yelled out that it was safe to come in.

The Talent was sitting on a wooden stool, his hands raised over what looked like a four foot tall blob of metal. Sparks were still shimmering around Lee's palms, and he shook them off, causing the metal to give a disturbing little *burp* and subside slightly in the middle.

No matter how many times P.B. saw humans use current, it always amazed him. He was, by his very existence, a creature of magic, but he couldn't use it that way. Few of the fatae could, as far as he'd ever been able to determine. And to use it to create something like the water sculpture that hung on Lee's wall…

P.B. slapped the awe away. Now was not the time.

Lee turned around and saw who it was. His expression, normally similar to a basset hound's anyway, fell even further. P.B. chose to ignore the commentary on his social welcome factor. Not everyone was as friendly as the Wren.

Demon, as a created species, didn't really have much in common with the rest of the fatae species. Maybe that was why he liked humans so much, despite his line's creator having been one of the crazier examples of their species. It was certainly why he'd gone to Wren in the first place when the fatae started to get their horns in a twist over the Council's most recent obnoxious behavior. And why he trusted Lee, now, to carry on, while the Retriever was out of the country. Trust that hadn't been misplaced. Yet.

"I've got news, and it's not good."

"Tell me." Lee stood up and went to the worktable, where he wrapped a dark red strap around his wrist and touched the hinge to a metal wire set in the ground.

Sparks flew. He closed his eyes and exhaled slowly until the sparks faded entirely, then unwrapped the band and put it back on the table.

"Two piskie pups went missing this week. Snatched out of their meadow. Mother was out hunting, left them hidden. Four of the litter were left untouched but couldn't remember a thing about what happened to their sibs." He paused, wishing the promised coffee were to-hand already. "And there's been a killing. A fatae."

"This is unusual?" Lee turned to face P.B., his now current-free hands held up to show the demon that he didn't mean to be insulting by the question.

"The pup-nappings? Odd, but it happens sometimes. People have weird ideas about what makes a good pet. The not-remembering part might be trauma, or it might be someone using current to cloud things. The killing? Yeah. You could say that's unusual." Fatae were too few, as a rule, to kill each other. They left that to the humans.

"Word is, the Council ordered it. Both things, although I haven't a clue what they'd want piskies for. Not pets, that's for certain. And nobody other than the piskie momma cares enough about them to pay ransom or give concessions; it just heated the tension level up in general. Maybe that's why the Council did it—if they knew progress was being made, they'd want to stop it, keep everyone squabbling, right?"

"Damn. The hounds getting restless?" By hounds he meant the five fatae leaders P.B. had been trying to sway to the more moderate stance regarding humans in general, and Talents in particular.

"The hounds are starting to yelp for blood."

But it wasn't all bad news. The work he'd been doing all summer, trying to get the fatae to think of lonejacks separate from the Council rather than lumping them all in the "humans bad, Talents worst of all," seemed to be paying off. A little, anyway. Enough that the elder had actually let him know what was happening, rather than just going off on his own, knowing that P.B. would tell his human friends. Okay, so that way the contact was square on his shoulders, and not the elder's responsibility. It was still more than he would have gotten two months ago.

What P.B. did with that information, though…that was going to depend a lot on Lee. And Wren.

The artist leaned against the wall, crossing his arms over his chest and looking down the full meter of difference in their height at the demon. "All right. What do you want me to do?"

P.B. grinned in relief, aware that his sharp canines weren't the most reassuring sight in the world. "I need you to find out what's going on over on your side of the fence. And I need you to do it fast."

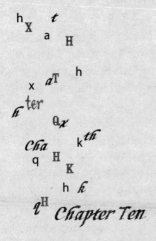

$t^H$ *Chapter Ten*

The faint sounds of a bird chirping arose from the pile of clothing.

"I hate them. Whoever that is."

Sergei managed to extricate himself enough to find his mobile and turn it on. "What?"

He looked over at Wren, and sighed. "Yeah, she's right here. Hang on, let me get the hookup." He looked for a place to set the phone down without risking losing the already faint signal, and finally with a sigh handed it to her. She took the clamshell gingerly, as though it might bite her. "Just…don't look at it, or something," he suggested, then touched his fingers to his lips and reached down to touch hers gently in turn. Stumbling ungracefully into his slacks, he went out the door. Wren could hear him opening the door to his own room, muttering under his breath.

The mobile phone made a noise that might have been someone at the other end saying her name, but Wren refused the bait. The way she had been sparking not fifteen minutes ago, it probably wasn't safe for her to even be holding this thing.

Her lips curved at the memory, and then she giggled. *Thank God whoever it is didn't call a little bit earlier....*

The door rattled, and she could hear Sergei swearing. He had forgotten to take the key. She opened the door for him, only realizing after he gave her a look that she was still naked. "Take the damn thing" she said, scurrying back to the pile of blanket. It only took him a minute to set up the speaker phone kit, and then Wren could hear P.B.'s voice coming through from her safe perch.

"Do you have any idea how much this call is costing? You couldn't have moved faster?"

"Actually, no. What is it?" It was after two in the morning back home, but only just. P.B. must have started dialing the instant he thought she might be awake.

"Hang on..." They could hear P.B. rattling around, and then a series of clicks. "You guys there?"

Sergei started to answer, when Lee's voice came over the speaker.

"Yeah, I'm here. Hey, Wren."

"Hi. And we ask again, what's up?"

"Chatter, girl. Lots and lots of chatter all of a sudden. Word came about an hour ago through the usual channels." Gossip, the staple of lonejack communication. There was a reason why P.B., a courier by trade, had decided to branch out. "Two 'jacks have gone missing in the past twenty-four. As in nobody's seen 'em, nobody's heard 'em, nobody can trace them."

Tracing was a basic skill set, one of the first things you learned from your mentor, because all it took was something that had touched the sought object, and a decent amount of concentration. If they couldn't be traced, that meant, likely, they were either dead or…

"People thinking it's a Council snatch?" Only thing that could hide a trained Talent would be a couple or more equally trained Talents forming a lockbox. Which when the targets were lonejacks meant, almost by default, Council.

*Although, let's be careful here. Assumptions get you killed. You and other folk, maybe. Could be anyone gunning for lonejacks, or maybe just those two in particular.*

"Who was it?"

"Shona Wills."

Irascible old woman, short-tempered and snappish, but one of the best Tracers in the city, for the money. She'd worked for the NYPD's Missing Person's bureau until they regretfully forced her to retire. Now she worked for private investigators, doing desk-work. Wren had worked with her, once. Smart, sharp.

"And?"

"And… Mash, Wren. Mash's gone."

Impossible. Mash didn't disappear. Mash *couldn't* disappear. Like Shona, he was one of the old-timers. Unlike Shona, everyone liked Mash. Any given day, half a dozen teenagers would be treating his brownstone's kitchen like their own, making snacks, drinking sodas, just hanging out. Half the mentors in Manhattan knew his phone number by heart—it was the first stop when trying to track down a missing student. His house was a Talented open house; if you knew to go there, you were welcome there.

How could Mash be missing? It didn't make any sense. Mash was *always* there.

"There's more," Lee said, and she could almost taste the grimness in his voice.

"Tell me."

"Pup-nappings, according to the piskies." Wren flinched. Piskie pups were the cutest thing to ever draw breath. Which was probably the only reason why they were allowed to grow up into the irritable adult form. "And Walter found a Nassunii last night."

"Alive?" Of course not. Alive, there's no news.

"Very dead. Asphyxiated."

Nassunii were water-fatae. Very shy. Also very strong, except when it came to pollutants in their gills. Having one live near you was generally a good sign for the health of the water. Wren had gone to the party Walter—a Coast Guard ensign—had thrown a couple of years ago the first time he spotted one in the waters around Manhattan.

"It could have been accidental, or something—"

"It wassssssnot."

The third voice was wet and slithery, and echoed oddly over the phone lines, like it was calling from somewhere really damp.

"Do I want to know what that is or where it's calling from?" Sergei asked quietly, just out of range of the phone. He was sitting on the edge of the bed, and she noted almost absently that his pants were zipped up but still unbuttoned. *Mind on the game, Valere,* she reminded herself. Poison was always a possibility, but it could just have been sludge getting into its water system, or something tragic but nonthreatening. Safer to assume a threat, but not always smarter. "You know something, eldest?"

Nassunnii didn't reach adult status until they were almost a hundred. It was always wisest to assume one had several centuries on you.

"No. But we sussspect."

"And by 'we' you mean...?"

P.B. took over from the serpent then. "We meaning the folk I told you about before," he said. "I've been doing a little...powwowing."

That had been back in May, when all hell was breaking loose around her ears. P.B. had told her that the fatae were becoming restless with the all-human Council and their attempts to control the *Cosa.* She had never actually gotten around to telling Sergei about that. Not in any detail, anyway. Between the Council, and the Silence, and then the lack of jobs and her trying to figure out what was going on between her oh-so-confusing partner and herself, the problems of the fatae had pretty much slipped to the bottom of the Things To Worry About list. She admitted to herself, now, that that might have been a mistake.

And what did he mean, "powwowing"? Damn it, she had trusted Lee to sit on him!

"So far, things seem to be pretty much local," Lee was

saying. "It's like having the mafia back in town. But whatsername, the Council flak—"

"KimAnn Howe," Sergei said, just loud enough this time to be heard.

"Yeah, her. Word is she's got hooks outside the area, maybe some pull with the West Coast and up in Ontario…but we can't get any definites."

That was worrying. Like the *Cosa*, the Council operated a little like old-time gangs, each area of the country having their own people and their own way of doing things. Until now, there'd been no hint that the New York-area Council was moving into other areas.

*Then again, for all the gossip we're not too good on sharing real information either. If any of us ever actually got off our backsides and got organized….* The thought made her shudder. She didn't want the Council running things, no, but she was pretty sure her fellow lonejacks would be just as bad. Their main appeal was that they were soundly disinterested in forming committees or making long-term plans that involved anyone except themselves.

And, "Hey, waitaminit." She said that last out loud, and Sergei looked at her. "Tree-taller, when the hell did you get involved in *Cosa* anything? Mister Don't Tell Me I Don't Play Politics?"

"Didn't want to, short-stuff. But this is my city too. Between the vigilantes beating up on innocent fatae, and Council trying to put lockdowns on mostly innocent lonejacks, and you getting shot at—"

"That was a job-related thing, Lee."

"It wouldn't have happened five years ago. Things are changing. Rules are changing. I'm not going to get caught unprepared, just because I don't like to think about bad shit going down. I'm a pacifist, not an idiot."

She knew what he was saying made sense, sort of, but Wren still felt like she'd swallowed a gutful of iron filings off the floor of his workshop, twisting and stabbing like betrayal. Lee was her partner in Don't Give a Damn, damn it. How was she supposed to not pay attention if she didn't have someone to go "la la la I'm not listening" with?

"Definites are what you need," Sergei said, taking part in the conversation finally. "Without it, all you have are suspicions and gossip and bad feeling. Which can lead to the wrong people getting lynched. I shouldn't have to remind you people of that."

"I've put the word out for people to watch their backs," Lee said. "And to pass along anything they see or hear that's…different. Or more intense of the same, in some cases."

"And the fatae?" Wren had to ask. P.B. had been of the opinion, recently, that a revolt was brewing among the nonhuman members of the *Cosa*. Sounded like he'd been right. What exactly that might mean she didn't know— and she didn't want to find out, either.

"We will…wait. For now." The Nassunnii seemed somewhat disappointed, but Wren took it at its word. "We sssshall ssssssseee you on the morrow, then, demon."

"I gotta name," P.B. protested. "Why doesn't anyone ever use it?"

The serpent's chuckling was the only answer as it went offline with a *snap* that indicated to Wren at least that the connection had been a current hijack, and involved no phone lines at all. Just as well, the thought of one of them maneuvering around in a phone booth…

"Um, P.B.? Where have you been doing all this pow-wowing?"

"We're not at your place, relax Wren. I wouldn't do that to you."

"All of it, because you know I'd be pissed, or this call in particular, because the serpent can't get up the stairs?"

There was silence on both other ends of the line.

"Talk to me, people. Who *have* you been meeting with in my apartment when I'm not around?"

"Ah." That was Lee, and she could practically see him shifting uncomfortably on that stupid stool in his studio. P.B. made a noise that might have been a faint whimper. They'd been busier than they were letting on, that much was clear.

She was *so* going to kill them both.

Sergei made short work of ending the phone call, and disconnected the speakerphone. By the time he was finished, she had almost gotten her temper under control.

"They're dead men. Demon. Whatever. Dead."

"And don't think they don't know that."

"Whatever possessed him? All right, P.B. has no sense of personal space, not when it's not his own. But Lee? He couldn't use his own space? No, much better to use Wren's apartment. Play on her reputation, play on her neutrality. Play on her being out of the country. Did they not think—God, no, don't answer that, of course they didn't." God, she was *pissed*.

He made a motion with his arm that was quickly checked. She thought maybe he had meant to touch her, put his arm around her, but thought better of it. Probably a wise move.

"You trust him?" he asked.

"Yeah, I trust him." Unfortunately. "You don't?"

"With your life, absolutely. Beyond that?" he shrugged. "Where is his loyalty, Wren? You said it yourself, just now. The fatae, overall, make selfishness into an art form. So what's his story?"

"I don't know," Wren said. "None of the demon I've met seem to have any kind of breed or clan loyalty."

"Demon, singular?"

"According to the little we know, yeah. Demon don't look much alike—in fact, the only way you can tell they're demon is in their eyes. None of the other fatae have red eyes. I never told you any of this?"

"No."

"Oh." She had told him, she knew that. Normally, he didn't forget *anything*. Sergei's fataephobia was something she had never understood, not when they met, and not now. "Anyway, P.B.'s only loyalty is to P.B., and what's going to benefit him. He's a demon. They're the nerds of the fatae world, and the only way they have to get ahead is to grow up and become Bill Gates.

"Look, I'm going to go take a shower." She knew she was being abrupt, but somehow she didn't feel like crawling back into their floor-nest to snuggle after this discussion. From the way Sergei just sort of nodded, his eyes focused somewhere else, she figured he felt the same way. God, she thought it would be simpler now, maybe—sexual tension resolved, back to the same old same old. But sex—having it, not having it, surviving it—complicated everything.

Grabbing underwear from her suitcase, and her bra from off the floor, she went into the tiny bathroom and stared at herself in the mirror.

Somehow she thought something might have changed there, too. She looked pretty much the same, though. More tired. There was that. And—she checked her right-side ribs—and a little more bruised. Sergei had a really strong grip. She liked that. And that was new, too. All in all, a very…interesting evening. She'd never had a lover who let her call the shots like that. And gotten off on her calling the shots.

Although he hadn't been shy about demanding what he wanted, either….

Her gaze met that of her mirror image, and they both blushed.

The sound of the door opening and closing again reminded her that she was supposed to be getting ready. She turned the shower on, grabbed the shampoo, and regretfully washed the smell of Sergei's skin off her own.

"Food, coffee, and an early start on tracking down our missing scholar?"

"Quacks like a plan to me," Sergei agreed.

They were way too chipper and organized and…awake, for this early in the morning. Wren hated mornings. Hated getting out of bed before eight, even when there was money in what they were doing. She was grumpy, damn it.

But it was very difficult to be grumpy when the sky was pale blue, the sun was warm, the air smelled like nothing she had ever smelled before, some fresh green tang, and the insides of her thighs were sore.

It really was a beautiful morning. But she still needed coffee. Badly.

"You want to track down our lunch companions, make sure they're okay?"

Wren snorted. "They're probably going to be sleeping standing up for a week, when their mentors are through with them. But yeah. A courtesy call, at least."

"Any idea where to start looking?"

Wren shook her head. "Partner, partner, partner. Did you not see everyone ignoring the hijinks last night?"

He raised an eyebrow, and she blushed. "Not those hijinks. I told you that the restaurant felt like a *Cosa* joint. The old men I'm not so sure about, but the woman who served us, and the cook—probably a married couple—they knew what was going on, and weren't too fussed about what happened. Which, added to the fact that there's not one but two Talented teenagers here, suggests there's probably an enclave nearby."

An enclave being a nice way of saying a coven, Sergei knew. Not quite the same, but the same concept of magic-users living together for mutual protection and aid. More common in Europe than the United States, simply because they had been doing it for so many generations, it became tradition. Also, much easier to find someone to marry, that way. But it had all been academic, until now.

"So, what, just go out into the middle of the street and yell 'yo, any Talent within hailing distance?'"

Wren gave a little shrug. "Bet it works."

It did.

"The boys, they're all right?"

"They have the headache, but *si*, they are fine. When they are better, I kick them around the piazza."

Ricard was Pietro's father, an older, slightly greying version of his son. In response to their query—asked by Sergei in Italian—the greengrocer had taken them by the hand and led them to the café where Ricard had been sitting, nursing what looked like an endless cup of cappuccino. They joined him at the table in back, and were joined a few minutes later by an older gentleman, balding and wrinkled but still walking upright and with a clear, insightful gaze, who apparently was 'Stagio's mentor.

"Don't kick them too hard," Wren said. "They were remarkably mild, all things considered. I shorted out a local movie theater my turn."

"And I brought down the only television receiver in the town. My friends, they did not speak to me for a month."

Wren gave her partner a "see? told ya so" look, which he ignored. Sergei seemed content to sit quietly, turning a slender cigarette around between his fingers, and listen to the two of them trade stories about growing up Talented, while the old man, who seemed to understand some English but speak none, stirred his coffee with deliberate precision.

After their second refill on the coffee, however, the old man finally spoke, rattling off what sounded like commands in an accent so thick Sergei couldn't make heads or tails out of it. Ricard looked taken aback, then somewhat embarrassed.

"Ah. Septus would like to know…he has asked me…" He visibly screwed up his nerve, and got it out on the next try.

"What is it, to be a Retriever?"

Wren looked at him, at a loss. Nobody had ever actually asked her that, before. Not another Talent, anyway. But running through her memory, she realized that all of the Retrievers she knew of, the ones with reputations—not that there were many to begin with—were either American or British. And one Spaniard, back in the '40s. No Canadians, no French, no Italians, no Germans—wait, there was that Argentinean, the one who wizzed in prison back in the seventies, took out half a cell block before his local *Cosa* shut him down.

"It's…like any other job," she said finally. "A lot of hard work, decent rewards, some downtime when you're bored, and occasional bouts of chaos when everything comes together all at once on top of you."

"But you live—off your Talent," Septus asked, through Ricard.

Ah. "Not always. Not even entirely. The way I think—

that is what makes me good at what I do. That's not Talent, that's just sneaky."

Sergei snorted into his coffee, but didn't say anything. She ignored him.

"Sometimes—" Not very often true "—I don't even need Talent to get the job done."

And sometimes she pulled down so much she could feel the burn marks on her neurons. Too many of those, lately. She was thankful for this job, she was, but a simple snatch-and-go of incriminating photos or something would have been nice, too.

Problem was, she acknowledged, she'd gotten too good. Too expensive. Even before the Council started messing with her, nobody came to her for the simple jobs any more.

"Are you here to solicit support in any move against your Council?"

Wren blinked in shock, turned to look at Sergei, who looked as poleaxed as she felt.

"No, of course not!"

Septus barked another command at Ricard, who replied with his own irritated comment, something about letting bread bake. Sergei had to assume it was a regional phrase.

"We will take no stand in what is a local problem. We cannot. There are no such as your lonejack here."

Hah. He had been right. The thought brought Sergei no real satisfaction.

"We have survived in this valley for generations because we do not call attention to ourselves. The Council of Rome placates the Papacy, and ignores smaller problems. You have stirred the pot, and made us seem a larger problem."

Ooops. "That was not our intent."

"We do not concern ourselves with intent." Septus's voice, even in Italian, was stern, and Wren had a flashback to her mentor, taking her down a peg or seven for some harebrained, seemed-perfectly-reasonable-at-fifteen stunt. The same age, more or less, as 'Stagio and Pietro, when you thought you knew everything, and weren't even a quarter right.

"Mea culpa, *magister*." The time-honored apology, equivalent of showing your throat and belly to the alpha Talent. Wren put her hands flat on the table and looked first at Ricard, then at Septus. "On my word, on my honor, we are here only to carry out a job that has nothing whatsoever to do with the Council, ours or yours, and should not involve you in any way, shape, or form."

Her words had a formal tinge to them that made Sergei think it was a ritual of some sort. It certainly seemed to quiet the old man down considerably.

"You will be leaving then?"

"As soon as we track down one last person we need to speak with, yes."

The old man spoke again, his voice less demanding, and Ricard nodded. "Who is he? There is a chance, no, that we can help?" And move you along more swiftly, was the implied undercurrent.

"That would be wonderful, thank you." She reached into her back pocket for the piece of paper with the scholar's name on it, then frowned, digging deeper and coming up empty. Sergei coughed, and pushed the folded piece of paper he had taken out of his wallet across the table to her.

"Oh, right." She unfolded the paper and scanned it to make sure it was the right information, then passed it over to Ricard.

"An American?"

"British, actually."

Ricard leaned back, and a young girl darted forward from behind the counter to take the paper from his hand. He spoke to her in a low voice, and she listened with the intent concentration only the under-ten set have, losing it when they reach their teens and become self-consciously world-wise. She looked up at Wren, her dark blue eyes wide, and then dashed away, clutching the paper in one fist. She disappeared into the back room, and they heard a door open and slam shut.

"With luck, we will have a direction for you soon."

Wren nodded her thanks. Then, with a glance at Sergei, she leaned forward. "Ricard, what do you know about the monks on the hill?"

By the time the little girl came back, they had moved on to espresso, and the *barista* had put a plate of some incredibly dense, rich cake on the table in front of them, with that one act moving it from a business meeting to a *Cosa* gathering. Wren was picking the last currants out of the crumbs on her plate and trying to think of one more question to ask, that might trigger the information she needed.

All Ricard and Septus knew about the House of Legend was that the monks kept to themselves, bought their supplies from somewhere else, and didn't get many visitors. The fact that she and Sergei had been there not once but twice seemed to fascinate Septus, and he and Ricard had another intense back-and-forth before Ricard finally shrugged and turned back to Wren.

"There was a rumor, generations ago. That a fatae had gone up the hill, and never returned. His kin came looking for him, but they refused to go up the hill to see for themselves. They warned us to stay away. And we always have. But why?"

Wren swallowed. *Fatae* had been smarter than she was.

"Dark space," she said, her throat suddenly thick with remembered fear. "They built a dark space. It's not safe for us."

Ricard's eyes opened wide, and he hesitated before translating her words for Septus. The old man looked at her intently when Ricard was done, then nodded, as though confirming something to himself.

*"Donna coraggiosa. Stupida, ma coraggiosa."*

That, even Wren could translate. She grinned, shrugged, and Septus grinned right back at her, showing an unsurprising lack of teeth.

"So…the fatae here, things are good?" It was hardly smooth, but then again, it probably didn't need to be. If everything was okay.

"Si, yes, they are…we do not see them often. This has never been a gathering place. But in the summers, sometimes, and when winters are bad we share our food with them, as we have always done."

"Good, good," Wren said. "I hadn't seen any here, and so wondered."

"You know many fatae?"

Sergei snorted, an unexpected, helpless sound of amusement, and Wren kicked him under the table.

"Yes. I ah…I know a number of them."

And then there was nothing for it but that she told them all about P.B., and piskies who lived in Central Park, and the other fatae-clans she had seen over the years. The *barista* moved closer, to hear while still keeping an eye on other customers as they came in and out, and even Septus seemed fascinated.

"New York. A most marvelous place."

"It can be, yeah," Wren had to agree. And she missed it, terribly. But it was nice to see that the relationships between lonejacks and fatae here were pretty good—something to bring back to P.B. and the others. She had been wondering what you got a house-sitting demon as a thank-you gift anyway. Not that she wasn't still pissed at him.

Just before she was going to suggest they order lunch, the little girl came back. A smudge of chocolate on her cheek indicated that wherever she had been, it hadn't been a hardship to her. She handed over a different piece of paper to Ricard with great solemnity, and was dismissed with the last piece of cake to go with her chocolate.

"Ah. *Aqui.*" Ricard handed the paper to her. It was a

thick sheet, flecked with bits of color woven in. Someone
had written an address in a strong hand, in dark blue ink.
Handmade paper, and a fountain pen, she guessed. Nice.
But she had no idea where the address was, or how to
get there, and said as much to Ricard after passing the
sheet on to Sergei.

"A town, north of here. Perhaps, hmm, an hour's
drive. Ruins, not much more. Not much of interest."

"Not to us," Sergei agreed. "But to a scholar?"

"Is possible, yes, yes."

Sergei looked over at her, sliding the paper into the
same pocket of his coat that the other slip of paper had
been in. "Our tickets were open-ended. We can go up
tomorrow, scout things out. If this guy does have it…"

"We can go home. Sergei, I want to go home." She, in
fact, was having a twinge that she thought might actually
be premonition that she *needed* to be home. It might just
have been her growing desire to have this Retrieval
underway, but—she didn't think so. Of all the times in
the world for her to start developing premmies!

Sergei nodded, understanding the emotion in her
voice if not the reasons for it. "So we'll go up this afternoon. It's on the way back to Milan anyway, more or less.
We can find a hotel along the way. And if we get lucky,
I'll see if we can get a flight home tomorrow."

Ricard walked them back to their motel; as much,
Wren suspected, to show the goodwill the local *Cosa* had
for the visiting Americans who weren't there to cause
trouble as to continue their conversation. It was a matter
of minutes after that to pack up and check out.

* * *

The town, Torillino, was in fact about almost two hours north, the way Sergei drove. The traffic was relatively light, with only one car behind them most of the way. Awake this time, Wren took advantage of the relatively slow pace and admired the countryside. It wasn't anything particularly special, although she loved seeing the little stone houses right up at the edge of the road, but it was Italy, and considering what it took to get her here, she was going to appreciate every moment.

"I wish…"

He took his hand off the shift stick long enough to touch her hand in sympathy. "Next time we'll book a cruise, and take our time."

The address they had been given turned out to be a lovely little house made of red stone, situated up a relatively low hill. Hills everywhere, Wren thought. Rolling and rising and must've been hell to walk, before cars, if you didn't have a trusty horse or mule. Vines and roses surrounded the front door of the house, and when Sergei used the knocker, a tiny black and white cat appeared out of the bushes to investigate them. Wren had just bent over to pet the cat when the door opened.

"Yes?"

"Doctor Ebick?"

"Yeah. Who're you?"

"My name is Sergei Didier." Sergei fished one of his cards out of his pocket, presenting it to Ebick with a subdued flourish. "A colleague of ours gave me your address. May we come in?"

Wren was pretty sure the guy had no idea what hit him, because the next thing anyone knew, they were sitting in the tiny living room of the house, surrounded by stacks of papers and enough computer equipment to make the hair on her arms stand on end. Thankfully, very little of it was turned on. From what she could sense, any three of them would be enough to short out the house's entire system.

"So, what's this about, then?"

Ebick was a short, very skinny man with hair so black it had to have been dyed and a pair of glasses perched over a nose that would have done a rabbit proud. All in all Wren thought he was probably the most unappealing example of mankind she had ever met. Not actively ugly, but off-putting. He scrutinized Sergei's card, then frowned and looked at him.

"What does a collectables and fine art gallery have to do with me?"

"Ah, you see, I am in the process of putting together a presentation of modern illuminated manuscripts; to bring the medievalist treatment to the modern eye, and we thought it might be best to show the actual work to educate the public where the inspiration rises from, yes?"

Ebick nodded automatically, then caught himself up as though to say something, subsiding when Sergei went on speaking. Wren just sat back in the somewhat lumpy sofa to enjoy the show. Her partner had such a lovely line of bullshit.

"It has been brought to my attention by that mutual

colleague, and no, I'm afraid I never betray confidences like that, I'm sure you understand the delicacy of such things, moving in the world as you do, yes?

"Ah, this colleague of ours passed along the fact that you had in your possession a quite remarkable manuscript suiting our needs, one loaned to you by the Monaci delle Sante Parole for your research—"

"No such thing!"

"I beg your pardon?"

Wren rather thought Sergei looked like a college professor unexpectedly and rudely interrupted by one of his more until-then-favored students.

"I don't have anything like that. They didn't loan me anything. I don't know who told you this but they're wrong."

*Methinks the man doth protest way too much, and too fierce,* Wren thought at her partner, not expecting telepathy to suddenly move from wishful fantasy to actual Talent skill set. But where magic couldn't do the job, the old partner brain-reading trick sometimes could.

Sergei frowned thoughtfully, tapping two fingers against his mouth as he thought. "Ah, most unfortunate. Could it be perhaps he meant that you had studied such a manuscript? Might you be able to give us a description of it, perhaps?"

Ebick stuttered a little, then, under Sergei's sympathetic gaze, it burst out of him.

"I saw nothing there! Nothing! Eleven years of research! The Church promised me full access to all the material I needed to complete my study, and yet those…so-called monks refused! They let me into one room, and one room only, and the material there was useless. Not a single reference in the entire room."

Wren desperately wanted to ask what he had been looking for, but she was afraid that any comment from her would shut the flow off. And what if he assumed they already knew, via Sergei's alleged mutual colleague?

"So you never actually saw…?"

"Anything. I didn't see anything." And he was clearly in a huff about it, still. "Oh, I have enough material to make my point; but I know that they have what I need to prove it. I could practically feel it there. But they are so jealous of their prerogative, their secret little society, that an outsider like myself had no rights to anything."

Ebick clearly could have gone on for longer, now that he'd started, but Sergei made a regretful-sounding tut-tut noise, and made to stand up.

"All this way, and only to bring up unpleasant experiences for you. I do apologize. Please, there's no need to go on, we quite understand that your time is precious. I do look forward to reading your eventual publication, yes, indeed. Thank you again."

Outside, with the door firmly shut behind them, Wren looked at Sergei, who was staring off into the pale blue sky. "So?"

Sergei sighed, and his shoulders slumped out of the pushy administrator pose he'd taken with Ebick. "So. We're still on the case, I guess. I'm sorry, Wren."

She shrugged. "We take on situations to finish them, right? So we finish." She was silent as they walked to the car, then tapped the roof to get his attention. When her partner looked up she said "They saved his life, you know. By not letting him near the second level. Because you *know* he's the type to meddle in what he hasn't a clue about."

"He won't thank them if it means he can never publish his theory."

She shook her head in incomprehension. "And you think the *Cosa's* weird?"

"'*Scusi?*'"

Sergei turned to watch the stranger walk toward them. Looking just past, he saw a car parked on the road a few yards away from the gravel driveway and cursed himself. It was the car that had been behind them on the way up.

"Yes? Er, *si?*" Wren said. The stranger was approaching her side of the car, and Sergei was judging the distance between them even as he put himself on an intercept around the back of the sedan, always keeping the newcomer in line of sight.

"You are Signorina Valere?"

"Depends on who is asking." She put her back to the car door, Sergei noticed with approval. If need be she could drain the car battery, but he doubted there would be a need. Not unless this guy pulled out an Uzi. Or sprouted big sharp teeth and a hunger for Talented flesh.

"I am Aaron. Of the Sante Parole."

"The monastery. Or whatever it actually is."

The stranger—little more than a kid, actually—nodded once, his eyes never leaving Wren's face.

"Signorina Valere, you are…you are of the select?"

Her face must have shown her confusion, because he hurried on. "Of our founders, you are the same?"

*Talented. He wants to know if she's a Talent.* Sergei had no idea what the right answer was. He held his breath, waiting for his partner's response.

"*Si.* I am."

Aaron's expression relaxed a little, making him look even younger, and Sergei let his own muscles go down off alert.

"I speak to you?"

Wren was quicker with the translation than he was. "Here?"

"*Per favore.* Is...better I not be seen."

Curiouser and curioser. Feeling like someone out of a low-grade cop movie, Sergei opened the back door of the sedan, and ushered Aaron in. Wren got in on her side, and he went around to get back into the driver's seat. Starting up the car, he pulled out of the driveway and started down the road, planning to do a u-turn at some point to drop the monk off at his own car when he was done with whatever he needed to say.

"The Nescanni manuscript. You seek it."

"We've been hired to return it to your monastery, yes."

Aaron took a deep breath, preparing himself for whatever it was he had to say. "Marco. A month ago, Marco told me a stranger came to him. Offered him much money for something. Something we were sworn to guard."

"The manuscript."

Aaron shrugged his skinny shoulders, his Adam's

apple bobbing up and down nervously as he swallowed. Sergei felt the sudden urge to shake him until the answers fell out, but kept his hands on the car.

"It was gone. I think so, yes."

"Who else knew about this?"

"No one." Aaron seemed very sure of that. "The man who ask, he buys for someone else. Marco take the money, gives him the manuscript. What can it hurt? Is not a thing ever called for, not a thing of specialness. Nobody will ever notice it is gone. But afterward, Marco not feel so…right about it."

"And he told you."

Aaron nodded.

Dear Lord. Did they not have a clue what they guarded? No, she knew the answer to that already. Please God, let Teodosio be meaning it when he said there would be changes in the guardianship. "So why didn't he come forward? We were there, he could have—"

But Aaron was shaking his head. "One week ago, Marco…" He swallowed again, and his gaze dropped to his lap.

"Marco's dead?" Wren's voice was very soft.

"They say…that he jump off the cliff. *Si e ucciso.* Committed suicide. But no, he would not. Even if he…" Aaron's voice trailed away, like he wasn't able to say the words, much less convince himself of their truth.

Sergei adjusted the rearview mirror and caught Wren's gaze in it. She gave a faint dip of her chin. She believed that Aaron's Marco might have been tossed from that cliff, rather than jumping. Or, maybe he really had been so overwhelmed with the guilt that he offed himself. If he knew—or even suspected—what he'd let loose in the world, but wasn't able for whatever reason to come clean…

"Leaving you to tell us."

"*Si. Ma si*… If you are of the selected, you can capture it, contain it, before any one else disappears, as Teodosio says this thing does?"

"I will," she promises him, taking some measure of comfort that Teo was saying that much already.

His eyes still directed down at his hands, Aaron seemed to be debating with himself.

"You've come this far," Sergei said. "The difficult part is over."

"*Si*. The man, he was an American. I think. He paid in euros, but Marco, he sent the parchment to an address in America. But I do not know where, more than that."

In the rearview mirror, Sergei saw Wren's lips in a single, heartfelt but silent expletive. He silently willed her to keep still. Yes, that left them a lot of ground to cover. But it was a start. And, more to the point, it was a start that would allow them to work from home, not here. Wasn't that what she'd wanted?

"*Grazie*," Sergei said to Aaron with absolute sincerity. "We know this was not an easy thing to do. And you have done a very good thing."

"You will return it to us, to safekeeping?"

He hated making promises he wasn't sure he could keep. "We will do our best. And our best is very, very good."

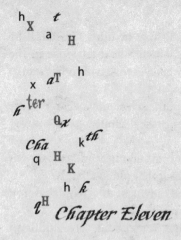

## Chapter Eleven

The glass door slid open, and the heat and humidity of the summer afternoon slid around them and coated their skin immediately. Sergei hadn't missed the weather on the East Coast, that was certain. Thankfully he had already taken his jacket off and folded it into his carry-on, and his khaki slacks were lightweight enough to be comfortable. He wasn't looking forward to putting his legit businessman facade back on in the morning.

Wren was sulky. "I *said* I was sorry to the flight attendant. In three different languages, thanks to your coaching. What more did they want?"

Sergei did not have unlimited patience, despite praying for it the past seven hours.

"I think that we need to just let it go." He loved her, he did, but that wasn't going to keep him from killing her.

The platform was mostly empty, only two dejected-looking teenagers sitting on their luggage, and a bored security guard talking on his mobile. He hoisted his suitcase, silently cursing Andre for booking them coming in and out through Newark Liberty rather than JFK. Newark was cheaper, yeah, and had more flights, but right now he wanted to pack Wren into a cab and send it off, not have to deal with the train back into Manhattan. But until they got paid for this, they also didn't have the ready cash on hand in the business account to pay for the cab.

He could have used his personal account—if the damn ATM in the Malpensa airport hadn't eaten his card earlier that day. Which meant he was going to have to go to the bank at some point and get a replacement.

*I'm too old for this,* he thought. Jet lag used to make him laugh. Of course, back in the Bad Old Days he used to be able to leave the Active agent in place and go home alone. Traveling with a Talent, especially one who... didn't enjoy air travel... was a situation in and of itself.

The train came, a few minutes behind schedule, and they got on. It was enough of an off hour that there weren't many other people in their car, just an old man in a filthy trench coat, and a young businesswoman busily dictating a memo into the speaker-tab of her mobile phone.

Wren had chosen a seat far from the phone user, he noted, but it might have been from the desire to not be near anyone as much as current-courtesy. He sat down next to her and proceeded to stare into the same space she was staring at. She had scraped her hair back into a knot on the back of her head, and strands were coming loose already, the soft brown seemingly absorbing the light in itself. Her skin had a delicate sheen of sweat on it that had only a little to do with the weather. He sympathized. But he still wanted to kill her.

They spent the entire twenty-minute trip in silence. As the train pulled into the city, his hand reached out and found her cold fingers, squeezing them gently. It hadn't been an easy trip, not for either of them. And it wasn't as though her phobia was anything she could control, exactly. A hesitation; and she turned her hand under his and squeezed back. It was enough.

At Penn Station they left the train and made their way through the labyrinth of hallways and stairs, wending their way up escalators to emerge into the reassuringly familiar noise and hustle of Eighth Avenue. Sergei was pretty sure that he could feel the cells in his body relaxing, and Wren looked like a cat finally home from the veterinarian's—still annoyed, but sure that the world would now run according to its proper order.

"Go home. Get some sleep. Spend an hour under the shower. Everything else can wait until we're human again."

Wren blinked, nodded. "Yeah. Yeah, okay, you're right. God, but it's good to be home again." She turned to him, and he cupped her chin with one hand, lifting her face up so that he could say goodbye. He knew it looked patronizing, and she was likely to kick him, hard, but despite being new to this entire Public Display of Affection thing, it felt like the right thing to do.

From the tiny, sharp sparks he could feel where their lips met, not to mention the way the tension practically slid off her body, he suspected that his instinct was correct.

"Mmmm. Yeah." She smiled up at him, jet-lag dead but happier now, and then stepped away. "You get some sleep too, mister."

"Absolutely," he promised, making a Scout's honor sign. She snorted, held up her hand, and a cab glided like a lemon shark to a stop in front of her. For a woman who made a living not being noticed, she had the most astonishing luck with cabs. She opened the door, got in, and was gone. Sergei sighed, and stepped to the curb to flag his own transportation for the trip uptown.

In the cab, Wren put her fingers up to her lips, and shook her head. She was going to have to do something about the current she kept leaking whenever Sergei touched her even remotely sexually. And never mind that he not only didn't mind it but seemed to like it. That was trouble just waiting to happen. In a lot of ways. Although it did give her a little more insight into her partner's psyche….

"Where to, miss?"

She gave the cabbie her address and heard him mutter in disgust at how small a fare it would be. She didn't care. Between the job and the travel and the fact that the sense of being watched came back like a slap the moment she got on the train out of the airport, she was too tired and too cranky to want to lug her bags *anywhere*.

Wren was seriously thinking about leaving them in the lobby of her building, in fact, rather than have to get them up the stairs. If she were even slightly better at translocation she wouldn't even bother with the stairs, and be damned anyone who might see her, but the thought of all the things that could and probably would go wrong, considering her limited ability with that particular skill, made the fifth-floor walk-up seem positively inviting.

There was a pile of mail waiting for her, which she shoved into the nearest available pocket of her carry-on, then gazed in disgust up the stairs. What the hell had possessed her to take an apartment on the fifth floor? *Privacy, and access to the roof without anyone seeing.* Right. There were days, though…

"If I leave them here, my clothing'll be for sale on the nearest corner table in half an hour," she reminded herself. "But…" A quick check inside confirmed that she had just enough reserves yet to maybe make things a little easier.

"Advantage to the girl who keeps up on her reading," she said, kneeling down by her suitcases. There had been an article mentioned in one of her listservs recently, about an experiment going on at one of the major universities, having to do with gravitational mass. She hadn't understood most of it, but had focused on the fact that while gravity only attracted, electricity could attract or repel.

She wasn't a scientist, by a long shot, but she had one advantage they didn't….

Looking around to make sure that nobody was coming down the stairs or walking in behind her, Wren sent a tiny tendril of current under the bags, willing it to infuse itself in the material.

"Heavy weight;

Tired arms need rest.

Give me ease."

Okay, so it wasn't deathless poetry. It didn't need to be. Intent was everything, intent and focus. The words just directed it.

There was a faint buzz in the air, the mental scent of ozone, and when she lifted the handle, the previously heavy suitcase lifted up into her hand with a minimum of touch. The bags weren't floating, exactly, but they went up the stairs with far less lifting on her part.

"Hah! I am lonejack, hear me mess with science as we know it."

Well, not really. As far as she knew even the most high-powered Mage couldn't actually affect gravity. But apparently you *could* confuse it for a bit.

*It's a shame I don't have a student. Someone to pass this along to.* She could, of course, bellow it from the rooftop for whoever wanted to hear it. But that wasn't how she was trained, or how her mentor had been trained. And even close friends like Lee didn't really share trade discoveries. They should…but it never seemed to occur to anyone.

*Some day. Maybe.* John Ebeneezer, her mentor, had been in his thirties when he dragged her—literally—into learning what he knew. There was time yet. And it had to be the right person. You couldn't just order one from eBay, after all.

Those thoughts kept her occupied for four of the five flights. On the landing before her apartment, however, something broke through to grab her attention.

*Something's wrong.*

She wasn't sure what made her think that; she had done the usual lockup, coaxing a few elementals into watching over the place. They were microscopic, current-eating entities that had taken to man-made electricity like dogs to domesticity. Low res, and barely smart enough to distinguish between human types and remember good (Sergei, P.B., Tree-taller, her mother) and bad (anyone else), but if something were seriously wrong, they'd be swarming over her the moment she came up the stairs.

In fact, they should be swarming her, anyway. Elementals were attracted to current, that's how she was able to coax them. And they liked the way her core "tasted."

Leaving her bags on the landing—anyone who wanted them badly enough to come this far could have them—she walked carefully up the last few steps, quieting her internal current to better sense if anything was going on behind the apartment door.

Nothing. No sense of anything at all out of the ordinary. Not even any elementals. Suddenly her exhaustion fled, replaced by a hyperaware tension.

"If P.B. effed with my settings when he was in here, or told the elementals to beat it, I'm going to skin the furry little bastard and dip him in boiling sesame oil before selling him as the newest lunch craze."

Taking the key out of her jacket pocket, she unlocked the door. Before opening it, however, she touched the wall and sucked up a quick hit of power. The lights dimmed slightly, and somewhere someone's stereo died midsong.

"Sorry," she whispered to the unknown neighbor, then pushed open the door.

Nothing. The hallway looked quiet. There were no lounging fatae, no angry Mages, no shimmering current traps or any other sign of anything being wrong.

And no elementals. Anywhere.

She took another step into the apartment, and peeked into her kitchenette. Even the dishes she had left in the sink had been cleaned up, and she made a mental note of that. P.B. might live, after all. Another step, and the sense of something being wrong rose up in her again, like fingers stroking her spine. She stopped in the hallway, breathing softly, her muscles tensed up and waiting for an attack that didn't come. Her mysterious, unseen watcher? A run-of-the-mill burglary attempt? Something worse?

"Right. You're freaked out by your own apartment. How sad is that?" P.B. had probably scared the elementals off, that was all. If he'd had other fatae in here, the little jerk, it would make sense that they'd overloaded or something, caught between his "okay" signature, and the fact that he was bringing strangers in. After all—

Something flew by her face and she shrieked, instinctively frying it with a thoughtless burst of current.

"Jesus, Valere. Way to overreact." Then she looked at the crisped remains, and her lips moved in a soundless curse. A sound like metal-on-metal made her whip around, ready for another attack, but nothing happened.

She looked up, and saw a thick black stream moving into the heating duct. Mottled grey bugs, about the size of a penny each. With a snarl of rage, she blasted them with a more selective flick of current, leaving a charred stain on the previously-white ceiling, and dead bugs falling to the carpet, where they began to smolder and stick.

"Arrrghh." Her immediate rage vented, she stopped to breathe for a moment, aware that her reserves were down to nil, and she was too tired to really be thinking straight.

The stream heading into the heating duct was stopped, but how many more of them were there? They could be anywhere….

And by now, whoever set them on her would know they'd been discovered. Which meant they knew she was in the apartment.

Shuddering in disgust, Wren forced herself to go get her luggage anyway, dropping both bags in the main room. Keeping the door open, she then went through the apartment anyway, giving everything a visual and magical once-over.

She found a few elementals huddled in the toaster, and calmed herself long enough to coax them out of hiding. "Why didn't you guys warn me?"

A quick flick over their surface memories, and she made a disgusted face, the disgust mainly directed at herself. Figured. They hadn't known what to tell her; she had given them the image of people breaking in, not bugs.

"The dumber the tool, the more explicit the programming needs to be." Odds were, the sense of urgency about getting home she'd felt the day before had been them fretting at the uncertainty of what to do. "Right. Okay guys, thanks. Now shoo, make yourselves scarce." She had nothing against elementals in someone else's home, or hers while she was away, but she'd rather have her space to herself, thanks anyway.

"Except you don't." Have it to herself, that was. The stink from the charred bugs was still in the air, and she knew that it would take some major cleaning to get rid of it. Not to mention the fact that there still might be bugs in the apartment she hadn't flushed out yet. The thought made her skin crawl. Giving someone else a voyeuristic thrill was so *not* on her to-do list.

And besides which, if someone had put them there to watch for her…

She looked around the apartment one last time, and made her decision.

Half an hour later, Wren wasn't so sure she'd made the right choice. She leaned against the metal pole of the subway car, trying to keep from coming into contact with her fellow passengers, all of whom seemed just as worn-down and sweaty as she was, second thoughts and indecision battling it out in her head. The train pulled into the station and jolted to a halt. She started to awareness just in time to slide through the doors before they closed behind her. The train pulled away, leaving her longing for its almost-breathable air. Someone had apparently hit the wrong button on the air filtration system, and they were pumping *warm* air into this station. Trying not to breathe, Wren climbed the stairs as quickly as exhaustion allowed, moving from one oven to another as she came out onto the street.

At least there was some air circulation up here, even if it was only caused by the traffic moving past on the avenue. She walked the three blocks to the modern highrise where her partner lived, thankful for the neighborhood watch group that was clearly still watering the trees that lined their street and keeping the leaves green. You could almost pretend, looking at green leaves, that the weather was going to break, soon.

Standing in front of the building, she took a deep breath, then started to weave current around her in order to get past the doorman without questions.

"Ah, damn." The current-snakes twitched sluggishly, but there was no surge in response to her pull. She was tapped out, totally. Which explained the dizziness, and how queasy she felt in her gut. Or was that jet lag? She hadn't been good about taking care of herself, lately. No gym time—too hot to even think about it.

"Ma'am?"

She smiled up at the doorman, a tall black man in a spiffy dark blue uniform jacket that was obviously not polyester. "Hi. Um, here to see Sergei? Didier? Apartment 16D."

The guard tapped a key on his desk and looked up at her again.

"Name?"

"Valere. Genevieve Valere."

"Right, Ms. Valere. I'll call up for you."

"Right. Thanks."

He was going to be pissed. He'd probably just gotten to bed. The thought of a sleepy, warm, maybe-naked Sergei made her smile, before more recent events took over her brain again.

"Mr. Didier?" The guard must be new, Wren noted. He pronounced the "r" at the end of Sergei's name. "Yes, there's a young woman…right away, sir." He replaced the phone and looked at Wren. "You can go up, miss."

"Thanks." She just hoped she could get up and walk across the lobby without falling over. Or throwing up. Or any of the other lovely things that sometimes happened when she got this depleted. The urge to pull from the building was overwhelming, but she didn't trust herself to do it delicately enough. Sleep first. Or some coffee.

The chrome-and-wood elevator door opened on the sixteenth floor, and Wren practically fell out into Sergei's arms. "What—no, talking later. Come on, inside."

She had been right, he had been sleeping in the nude. The sweatpants he had obviously just dragged on were loosely tied, and sat low on his hips. The freedom to look, and not look away, was still new enough to be intoxicating.

His apartment had an open space plan, with a loft bedroom. The walls were some faint pearl tone, there were gorgeous paintings on the walls, and the furniture came straight from the showroom of some obnoxiously expensive store. It looked sophisticated, modern, and very expensive, and Wren was always afraid she was going to break something there. In the ten years they'd worked together, she had never been in his apartment before the Frants case, as though something in her had told her she wouldn't fit there. Since then, they'd continued to meet at her place, just out of habit.

Or maybe, she thought, not for the first time, because he didn't want her here, in his refuge.

He was in almost every aspect of her life, now. But there were still bits of his that she didn't see. She thought that it probably shouldn't bother her as much as it did. Or maybe it should bother her more. Or maybe she was just delirious.

He deposited her on the nearest sofa and went into the kitchen, fussing around with something. The smell of coffee hit her brain, and she inhaled deeply. "Bless you, my son." It would be crappy—he'd only bought the coffeemaker a month or so ago, and still hadn't got the hang of how much ground to use with how much water, but the thought was almost enough.

"You haven't been recharging." It was a statement, not a question.

"Airport not exactly a good place—"

"Bullshit." That was crude, coming from Sergei, in English, and it stopped her in her verbal tracks. "I've seen you skim a hit off a police station, Valere. While we were in the damn holding tank."

True. "It's…" She hadn't really thought about it. Not until now, and the thoughts were slow to turn over in

her head. Sluggish. Slow. Not good. There had been no
hesitation in taking a charge from her apartment
building, where the wires and she were old friends. "I
think…the dark space maybe freaked me out a little
more than I thought. I didn't…I didn't want to reach out
and touch a strange place, in case…well," and she
shrugged. "You know." Except he didn't. He couldn't,
unless he'd one day tried to speak and had no voice. Had
tried to see, and had no vision. Tried to breathe, and had
no lungs.

Sergei came back carrying a square object, and put it
on the coffee table in front of her. She took a look, did
a double take, and started to laugh weakly.

"Shut up and use it," he said. "And tell me I'm a genius."

"You're a genius," she said obligingly, leaning forward
to put her hands on the car battery. "Absolute, unques-
tioned genius."

The charge in the battery was slight, barely twelve
volts, but it soothed the inner core with the promise that
it hadn't been forgotten.

She sat back with a sigh, and contemplated her partner,
who had taken the easy chair opposite her. His legs were
stretched out in front of him, crossed at the ankle, and his
hair was mussed, as though he'd been running his fingers
through it endlessly. She liked the longer look on him, remembering how it felt to run her own fingers through it.
Much nicer than the much shorter, almost military-style
cut he used to have. She'd have to remember to tell him
that, make sure he didn't go short again.

"I assume there's a reason you're not tucked into

your own bed, visions of thunderstorms dancing through your dreams?"

The memory crashed down on her again, and she leaned her head back and closed her eyes.

"My apartment was bugged. Literally."

He frowned, a lot more alert now. "Bugged? As in, electronics?"

As tired as she was, the thought of someone bringing more electrical devices into her apartment made her snicker. "As in bugs. Oh-so-cutely-named spybugs. Small, swarming, magically trainable, and all over my apartment. God, they're really beginning to piss me off."

"Who?"

"Council. They're the only ones with the money and the reason to do something like that. Unless there's another player in the annoyingly stupid game my life is becoming that I don't know about?"

Sergei shook his head at her mostly unvoiced question. "The Silence relies on human agents, not magical ones. Mainly because they don't have access to them, but I suspect there's a trust issue there, too. Magic's too often the bad thing in their situations, something they're working *against*."

Sounded like they'd run into their fair share of old magics, she thought. There was something else he wasn't telling her, she could hear it under his words, but it was too much effort to switch gears and ferret it out right now. Odds were; it could wait.

"So, what now?"

She yawned, not even the promise of coffee keeping

her eyelids open. "Now, I need to get the place fumigated. Which is a pain in the ass like you wouldn't believe. Nailing those bastards would fry every single electronic I have; they'll need to move everything out and cleanse and then move everything back in, and then I'll have to have the entire apartment cleaned. Spybugs stink to hell when you fry them." She managed to pry her eyelids up long enough to look at him, trying to find the best way to phrase it. "The place *really* stinks now."

Sergei shook his head, his lips curving into a narrow smile. "Hotel Didier, at your service, for as long as you need it."

From the way his gaze focused on her then, she didn't think it was just the apartment that was going to be at her disposal. *Mmmm. Coffee first. Then sleep. Then sex.*

She looked up at him again, and thought, *Okay, coffee, then sex. Then sleep.*

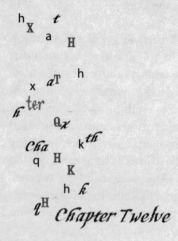

# Chapter Twelve

The alarm went off, and Wren slapped down on the top of it to shut it off.

But instead of hitting the plastic top of the clock, or even the hard wooden surface of her night table, she came down hard on…something soft.

Bed, her brain told her fuzzily.

Specifically, Sergei's bed, which was wider by half again than her own. And had the alarm clock on the other side. She crawled the six inches across the rumpled bed-spread it took to reach the clock, and turned the alarm off.

Silence reclaimed the room.

No Sergei. No sound of Sergei. She had a vague memory of the shower running at some point, but being too comfortably asleep to investigate. She shoved her hair out of her face and squinted at the clock—8:45. He must have reset it before he left for the day. Sweet of him. In that annoyingly business-minded way. Her body didn't want to move, and her brain was totally unhappy with the thought as well, but there was still a job to be finished.

The night before they'd managed to sort out a rough plan of action, before they both crashed. Sergei was going to handle the bureaucratic side of it, while she went on the direct attack. To each her—or his—their own strengths. But first, she had to sort out the deal with her apartment.

Sliding out of bed, she padded naked down the spiral staircase that led from the loft to the rest of the apartment. If anyone really wanted to stare at her from the building across the avenue, they were welcome to. She wasn't putting on her travel-grubby, sweat-stained clothing again.

The coffee machine was on, and there was a decent amount of black sludge in the carafe. Wren hunted through the kitchen cabinets in search of a sturdy, unbreakable mug before giving up and going back to the expensive-looking black china mugs. They managed to be delicate and masculine all at once, and she suspected it took a lot of money to manage that.

She'd grown up in a household where coffee was served in plain white mugs like they used in the diner where her mother worked, and China was a country, not what you ate off of. Wren had gotten used to better living since she started working, but it still wasn't second nature like it was to Sergei. She didn't think it ever would be.

Which was funny, when you thought about it. From what he said, his folks were solid middle class, not the sort to have fancy china for everyday. But that was Sergei for you, she guessed. Full of surprises. Even to her, even after all this time.

With a long pour of coffee, black, down her throat, it was time for the shower she'd been too wiped out to take the night before.

The bathroom was a sweet indulgence to the art of getting clean. Sergei even had a spare toothbrush under the sink. Okay, so it was probably a replacement, not a spare. It was hers, now. And there was, blessed be the designer, a tiled shower stall with two shower heads, and soap that smelled of warm spice. Now she knew where that underlying tang on Sergei's skin came from.

She lathered up twice, aware that it was silly but finding comfort in the smell.

Wren placed both hands palm down on the white tile and let the hot water sluice away the last of her grime and travel sweat. Without conscious decision, she began to oh-so-carefully tap into the electrical wiring she could feel behind the tile and greenboard. Deep in the building, it hummed to her like a mother calling her child. Unlike her own walk-up apartment, this place was both state-of-the-art electronic, and extremely well insulated. She could feel the fail-safes built into the system *there,* and *there,* and straight down the middle of the building, what must be the elevators.

Reassured, Wren narrowed her awareness to the disturbingly faded core inside her, and then let a careful flicker rise up, splitting to go down both arms, out through her palms and into the building, scooping up the current that ran alongside the electrical wiring without too much fear of shorting things out.

*Hello there, sailor….*

When she came to, the water had cooled down to an almost uncomfortable temperature, and her inner core was sparking and shimmering again.

"I take it back. I could get to like this place."

Rinsed, renewed, and wrapped in a spotless—and huge—white towel, Wren sat at the kitchen counter, combed out her hair and considered what her first move should be. The act of combing and braiding were familiar, allowing her brain to suck up some of the current zooming in her veins and put it to good use.

"Given: that the VDA—" Very Dangerous Artifact, a term Sergei had coined in the first year of their partnership "—is in this country. We need the point of entry." Sergei's job, that. "Also given: that whoever has it, or is about to receive it, will need a place to store it, even if just short-term. And it will either have to be pretty damn well shielded, or the same stuff I felt there will leak out—and maybe draw something bigger and badder to it."

Assuming it wasn't already in the hands of something bigger and badder. In which case she might as well just go back to bed and wait for the world to end, because the Silence wasn't paying her anywhere near enough to take that on.

By the time she had the strands tangle-free and

braided, though, she thought she had a pretty good plan of what she *could* do.

First, clothing. She'd stored a pair of jeans and a sweatshirt here a couple of months ago, for emergency measures, but the weather didn't feel like it was going to break any time soon, and besides, that was the wrong look for what she wanted.

Going into Sergei's closet, she found a worn but still wearable pale blue button-down Oxford, and pulled it off the hanger. She collected two ties, one a darker shade of blue, the other white and blue pinstripe, and prayed that she had remembered…

Yeah, she had. There was a pair of panties in with the spare jeans and sweater. That she would use, and be thankful. Now, where would he keep a pair of scissors?

Twenty minutes later, she was considering herself in front of the full-length mirror in the bed-loft. The shirt came down to midthigh, and with the sleeves removed, looked like an acceptably funky sleeveless shirtdress. A little '80s, maybe, but that had been long enough ago for the retro look to come and go, and be acceptable again. She experimented with twining the ties into a belt, but finally decided that the result wasn't good enough to justify ruining two probably outrageously expensive ties.

Anyway, with her sandals, the look worked. Mostly. She wished she'd thought to bring her toiletries kit with her when she left the apartment.

*I'll hit the cosmetics counter for a makeover on the way over,* she decided. It was about time she bought some new lipsticks, anyway.

But before she did that, one very important phone call to make.

Sitting down on the side of the bed, she reached out to pick up the phone. She hoped Sergei'd listened to her, and put in surge protectors. Not that she thought anything would happen; she was calm, and she was rested, mostly, but you shouldn't take things like that for granted. Ever.

Dialing a number from memory, she mentally crossed her fingers and hoped for the best as she put the receiver to her ear.

"'lo?"

"Hey, Tree-taller."

"Valere. When'd you get back into town?"

"Last night. Which is why I'm calling."

"I told him to clean his hair out of the shower," Lee moaned, and Wren rolled her eyes, mentally making a note to kick P.B. if he really had clogged her drains again.

"Nothing so easily fixed, amigo. You may note your caller ID has an unknown number on it, if you actually bothered to look at the damn thing before you picked up."

She could practically hear the other Talent blush.

"I'm at Sergei's. There was a little problem with my apartment that didn't directly involve white fur."

"Oh?"

"Spybugs. Many but not all of them currently crispy-crittered and stinking up my home. You know the name of a good fumigator?"

"Hang on. Yeah. One of the Mackenzie brothers went into that biz, he gave me his card last time we had dinner, where the hell is it?"

There was the sound of drawers being opened and closed, and papers being shuffled. "Right. Got a pen?"

"Yeah, give."

She scribbled the number down, as well as the Mackenzie brother's name.

"You think they ah, bugged your place because…"

No need to ask who he thought "they" were. "Yeah. Probably. This is why you're supposed to hold important powwows somewhere people don't live, okay? Remember that, if you guys intend to stay in the business."

"I'm not…I was just—you said to keep an eye on him!" Lee sounded a little harried, and she took her vengeance in that, letting him off the hook a little.

"Yeah, yeah, I know. And he knew that too, I bet, the little creep." Her kill the demon/don't kill him meter was wobbling again, this time toward kill.

"Speaking of fumigation…did this little powwow of yours discuss the possibility that the source of their most recent problems might be coming from another direction?"

There was silence on the other end of the line.

"The folk who showed up again this spring?" she reminded him. Antifatae vigilantes, who had attacked at least one fatae that she knew of, having stumbled onto the attack as it was happening.

"Oh, yeah, right. It was brought up, actually."

"And?"

"And, they're still around, but they're a little more cautious now. That cop you talked to, Doblosky, he put the word out that these guys were trouble, and between that and what P.B. did to that guy's dog—"

Wren winced. She really didn't want to think about that, even now.

"—they've been sighted but not felt, if you know what I mean. The elders didn't think it was them. Anyway, I think they don't think anyone except one of us could take down one of the Nassunii."

"What, only Mages are able to kill magic? Oh yeah, 'cause that's been proven down throughout their history. Not." There were days when Wren thought she pretty much hated everyone. If she hadn't woken up feeling so good, this would be one of those days.

"Right. Stupid people not being limited to humanity, this we knew already. So. You get whatever it was that took you away cleared up yet?"

"I wish. No, about to get back to it, in fact. So do me a favor?"

"Let me guess. You want me to keep your demon sidekick busy for a few days more?"

"Be a pal, willya? I just don't have time to get into the whole fatae politics thing right now. And you're a lot better than I am at not telling people to take a long leap off a short stair."

"I'll try. But no promises. He was really pissed you didn't tell him anything when you took off...."

"Yeah, right." Wren picked up the paper with the name and phone number on it, and folded it, then realized that she didn't have any pockets to put it into. "P.B.'s a freelance information-monger. I trust him with his business, but not my own."

"Not saying you're wrong," Lee said. "Just that—"

"I know." She sighed. P.B. was a conniving creature, but who was she to talk? There wasn't a lonejack alive who wasn't, one way or another. Even Lee, much as she loved him, always had an eye on the main chance. And P.B. had always come through for her; more to the point, in the past year or so he'd started coming *to* her, even when he saw it as a question of fatae versus human. She had to respect that. More, she needed to *reward* it. Or find someone else who could, anyway.

"Dodge the question. Keep him on the elders, try to work out more info on them, about the dead fatae. Information's what he's good at; stroke his ego a little, tell him we're depending on him to be the conduit."

"You really think that's smart, setting him up against the other fatae like that?"

Jesus wept, she couldn't win! "He came to me, first, Lee. He's the one who wanted me to get involved. Remember? So quit with the guilt thing. P.B.'s old enough to know what he's doing. In fact, as a point of reference, he's older than both of us added together. Okay?"

"Okay. Right. You're the boss."

"Let me know if anything comes up. Um, call here," and she gave him the number, "or call Sergei's cell. He'll get word to me."

She hung up the phone, only now aware that her hand was shaking. One of the things she loved the most about her job was not having to deal with anyone other than her partner. No consensus-building, no coaxing, no chivvying people along despite objections. That was Sergei's job. That was why he got a hefty chunk of the action.

Grabbing her bag off the sofa where she'd dropped it last night, Wren pulled the key to his apartment out of the bag, locked the door behind her, and headed for the elevator.

"Ah yes, I was wondering if that would catch your eye. It's new to the gallery, in fact, the artist only brought it over last week."

Lowell was busy guiding a customer through the newest display. Sergei watched him on the close-circuit monitor over his desk for a few minutes, then, satisfied that the boy knew what he was doing—and of course he did, for all Lowell's faults he was a first-class salesman— muted the sound and turned back to the paperwork on his desk.

Days like this, he remembered why he generally left the fieldwork to Wren, and stuck to the negotiations and payment details. Paperwork bred like rabbits. And while Lowell could sell even the most god-awful avant-garde mishmash to otherwise discerning customers, he was a total failure when it came to actually running a business. Especially a business with so many small details to co-ordinate. Tax forms, customs forms, verifications, and authentications, also known as provenance.

Didier Gallery only handled original artwork. But Sergei had spent four years working in an auction house, and he knew how complicated things could get, once works of art left the original creator's hands. And, more to the point, he had kept up certain of the contacts he had made during those years. Everyone was useful, eventually.

Putting aside the sheaf of sales invoices Lowell had left for him to enter into the computer, Sergei picked up the phone, touched the switch on a small box that kept casual interlopers from listening in to his conversations, and dialed a number.

"Karl, yes, hello, it's Sergei, from Didier—yeah, I'm good, thanks." Karl rooted for the Rangers, but was otherwise a pretty good guy. Knew the ins and outs of the ACS like nobody's business. "No, everything's good here, I was actually trying to track down something a client came in asking about."

Karl worked for the U.S. Customs Service. ACS—the automated commercial system—was the software they used to track goods imported into the United States. Technically speaking, what Sergei was about to ask was a gross violation, yadda yadda yadda. It was also harmless, and certainly worth tickets to see a hockey game next Tuesday night.

"No, not a sculpture, thank God." The last time he and Karl did business, it had been to determine that a sculpture the alleged artist had been trying to get him to take on was actually a replica of an Italian marble that had recently been brought into the country by a private collector. "But Italy again. A manuscript, illuminated. About the size of a legal document, no, I don't know what the illustrations are of. Gold and green, I think," he checked his notes again, "and a reddish-brown ink. Yeah well, it's an old and valued client with *beaucoup* bucks. If he wants to use me as his research boy, I'm willing to make him happy. And then he makes me happy, and we're all happy."

Karl said something, and Sergei laughed. "Well, I can't help it if they're playing like shit. You need to pick a better team."

Picking up the sheet of paper with the details Aaron had given them, Sergei gave the customs agent what he knew.

"Basically, I need to know if anything like this has come through in the past month or so. I don't know; the guy's a straight shooter…I have a bad feeling he thinks he got rooked on a deal, maybe was sold something with a provenance his gut doesn't like? Why they can't just use a reputable dealer… Of course someone like me. Better yet, exactly like me. I have bills to pay too, you know. Yeah, everyone's an expert. Yeah, absolutely. If nothing shows up on your screens I want to know that, too. If the client's gotten his hands on something that he shouldn't have… Yeah, as always. Right. Stop by for dinner when you're in town next. There's a fabulous new Indochine place that's opened around the corner. Right. Bye."

He hung up the phone, and switched off the jammer. Leaving it on too long made it that much more likely someone would wonder what you were trying to hide, and why.

Speaking of which, he needed to have a talk with Lowell—again—about staying out of the office when Sergei was out of town. There was a certain style to his clutter that made it glaringly obvious whenever Lowell came in and snooped around. It wasn't so much of a deal—anything not for outside eyes was locked inside a safe that needed both his retinal scan and Wren's electrical signature to even see, much less open. But it was the thought that mattered.

He glanced up at the monitor again, and noted that there were two new customers looking at the case of exquisite metal sculptures Lee had brought in last week. Priced to sell, to get people talking about his work, build demand for his larger pieces. Although, personally, Sergei preferred these: miniature spiders and preying mantises and dragonflies, in such tiny but perfect detail you'd swear faeries had crafted them. Sergei had seen faeries. They were ill-tempered little shrew-faced creatures who didn't have the patience to flatten a tin can, much less do work of that sort.

The thought made him put his hand to the phone, then take it away again. It was almost ten o'clock; Wren would have left the apartment by now. And he had a gallery to put back in order.

A discreet vibration drew Andre Felhim's attention out of the attack of papers in front of him. He placed the topmost sheet down carefully, squaring the edges of the pile and tapping one slender dark-skinned finger on the top before removing the mobile from his jacket pocket. Opening the phone, he noted the number calling him and tapped the button on the side of the special-issue unit that distorted the signal just enough to make it annoying to eavesdrop. It wouldn't stop anyone truly determined, but little shy of Esperanto sign language spoken backward *would*.

"No, Alessandro," he said into the phone before the other man could say anything, going on the attack immediately, but to no avail. He listened for a moment, too well-bred to do what he truly wanted to do, which was to roll his eyes and make "yap yap yap" motions with his hand. But his index finger did tap the pile of papers once, sharply, as though to say "why are you wasting my time with this?"

Darcy, sitting in the chair on the other side of his desk, had no such mannerly hesitation. His scowl tempered the face she was making, but not by much. His researcher was good enough at what she did that she got away with that sort of behavior. But it was also why she was still where she was, and not higher in the ranks.

Then again, she took such pleasure in her job, it was questionable if she actually cared to rise any higher, making her an anomaly within the organization, and therefore unpredictable and potentially dangerous. A reaction she probably took greater pleasure in than any sort of promotion or perk.

Andre spoke seven different languages, and had an MBA from Wharton. He had no idea how Darcy's brain worked. He suspected, however, that she understood him perfectly.

Pushing that thought aside, he responded to the questions being asked of him over the phone. "They're home, yes. No, they haven't reported in. Alec, you know better than to push an Active. They do the job and report in.

That's how they work. It hasn't been all that long since you supervised directly, you know this. Unless it's true, that being pumped up to upper Admin these days really does require a lobotomy."

He was probably going to pay for that comment, but it felt good to let it loose. While Darcy was smiling in appreciation, Jorgunmunder would be terribly disappointed in his boss, no doubt. And with cause—bad form, to snipe. It showed a weakness in your own position, even if you scored off theirs. Besides, reminding Alec *again* that he was junior in seniority, if not in current project-load, was just cruelty without purpose.

"Alec, for Heaven's sake." He tempered his tone, inserting a fatherly, sympathetic, "I know you want to do your best but don't jostle the workers" vibe into his words. It was guaranteed to piss the hell out of the other Admin, but there wasn't anything specific he could object to, not without being seen as a whiner. "You know what Actives are like. Hovering doesn't move them, and it's beginning to really annoy me." *That was more like it, old man. Remind the pup that you're the Admin on this case, not him.*

Alessandro talked at him a little while longer, then signed off abruptly, having not gotten whatever he was looking for from the call. Andre replaced the phone in his jacket, his patrician face serene while his mind worked overtime underneath. Alessandro had reason to be uptight, since Italy was his area of oversight. But the situation had been channeled through the New York office, and Andre's people were on it. So he really had no leverage. Normally, it wouldn't have rated a second thought on Andre's radar. But Duncan's arrival, his interest in this case, was making everything worthy of not only a second thought but a third look.

When the tide changed in the Silence, it changed fast. You had to watch your footing, or risk getting knocked over. And he'd worked too hard, for too long, to get wet now.

"All right." He looked across the desk at his diminutive researcher, and raised one narrow eyebrow. "What do you have for me?"

"The FocAs is refusing to come in for debrief."

"Excuse me?"

She didn't sound any happier repeating it than she had saying it the first time around. "He has refused both a request and an order to return for debrief."

"His Handler?" They had originally planned to bypass the Handler to prevent placing any undue stress on that relationship, but Andre trusted in Darcy's initiative.

"Has—under mild protest—been to see him in person. The result was the same. The operative respectfully declines to cooperate with us in this situation. And no, we hadn't told him anything other than it was a routine debrief on a past case."

"So…"

Darcy's eyes lit up and she shuffled the papers in her lap without looking at them, finally getting to the meat of her report. "Either someone has gotten to the FocAs, and scared him so badly that he will be of no further use to us overall, on any front, or the details of what you had me looking into have been leaked, either from inside the Silence, or the *Cosa Nostradamus* itself."

"Or both," Andre said, almost to himself.

"Or both," she acknowledged. "Although that would seem somewhat overly coincidental, unless the source of the leak is in both camps."

"Sergei."

"Unlikely," she said, dismissing the thought as quickly as he raised it. "There is no profit to him in any of it, even assuming he has the time for that game in addition to his own."

Andre wondered what game Darcy thought Sergei was running, specifically, but didn't distract her from the topic at hand by asking. If it was germane, she would tell him. If it was off-topic but of potential interest, she would keep digging and get back to him if anything showed up.

"So we're looking at the likelihood that someone doesn't want the boy speaking about what's going on within the *Cosa*. It may be specific to us—the person or persons in question may know the boy's connection to us—or it may be a general shutdown of speaking to any outsiders. Either way, I don't like it. I don't like it at all."

He tapped the desk once, sharply, with a forefinger, then looked up at Darcy. "Get the information. Willing, or not." In the scheme of things, one FocAs was less important than having the full picture.

Darcy absorbed her instructions, and left.

With a sigh, Andre returned his attention to the

papers in front of him. Out of the hundred applicants passed on to him last month, he now had to winnow it down to the twenty they had available slots for. And, as he did so, choose which one he was going to personally oversee, to replace Jorgunmunder when the boy moved on to his own assignment.

You left nothing to chance, not from the very first step.

Her suitcases were still in the music room, seemingly untouched. The apartment *felt* still. But she didn't trust it. Leaving the front door open again, just in case, Wren walked from one room to another, giving it a much more thorough once-over than she had before. Now that she knew they were there, she could feel the skittering of the bugs, like the whisper of wind over her skin, the heaviness of the air before a storm. And the carcasses on the floor still stank like a bad chemistry experiment gone terribly wrong.

Spybugs, like demons, were bastardizations of current and flesh. They were more recent, though; the result of a lab in the southwest of France that had survived by selling their product to both the Allies and the Axis powers, neither of whom asked any questions than "how do we use them?" Useful things, if you had the money to buy an entire batch—singletons got squashed, there went your investment. A swarm was the only way to go.

"Ugh." She hated bugs. If it flew, if it crawled, if it had a carapace and more than four legs. If it hadn't been for current being a significant cockroach deterrent, she would never have been able to live in Manhattan.

Satisfied that nothing had been disturbed other than her privacy, Wren took the folded paper out of her bag and picked up the phone in the kitchen. The extension in her office was better shielded, but she felt uncomfortable being out of line-of-sight of the front door.

"Hi. I need to schedule a fumigation. Spybugs. Yeah."

The Mackenzie brother, if that was him, had a lovely voice. He was probably four foot seven and as wide across, with warts and hairy ears, but his voice was worth the cost of the call.

"No, I'm not staying here…yeah, I killed a couple. Fried 'em. Oops."

He had a nice laugh, too.

"You can? Bless you. Yeah, I'm here now. I'll wait and let your guys in. Fifth floor, it's a walk-up, I'm afraid. Oh, good."

She rummaged into her bag again, pulling out her wallet and reciting her credit card information. The cost made her wince, but if this wasn't a reason to carry a balance, she didn't know what was.

Hanging up the phone, she hesitated a moment, then went into the music room to turn the stereo on. The CD player rotated, and the sound of Sting's voice floated out of the speakers at his bluesy best.

Checking in with either Lee or Sergei might be a good idea, but she wouldn't feel comfortable doing anything with the bugs still in residence. Which reminded her…

Walking down the hallway to where three tiny shoebox-shaped bedrooms lined the back wall of the apartment, she went into her bedroom and threw clean clothing onto the bed, hesitating over a pair of jeans before throwing it into the pile along with the dark blue sundress and a pair of black cotton leggings and a handful of T-shirts and cotton vests. The weather could break any day now, right? It's not like the forecasters knew what they were talking about when they made noises about the Drought of the Century....

But, God, she needed a thunderstorm. Something heavy-duty, with sheets of water coming down afterward. She could feel the dryness inside her. Neezer had originally thought she would have a weather affiliation, maybe give her a second career option other than Retrieval, but that sensitivity ended up being remarkably limited; still, nothing drew her the way a thunderstorm did.

Gathering up the clothing, she lugged it down to the music room, dumping it on the one chair, then went back down the hall to the second bedroom, which doubled as her office. Booting up the computer, she took a memory stick out of a shielded case and inserted it, tapping her fingers impatiently until everything finished loading. With the fail-safes she had this desktop hooked into, it took almost twice as long as an unaugmented machine. On the plus side, she had only lost the system three times in the years since she had set it up. Logging in, she transferred all her current files into the stick, checking her e-mail while it copied and saved.

"No, no, no, no, no...yeah, all right, no, no..." She pulled out the chair and opened the e-mails that probably couldn't wait; two from her mother asking if she was home yet, and a third from an old friend of hers from college.

She skimmed the ones from her mother just to make sure there wasn't any dire maternal wrath coming down on her head, then opened Katie's e-mail.

"Oh, most excellent!" Katie lived in California, and they hadn't seen each other since graduation. But she expected to be in town in October for a trade fair, and wanted to get together, "in lieu of the reunion I know neither of us has any plans to attend."

Katie knew her far too well—Wren had tossed all the alumni stuff that came her way without even looking at it. Dashing off a reply in the affirmative, Wren did a quick check into the various mailbox folders to make sure that she hadn't missed anything, then logged off. She removed the memory stick and put it back into its insulated case, stopped in the kitchenette to put the case into her bag, and then went to deal with the great clothing exchange.

Pulling the suitcase into the room with her, she sat down on the hardwood floor and, while the CD player changed over to Sting's most recent album, she opened the bag and started sorting laundry.

By the time she had emptied out both bags and her laundry basket and built piles of "hand-wash," "goes to the Laundromat," and "dry clean," and started putting the clean clothing into the suitcase, the downstairs buzzer rang.

"Who is it?"

The static was even worse than usual, which made sense if the cleaners were also Talents. She *thought* they had said they were from Mackenzie Cleaning, anyway.

"Come on up."

Three of them tromped up the stairs, carrying what looked like an elongated elephant's trunk attached to a squat, square box tied around with copper wires.

"Catchbox," the first workman said, seeing her look at it curiously. "What the nasty creepie-crawlies go into." The guy holding it put it down carefully at the door, and fiddled with a couple of knobs on the side, then gave the speaker a thumbs-up.

"We're good to go."

"Excellent." The speaker turned to Wren, and she was treated to a full-on blast of Irish Boy charm. "I'm Dar Mackenzie, Junior." And he wasn't short or squat, although his ears were a bit on the large side. And she'd never been partial to redheads. "It'll take us a couple hours to prep, then we have'ta let the thing run. You might want ta get your stuff and scoot. Place should be cleared in two, three days. It'll take another day for the stink to clear, though. Longer if this heat sticks around. You should be able to move back in by next Monday, latest."

Wren nodded. The guy on the phone had warned her about that.

"Long as we're here," the third workman said suddenly, "you want us to dehex the entrances, too?

"I've been hexed? Huh. Yeah, do a full sweep." Wren ran a hand through her hair, lifting it off the back of her neck with a grimace. She had no doubt that would cost her extra. But it would explain the feeling of unease she'd gotten that first day on the landing.

Although…why would anyone hex her to make her wary? Unwary, maybe, she could see that. But something that specifically made her normally suspicious mind perk up even through the jet lag and the emotional turmoil to note that something subtle wasn't right? *Because, let's be honest here, Valere, if you hadn't been on alert, the bugs could have gone on eavesdropping for a couple of days, maybe longer without your noticing.*

So it would stand to reason that whoever had planted the bugs… "Wasn't the person who planted the hex."

Junior, clearly understanding the antieavesdropping nature of his job, pretended he hadn't heard anything she said not specifically directed at him. He and the unnamed workman were busy lugging the elephant's trunk into her apartment, anyway. It really did look rather worrisome, this grey and rubbery extension snaking its way down her wall. She tried to remember if there was anything incriminating lying about, then decided that running around trying to clean up one step ahead of them would be worse than leaving anything out where they might or might not take notice of it.

"You have a cell phone I can use?"

He looked at her dubiously, and she tried to look innocent and static-free.

"Local call?"

"Yeah."

"Hey, Klein." The guy fiddling with the box looked up, and the first worker made a gesture. Klein looked like he was going to protest, then sighed and took a clamshell mobile out of his pocket and tossed it to him.

"Here. He never use all his minutes, anyway."

Flashing Klein a thank-you smile, she took the phone and, going out onto the landing to get away from any bugs, not to mention the workmen themselves, dialed Sergei's mobile number.

"This is Didier. Leave a message."

"It's 3:30. Hopefully you're off kicking Lowell's prissy ass. Anyway. I'm at my apartment, and the cleaners are here. Looks like you've got me the rest of the week, lucky you. I'll stop by in about an hour, see if you're ready to kick out and grab some dinner. Or we could just do take-out. Your choice."

She handed the phone back to the cleaner, feeling a sudden wave of domesticity sweep her. God, had she really just left that message?

Yeah, she had.

Grinning and shaking her head, Wren closed up the suitcase and her pocketbook, and headed down the stairs. On the second landing, the door opened and the male half of the couple who lived there stuck his greying head out to see who was making all the noise. Considering he and his other half fought on a regular basis, and had noisy sex the rest of the time, Wren didn't think the regular thump-thump-thump that was now coming from her apartment really was anything to complain about. So she gave him a cheerful grin and a wave, and continued down the stairs.

"Hi honey, I'm home!" The thud of a suitcase hitting the carpeted floor accompanied the jingle of the door chimes and the forcefully cheery voice.

Sergei looked up from the reception desk where he was going over a screen invoice with Lowell, fighting down the urge to snatch the glasses off the end of his nose and put them away. "Hello yourself." He looked back down at the screen to finish pointing something out to Lowell, then did what he realized a second later when Wren started giggling was a perfect cinematic double take.

"Is that my shirt?"

"It was," she said unrepentantly, doing a slow twirl to show him all sides. "Looks better on me, don't you think?"

Actually, he did. But he merely offered up a silent prayer that she had been kind enough to take one of his older shirts, pushed the wire-frame glasses farther up on his nose, and went back to the screen. *If you leave a thief in your closet...*

"You look like a streetwalker."

Clearly, Lowell didn't find the length of leg showing as enjoyable as he did. *Even if he had, the idiot would rather die than admit it.*

Fortunately, Wren long ago stopped giving a damn what Lowell thought.

"Streetwalker? Where did you pick that phrase up, the 1950s? Ho, maybe. Come on, say it after me. Ho. Hhhhh—ohhhhh."

Realizing that he wasn't going to be able to finish explaining the problem to Lowell until the two of them had had their spat, Sergei straightened up, took his glasses off and folded them into the pocket of his shirt, and crossed his arms and leaned against the back of the counter, spectating.

"That fits," Lowell agreed, his expression changing from his normal How-May-I-Help-You? expression to a distasteful sneer. "Cheap and easy."

"You would know about that," Wren agreed. "Seeing as how you have to pay for it."

They'd been at each others' throats since the first moment they'd met, and he couldn't quite believe it was over territorial rights to him, alone. Some people just didn't take to each other, he supposed.

Pity. It would have made his life far easier. Then again, it's not as though they ever did each other any permanent harm for all the hissing and scratching.

"At least I bed clean partners, not just any—"

"Okay kids, enough for tonight." They were getting into a discussion he really didn't want to be around for. Eventually, since the boy wasn't as much of an idiot as Wren thought, Lowell would figure out that the relationships had shifted. Sergei personally didn't want to be anywhere near the detonation point when that happened.

"Lowell, do you think that you can finish the rundown on that invoice, and make sure we're in the clear on the insurance?"

The blonde pulled his claws back in, and collected himself back into the well-bred fashionista pose he had perfected at birth. "Of course."

"And how could you think otherwise?" Sergei translated in his head. Lowell would be far less irritating if he wasn't almost as competent as he thought he was. He would also be easier to get rid of if the need arose. And it might, eventually.

"Genevieve?" Her full name, to let her know she wasn't getting off blame-free either, in this particular spat. "My office."

She raised an eyebrow at that, but picked up her suitcase and lugged it across the gallery floor, carefully avoiding the delicate hydra-in-flight sculpture that currently had the space of honor. He let his hand drop onto Lowell's shoulder, giving him an encouraging touch, and turned to follow her. Behind him he heard Lowell start to mutter under his breath, picking up the data correlation where they'd been interrupted.

The balance of his universe restored, he followed Wren in through the sliding panel door of his office, and touched the panel to make it slide shut again behind him. She had already taken her usual place on the black leather sofa, although not in her usual sprawl as a courtesy to the shortness of her makeshift dress.

"Sorry about that."

"No you aren't."

She grinned, a quick flash of even white teeth. "Well, no. I was feeling the urge to be polite, though. Otherwise you might throw me back outside, luggage and all, and it's too damn hot for human beings to be out there." She paused. "You got my message?"

"I did. And yes, I meant what I said. You're welcome to stay however long it takes." He moved a pile of papers and a blue and red Murano blown-glass bird and sat down on the edge of his desk. "Um, how long might that be, again?"

She looked up at him, shoving the hair out of her face in order to give him an indignant glare, then rolled her eyes when she realized he was teasing. Turnabout was fair play. He knew how much she enjoyed yanking his chain on occasion, too.

And that thought led him to another, that made his smile change tenor slightly. The casual comfort of where his mind went was astonishing. A week ago, he would have been frustrated at the thought, not—

"A week," she said, sitting forward and crossing her legs at the ankle. "So we'd better pick up a couple of surge protectors and stuff."

"Already ordered and being delivered, courtesy of our friendly neighborhood office supply store. It's something I should have done a while ago, anyway." And he hadn't thought of it; and more to the point she knew he hadn't thought of it.

*Later. Deal with all this later.* It wasn't as though he hadn't years of practice shoving everything into little locked boxes. The difference was that now he could take them out and open then.

*After* they'd tracked down this damn manuscript and gotten it back to its damn stone drawer. Which meant passing along what Karl had been able to discover.

"Karl called me back."

"Already? That was fast. Even for the god of information himself."

"Apparently, our unknown collector is a fan of *The*

*Purloined Letter.* His paperwork was completely in order, from the description to the place of origin all the way through to the shippers' credentials. Forged, of course, but totally in order. Nothing that would tip anyone off or set off any warning bells at all."

"Professional."

"Absolutely."

That was a relief, in a way. Professionals dealt with things in certain ways. Amateurs were more likely to go off half-cocked and crazy, especially if they got spooked.

"So we know where it is?" Wren was practically salivating, whatever news she had walked in here with tossed to the side for the moment. The Retriever on-point. Not that he'd ever share that visual with her; he wanted to live, thank you very much. He merely handed her the sheet of notes he had taken during that second phone call, and mentally stepped back. His part in this job was over. Hers was kicking into high gear.

"You want dinner?"

"Hrmmmm?"

"Dinner. Food. Things to eat?"

"Dragging this?" And she indicated the suitcase. "I was thinking we'd just grab some take-out on the way back to the apartment. Or, hey, you could cook for me."

He did his best "annoying child" glare, which had worked for about the first eight months she had known him, and no further. She had already gone back to his notes, reaching into her pocketbook to take out a pen and scratching notes and arrows over his much neater handwriting.

"I'm assuming you won't want Italian. Mexican or Thai?"

"Ooo. Thai." She looked up at that, and he could swear he saw her eyes flicker with greed. That answered that, then.

Nice to know that even in the depths of her most focused, he still had a way of getting her attention.

*Chapter Thirteen*

The morning had, wonder of wonders, actually started out on a cooler note. "Cooler" being a vastly relative term, but Wren had been able to go out for breakfast— a Starbucks grande with an extra shot—without coming back feeling like she needed to be rehydrated with a fire hose. Hot, but not suck-the-life-out-of-you dire.

By the time she left Sergei's apartment again it was midmorning, and the respite was over. The subway was a day more disgusting, the air thick with human sweat and machine heat, but she was able to get a seat at the end, the hard plastic bench-end allowing her a modicum of distance from her fellow passengers, even as the position put her at the mercy of swinging pocketbooks and careless backpacks.

She was heading into the guts of Midtown, an area she generally avoided, as the only things there were office buildings and overpriced restaurants that catered to people who worked in those office buildings. And Grand Central, which, even with the gorgeously restored starscape ceiling, ~~echoing pit of too many people thinking they~~ ~~Now, nothing except~~ echoes a~~nd~~ ~~~~

They must have taken everything down during the renovations. Adding artwork would make the place echo less, she suspected. But still, you'd think there would be someone here, to take donations, or give directions, or something. She looked around, at a loss, then saw a man sitting behind a small desk set into an alcove under the stair. She had missed him, at first, because it was all so…empty.

The guy was forty-something, and not wearing it well. Balding, underweight, and as bland and dusty as the bare walls around him. He looked up from his newspaper, blinking at her as though surprised that anyone might be bothered to be looking at him.

"Hi."

"Yes?" Borderline rude for "how may I help you, in the unlikely event that you could possibly be asking me for assistance?" The guy obviously didn't want to be bothered, and had already dismissed her by the time he looked up. Current surged to her call, sliding up her spine and into her hands, making each finger tingle. It was the first time since the dark space that she had intentionally called current, and the sensations threatened for a moment to overwhelm her.

*Steady. Ground and center. You control it….* Her mentor's voice, as always when she recalled that very first lesson. The pain she always felt when thinking about

To the left and right, hallways led off into the distance. The foyer was disturbingly empty; nothing on the walls except shadows and hooks where things used to hang, no carpeting on the hardwood floor, no any~~~~~ was still and dust. ~~~~~

had somewhere important to go Right ~~~~~

She was going to the library.

Wren admitted to a certain curiosity about her destination. In Manhattan, you didn't really build up any expectation of what a library could or should look like. Not when you could compare those famous stone lions of the main building just a few blocks away with some of the tiny, run-down branches. But the Friesman-Stutzner building looked even less like a library than most, and more like a private home. The private home of someone very, very wealthy. And undergoing a lot of renovations, based on the construction walls that were up around most of the brick building, and the number of hard-hatted workers yelling and gesturing at each other.

This was where the parchment had ended up?

Wren ducked around two workmen carrying a load of what looked like wrought-iron fencing and walked up the white stone stairs and through the double-hung wooden doors, the weight of them causing her to struggle for a moment until it swung open.

Inside, the entrance foyer was larger than it looked from the outside, with high ceilings and off-white walls that glimmered in the surprisingly soft lighting. It was also surprisingly quiet, after the hustle and clamor outside. A huge staircase was directly in front of her, leading up to a landing with a huge stained glass window.

Neezer seemed more muted than usual somehow. She wasn't sure if that was a good or a bad thing.

So. Soften the power. Soften it to water flowing over stone, wearing and smoothing rough edges, making the way clear. "I called this morning? Asked about talking to someone about an Italian manuscript the library has in its collection?" She had read somewhere that a southern accent set people at ease, especially in a woman, and so let each sentence end on an upward note as though asking a question, the way she'd heard people talk during her one visit to Atlanta.

It seemed to work, at least enough for the self-appointed gatekeeper to unclench his asshole long enough to give her directions down to the curator's office.

To get there, she had to walk down the hallway which seemed to take her three-quarters of the way around the building. The only people she passed were more construction workers, although through an occasional frosted door window she could see what must be employees going about their daily routine. Wren had never actually worked in an office. She didn't think slinging hash at a twenty-four-hour diner back in high school and college counted....

And this, according to the shiny silver nameplate, was her destination. She knocked once, then opened the office door and looked inside.

"Mister Taibshe?"

The guy behind the desk looked up from the neat piles of paper in front of him. "I am. Ah, Ms. Valere?"

He thought he was a smoothie, in the bluff bear way

so many women got wet for. She could see the appeal, but not when on the job. And not when it was so obviously turned on and aimed for intent.

"That's me." She stepped inside the office at his "come in" gesture, and took the seat he waved at, reaching across the desk to shake his hand. It was fleshy and a little wet, as though he had been sweating, even though the temperature inside the building felt like it was being maintained at a comfortable high sixty-something, and a little on the dry side, just the way Sergei always told her valuable papers should be kept. The dark space had been too dry, she thought in passing. She was going to have to have words with Brother Teo, maybe add something to the slate-spell, to keep everything well preserved. Once you put magic into solid form, you didn't want it to start falling apart, unexpectedly. Who knew what might leak out of a dissolving parchment?

"Were you able to scare anything up for me?"

The curator steepled his hands in front of him, and looked professionally regretful. "I am sorry, I know that when we spoke this morning I said that it would be no problem in finding the manuscript you referenced, but I am afraid that our records show no such item in our collection. Are you certain that it was on loan to us?"

"Oh, yes." Wren nodded her head emphatically, rock-solid in her own conviction the way only someone who never doubted her source could be.

"Hmmm. Interesting. Might I know the name of the original owner, perhaps? Or the person who gave you that information?"

"Oh, no, I'm afraid I couldn't…that information, you understand, I had to promise never to tell anyone who told me, so they wouldn't get into trouble. I think maybe there are tax things going on." She didn't do dumb very well. But he seemed to be buying it. Idiot. "But I had spent so much time trying to find it, to see if the information I needed was there, that it seemed silly to stop when it turned out to actually be in my very own city. Are you sure you don't have it here? My source was *very* certain."

She was starting to feel the stress of all this playacting. Retrievals weren't real big on the interpersonal contact, mostly. It was so much easier to simply fly under their radar. The effort it took to make people not look directly at you was so much less than making sure they were looking nowhere *but* at you. The idea that some people did this their entire lives made her exhausted just thinking about it.

"Mmmm." He sucked on the insides of his lip when he did that, and Wren tried not to roll her eyes. Either you have the damn thing on record or you don't, schmuck, she wanted to yell. But she kept her polite, cutely confused expression on her face, even though her skin felt like it was going to crack from the effort. "Without more detail, I'm afraid I won't be able to help you. I'm sure you understand—the manuscript might have been entered under the donor's name, or some other piece of information, and not the commonly-used name of the document. We have a multirelational database, and while we're supposed to use all known terms, it's quite possible that the name you have for the document is not the official one, or was misspelled or—" he looked slightly, professionally, embarrassed "—it could be that they just forgot to enter it. If I had more information, but…" And he made a palms-up gesture with both hands to indicate his helplessness.

"Ah well." Sergei had told her once that pouting made her look like a hung-over basset hound, so she just let her shoulders sink in not-entirely-feigned disappointment. "I'm really sorry to have taken up so much of your valuable time, and I do appreciate it. Might you, maybe, have a secretary or someone who could give me just a little tour, so I don't go back to the magazine totally empty-handed? Even if we can't feature you, I can certainly make sure you're mentioned, as a thank-you for your time and effort."

She could almost see him weighing the benefits versus annoyance in his mind, then he nodded. "Of course. I'll have one of our interns show you around. Although you must understand that things are somewhat chaotic at the moment, as we're in the final stages of some rather major renovations to areas of the library."

"Of course." Like she'd somehow missed all the activity outside. This guy might be in charge of the collections, all the things on display here, but she wouldn't trust him to give directions to the nearest Starbucks.

He stood up to indicate they were done, and she followed suit, reaching across the desk to shake his hand again. It was a lot dryer now, as though he'd been wiping it off on his pants leg. Or she hadn't asked the questions he'd been afraid of. Interesting. Ver-ry interesting.

The intern was named Heather, a bright and friendly girl, almost half again Wren's height and with skin the color of old-fashioned black licorice and startling hazel-green eyes, dressed in a dark black tank and long skirt, clunky silver-tone earrings, and comfortable-looking clunky black sandals. Beach-goth.

"You're a reporter?" She was wide-eyed, too, and Wren mentally marked a couple of years off the girl's probable age and changed her Retrieving persona from Dumb-but-Likeable to Just-Another-Professional-Girl-Like-You.

"A stringer. I write stories and then try to sell them. I was hoping to get some information on really old manuscripts, maybe something with a spooky story attached to it, you know? Like ghosts? It would be a neat Halloween article, I thought."

"In August?"

"You've got to pitch and sell early," Wren said like she knew what she was talking about. Her mother had dated a newspaper editor once, for about six months, and everything she knew about the industry came from him.

She'd give her mom credit; not much in the finding-a-steady-partner category, but every guy she brought home was awesome stepfather material. Wren still kept in touch with a couple of them, years after the actual relationship went flop.

"Well, this is the main hall, where you came in," Heather said, picking up her tour guide duties. "Normally there are paintings on the wall, showing what the house looked like when it was first built, and the

neighborhood surrounding it. The first room of interest
is the Main Reading Room, where the original Stutzner
collection is displayed...."

The Friesman-Stutzner Library was actually a neat
place. Wren got to see the club-room-like Reading Room,
with its overstuffed leather chairs and glass-fronted
display cases, and three smaller galleries that followed
the American written word from the pre-Revolutionary
War broadsheets on up to the current publishing scene.

Then they walked up the staircase, past the disinterested guard, and paused for a moment to admire the
stained glass window before going up to the second
floor, where, as Heather said, "the really cool books
lived."

Wren had lived in the city for almost a decade now,
had grown up across the river, and she'd never even
known about this place, much less been inside it. She
wasn't more than a casual reader, but the feel of some of
the rooms they walked through made her want to settle
down with the nearest book and just start turning pages.
It wasn't current, but there was a kind of energy here that
she'd never felt before. It was warm and sharp and
shivery and she thought maybe it was a little like the
thing Lee talked about when he'd told her how he got
ready to work on one of his sculptures.

"These galleries are closed—they're being fitted with
a new security system, and we're not supposed to go
into them until it's all coded," Heather said apologetically.
"But the Wilgarten Room is open, and you can see how
the renovations have changed the way the building looks

inside, because this is still an original—you could use that in your article, maybe? You think any ghosts would mind that we updated their surroundings?"

"Who can say what ghosts mind or don't mind?" Wren said, probably more seriously than Heather had intended her question to be taken. But then, she knew ghosts. Heather didn't.

The intern smiled, a little nervously, and held open the door to the next room. And that was when Wren felt something completely different settle in the air around her.

No, not felt. Tasted. Smelled. Heard. And none of the senses she was accustomed to, but not the way she sensed current, either. This was like…being choked in mud. Thick, greasy, old mud. Oh, badness. Much badness.

*Calm. Stay the hell calm, Valere.*

The first trick was going to be tracking it. And she couldn't do that if she was freaking out.

The intern was still walking and talking. Wren forced herself to breathe normally, wishing that she could just make herself fade out of notice and search the building on her own. But there were too many people moving about, and she didn't know where she was going. Recipe for disaster.

"What is this room?" she asked, barely keeping herself from gagging at the psychic residue

"This?" Heather looked around the bare walls quizzically, as though having to think about it. "Well, normally this is where we put all the recently arrived shipments, because it's got the best workspace—" three long wooden tables set directly under the lights "—and the dumbwaiter over there goes directly to the loading dock, what used to be the kitchen, so it's really convenient. But with all the chaos of the renovations I think they've put all the stuff that came in recently into storage in the basement. Nobody had the time or the space, really, to do the usual cataloging. I'm sorry, because we got some great materials in, but I can't take you down there. I'm not even allowed down there, right now."

"No, I quite understand. And it's probably all still in its original shipping boxes, right?"

"I guess. Yeah, they would have opened it to make sure the right stuff arrived, before they signed off on it, but they wouldn't have actually taken anything out."

"Ah." So Taibshe had been shining her on. Or at least not giving her the full skinny about everything being tagged and filed. Was he hiding something specific to the manuscript? Or just playing cover your ass in general, in case she was some sort of procedural inspector come to hand out fines for improper document management?

Having heard Sergei's friend Karl's stories about some of the more magnificent fiascos involving materials on loan to public and private institutions in the States, she was pretty sure that there actually *were* people who got paid to make life hell for people who screwed up like that.

"Thanks, you've been great, I really appreciate it. What's your name again? And how do you spell your last name? I want to make sure I get it right, if they take the story."

Intern thus duly flattered, Wren got herself escorted back to the front entrance. The heat took her breath away the moment she stepped outside, but it felt healthier, somehow. As though the sunlight were burning away the last of the cold, ugly mud still left on her psyche from that quick brush.

"Right." She started to tick off the possibilities on one hand, keeping to the shadows the building cast in the hopes that it was slightly cooler there than on the sidewalk. "So, assuming neither of them are our mystery importer—" he or she was probably long-gone from the action, and even more probably had never reentered the States after arranging shipment "—are they idiots, criminally careless, or yanking my chain? And which one would be easier to deal with? And why the hell, if they've sent everything else on tour, are they still taking in shipments? And why am I even asking questions about the relative cluelessness of any non-profit organization?"

One thing she knew, though. Even in the shade, it was too damn hot to be standing here debating with herself. Time to go somewhere cool, safe, and with a brain she could bounce everything off of. Which, at this time of day, meant the gallery.

For a change of pace, she took the bus that stopped just outside the library. It was slower than the subway because of midtown, midday traffic, but at the moment, some time to sit and think, with the city as white noise, wasn't such a bad thing. And by the time she had gotten off the bus and walked through the sticky afternoon heat that passed for air in the city these days, she had calmed down enough to come up with a potential plan.

"Absolutely not."

"Excuse me?" Wren stopped luxuriating in the wonder that was cool air to look at her partner. She was sprawled out on the couch in his office, the long cotton skirt and top she had put on this morning more conducive to that position than Sergei's shirt-dress the day before.

"Wren, I am not going to be able to just waltz in there…yes, I have some contacts. But I'm an art dealer, not a scholar. They're not going to let me down there any more than they let you." He was sitting behind his desk, the paper-wrapped remains of his lunch shoved off to one side, the computer screen powered down. "And it's not as though you know that it's there for certain. No matter what the paperwork says."

Wren shook her head once, not having the energy to be more vehement. Just thinking about what she had felt in the library made her feel drained, tired. "It's there, I know it is. I can *taste* it, the same flavor from the House. And yeah, I know; I thought the same thing, that maybe it's just stronger because it was more recently there but…no. It's there. Still."

"All right, say you're correct. Worst-case scenario: this Taibshe's in on it, whatever 'it' is. In which case, he's now alerted to the fact that someone's snooping around. Which means that he's going to be on his guard. And if he's just your run-of-the-mill idiot administrator, he might still get curious, which means poking around. Which is bad, for him, and for your plan." He tapped his fingers on his desk. "And then there's the possibility that our original buyer, or at least the go-between from Italy, is using this place as an import blind."

"Even if you're right, and the library's just being used as a bypass for a third party, it hasn't been picked up yet. It's too soon. And it all fits. It gets shipped through to them through the library's contacts, and then the third party sneaks in one night and takes it. And since they never actually ordered it, they won't even know it's gone. But they've got to get to it before anyone opens the crates and actually starts documenting things...."

She had a terrible thought, and stopped. "What if someone was smart and already noticed it wasn't anything they were supposed to be getting?"

"That would have come up on Karl's search. As far as the records show, the manuscript came in, passed customs without a hitch, and hasn't been heard from since."

"Yeah, but if someone got smart and illegally minded? As in, 'wow, this isn't on the manifest, but hey I've got contacts, I can make some money on the side with it?' I bet they don't pay for shit."

"You're thinking like a thief. Librarians aren't thieves. They're librarians."

"Anyone's a thief with the right incentive, Sergei. They're just usually not very good at it."

Sergei snorted, then got up to pace. She expected him to break out the cigarettes any moment, but the case was probably still in his coat pocket, which was draped over the back of his chair. "Wren, you would know—could this be a weapon?"

She shrugged helplessly, as much as she could while lying down. "Oh God, I have no idea. *Anything* can be a weapon. Especially anything that's clearly got major mojo woven into it. It would help if we just knew what the hell it was. I mean, okay, people disappear if they read it. We presume."

He came back and shoved her over enough that he could sit down next to her. She shifted so that her head now rested on his leg. He reached down to stroke the back of her neck and shoulders the same way he might a pet. The overhead lights were turned off in favor of the lamp on his desk, and the softer light made the office seem cozier than usual. "Don't presume. We've been presuming ever since we took this job. Presuming it would be simple, presuming the Silence would share whatever information they had with us. Stupid. We know better. I sure as hell should have known better. We would never have treated a walk-in job like this."

There wasn't anything to say. They'd been in a bad place and Andre hadn't given them time to think about it. That was why he'd wanted them on a flight right away. Not just because time was of the essence. Manipulative bastard.

"So what do we know, for absolute fact?"

"The manuscript was deemed dangerous enough to be held in a dark space, and bound by low-level magics within that dark space, and can I say, by the way, that I don't want to meet the Talent who could do that in a dark alley? We know that people who come into contact with the manuscript disappear, although not how…"

"Actually, we were told that, but we don't know it."

"At some point, we have to trust something. Otherwise I'm going to stay in bed all day, every day."

"Point taken. All right, something bad, probably deadly happens to those who come into contact with the manuscript, but not merely by proximity, otherwise there would be a wider trail of missing persons."

"We know that someone wanted it enough to suborn a monk with enough money to get him to take some major risks and break a whole bunch of supposedly sacred oaths that he felt bad enough about breaking that he threw himself off a cliff afterward. Or," she added without missing a beat, "that someone wanted it badly enough that, in order to cut any connection between himself and the missing manuscript, he threw a greedy but remorseful monk over the cliff."

His hands had strayed off her hair and were currently sliding along the vee neckline of her shirt, making it difficult to concentrate. But she didn't want him to stop, so she didn't say anything.

"And we know that whatever this manuscript actually is or does, the Silence has a vested interest in seeing it back where it came from. They don't take jobs for the money—there's always a reason for it. And that reason, historically, has been on the side of humanity's good, as annoyingly pretentious as that sounds."

"Annoyingly pretentious sums it up pretty well, yeah. But the check's deposited?"

"You're slipping. It took you how many days to ask?"

"I got distracted," she said, defending herself. "You know. By going to Italy. And…other stuff."

"Other stuff, huh?" His hand reached down a little further and she yelped in surprise, then, "Hrmmmm. Yeah, like that."

She arched her back a little and he bent forward to meet her halfway, their lips touching with the by-now-expected tingle of sparks.

"Gotta do something about that," she tried to mumble, but his tongue and teeth silenced her, his hand still stroking her breast.

"Hrmmmm-mmmm. You taste good," she said when they separated a few inches, more because of back strain than any desire to stop kissing. *Bad Wren! No time for distractions!* "What did you have for lunch?"

His eyes closed briefly, as though holding back a laugh with his lids, then opened them and said, "pastrami."

"Mmmm, yummy. C'mere."

But their lips had barely touched again when the chirping of a bird disturbed them. Sergei lifted his head, dislodging her hand from where it had reached up to tangle in the dark hair. "I have to—"

"Yeah, I know," she said in disgust, letting him get up to retrieve the phone from his desk. "Y'know, I think you need to download another ring. It was flattering for a while—" how long did he have to search to find a wren's song, anyway? "—but a few more times of that and I'm going to start getting a complex."

"Didier. Yeah," he looked over at her, making a "get up" gesture with two fingers, "she's here. Hang on, I'll hook the phone in." He put the mobile down on the desk and reached into a drawer for the speakerphone hookup. "It's Lee."

Wren sat up, as though the other Talent might be able to see her, and straightened her top so that she didn't look quite so slut-worthy.

"Heya Lee," she said when Sergei finished hooking the wires up. "What's up?"

"The entire damn world has gone insane."

Wren looked at Sergei in shock. Her partner was doing a pretty decent impression of Mr. Spock, with eyebrows rising up almost to his hairline in surprise. Lee was normally one of the most mellow, *c'est la vie* types imaginable. The frazzled, end-of-my-rope voice coming out of the speaker did not sound like him.

"Deep breath, then tell momma what's wrong. Is it P.B.?" God knew the furfaced ratfink could drive anyone insane, and she felt a momentary flinch of guilt for having given the demon Lee's home address. But…

Lee almost laughed at that. "No, believe it or not, he's not the problem. It's Baxter. You remember, the critter specialist?"

Baxter… Wren flipped through her mental Rolodex. "Right, Holistic veterinary practice, up on the East Side. He's okay?"

"He's insane."

"Lee, the guy spends his entire day talking to the animals. Of course he's insane. Wouldn't you be?"

"No, I mean it, Wren. He's calling for a meeting. A moot."

Wren gaped at the phone, her brain going into a complete and total blankness.

"He's…what? Jesus wept." Her favorite swearword, the only one that her mother allowed in the house when she was growing up, was getting a workout these days, it felt like. "When was the last time there was a moot?"

"1973. I looked it up. Wren, he wants us to organize. Against the Council. And there are a lot of people who're talking like it's not a bad idea."

"We'll get killed. All of us." Wren ran her hands through her hair, tugging at the ends in her distress. A gather was a social get-together, a way to vent and share and blow off steam. A moot was something else entirely. "Lee, we're not going to get any support from anyone. Not locally, not anywhere. When we were in Italy the local *Cosa* was very clear on the fact that they didn't want in on our troubles. In fact, the feeling was that we needed to settle it among ourselves, and soon. I can't see anywhere else taking a different stance."

"Preaching to the choir, Wren. But that's what Baxter's talking about. Settling it."

"How? By pushing back at the schoolyard bully and saying 'I'm not scared of you?' That's not settling it, that's writing a suicide note!"

"Come to the moot, Wren. Talk to them."

Wren sat back against the back of the sofa, barely noticing, as she always did, the resilient buttery softness of the leather.

"I don't talk, Lee. Hell, I could stand in front of them and yell my damn fool head off, and it's not like anyone would listen."

"Of course they would. You're—"

"Invisible," Wren cut him off. "I'm invisible, Lee. That's my skill, that's what current does to me."

"I see you." Tree-taller sounded so absurdly confused, Wren's voice cracked when she spoke.

"Sweet guy. Yeah, you do. You see me. But you look with your heart, not your eyes. Most people don't. And even the ones who do, the current sends them right through me, like I'm not even there.

"It's always been like that. Always."

The artless pain in his partner's voice cut at Sergei sharply. She had talked about how people never seemed to see her, but always in the context of the job, of it being an asset. He had never stopped to think that maybe it was something she couldn't turn off. Something that she felt bad about.

Lee made a sound of protest, but plowed on. "Try. For me. Try. Please? You're The Wren. When it comes to dealing with the Council, they'll listen to you. They'll have to."

Wren looked at Sergei, who gave a little shrug to indicate that it was her call. He tried to keep his features as still as possible, to not indicate his preference one way or the other, because what he really wanted was to lock her away somewhere well out of this entire mess. The lonejack code, what there was of it, could be summed up as: "Don't get involved. Don't join anything large enough to become a target. And most of all, don't get tangled up in the Council." She had taught him that.

But the Council was already gunning for her. Bugging her apartment, that was almost certainly their work. The Council's ire had forced them both into this devil's bargain with the Silence in the first place, to make sure she was protected.

How could you stay unentangled, when you were already caught?

It didn't take her long to come to a decision, the one he'd already known she would make.

"Yeah." Her voice was dark and thick, coming from her throat only with effort. "Yeah, okay. I'll try."

Lee's breath of relief was audible even over the tiny speakers. "I wouldn't ask this, Wren. But I really think you're the only chance we've got to stop this now, before more people get hurt."

Her head sank forward, until the tip of her chin rested on her chest, and a shining curtain of brown hid her from view.

"When and where?" Sergei asked, taking over the conversation. Lee gave them the time and place, letting Sergei know that there wouldn't be any problem with him attending as well. "If anyone gives you grief, send them to me." The Talent might be mild-tempered, but he came by Wren's nickname of "Tree-taller" honestly, from his height and shoulder-width, and his first career had been as a martial arts instructor.

Sergei disconnected the call and put the speaker set back into the drawer, carefully not looking over to where his partner was still motionless on the sofa. He didn't know what she was thinking about. He wasn't sure he wanted to know, only that if he needed to, she would tell him.

There was a difference between being invisible, and not being the focus of attention. And right now, he thought maybe she needed the latter.

Sitting back down quietly at his desk, Sergei pulled out a pad of paper with a series of notes already on it, in his precise handwriting, took up a pen and started adding to it. He thought better, with things on paper. He'd memorize the details and shred the paper after; leave no details for trash-surfers or snoopers, but the act of putting it down, black on white, made his thoughts fall into line.

Too many distractions; Silence, and *Cosa*, Council, and now lonejacks. Everyone was putting their paw in to stir things up. Why now? This job was important, damn it. That was what he hadn't shared with her, what he thought she was beginning to realize: that any job the Silence took on had that urgency to it. Maybe not end-of-the-world status, but more than her usual property Retrievals.

But she couldn't say no to Lee. Not to P.B. Not when they had stood by her in the past, when she needed them. So he was going to have to pick up whatever slack he could, and be silent support when he couldn't.

About ten minutes later, he heard a soft sigh, and looked up to see Wren stretching, her arms held straight above her head, neck and back arched back. She relaxed, and he could almost hear everything snapping back into place from ear to hip.

"We have time to grab some food before the meeting?"

Sergei checked his watch, the gold glinting in the lamplight. "Something quick, yeah. If we go now." He folded the paper, put the pen back down, and stood up, stretching a little himself. "Why the hell they have to be all the way up in the Bronx…"

"Council's in Manhattan. Having some running water between us and them is probably a good idea."

He stopped with one arm into his suit jacket. "You mean that actually works? Running water?"

"I never told you that?" She gave him her best Innocent Child look.

"Not once in ten years, Valere."

"Well, don't worry. It doesn't." She slipped away from his mock-threatened backhand, and grinned, her earlier mood seemingly vanished. "But I can't imagine too many Council members wanting to take the 2 train into the Bronx, do you?"

The streets were still light when they emerged up out of the subway station ninety minutes later. But Wren wasn't thinking about the wonders of short summer nights.

"He's still there."

Sergei hadn't seen anyone following them when they left the gallery, but somewhere between there and Sue Cho's, they had picked up a tail. A very good, very professional tail who had yet to be seen, but Sergei's neck hairs had started prickling. When they left Sue Cho's,

Wren had noticed something was wrong as well, although she wasn't sure if she was picking up on the tail's presence, or her partner's unease.

Taking his hand in her own, Wren leaned against his arm, breathing in the evening air with relief. It wasn't significantly cooler, but the sun was behind the buildings now, and that made a difference in how it *felt*.

"We're only a couple of blocks away, according to Lee's directions," Sergei said. "I really don't feel like leading whoeveritis straight to them. Even if it's nothing whatsoever to do with the Council…."

"You know, I'm pretty sure that not being certain *which* shadowy organization put a tail on us is a warning sign that our lives are just too damn complicated."

Sergei's laugh was a warm flow of current as much as it was sound. Wren had told him, long ago, that she could sense the inner current of "normal" humans, the same way that Kirilian photography claimed to. But she had never gotten around to telling him how much of his natural current had been siphoned off over the years into her own core. Nothing major, nothing he would even notice, although if you took too much a person would come down with a splitting headache, maybe even a migraine if they were sensitive. But it made his laughs into a physical pleasure for her.

"Okay, when we get to the end of the block, I need you to make like you stumbled a little, okay? Not a full fall, but maybe go down on one knee?"

Sergei didn't bother asking why, or what else he should be doing, or do anything other than squeeze her hand and keep walking forward, turning occasionally to look into a storefront window to see what the display was—as if their shadow would slip up enough on the sparsely crowded streets to be made.

Two sidewalk squares before the corner, Sergei tripped over a crack in the pavement, seemingly falling forward without actually pulling Wren off balance at all.

"Into the Shadows;
Rise a Veil of Deceit
And slip us away."

You didn't even need words, much less say them in any kind of formal structure, but it was easier to focus when you had everything visualized just so, and the fondness Wren had for the haiku form only strengthened her casting.

Sergei caught himself and started walking again, giving the impression of a man angrily embarrassed at having looked foolish in public. Wren had to run a few steps to catch up with him.

"We clear?"

"Yeah. As far as he's concerned, we just *poof* vanished. If he's from my side of the family—" meaning a Talent, or accustomed to Talents "—he'll know what I did but not be able to follow. And if he's your side, he's going to be very confused."

"How did the fall work into your spell? I've seen you cast at a full-out run, so I know it wasn't just to make me stop."

"You're too tall."

"Excuse me?"

"You're too tall. The Veil is cast around me. If you

hadn't bent over, your head and shoulders would be outside the veil."

Sergei was still laughing when they knocked on the garden gate of a discreet little two-story brownstone, and were let in.

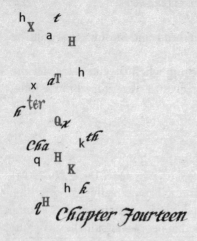

## Chapter Fourteen

Wren woke suddenly, eyes open and her entire body alert. Beside her, Sergei was sprawled on his stomach, his arm thrown over her chest like a safety belt. He was large and warm and she had the urge to turn on her side and snuggle into him. But moving right now seemed like too much effort.

The meeting the night before had been just as bad as she thought it would be. Baxter had called the moot, so he was allowed to open the floor. But that had been the only moment of calm all evening.

Wren groaned, wanting to block out the memories. It hadn't been bad enough that Baxter started by calling for a complete and total change in their society. No—he had to demand that they enforce it on everyone! Some rat-assed idea that they could only stand firm if everyone stood with them, and anyone who didn't stand with them was the enemy. Wren had almost walked out then. Only Lee's eyes, intent on her from across the room where he sat with a few others, kept her there.

"They're picking us off, one by one. Locking us in our homes, preventing us from earning a living!"

That much was true, Wren admitted to herself. Over the summer there had been several reports of lonejacks being Mage-locked into their homes for acting in a way the Council disapproved of. Low-level Talents, mostly— she didn't think the Council could really restrain a high-powered Talent, not without drawing down enough power to make a stink that people outside the city would have to take notice of. And she didn't think they wanted that. The pieces didn't add up that way.

Not that the pieces were adding up all that well to begin with. She hadn't given it much thought, being too busy first with surviving her own problems with the Council, and then trying to scare up some work. But there was something here that she was missing, or something that should be there, and wasn't. It bothered her. She didn't like mysteries or puzzles. She wanted everything neatly researched and laid out for easy comprehension, so she could just get her job done.

"And what do you expect us to do?"

That was Lee, finally standing up to speak. His voice barely cut through the din of discussion in the small living room, but just the fact that he was talking got peoples' attention. That, and his height.

"You say we should arm ourselves, cut them down before they come for us. How? Power for power, you've said it yourself, we're outgunned. Bring in people from outside? Then what's to stop them from bringing in people, too? Right now, it's a local thing. Escalate, and you're damning us all to a war we are not going to win."

A woman sitting a row over nodded her head in agreement, but everyone else started arguing with him, all at once.

"You'd rather just sit there and watch while they destroy our way of life?" Baxter was an ape of a man, but his voice was an orator's blessing, cutting through the babble. Wren thought he would be far less dangerous if his voice squeaked, or was low and soothing, rather than a well-tuned trumpet's call to arms.

"Looks like you're doing a pretty good job of that yourself," Wren said loudly, in her best disgusted voice.

Baxter went on as though he hadn't heard her, and he probably hadn't. She sat back and let it wave over her until he got to his selling point. "If we do nothing, we're destroyed. If we take a stand, together, unified, we at least have a chance. And no one will be able to say that we went like sheep to the slaughter."

That hit notes with a lot of them. No Talent got away without learning of witch hunts, of what had been done to their kind in earlier generations, simply for being different. The aversion most Talent shared for causing harm had gotten a lot of them killed, over the years.

"If we form a single body, yes, we are a greater target. But what is our option?" someone asked.

"To *think!*" Wren yelled, finally losing her patience. She

got off the folding chair she had been sitting in and strode into the middle of the room. "Who here knows me?"

Two men and a woman had been arguing, they turned and looked at her, then shrugged. Baxter went on talking as though she hadn't said anything. In a room filled with people intent on their own destruction, her protective coloration kicked in instinctively, shielding her from what her core recognized as harm. It had saved her life in at least one ugly situation, but right now, as she expected, it was keeping her from being even remotely effective. She threw her hands up in an expressive shrug, mentally damning them all to perdition, when she saw Lee's face again through the crowd.

Lee was a good man. A gentle man. But if this moot decided on action, if his friends and fellow Talents decided on this course, that wouldn't protect him. The Council would hunt them all down, and call it self-defense.

Taking a deep, shuddering breath, Wren shoved a mental hand deep into her core, gathering up the staticky, agitated strands of current and forcing them to do as she willed. The lights around them flickered, and everyone looked up, alert to the signs of major power use. It would have been so easy at that point to pull from everyone in the room, to siphon off their current the way she did from Sergei. But she needed to make a point. And it needed to be done solo.

"To me now," she whispered harshly, the strain making her sweat more than the day's heat had. "To me now, source of my own self. To me now!"

And with the last word of the spell, she reached up

with her left hand, toward the white-washed tin room, and *pulled* down.

And lightning ran from the four corners of the room, shimmering along the metal of the ceiling before joining in the middle, directly over Wren's hand, and then jumping from the ceiling down into her open palm.

Lying in Sergei's bed the next morning, feeling his comforting warmth beside her, Wren sighed. Calling lightning was considered quite unforgivably rude, a public statement of Mine's Bigger Than Yours that absolutely could not be ignored. Nor, given the egos Talents tended to carry around with them, forgiven.

But it got their attention.

She had stared them all down, willing them to see her, not through her, for once in their misbegotten lives. Or at least *hear* her. "Organize? Take action? That's exactly what they want. For us to create a single target that they can take down. Don't give 'em what they want. Frustration is our best weapon. *Their* frustration, not ours."

The meeting might have gone on for hours after that, Wren didn't know. She had stalked out, Sergei close on her heels. The effort—and the anger she had to summon to make the effort, left her shaking and shattered, and Sergei had ended up carrying her up the stairs to bed.

Now, however, she was wide-awake. And hungry. Sliding out of bed as quietly as she could, Wren threw on her shirt from the night before, slipped on her underwear, and went downstairs to use the bathroom and find something to eat.

The hardwood floor was cool under her bare feet,

and the early morning air was cool enough that the central air hadn't come on yet. Wren went to the wall of windows and looked out into the city. Sergei's neighborhood was a combination of high-rise apartment buildings and equally sleek offices. Half the lights in each building were on already, some with people getting ready to go to work, others with people already at work.

"The city that never sleeps."

She had known someone once who didn't wear a watch, not because he didn't care what time it was, but because he was existing simultaneously in two different time zones, tracking the markets in Japan at the time he was trying to have a social life in Manhattan. It hadn't worked very well, from what she recalled. But he kept trying.

A few more lights went on in the apartment building across the street, and that broke Wren from her memories. She went into the kitchen and started the coffee, then used the toilet. By the time she came back, the first caffeinated aroma was starting to warm the air, and the morning began to look a little better.

Some bread into the toaster, a chunk of smoked Gouda and leftover steak from the stainless steel refrigerator, and quick application of a sharp knife turned up a decent enough no-frills breakfast. She piled it all onto a plate, then poured herself the first cup of Colombia's Finest into one of Sergei's delicate-looking but sizable black china cups, and seated herself at the breakfast bar, digging in with enthusiasm.

By the time she was done, the soft thumps and thuds from the loft indicated that her partner was awake. She found herself getting up and moving toward the cooktop without conscious thought, and, as she filled the teakettle with fresh water, finally accepted the fact that in some way at least, she had been domesticated for years.

If the urge to make tea whenever he got near was the price she had to pay, well, that wasn't really a bad deal at all. Although having to resist the urge to turn the music on so she could think, because he was sleeping, was starting to wear on her. And why couldn't the man get around to current-proofing his electronics? It wasn't all that difficult, if every Talent in the city could do it!

"Morning," she said. He woke up better than she did, as a rule, but with a rumpled little boy look that was only worse now that his hair had grown out of the short cut he used to favor.

Sergei grunted at the mess she had made in the kitchen, saw that the kettle was on, and shuffled into the bathroom. A few minutes later, the shower came on.

Dumping her dishes in the sink, Wren poured the now-boiling water into another cup, adding a tea bag and set it aside to steep. *Domestic, domestic. Someone shoot me now.*

Pouring another cup of coffee for herself, Wren went out into the main area of the loft and curled up on the sofa, tucking her feet under her. Sipping at the steaming liquid, she let herself relax, reaching out past the walls to see if there was even the suggestion of a hint of a thundercloud anywhere.

Nothing. The air was still bone-dry and flat. A Talent

could recharge off anything, yeah, but some things were easier than others. And some could feed more than others. Without a thunderstorm—the original cornucopia, in terms of current—people were going to be pushed toward man-made sources. And those had a limit on how many they could feed before *ffffft* and the entire city goes blackout.

"It's no wonder half the lonejacks in the city are going nuts. If we're really unlucky, the Council isn't doing anything to help their people, and both sides will snap on the same day."

"What?"

"Nothing." She turned slightly to watch her partner as he came into the room wearing nothing but a pair of boxer shorts, a white towel around his neck. One hand was rubbing the end of the towel over his wet hair; the other held his tea mug.

"Wren, how many times have I told you, use a coaster?"

She sighed, picking up her cup of coffee and replacing it on top of the marble square he handed her. *Domesticity. And Sergei's Mister Good Housekeeping, matching china cups and all.*

"What's on the agenda for the day?"

He sat down next to her, putting the damp towel on his lap so that it didn't touch the leather.

"Need to go over the newest installation with Lowell. And don't make that face. I know he's a putz, but he's also a damn good assistant and I can trust him with the gallery when we're away." An expression crossed his face that she couldn't quite decipher, and then was gone. "You?"

"I want to take another shot at the library. No, I'm not going to break in." *Yet,* she added silently when he looked like he was about to protest. "But I thought I'd bring Lee along with me, use him to sweet-talk me past the guardians."

With luck, nobody would ask for details about his doctorate, which was actually an honorary one from his art school alma mater.

"Be careful." His eyes were half-lidded with sleep, still, but his expression was that poker face she knew meant he was repressing more detailed comments that he knew better than to say.

"So what are we looking for, anyway?"

"I haven't a clue."

"That fills me with an incredible amount of confidence."

"I'm the sarcastic one here, Tree-taller. You're the 'loves life, puppies, and raindrops' type."

He lifted his arm and touched her hand lightly where it was holding on to the metal handrail to maintain her balance. To the casual observer it looked like an affectionate touch, but the sudden zing that went through her nerve endings made her utter a short and rather pithy swearword in Russian. "Bastard," she added for good measure. But she refused to move her hand from the metal. It was a petty game of one-upmanship, more suited for 'Stagio and Pietro than two alleged adults, but be damned if she'd let an overtall mutant artist win.

They were in the subway heading toward midtown and the Library. Lee hadn't been happy about being dragged out of his studio, but when she'd mentioned, oh so casually, about how some people asked favors of their friend and then didn't return them, he had put the metal bar he was working on back down on to the static-guard pad and taken off his leather apron and gone with her.

Sometimes, you only needed a little bit of guilt.

"Here. Catch this." Her right hand had been holding the strap of her bag, but she extended it to where he sat on the molded plastic seat at the end of the row next to her. He looked at her dubiously, but reached his own free hand up to touch her fingers.

*A sense of foreboding, like the classic "getting a bad feeling" about something. Unease, distraction, a nervous flutter deep in your gut where instinct reigns supreme. The sense of metal bending wrongly, of the second before an unforeseen disaster strikes.*

*Another step, and foreboding becomes rage. Thick red heat, a sullen morass that simmers in on itself. There is no air to breathe, and you suck in instead the rage, until it sears your marrow and settles into your cells and that would be the end, my friend, the very end, so come closer, come here....*

"Gah!"

Lee's revulsion was perfectly expressed, and he jerked his hand away as though Wren were the source of the emotion, rather than merely conveying the memory of it.

"Fucking hell."

"You see why I think the parchment's still there?"

"Something's there, yeah. But why assume it's the parchment?"

"It matches what I felt at the…original site. Not that strong, it was way more faded there. The bindings helped, a lot more than the monks had any idea. God, if I'd felt that when I was there…" Wren's eyes went blank for a moment. "If more of the stuff in the place is like this, the whole thing should be burned to the ground, and good riddance."

"Uh-huh."

Translation: "That's stupid thing number three you've said today." If the other manuscripts in the House of Holding were like this, all burning them would probably do was release whatever magic was in them. A smart Talent tried not to do shit like that.

By the time they got off the subway and walked up Madison Avenue to the library, Lee had gotten himself under control, and was walking like a man with a purpose. Wren trailed behind him, projecting the air of a brow-beaten research assistant or TA, as far from the brash arts reporter facade she had used on her last visit as she could manage. With luck, nobody would notice her at all, except as an adjunct to Lee's more commanding image.

"I don't care who you spoke with! The library is closed. There are no tours, no research trips, no sniffing around so you can come back later." The security guard looked, Wren thought, as though he were about to burst a blood vessel in the side of his face, and she mentally ran over the ways she could push him, without risking his taking serious medical damage. Was Lee any good at the Push? She honestly didn't remember.

"It's okay, Danny, I'll take responsibility. You go on back to your post, thanks."

The man standing in front of them in the doorway was about five-ten, and looked more like a short linebacker than an office worker, with broad shoulders and relatively short but powerful legs. But his expression was alert and curious.

"My name's Saul," he said, not offering his hand to shake. "Saul Haven. I'm the Exhibit Preparator. You said that you were interested in one of our displays? You know that everything that came in recently is in storage right now, yes? I'm afraid that we can't— Who are you?"

Wren looked up at that, and their gaze locked.

Haven's gaze sharpened, and now he did extend his hand. Wren looked at Lee, who gave back his best wide-eyed, you're-the-boss look. Wren sighed, and took Haven's hand.

"Oh." Haven took a step back, almost as though he'd gotten a sudden shock.

"Ah, shit," Lee said with feeling.

"Shut up, Lee." Her brain was racing, trying to figure out what to do if the guy started screaming, or fainted or—

No, Haven looked like he'd recovered himself pretty well. Wren was going to go to Plan B and do her usual "welcome to the *Cosa*" spiel—finding someone who was sensitive to Talents wasn't unheard of, although they usually figured it out well before they were in their fifties, like this guy, but apparently it wasn't needed.

"You're here about the curse?"

"The…" Wren shot a look at Lee, who looked back, as totally blank-faced as she felt.

"Oh." Haven regrouped himself quickly. "Yes, well, there is a legend that the library is haunted by a—"

"No, there isn't." Wren didn't know that, actually, but she knew lying. "What curse?" She frowned at him. He wasn't a Talent—she wasn't picking up that particular vibe. But he was one of theirs, no doubt about it. "You feel it, don't you? That there's something wrong, here?"

Haven nodded, furtively, as though afraid someone would see and catch him out. "There's something in the library. I've worked here for almost nine years, and this has always been a wonderful place, barely any negative vibes at all. But then they started the renovations, and everything changed. And all I could think was that one of the workers had done something, or brought something, or…" he trailed off. "I'm not crazy. I mean, no more so than anyone else who talks about vibes and negative energy, or—"

"Anyone in your family ever burned at the stake, Mr. Haven?"

His hazel-brown eyes darted from Wren to Lee, then back to her. "According to family legend. Pressed, not burned."

It happened, sometimes. Not-quite-Null, but not Talent, either. The hedge-witches and conjurors of previous ages. There had been inconclusive studies,

Neezer had said, about the genetic basis of Talent. You could pick and choose your opinion. Neezer, a scientist, a biology teacher, had come down hard on the genetic side. Wren wasn't so sure. But where you found one in a family tree, pretty often there was another.

Haven nodded once firmly, a decision made. "Come with me, please."

Inside, the building was empty of even the few workers and staff who had been visible on her last visit.

"Everyone's at a reconstruction meeting," he said, seeing her look around and correctly interpreting her expression. "You're lucky I decided to take a bathroom break."

He led them into a small office filled with boxes and piled high on top of that with papers and bubble wrap and what might once have been pizza boxes, and closed the door behind them. The difference between Haven's office and that of Taibshe's made Wren relax slightly. This was a place where *things* got done, not meetings.

"You can do something about the…whatever it is?" He sat in the chair behind the desk, having to shove a small, securely taped file box out of the way so he could see them clearly. Lee sat down in the one chair available, while Wren stood off to the side, forcing Haven to move his head from side to side to keep them both in his line of sight.

Unsurprisingly, once Wren stopped speaking directly to him, he kept his attention totally focused on Lee. "Because I can't. Do anything about it, I mean. I tried the few little cantrips and castings my grandmother taught me, but they didn't manage anything except set off one of my coworker's asthma. As though the dust in this place from the construction wasn't doing that anyway."

"Can you get us into the basement?" Wren asked.

"You think that's where it is?" He shook his head, still directing his answers to Lee. "No. Anywhere else, probably. I could find some reason, some way to sneak you in, through all the confusion. But the storage area is off-limits to everyone without a real reason to go down there, unless you're higher up in the food chain than I am."

"Alarm system?" The intern had mentioned something about that....

He nodded. "The same as the rest of the library building proper, plus an extra level they installed when the renovations began."

"Damn." Not that she couldn't get in, if she needed to. But it would have been nice to bring some backup with her, if this thing was as nasty as it felt. Nasty on that scale, and with the background they'd picked up from the monks generally meant the parchment had originally been the work of either a seriously high-mojo Talent, the kind that leveled small countries for kicks, or an old-timer fatae, one of the breeds that used magics the way humans did. The old-timers generally had very little use or liking for humans, so anything that they had a hand— or paw, or claw—in wasn't anything Wren wanted to be taking on alone. Or even two-on-one, for that matter. Twenty-on-one sounded a little more reasonable.

Or—a thought she hadn't even allowed herself to think, much less mention to Sergei—it wasn't a parchment, per se, they were going after, but an old one, to use the fatae's term. *God be kind, don't let it be an old one.* The last time one of the ancient beasts took notice of the world, there was a flu epidemic that wiped out almost thirty million people. Her only consolation was that that had been in 1918, and the Talents of the time were pretty sure they'd gotten that bastard, down to the last fetid breath.

Lee leaned forward in the chair. "Do you have access to the inventory?"

Wren could have kicked herself. She was too distracted, too caught up in what might be when she needed to be thinking about what was. What, as Sergei said, they *knew.* Invoices and inventories were a godsend to fact-seekers, Sergei had taught her that much. Shame on her that Lee was the one to ask.

"I…yes, I could. It may take a few days, but I can do it. You think it came…of course. In the chaos of the renovation, anyone could slip something in, and it would merely be recrated and sent below."

And the person who had paid for all this could then take his or her time in claiming it.

If nothing else, having the actual invoice paperwork, not just an electronic rendition of it, might lead them closer to tracing the person who arranged the shipment. And then she could pay that person a visit, preferably on a dark and very stormy night.

"It's strange, though," Haven said.

"What is?" Lee asked.

"That no one noticed when such an evil thing came in. Surely that could not have been on a legitimate manifest."

"You'd be amazed what people sign for," Wren said, speaking from long years of experience. "Really."

Haven looked as though he wanted to argue the point, but a beeping noise came from his belt and he grabbed at it, looking abashed.

"I'm summoned back into the pits of boredom." He rummaged through the piles on his desk until he found what he was looking for, and then thrust it into Lee's hands. "Please, let me walk you out."

Haven dropped them at the front door, disappearing back down an empty hallway and leaving the two of them no choice but, under Danny's glowering attentions, to walk down the steps and back out onto the street.

"That…y'know, I'm not exactly in any position to pitch stones. But I *warn* people when they're asking me to get something icky. And I sure as hell don't leave it in unsuspecting go-between hands."

"You're the very model of a morally upright Retriever."

Wren just glared at him. "You really do have a death wish, don't you?"

"Mellow, Valere." Nice to see that Lee, at least, was back to his usual self. "You think he's going to be okay in there?"

She shrugged. "As much as anyone there. Maybe even more, since he'll be able to sense what it is if it gets near enough to be really dangerous." She hoped. But then again, horror movies were filled with otherwise likeable people who, when faced with something dire and dangerous, went right into the cellar without an Uzi or a squirt gun of holy water. So who knew?

On the street outside, Lee paused, looking up as though he were seeing something there besides a slate-blue afternoon sky. "You want to have dinner with us?"

"No, thanks. I think I want to go home and crash for a while." She caught the look Lee gave her, and shrugged. "Right, Sergei's apartment. Don't look at me like that."

"Like what?"

"Like 'does she realize what she just said.' I'm tired, I'm probably still jet-lagged, I spent all afternoon lurking around the edges of some icky current, and there's not a thunderstorm in sight to clean off in. Plus, thanks to you, I had to drain myself way too much last night just to make myself seen, to maybe crack some sense into the heads of people who really damn well should know better. So don't even start on the totally uncertain and probably screwed up state of my relationship with Sergei, okay? Right now I'm crashing there while my apartment's set straight."

Lee kept looking at her.

"Jesus wept." She stared back at him, but he didn't blink. "Yes, okay? We're sleeping together. News flash. Yes, I love him. Totally not a news flash. No, I have no idea what's going to happen tomorrow, much less down the road. And yes, the control freak in me is going insane. Anything else you want to know?"

He didn't laugh the way she had intended him to. "Does he make you happy?"

She had to think about that for a moment, taking her turn to stare into the sky while adjusting the strap of her pocketbook over one shoulder. The air was—surprise!—significantly warmer than it had been inside. Despite that, she could feel goose bumps forming under her T-shirt. "There's a place in my soul I always knew was empty. I thought that was just sort of the way it was going to be. And then something cracked, and there he was, and it's not a perfect fit and it's scary sometimes, thinking about it being empty again, or worse, if he moves wrong and breaks it all open and how much that could hurt."

"So, not happy."

She looked at him, shrugged, felt her lips quirk in an almost-smile. "Not happy, no. But there are moments of this…this incredible, painful joy. And if you ever tell him any of what I said, you are totally a dead man."

## Chapter Fifteen

The jackals were out tonight. Andre could feel them in the shadows, watching. The Italian situation was worse than expected; the client was blaming them for not taking the theft seriously enough, for not sharing the information they knew. Who knew that the guardians had no idea what they'd guarded? And yet, somehow, blame would land on the Silence—or the designated scapegoat thereof. Nobody would do anything, not until they knew for damn-sure certain how things were going to fall out. But then they'd be on the meat, fighting for their unfair portion. Alessandro's concern had been his first warning, and he'd heeded it, covering his ass and making sure no loose ends were left to trip him up. He fully intended not to be the spoils they fought over.

And if that meant that he had to sacrifice other players...he would regret it, but regret would not stop

him. Not even if those players were people he was personally fond of.

His blinds pulled against the midday sun reflecting off
a dry blue sky, Andre skimmed through the reports
filtered onto his computer screen. The monthly
download of reports from active Handlers had to be
entered into the database, and before that could happen,
he had to sign off on every single one under his watch.
Allowing someone to slip in unauthorized conversation—or worse yet, allowing something to be recorded
that should not be made official—could be deadly.

But still, his thought kept returning to Duncan's appearance after his meeting with Poul. What was the
bastard up to? Even though nobody else had been in the
coffee shop with them rumors were already spreading,
as he'd known they would. As Duncan had to have
known they would. You didn't get a casual stop-by from
the Man himself. Not without reason. And the reason
could as easily be bad as good—and deadly either way.

A small icon flickered on his screen, and he clicked
on it, bringing up his mail program. Sergei had reported
in. Finally. It would have been nice if he'd actually come
down to do it in person, but Andre would indulge him
in that small rebellion. For now.

*"Silence contact injured in car accident prior to
arrival. Later died. Doubtful it was coincidence, based on
later findings."*

Andre's pitch-black eyebrows raised into his salt-and-
pepper hairline.

*"The organization contacted had very little idea of the*

*value of their stolen item. Suggest insurance evaluation immediate, for future reference. Also, suggest increase in vigilance on dry lines, which would have been useful in this case."*

Dry lines were Silence-speak for international boundaries, specifically official ports of entry.

*"We believe that the situation is currently contained and will be resolved within the allotted time frame."* Humor, Didier-style. He had not given them a specific time frame.

*"Strongly suggest alerting other operatives to be alert for indications that situation is not fully contained."*

In other words, if anyone heard of anyone disappearing suddenly, to let them know. A lot of false alarms, with an M.O. that vague. But since he'd already instituted the alert when the situation was first taken on, he couldn't disagree. And did Sergei believe that he was losing his touch, or was that another intended-as-humorous poke?

*"Updates to follow."*

As reports go, it was sparse, spotty, filled with useless material and lacking anything even close to justifying the cost of sending them to Italy. Andre shook his head, moving the report into the correct file. Which, since Sergei was neither careless nor foolish, meant that the real report was in what wasn't being given.

Another icon flashed on his screen, a different one this time, and Andre passed the cursor over it, making the telltale disappear. Someone had just accessed Sergei's report without permission. Possibly, nothing untoward at all. Possibly…something more. And again, the Silence bureaucrat felt the hyenas shift in the grass behind him.

* * *

Somehow, it seemed longer than a week since she'd been home. Well, technically Wren supposed it had been. They'd left for Italy on Friday, and come back on Monday, and here it was Saturday again. So a week and a day, counting the blur of that first Friday as being "away." She said as much to Sergei, who was putting the groceries they had picked up on the way over into the fridge. She was going to have to go through and reorganize them, later. After he'd gone, so he didn't feel bad.

"You look like you want to go around and pee in all the corners, to make sure your scent is properly marked," he said over his shoulder, bending down to put the veggies in the drawer she usually used for cheese.

"Very funny." It was, actually. She admitted to feeling a little raw about the relief she felt at being home. Sergei's place was nicer, yeah. She'd kill for that bathroom. And having a warm body in bed beside her every morning…

Well, it was nice, but not as nice as she'd thought it would be. Oh, she loved him, yeah, not trying to back away from that. And the sex was…well, the current-sparks still had her worried, but other than that it was fabulous. Certain parts tingled when she even thought about it. The truth was, though, it felt a little confining, too. Waking up with him so *there* and so…unavoidable.

Feeling that way didn't make her a bad person. Just, she supposed, used to having her own space. And if the way Sergei had gotten so very precise about the placement of coasters and laundry and dirty dishes, she sort of suspected that he was going to be kind-of glad to get rid of her, too.

*Back to the modern Manhattan pattern of long-term relationships. Your apartment or mine?*

"You hungry?"

"Am I ever not?" The Mackenzie son had called around midmorning to say that the apartment was clear and fresh-daisy-smelling (his words). She had wanted nothing more than to rush over and check for herself, but Karl had come through with the analysis of those shipping invoices he had promised, plus the additional bonus of another packet sent under the same import company's name, and Wren needed to look them over to see if anything jumped out at her. There had been more than she expected—Karl was probably using her to clear away a backlog of suspicious activity or something. Still, since all it involved was sitting in the cool quiet of Sergei's office, on the sofa, and letting her eyes flick over reams of paper, she supposed it was an easy enough way to pay back, and maybe grease the wheels for later use. And there had in fact been a couple of names that she had been quite surprised to see listed on those papers as rare art dealers. Dealers, certainly. But Pigskin shouldn't have been anywhere near anything even remotely qualified as "art." She had red-tagged that one, and hoped that Karl would be able to nail his ass. Piggy was a disgrace to the name Retriever. She knew for a solid fact that he had undersold his client on at least two occasions, which was three more than was acceptable. How he was still alive and breathing was a wonder for the ages.

"Let me guess—Noodles?"

She hadn't thought about it until he mentioned the name, but her taste buds immediately began to salivate at the thought of Chinese food. "You do know what I like."

"You're not exactly subtle about it."

She tried to raise an eyebrow at that comment, and failed, as usual. Filing it in the back of her memory for dissection later, Wren grabbed her suitcase and upended it on the floor in the main room. Where, she was disgusted to notice, her laundry from the Italy trip was still dumped in a pile on the floor. "They do windows, but they don't do laundry." She should have thought about that before she left, but getting the hell *out* had seemed more important.

She picked up a shirt, and sniffed at it suspiciously. "I'll be damned." Fresh-daisy, indeed.

"You want Chung Pao, or—?" Sergei stuck his head into the room, his mobile already at his ear.

"Extra spicy, yeah, thanks." She let the shirt drop, and sat down on the floor. She should really cart it all down to the Laundromat tonight. But it was still too icky outside. Not quite tar-melting levels, the way it had been earlier in the month, but the air really felt unhealthy. And the cops had cracked down on the hydrant-opening, so everyone was even crankier than usual without the chance for a splash-down.

"Chung Pao, extra spicy, a day's special, and a small egg drop soup."

"And a won ton!" she called.

"And a won ton soup. Apartment.. right. Yeah. You too."

He clicked off the phone and came into the room, sitting down on the one chair, an overstuffed and heavily battered armchair, and looked at her bemusedly.

"Are you sure Jimmy's not a Talent?"

Wren snickered. "Less Talent and more tech. I'm pretty sure Jimmy's got caller ID just to freak everyone out."

"I was calling on my cell!"

"Yeah and you've never called in an order from your mobile before?"

Since he had, and many times, Sergei had no comeback to that.

"Don't worry," she said to reassure him. "I'm sure you're still plenty sneaky for the Silence. And speaking of which, shouldn't we, I don't know, check in or something?"

Sergei raised a hand, then let it drop. "Or something. Yeah, I let Andre know we're home, not that he doesn't already know all that. Generally you're set on the situation and told not to come home until it's done. Or, if you need backups or further information. But since they didn't give us anything to begin with…"

"Do we smell setup?"

"Probably not. Although I suspect there will always be a section that would not be displeased should we suddenly disappear on contact with the Nescanni Parchment."

*Okay. There's stuff behind that.* He had been pretty forthcoming about how the Silence worked, and what she could expect—and not expect—from them in terms of the agreement he had hammered out. He had even 'fessed up to the work he had done for them, which was pretty much what he was doing now, only hopefully without the sex-with-the-operative-he-was-running part. But why he'd left, and what kind of terms he'd left on, and the reactions to him coming back, that had been pretty much do-not-discuss territory.

And you couldn't push Sergei. Or, you could, but that way led to tight-lipped silence and unhappiness all around.

"Okay, I think we need to stop worrying about the whos and the hows. Personally, I don't give a damn who bribed the monk or what they're planning to use it for. It's a nasty piece of work, and I want it back under slate and totally out of reach of anyone."

"I agree," Sergei said. That surprised her. Not that he wouldn't want this dealt with soonest possible, but that he'd be okay with not knowing every detail. "I've no doubt that Andre has people working on this as well—the whys and the wherefores, that is—to ensure that it doesn't happen again. In fact, when the Silence is done with our Italian friends, I suspect that there will be a neatly listed and carefully protected inventory done, with annotated histories and suspected side effects."

"And then they'll bury that list deeper than anyone can dig?"

"Burying things is one of the tasks the Silence is best at."

And for once, Wren actually did feel reassured. Or as much as you could be when you've got stuff that nasty waiting for you to come and try for a piece of it.

"So all I need to do is figure out how to handle the actual Retrieval without getting vanished or otherwise hurt myself. And the clock's ticking. Damn. Speaking of which. You want to go get it, or should I?" She rolled her eyes at his blank look. "The food, Didier! The food!"

"I'll go. You need to look those over."

He gestured with a jerk of his chin, not at the piles of laundry, but the two slender, leather-bound books she had stopped to pick up on the way over. Sergei had stayed outside while she went into a storefront and, through their back door, walked up two flights of stairs to a small, windowless apartment. Daishia wasn't the most paranoid Talent Wren had ever met, especially with the city braced and paranoid with Mash and Sasha still missing, but she was close.

That level of paranoia made sense when you remembered that there were not one but three angels who had sworn to rend Daishia into tiny bits. Nobody knew what she had done to so piss them off, but of all the modern fatae, the wrongly named angels had the least amount of fondness for humanity, and it was generally considered a good thing that they usually showed that lack of affection by just staying away.

Earlier in the spring, a band of antifatae vigilantes had killed an angel. Wren and Sergei had been there in time to see him die. They hadn't hung around longer than that, for fear of what his brothers might do when they found him.

Wren frowned, wondering suddenly if the fatae leaders P.B. had been hobnobbing with had actually talked to any of the angels. It wasn't like *anyone* got along well with angels…

Anyway, Daishia had the best library of anyone about particularly malevolent critters. And she was an old friend of Wren's mentor, John Ebeneezer. Neezer had long wizzed, gone crazy from the current, and disappeared, but his network still remembered him, and through him, her.

"Right. You go into the heat, and I go into the craziness." The two volumes were the writings of an Irish magician named Elspethian, who died in the eleventh century, reportedly of rabies. It was generally accepted that he'd been frothing mad long before then. But part of that madness had left him open to visits from things that might or might not have been what were euphemistically called the Upstairs Neighbors; the original, very very human-unfriendly fatae. Not many saw them and survived, so if this did have a touch of them about them, God forbid… And firsthand resources were always to be preferred, anyway.

She reached for the topmost volume, hiking up the skirt of her sundress to her knees so that she could sit comfortably.

"Quit leering and go get me some food," she told Sergei without looking up.

"Yes ma'am," he said, and hoisted himself out of the chair with a grunt of effort. The door closed behind him, and everything was silent except the scratching of paper as Wren turned the pages.

* * *

"Lookey lookey what we got here."

The voice was male, flat, and carried the faintest hint of a southwestern accent, as though the person had tried to erase all traces of their past but hadn't been able to go that last step.

"What do you think it is?"

"Gross, is what it is. Man, how does anything that ugly manage to breed?"

There were five in the group, three men and two women. All well-dressed, young urban professionals out for dinner, drinks, maybe some theater. Two black, the others white. They were walking slowly up 38th Street as though the warm summer's evening air was making them sluggish. But their faces were sharp and intent, like ferrets scenting a treat.

The fatae they had spotted froze against the red brick of the building it had just come out of, the visible skin shading into a pattern that almost but didn't quite match the pattern of the wall. Unfortunately, the long pastel dress she was wearing didn't change with her skin, and she remained clearly visible. The knapsack slung over one sloped shoulder was released slowly to the ground, and the narrow, salamanderlike head dipped once, as though scenting the ground.

"What's it doing here, rather than in a swamp where it belongs? With all the other lizards."

"We could make sure it gets back there. Safely."

That last word caused the two women to giggle, and the leader, who spoke first, to puff his chest out with pride at his wit. He seemed to almost glow with personal satisfaction, the way the others all nodded their heads in agreement. The burliest male in the group, a blonde with a heavy moustache and sharply trimmed beard, moved away from the group slightly, stepping into the gutter and walking slowly to where the fatae waited, still frozen in fear. Her round eyes watched him move forward, flicking back every few seconds to look at the others as well.

"I say it's here, it's fair game," the youngest male in the group said, his voice high and thin with malice. "'Sides, look at the way the skin's all sparkly. Bet it would make a really nice bag, huh? Never lose that in the airport."

The leader pursed his lips, looking carefully at the creature as though weighing options. "Jack, I do believe you're right."

The two women fell back, moving into lookout position, one on each side of the street looking in opposite directions. Jack and the unnamed leader stepped forward confidently, Jack reaching into his slacks pocket and pulling out a jackknife, which he opened to display a thin, well-honed blade. The metal caught the sunlight, reflecting it back onto Jack's face. But he didn't flinch away from it, instead seeming to absorb the glow until it settled just under his skin, pulsing with the rhythm of his walk.

The blond man lunged forward just as the fatae realized that holding very still would not dissuade these predators and tried to dart away. He caught hold of the rayon of her dress, and yanked hard enough to tear the fabric. One slender, seemingly frail arm grabbed the knapsack and swung it hard in a half circle, landing a blow on the blond man's shoulder and making him stagger slightly sideways.

The female, seeing her escape route cut off, put her back to the wall, and opened her eyes very wide, the pupils expanding until the red centers almost filled in the black. And then she opened her mouth, a narrow pink tongue flickering out, and she hissed, a sound that should have put fear into the hearts of less determined individuals.

The second rule of intelligent survival among fatae encounters was to never annoy a basilisk. The first rule was especially to never annoy a *female* basilisk. Not that the female of the species was any more determined, more aggressive or more vicious than the male. But they were the brood-raisers, and genetics had therefore given them the tongue that spat poison that could stun an egg-stealer—or a full-sized human—for days at a time.

"Watch it! Come around the back!" The leader called his orders in a soft voice that carried just far enough for his companions to hear, but no farther. "Don't let this stinking animal get away. Teach it not to walk on *our* streets."

"Leeeeeezard!" Jack called, moving his knife just enough to draw her attention to it. "Leeeeezard leeezard leeezard! C'mere little leeezard."

In another area, perhaps a few decades before, they would have been wearing white hoods. Or the robes of the Inquisition, ferrying souls to the fire not for the glory of God, but the fear of things Other.

But the basilisk was no terrified child, for all that she was young for her kind. The knapsack was filled with textbooks, and made a dangerous weapon, and only the fact that her aim wasn't very good had kept the human attackers from failing already. Small puddles sizzled on the pavement where her failed poison pooled.

"Vigilanteeessssss…" she hissed, her scales flickering in the dusk with an unholy light. "I know you, vigilanteeeesss. I kill you, kill you all, and dance on your bonessss."

Word had gone out months ago, courtesy of The Wren and the demon known as P.B., about the antifatae vigilantes hunting the streets and alleys of Manhattan. Some masqueraded as a pest-control service, sending around flyers and making cold call solicitations. Others, or maybe the same ones off the work-clock, preferred a more direct approach. The word from the elders was not to attack—but be prepared to defend yourself. Lethally, if need be.

The blonde lunged, taking advantage of what he thought was her distraction, and she spat at him, the stream of venom missing her goal—his eyes—and splattering into his mouth, open to spew his own type of poison at her.

The word "bitch" barely escaped before his face froze in its rictus of hate, fulfilling at least one long-ago motherly scolding about faces freezing that way. But the rest of his body kept moving, and with a desperate burst of speed he lunged against her, crashing them both to the pavement.

Jack rushed the pile-of-two, his knife held off to the

side slightly, to avoid hitting the other human, but the other man gave a short, sharp whistle and he halted.

"Let Stevie have his fun. Only female he's had a chance to grab in a while."

Jack looked disgusted at the thought, but looked willing to hold off until the basilisk's tail swept out from the pile and knocked him off his feet. She might have been down, but she was definitely not out. And Stevie, with his eyes getting the next stun-poison dose, wasn't able to hold his own in the scuffle.

"Fuck this," he said, shifting his knife to the other hand and reaching down to grab at the scaled tail. "Gonna get me a souvenir. Handbag for Julie!" he said, loud enough that his lady-friend across the street could hear. A swipe of the blade barely cut through the scales, and she roared in pain, pushing aside the now-staggering Stevie and lunged on her knees at the younger man. Gone was any pretense at human civilization: the dress was long-shredded, her claws extended and glowing.

Basilisks didn't glow. Nor did humans. But the two of them were clearly glowing in the growing dusk, a dark, shimmering light that seemed filled with even darker specks that somehow threw off light nonetheless.

"What the hell?" the leader muttered, taking a step back from the two still too occupied to notice anything. Then he looked down, and noticed a similar dark sparking coming off his own skin, fainter, and fading even as he watched.

"Screw this. Haul off! Leave it, Jack. Haul off!"

The two women started walking quickly down the street in the other direction, while he grabbed Stevie by one arm and hauled him awkwardly to his feet. "Jack, leave it! Let's go!"

The glow around the two fighters intensified, so bright that even they, caught up in their snarling scrabble, noticed.

"What the hell?" Stevie managed, then grabbed at the female, his attention too tightly focused in rage to let anything distract him for long.

The basilisk, more accustomed to magic and what it might mean than the human, clamped her mouth shut and slithered out from under him, trying again for escape, not attack. Jack lunged after her, the knife landing a blow across her face, and her anger surged again, over-riding all logic and turning her to the fight again.

"Jack!"

Jack was too busy to answer.

"Ah, the hell with you, then," the other man said. "No," he barked at the woman who would have gone back to help them. "He's on his own, stupid shit."

She looked back once, then took the other side of Stevie's staggering body and helped him walk down the street, away from the continuing combat.

"Stupid thing. Teach you to mess with my city. Teach you to mess with a human."

The basilisk hissed something in her own language, and spat once, her aim improved at such close range so that she hit him directly in one eye.

"Bitch!" His arm wrenched free of her grasp, the knife rising high over their heads and coming down in a perfectly executed killing stroke that failed only because she shifted in a way no human could have managed.

The glow took on an intense golden tone, radiating like heat waves off their bodies, until it seemed as though there should be sound breaking from it as well, a scream or a bellow or the sound of steam escaping. The basilisk twisted and rolled, her serpentine heritage in full view, and sank her teeth into Jack's exposed neck just as he jerked upwards, driving the knife into the relatively unprotected softness of her belly.

There was a soft puff of air that somehow muffled their cries. The glow went up a notch, and then disappeared.

The two bodies lay sprawled, tangled together, on the sidewalk. Blood pooled around them, creating an inhuman outline of legs, arms and tail.

And two blocks away, in the Stuzner-Friesman Library, a small plastic case lined with lead let out what could only be described as a satisfied burp. A good beginning. But only the beginning.

"Hey. That was fast." Wren looked up from her reading, expecting to see Sergei coming back with the food. Instead…

"Mom. Hi!" She closed the book in her hand and, thinking madly, shoved it and its counterpart under the nearest pile of laundry. "Why didn't you tell me you were going to be in town? You should have called!"

Margot Valere raised one perfectly arched eyebrow at her only child. "And you would have answered the phone?"

"I answer the phone, " Wren defended herself. "Mostly.

And I would have if I'd heard your voice on the answering machine!"

Wren loved her mother wildly. But they both agreed that their relationship had taken a turn for the better when Wren moved across the river into Manhattan, and they were able to put a little distance between them.

Margot placed the shopping bag she was carrying down carefully by the door, and came in to give Wren a gentle hug and a kiss on the cheek. She smelled, as she always had to Wren's memory, of warm baby powder and the faintest hint of orange spice. Her white cotton blouse and floral skirt were simple but perfectly fashionable, and you wouldn't know they came from Sears unless you had looked at her shopping receipt.

"Sorry, things are a bit of a mess."

Margot sank into the chair Sergei had just vacated and glanced at the laundry, somehow in true mother fashion managing to speak an entire lecture without opening her mouth.

"I've been on a job," Wren said in self-defense, knowing the moment she spoke that she had already lost the battle and the war.

"Did I say anything?"

"Mom. Deaf children in India heard you not saying anything."

Her mother really had the most beautiful laugh. Her life had pretty much sucked, but she was still totally a lemons-into- lemonade kind of person.

"So, did you have a fun trip to Italy? And I didn't even know you had a passport!"

Okay, that was the sticky part. Her mother knew what Wren was, and what she did. Neezer had insisted, as part of taking her on as a student. "Bad enough you're underage and I'm a teacher," he had said. But, with the awesome mental powers only mothers possess, she somehow managed to block out anything that she didn't want to know about her daughter's life.

"Yeah, it was interesting." *True.* "And too short." *Also true. A trip by cruise ship would be much longer. Also smarter.*

"I don't suppose you met anyone while you were there?"

*Oh God.*

"Mother. Please. I really think you need to let that go." *Especially now. This wasn't going to be pretty. Mom was okay with Sergei as a coworker, as much as she ever really understood it, but I know she grilled him pretty hard when he proposed the partnership deal in the first place. And she totally blames him for me not getting a four-year degree like she wanted me to. Gonna have to break that news slow and gradual-like....*

"Hi honey, dinner's home! You want to eat in there or in bed—and hello Ms. Valere, what a pleasure to see you so unexpectedly."

*Oh, fuck.*

Margot stared at Sergei as though she had never seen him before, then turned to her daughter.

"Mom..."

"Tell me you're not."

"I'd be lying."

"Genevieve Marie Valere!"

"Margot Elizabeta Valere!" Wren responded, in exactly the same tone of voice. Sergei had the sudden urge to hide under a chair. In Kosovo. It would be safer.

"You're always after me to get a social life."

"That wasn't what I meant!"

"Why? Mom, it's Sergei. You know him. It's not like I picked up some half-trained kid off the street."

There was an undercurrent there that made both Margot and Sergei flinch. Sergei knew why he did, but wasn't sure what it had meant to the intended target.

"That's not... Genevieve, think about this, for God's sake."

"What? Because we work together? You dated a coworker or two in your time, if I recall correctly."

"And if you will also recall, it was a mistake. But... think this through, please."

They had both forgotten he was standing there, a plastic bag of Chinese food in his hand. "I'll just go put this in the kitchen, then," he said, and got out of their line of sight. He could still hear the conversation, though.

"What's there to think about? Mom, this is a good thing. It could even be a long-term thing. I think maybe it is."

"How long-term could it be?"

"Wha?" And Sergei found himself echoing his partner's confused reaction.

"Genevieve. Please. I know he's a nice man, and you two have a good relationship, but you're twenty-eight. And he's—"

"Not," Wren finished. He was, in fact, pushing forty with a very short stick.

"And where does that leave you? You should find a younger man, Genevieve. Someone closer to your age, who—"

"Mother? Leave. Now, please."

"I'm only thinking of your future, sweetie."

"I know. That's why I'm not yelling right now." Her voice was, in fact, particularly calm and flat. "Please? We can…we can talk some other time. But not right now. Okay?"

The sound of movement, and a heavy sigh. "You'll call me? We'll have lunch? Or maybe you'll come out for dinner? You haven't been by since the spring."

"Yeah, okay. That'll be nice. Probably cooler out there, anyway. Good night, Mom."

The sound of the door opening, and a yelp of surprise.

*Oh God, what now?*

He deposited the food on the counter and came back out into the hallway in time to see Margot and P.B. doing an awkward sidestep around each other, her trying to leave, him trying to come in. He was wearing a coat today, thank God, a long windbreaker sort of thing, with his usual messenger's bag over it. But his head was uncovered, and there was no way in hell that anyone could avoid seeing his flat, white-furred face, or the rounded, bearlike ears, even if they somehow missed the fact that his eyes were the color of dried blood.

"Oh. Sorry about that." P.B. seemed flabbergasted, and if the situation were a little less potentially disastrous, Sergei would have laughed at how the demon, clearly uncertain how to react, was hedging, looking to Wren for rescue.

"You were leaving, Mother," Wren reminded her, taking her by the arm with one hand and picking up her shopping bag with the other. "And yes, I will call you." P.B. looked up and saw Sergei standing there, and made for him like a safe zone. Considering that P.B. knew how Sergei felt about fatae in general, and demons in particular, that was a sign of his panic.

The door shut behind Margot, and Wren turned around to put her back to the door, looking at the two of them with a wide-eyed look of disaster averted.

"Jesus wept."

"Valere. Your mom's a babe. How come you got all the short, boring genes?"

"Shut up, P.B. You got the goods?"

"Handy and dandy." He laid one clawed hand on the messenger's bag. "Am I not da man?"

"You da demon, that's for sure. And I am totally tapped out, so you're going to be da demon who takes it on credit."

"Wren!" P.B. actually did look horrified, and for a moment Sergei thought that he was going to have to dig into his wallet to pay the furry little bastard off. Assuming he had enough cash on him, that was. Would P.B. take a credit card? Probably.

Then P.B.'s jaw dropped open in what passed for a grin with him, and Wren held out her hand for the packet he took out of the bag and handed to her.

"You get a month, Valere. And that's only 'cause I like you."

"I'm good for it. Soon as the job's done."

"Right. Y'know, I think I'll take my usual route home. Seeing as how the stairs are so crowded tonight."

"Sorry about that," Wren said as she walked P.B. the half-dozen steps to the kitchen window, opening it so that he could crawl out onto the fire escape. "Watch your back."

"Always do," he said, and was gone, the only mark of his passing a faint tap-tap of claws on metal.

"Damn."

"What?"

"I was going to ream his posterior for using my apartment. And I totally forgot."

"Come have dinner," he said. "You'll feel better then."

Food parceled out and consumed—on the floor of the main room, because the bedroom was too hot for comfort despite the small floor fan and the rice paper shades over the window.

"Fortune cookie time," Sergei said, holding up two paper-wrapped objects as she was slurping down the last of her soup.

"Why does hot soup taste so good on hot days?"

"It creates an equilibrium of temperatures, inside and out. Which fact you well know. Come on, pick a fortune. You know it only gets worse if you don't."

Wren put down her soup carton and glared at the two innocent-looking objects in Sergei's open palm. Jimmy, the owner-chef of Noodles, had a Seer writing his fortune cookies. It was a gimmick most of the regular customers loved. Wren, having had firsthand experience with the cryptic accuracy of the Seer, was less enthralled. But if you tried to not open it, things just got worse. Sometimes it was better to have advance warning, no matter how obscure it might be worded. And sometimes…

"Fine. Right. Okay." And she reached over to snag the left-side one from him. He took the remaining cookie and opened it, smoothing out the small square of paper.

"So?"

"I'm not sure if I should be worried, or terrified."

"What?"

She looked up, shrugged. "'The heart is the only thing that can hurt you.' So, either I'm invulnerable, about to have a heart attack, or I'm going to get killed by a surfeit of sweetbreads. Ugh. Yours?"

He frowned down at the paper. "If you must curse the dark, remember it is only fallen light."

"Oh, good. I'd hate to think the Seer was slipping and making them all, y'know, sensical."

"Speaking of which." It was a risk, but it seemed a good time to take it. If nothing else, it would get her mind off her eventual demise from sweetbreads.

"Yeah?"

"What your mother said."

"Oh God, don't you start." She crushed the remains of her cookie in her fist and shook the crumbs into the empty soup carton. "Look, my mom…has issues, okay? In fact, when it comes to guys, and relationships, she's got a subscription. She's not happy when I'm not seeing someone, and she's never going to be happy with anyone I am seeing. I know the routine."

"Why?"

"Why is she such a freak?" Wren started to fuss with the debris, until he leaned over and put one finger under her chin, bringing her gaze up to meet his.

A heavy sigh. "You remember what that monk said?"

"Freddie? He said a lot of things, most of it stupid junk." Sergei thought, remembered. "Most of which went right off your back. Except that last one."

"Devil child. Yeah. You know anything about my dad, Sergei?"

The question took him by surprise, and he had to think about it. "No."

"Me neither. Mom would never tell me word one, except that he was gone." She held up her fingers to make dialogue marks around that last word. "He came and he went—literally, apparently."

A flashback: a night only a few months ago, a crisis and a phone conversation across town, and Wren's voice, asking him not to leave her. He had thought at the time that she had been referring to her mentor, John Ebeneezer, who vanished when she was still in high school. Apparently not. Or at least, not entirely.

"Anyway, guys are a button that it's real easy to push, with my mom. Not that she didn't date a lot when I was growing up. But it was like a lioness bringing kills home for her kittens, not like she wanted them for herself."

A rueful grin up at him, her brown eyes tired and

shadowed with memories. "I guess that this counts as disclosure. I didn't have the very best role model for relationships, as a kid."

"That doesn't explain why the monk's comment bothered you so much, though."

She shrugged, and now she did begin clearing up the plates and cartons. He let her be, suspecting the words would come easier if her hands were occupied.

"Mom's about as Null as you can get. You saw how she didn't even see P.B., standing there in front of her. So I always figured my sperm donor was where it came from. Neezer was big on the whole genetic theory thing, and God knows there's no sign of it anywhere in the Valere line. And I didn't know what it was, when I was little. Only that was back when Mom made me go to Church, sort of regularly, and I was pretty sure whatever it was that let me do the things I could do, wasn't something the minister would approve of."

"Devil child."

"Yeah. So I grew up wondering if I was going to go to hell for it, especially since I pretty much used it to steal. I know better now—it's what I am, and it's natural, and it's a wonderful thing—but the early stuff is…hard to forget."

He stood with her, and she let him gather her into a hug, but he could feel the tension in her body.

"You want me to stay tonight?"

"I don't think so. I'm not going to be very good company and…let's be honest, we could use the break."

She was right, but he felt that he had to make the offer. "You going to at least try and get some sleep?"

"In this heat? All right, yeah. I'll try."

But when she kissed him at the door, a long, suggestive kiss so much better than the furtive, half-braced-against-disaster ones pre-Italy, Wren knew she wasn't going to be able to sleep. Her mother's words, stupid as they were, had shoved themselves into her brain, and they wouldn't go away.

"Thanks, Mom," she said to the empty apartment. "Because, you know, this relationship didn't have enough luggage going into it, you had to add more."

God, but it was hot in the apartment. The thought of even trying to go into her bedroom was oppressive; its normally soothing dark green-painted walls seeming to hold the heat in rather than reflect coolness the way it was supposed to. For a moment she let herself think longingly of Sergei's apartment, with its current-resistant central air, then gathered her hair into a rough braid and went into the bathroom to grab a butterfly clip to keep it off her neck. Her sundress was sticking to her back, despite it being the lightest rayon fabric she could find in her closet. Pulling it over her head with a sigh, she wadded it up and tossed it into the laundry basket, currently empty since more than half her summer wardrobe was collecting on the floor in the main room.

Dressed only in a pair of panties, Wren stretched, feeling sinews and bones crack and move back into place. Padding down the short hallway to the bedroom, she dared the enclosed space long enough to pull a sleeveless button-down shirt and a pair of cotton shorts out of the wardrobe, then ducked into her office next door to pull half a dozen books off the "history" shelf.

The books were added to the material retrieved from under the laundry and placed on the tiny tray-table next to the chair. Then she went into the kitchen and got out the jug of iced tea she had brought home with her, pulled a package of frozen Mallomars from the freezer where she had stored them during their brief on-sale season, and settled in for some research reading.

Two hours later the iced tea was gone, a half-eaten Mallomar was forgotten on top of the discarded pile of books, and Wren was curled up in the chair, a book with yellow-edged pages open on her knees, one hand marking the page while her other flipped backward to check an earlier reference.

*And the Magi came to princes of might, and worried them so that none might say no to their demands. And so a place without worship was created, under princely name but not of their authority.*

She flipped back to the page she had marked.

*The Toscana Magi refused to bow to any man, neither secular nor religious nor power, but held themselves outside all else, in their charge and their cause. And none might gainsay them, and none dared try.*

"Huh." She looked up, glaring at the heat-heavy air in front of her. "Monastery and men of God, my firmly grounded *ass.*"

*Chapter Sixteen*

"Good morning, Lowell."

His eyes narrowed suspiciously at her cheerful tone, but there wasn't anything he could say with a potential customer in the gallery. She flashed him a toothy smile, flipped her shoulder at him in a move she'd stolen from The Girl Most Likely To back in high school, and walked right past the reception area into Sergei's office, palming the entry-lock with studied nonchalance, knowing damn well that it was off-limits to lowly assistants named Lowell.

Of course it was cruel. That was the point.

"You're up and out early."

"Beating the heat. Trying to, anyway." They were predicting another ninety-degree day, making the total eleven for the month. She had slept with her windows open that night, what little she had managed to sleep, and been woken at dawn by the sound of the garbage trucks coming around. On a normal day, she would have pulled the sheet over her head and gone back to sleep, just to say screw you to the regular suited work-a-day. But the book still open on her nightstand was enough of a prod to get her up, showered—blessed cool water on her skin—and out the door. "You look like hell."

He did, too. Normally his skin was so smooth you'd swear he'd had treatments, and his ever-so-slightly-oval eyes were clear and well defined. Looking at him now, though, she could see the hints of sag in his jaw and around his mouth, and the skin under his eyes was lined with the faint red of irritation, exhaustion, or tears.

Knowing her partner, she was betting on the first.

"You tell me your news, I'll tell you mine," she said, taking her usual perch on the black leather sofa and leaning back to savor the almost-magical cool.

"It's nothing." Yep, irritation. "I just… I keep thinking something's been disturbed. But I can't find anything. And I know Lowell hasn't been in here, he's just not good enough to lie to me about that."

"You think someone's been snooping as they shouldn't?" She was too well trained to look in the direction of the current-warded safe, but her eyebrow arched in a way that transmitted her concern. Sergei tilted one hand up as though to say, "who knows?" "Probably just my imagination. Or maybe I moved something before I left and can't remember it, so that's what's making me crazy."

"Or maybe it's just the heat. Everyone's hallucinating. I saw a salamander on the way over insisting that the buildings were burping."

"Salamanders shouldn't be bothered by the heat." He frowned. "Salamanders can talk?"

"Not much and not often, but yeah." The foot-tall fatae were the only land-living creatures not desperately unhappy this summer, coming out from their usual restaurant kitchen hideaways to bask on sticky tar and boiling-hot canvas awnings.

"Learn something new every day. You've got something?"

She pulled the book out of the tan canvas bag she had dropped by her feet when she came in and handed it to him. "Where it's marked."

He opened to the page indicated by the red ribbon and skimmed. When he got to the part that had stopped her she could tell, by the way his eyes continued on for a line or three, then jerked back up as his brain processed what he had just read.

"Bells, prayers, etc. Window dressing. They may be supported by the Church, they're certainly protected by the Church, and yay for the Church keeping that stuff out of circulation—I wonder if any of them actually were priests sent there, or if they're picked for an utter lack of curiosity about what they're not supposed to be reading? And that must be why they could tell the Vatican guy where to punch his ticket. I know, we agreed yesterday that we weren't going to worry about anything except how to do the actual Retrieval. But everything they're presenting is a lie. So do we assume everything they told us was a lie, too? And if we do, I've got to rethink everything else, too."

Sergei held up a hand to indicate that she should let him finish reading, first. She settled back into the sofa, closing her eyes and trying to let the tension in her body fade away. It wasn't working. She needed a thunderstorm, bad. And if one didn't come soon, she was by God going to *make* one, and fallout be damned.

"Interesting. But it doesn't really change anything. They're arrogant and elusive with the truth, maybe, but they're still on our side, more than not. And from what you've said about the magical scent of that parchment, it's *not*."

"Mmmrrppphh. They lied."

"They're operating under a useful, passive cover. Got something to say about that, Ms. Kettle?"

"You're the kettle. *I* never pretend to be anything I'm not."

Sergei chose to not even dignify that with a response.

"You think Andre knew about this? That they weren't what they claimed to be?"

He didn't have to think about the question for long. "Assume the worst. It's usually true." Then he shook his head, rolling his chair around the desk and handing the book back to Wren. "He might have. The Silence usually does their research and does it almost obscenely well. But based on the level of Teodosio's ignorance, I could see it being so deeply unknown down the years that even a Silence review didn't catch it. Either way, Andre's promised to address the situation, and I do trust him to do that."

He paused. "Like I said, does it really matter to the job?"

Wren shrugged, putting the book away. "I don't know. Probably not. It shouldn't."

"But?"

"But there's a prickling in my thumbs."

"I trust your thumbs," Sergei said, the lines on his face deepening as he thought about the implications.

"Yeah. Me, too." She took a deep breath in, held it, let it out. "Hey, what with all the other shit flying around, it's probably the least of the prickling to come. And isn't that a cheery thought?"

"Truthfully? No." He pushed back in his chair and leaned his elbows on the desk. "You going back to the library today?"

"Not right away, no. I want Lee with me, since he seems to have the charm, and he's all tied up with his other business." Translation: he was busy with P.B., out on the street mining all the gossip coming from the moot they had attended. She had no doubt at all that, once he had an idea of how things went, they would update her. Whether she wanted them to or not.

She wasn't sure if she wanted them to or not.

"So…" She scuffed one sandal-clad foot on the carpeting, thinking about how she was going to say what she was going to say.

"So…?"

"The other reason I had to get out and about early. P.B.'s having another powwow."

"At your place? And you're letting him?"

"At my place, yeah. Because I'm supposed to be there." She shrugged away his look of surprise, feeling irritable and trapped and more than a little stupid. "They trust him. And he trusts me. So, apparently, they trust me. A little. And I hate the thought that they think maybe Talents had anything to do with what's going on."

"And you're going to be able to make them differentiate between lonejacks and Council."

"I'm going to try, anyway."

Sergei looked dubious, which was pretty much how she felt. Especially after the moot fiasco. If it had been anyone other than P.B. and Lee pulling the strings on her…

"All right. But be careful."

*And that, partner mine, was a serious* duh *statement, and from the look on your face, you know it.* "Right." She stood to go, and suddenly felt awkward as hell. Normally, before-with-capital B and that stands for Sex, she'd report in, they'd confab, she'd go on her merry way and he on his. Mostly. Now…

"I'm going to be meeting a rep for drinks tonight, probably won't be home until late. So let me know how it goes tomorrow, okay?" He was already back at his desk, mentally as well as physically. Wren swallowed a sharp, totally unexpected splash of pain in her chest. It wasn't as though she had even necessarily wanted him to come over, was it? They'd had a weekend together, and two long plane trips, and then a week sharing a bed, and it wasn't as though he was saying, "thanks been fun, now scoot." It wasn't even "I need some space, okay?" She had stuff she needed to do, and he had stuff he needed to do. And it wasn't stuff they could do together. That was all. No brush-off intended.

"Yeah. I'll check in tomorrow." She was proud of how steady her voice was. How normal.

Her sneer at Lowell on the way out was returned in full measure, since there wasn't anyone demanding his perfect-faced attention, and that made her feel a little better. He really was such an unctuous little prick.

But the moment she stepped out onto the sidewalk, any good will toward the universe fled. The sun was up in a slate-blue sky, not even a hint of clouds, and she could feel the sweat beading on her neck and face even before she started walking. The rayon sundress and sandals that had seemed so light and comfortable that morning could have been burlap for all the breeze they caught. Adding insult to injury, just as she reached the cross-town bus stop the inevitable-in-the-summer aroma of overripe garbage rose up and slapped her in the sinuses.

It never seemed to matter how often they carted trash away. There wasn't even any trash around, that she could see, just glass storefronts and sun-baked sidewalk. But the thick, putrid smell was unmistakable.

Her mother had told her stories about the trash haulers' strike, back in the 1970s. The thought of living like that for even a day made her skin crawl.

Thankfully, a bus came along and she was able to exchange the trash-scented air for the press of human flesh and overrecycled half-cooled air. It was a fair trade.

The bus let her off at the beginning of her block, and she stopped at Jackson's for a gallon of iced tea and a pound bag of M&M's. As fast as the heat was melting pounds off, that was nothing compared to the calories burned by one hot burst of current. There were ugly Talents, but there were very few fat ones.

The dark coolness of the lobby was a welcome treat, and she almost didn't mind the walk up the stairs. The air might have been stale, but thanks to Mrs. F. on the second floor the entire stairwell smelled of oranges and mozzarella, two aromas that shouldn't have blended so well but did.

"Hey." A voice came out of the shadows, a lump of greyish white in the darkness.

"Hi."

"You said something once about getting me a key?"

"I lied."

P.B. took it with good humor, rising from his cross-legged position on the floor by her door with more grace that you'd expect from a four foot demon who looked disconcertingly like a mutant polar bear standing erect.

"You gonna share those M&M's?"

"Maybe." She got her keys out and started unlocking the door. "Tell me who's coming to this shindig."

"Me. You. Eshani—he's an earth-walker. Someone to represent the air-walkers, I don't know who. Forrey." Forrey was weird but okay, she'd met him a time or two. She hadn't realized he was high up enough on the food chain to warrant inclusion. Then again, she'd never thought she would be high enough on the chain, either. "Rorani, of course. And Melanie."

Wren contemplated slamming the door shut on P.B.'s flat, furry face, but decided against it. "She gives me hives."

The demon followed her into the kitchen and hoisted

himself one-handed onto a stool. "She gives everyone hives. But the wees trust her." The wees being the smaller fatae, the generally nonaggressive ones who otherwise might be overrun or shouted down in a gathering like this. Wren could see where Melanie might come in handy in those situations.

"No angels?"

P.B. made a rude noise. "Yeah, right. Like they'd actually give a damn…. You ever read Ven Russell's *On the War in Heaven*?"

"I did, I'm surprised you have."

"Anything that disses the angels, I'm all for. Who do you think stuck us with the genus 'demons,' anyway. They think they're so damn…something."

"'Too good to dwell amongst the dross of mortal souls,'" Wren said, quoting Russell.

"Yeah. Personally, I say they can stick their attitude up their—"

"Hello?"

"It's open, come on in!"

Wren gave P.B. a "who lives here, you or me?" look that totally failed to have any impact whatsoever.

"Hello, hello. My dears, it's miserable out there. And for me to say that, it's seriously miserable out there."

Rorani was commonly referred to as the First Lady of the fatae, among the Manhattan clans. Not because she was older than them all, although she was. And not simply because she was wiser than almost anyone else, although most suspected she was. But simply because she was Rorani, which meant that she gave a damn about *everyone*.

"Genevieve. Bless you for opening your home to us this way."

"My soil is yours, Rori, same as it will ever be."

The dryad smiled acknowledgement. "Still. I know that this places you in a certain…discomfort among your own species."

"Wren being Wren does that, even without us."

"Bite me, Polar Bear." Wren had learned his actual name years ago, but nobody using human vocal cords could pronounce it without serious strain. She knew, she'd tried.

Rorani reached out one impossibly willowy arm and tapped P.B. on the nose, her oddly-jointed green fingers contrasting with his white fur and pitch-black nose. Wren blinked, but the image stayed clear and real in front of her.

*You've got to love a world where I'm going to be the normal and ordinary one in this meeting.*

Three hours later, Wren wanted to amend that thought to "normal and not insane." Even Rori, who had watched generations of squabbles from her rooting in Central Park and so should have some concept of moderation and rational thought, had raised her voice no less than three times. Two of them, unsurprisingly, to Melanie.

Eshani, a squat, grey-haired troll, had come in with a chip square on his shoulder. The fact that they were meeting in a human's apartment set him off from the start, and nothing had pleased him since. The air-walkers' rep, named Illy, was sweet-voiced but foul-mouthed, and seemed to want nothing more than to take the offensive against everything that looked cross-ways at any fatae anywhere. The fact that every time any fatae did this they ended up near-slaughtered and vilified didn't seem to have made an impact on his brain.

"And that is another thing. You say the unaffilates have nothing to do with this. But how may we know that? How may we believe that? It might all be some sort of trick."

"Forry. Give it a break, okay?" Five sets of fatae eyes turned to her, and she was sorry she'd said anything, but *honestly*. "Lonejacks? Spending that much time and energy on something that would bring them no cash value? One, maybe three or four, okay, we all have our eccentrics. But a *Cosa*-wide conspiracy against the fatae? Do you really think we're capable of sustaining that much prolonged unpaid sneakiness?"

The feathered serpent studied her, then flickered its tongue at her in what passed for a laugh among its kind. "No. It is hot, and we're all tired, and we are grasping for straws in the dark. I apologize."

"Well, I don't." Eshani crossed thick-hewed arms over his chest and glared at them both. "No humans have been killed. No human children have been taken. I see no reason to think humans are not the cause of the problem."

*I begin to understand the Council's attitude,* Wren thought uncharitably, as Illy, Forry and Eshani turned to squabble with each other again. Melanie sat back and grinned uncharitably. The gnome had been unusually silent all afternoon, which worried Wren, but she took what small mercies life gave her. Lunchtime had come and gone, but she refused to offer them real food. Cool liquids and snacks were enough to satisfy the hospitality protocols.

"Gentles, please." Rorani clapped her palms together, the sound like aspen leaves in the wind, but enough to halt everyone midsyllable. "We have been speaking for—" she cast a glance at the blank wall, seemingly able to see through the plaster and brick to the outside "—for three hours now. And in all that time we have done nothing but point and accuse and deny. The Wren says that the unaffiliates have had nothing to do with the troubles we have been experiencing. Is there any reason to doubt her word?"

"She does not speak for them all." Melanie, coming in to cause trouble just in the nick of time.

"No one speaks for them all. You have all heard of their moots."

*They had?* Wren suspected that they hadn't heard what was discussed in the most recent moot. If they had, the tone of this afternoon might have been a little different. She was tempted to tell them...but only in passing. There was that much truth in their distrust— the *Cosa* was the *Cosa* only against the Nulls. Within, it was...well, a lot like this powwow, actually. Lots of sniping and snarling and the occasional moment of humor and involuntary trauma-bonding.

*And here I used to think that I was an only child.*

"Someone's coming." Illy sat upright, what Wren knew was a sign of distress or anger among fatae of his type, and his scales shimmered faintly in anxiety. "Someone human."

Wren glanced at P.B., who had just come back in from the kitchenette with a refill of iced tea. He shrugged, not having heard anything. But Illy's irritation was real, so Wren hauled herself up from her cross-legged seat and went into the hallway. Anything to get away from the fatae for a moment. She was starting to get a headache, a coil of intense pressure between her eyes that any moment was going to turn into an icepick, she just knew it. The temptation to let loose with an equal spike of current, to try and release the pressure, was, well, tempting. Stupid—pain-release was damned difficult to control and typically rebounded—but tempting. The moment she kicked everyone out—which was going to be soon, manners or no—she was going to turn on the new jazz CD she'd just picked up, put her feet up, and soothe her severely frazzled core with a nice, slow, steady drain off the building. Okay, maybe not her building. The one across the street had a much better—

A sharp, impatient knock on the door interrupted her thoughts.

"Ah, hell." Looks like Illy had been right.

She opened the door, and had to step back or be run over as a slender, elegantly dressed woman moved into the apartment with the irresistible force of a well-mannered hurricane.

"Madame. This is…unexpected."

Unexpected was one word for it. Wren felt her current bristling like a cat's back when another feline decides to stroll into its territory. Which, in point of fact, was exactly what had just happened.

KimAnn Howe. The very very quietly acknowledged head of the East Coast Mage's Council—the actual Council that led the group the *Cosa* referred to *in toto* as the Council. One of the most powerful Mages in the entire country, and probably in the top twenty-five worldwide.

In Wren's apartment.

In Wren's apartment, not ten steps away from fatae leaders who were already convinced the Council was out to destroy them.

*What?* Wren demanded of the Heavens. *What did I do to you?*

"Is this a bad time?" KimAnn was barely as tall as Wren herself, but with twice—all right, Wren admitted it, ten times the presence. White-haired and regal, she had a direct gaze and skin that was still smooth as a woman half her age. She was by reputation also an excellent poker player, so her patently disingenuous expression was meant to convey to Wren that she knew exactly what was going on and that was why she was there and she wanted to see how Wren was going to handle it.

So Wren did the only thing she could do.

"Hey, guys! Look who stopped by to meet with y'all!"


"You're a brave woman."

"I'm an idiot. But I was an idiot without any other choices."

"You could have killed her. We would have helped you hide the body."

"Gee, thanks." But Wren smiled as she said it. Melanie had dived into the silence that greeted KimAnn's appearance with a snide comment that KimAnn had fielded so swiftly even the gnome was impressed. And that had gotten things off to a suitably rocky start.

Two hours, seven minutes and a seriously pounding headache later, Wren was pretty sure that she hated everyone at this point, and was willing to send then all to the devil, P.B. included, since the furry turncoat had said something about having a client to meet and scooted out the kitchen window the moment KimAnn was introduced.

"Anyone who is still here in three minutes is going to find themselves standing in the dark, listening to me snore," she announced suddenly. Since the only ones left were Melanie and Rorani, Wren wasn't too worried about not being taken seriously. Rory was only there because Melanie hadn't left yet; she would escort the gnome out, forcibly if need be.

"Because, y'know, I'd hate to have to go around saying that a Council member knew when to leave and the fatae didn't."

"Except the demon."

"The demon will get his comeuppance later. Mel, that wasn't a hint, that was a sledgehammer."

"All right, all right, no need to twig-march me out, Rorani." The gnome held up iron-hard arms in a gesture of protest, then stopped for a moment and stared at Wren, which was attention of the sort Wren didn't want, to go with her headache. "You are brave. Stupid, but brave."

"That's the second time in a week someone's said that to me."

"Maybe you need to think about that, then."

"Don't you dare go Yoda on me, Mel. Rory, get her the hell out of here."

Finally alone, Wren locked up behind them and rested her forehead against the door, her hands palms down on the wood as though bracing against someone coming back. The words to an old song came to her mind, suddenly, about the Catholics hating the Protestants and the Hindus hating the Moslems, and everyone hating the Jews. Tom Lehrer, "National Brotherhood Week," that was it. That was what this city was turning into. The fatae hated the humans and the Council hated the lonejacks and everyone, it felt like, hated *her*.

*Why me, Lord? I ask again, why me?*

It wouldn't be so bad, she thought, maybe, if she could figure out what they wanted. Ideally something she could go out and Retrieve without too much stress, and maybe even get paid for it. Something that didn't have unknown and maybe Upstairs Neighbor mojo on it. At the very least, to get the fatae out of her hair and never, ever please God ever have a Council member show up just to show that, fumigation or no fumigation, she didn't have any damn secrets in this town.

But it all seemed to circle around to being respected, and the fact that respect had to be earned and freely given wasn't something either side wanted to hear. They wanted theirs without having to sacrifice anything. And

God help anyone who told them that the world just didn't work that way.

Sometimes, she thought wryly, you just have to duck and cover. And next time she was sneaking out the kitchen window with P.B.

A

h
X    t
   a    H

      x   aT    h
ħ ter
         Qx
   Cha         k th
    q    H    K
       h   k
q H   *Chapter Seventeen*

"You know their entire complaint is bullshit."

The client's voice was equally reasonable. "It may be bullshit but it's public bullshit. And I don't want anything public involved in this deal."

Once, "Wren" had just been a nickname. Then it had become a title. Now, thanks to the Council's damned games, it was becoming a byword. Sergei was not happy with that turn of events, but he didn't see how he could stop it. As shown by her reception in Italy, of all places, his partner was getting a profile to go with her reputation. Not good. Of all the problems he had foreseen getting into this business, being chased into early retirement by success wasn't one he'd thought he'd have to deal with.

On the other hand, there was no bit of bad news that wasn't useful to *someone,* somehow.

"Michael." Sergei slipped into French almost unconsciously, his tone reasonable and persuasive at the same time. "Think of it. The perfect cover. While everyone knows that you cannot, will not hire a Retriever who is under such scrutiny, others will be waiting for you to hire another. And then, voilà, The Wren goes forward and performs the Retrieval while others are waiting for you to make your move."

"Mmmm."

That wasn't a "get out of my face" mmmm, so Sergei let the client mull it over by himself.

He'd had such a marvelous meeting the night before, Wren seemed back on track with the current situation, and it was only supposed to be in the upper eighties today. If Michael would only see reason, he could call it an excellent day, and it wasn't even five o'clock yet.

"Boss?"

Sergei's hand came up, index finger pointing in the international "out!" sign. Lowell opened his mouth to say something and the finger repeated the movement with emphasis. The door closed behind him with a distinctly if impossibly peevish sound.

"Michael. You know that I am right."

"Mmmm. You are always right. It's quite annoying."

"So, we are in agreement?"

"Maybe. I'll get back to you."

Sergei stared at his mobile as though trying to force Michael back on the line, then shook his head and closed the phone with a quiet snap.

"Lowell."

The door slid open far too quickly for Lowell to have

been more than an inch away from the control. "What have I told you about my office?"

"I didn't go inside. I just opened the door." He could have been more petulant, but he probably would have had to regress back to five years old to do it.

"And you've never come inside?"

"You said you'd fire me if I ever did."

"So if you did, you'd lie to me about it?"

"You said you'd fire me if I did that, too."

Sergei glared at Lowell, then gave up. Lowell was a lot of things, many of them annoying, but he had always been trustworthy. That was why Sergei had hired him in the first place.

"You've never crossed that doorway."

"Never."

"And you resent that."

The look Lowell gave him was half incredulous, half furious. "Yes. I resent it. But you're the boss."

"That's right, I am. What did you want, Stephen?"

"Mrs. Rehoney called about the pickup this weekend. She wanted to know if you were going to be here when she came by. I wasn't sure if you had other plans or not—" the look on Lowell's face made Sergei's palm itch to slap it off, and he curled his fingers into his palm to keep the impulse from traveling up to his brain "—so I thought I'd pass her question along to you. In case you decided to grace us with your presence."

Somehow, Sergei didn't know how, assistant radar maybe, Lowell knew that his relationship with Wren had changed, and was...not jealous. He was pretty sure his assistant didn't think of either of them that way. But there was definitely property issues going on with both of them, and like two cats in one territory, there was too much hissing going on for a sane man to think when they went at it.

"I'll be here," he said abruptly. "Close up the shop will you? I'm out of here." He touched the screen to shut down his computer, and stood up, noting that Lowell was still standing in the doorway looking at him. "What?"

"Nothing."

"Good."

Lowell was an average-sized guy, but Sergei always felt uncomfortable around him, as though he might break if anyone hit up against him in the commuting crush. Now, he seemed even more slight, standing there clearly wanting to say something but—for once in his career—not able to open his mouth.

*Oh.*

"And we can talk about your review on Saturday morning, too. If that's okay with you?"

"Yeah. Yeah, that'd be fine."

Sergei nodded, getting his suit jacket out of the closet where it was neatly hung up, and shrugging into it. He would be sweating the moment he stepped outside, unless a miracle had occurred and the temperature had dropped, but he felt undressed in shirtsleeves.

"I'll see you tomorrow then." He moved Lowell out of the doorway by the simple expedient of moving through the doorway and closing the door behind him.

"And Stephen?" When he had his assistant's attention, he looked him in the eye and shook his head ever so slightly. "Whatever it is? Get over it. She's not going anywhere."

He escaped into the heat while Lowell was still spluttering. *That was cruel. Fun, but cruel.* Wren actually enjoyed Lowell's hissing and spitting, at least enough to make her taunt him even worse, and yeah, now he knew where Lowell's mood came from.

"Damn the woman, anyway." But still. They'd enough hints already that the relationship was not going to be easy sailing. If he could take one potential annoyance out of the way, he would. Even if it meant paying Lowell what he was actually worth.

And with that thought he took his mobile out again and hit speed dial, thinking that he hadn't wanted to go back to his apartment just yet. Not alone, anyway.

Marianna's was busy, even though they relied on ceiling fans instead of air-conditioning, and as always the tables were far too close to each other for truly private conversation. The food was that good. Wren had a moment's mournful regret for the days before Zagats spilled the beans, and you never had to wait for a table. "Hey."

Callie looked up from the hostess stand's display, then did a double take. "Welcome back, stranger."

"Yeah, I know, I know. Been a while."

"Too long. Someone else is at your table."

Wren feigned a heart attack, and the waitress laughed. "You want I should kick them out?"

"Nah. I'll let 'em trespass this once. Just don't put us in the window, okay? The man would freak." Neither of them were comfortable being on display, but Sergei had an almost pathological dislike of being anywhere near ground-level windows. Having been exposed to just a hint of what life was like within the Silence, Wren thought she could maybe understand his paranoia a little better now.

"No problem. I'll shuffle reservations a little."

There were, Wren thought comfortably as she waited at the bar, real benefits to being a regular, even if they'd been absent most of the summer. Being greeted when you walked in the door, even it was with Callie's professional Manhattan waitress rough-edged affection, gave the most deflated ego a boost.

"*Buona sera, bella,*" Nate greeted her, passing a glass of ginger ale over cracked ice across the bar to her.

"*Buona sera, signore,*" she responded, a little more confident in her accent now than last time he'd tried to coax her into responding. From the delighted grin that took over his face, it *was* better.

"You have been practicing! *Bene, molto bene.* So where is the tall and snarky one?"

"On his way. Yes, for once I'm actually here before he is. Mark it down in the books." She tilted her head a little in order to look at Nate's watch. Sergei was punctual to the point of being obsessive about it, and she…wasn't, generally. So where was he?

The door opened behind her, heralded by a wave of warm air.

"Hey there."

She always knew when Sergei was around. Even without the tea-making instinct, something in her nerve endings just *knew.* She had always written it off to the amount of sampling she had done off him, the number of times she had used him to ground in, the most recent incident in the monastery the most extreme of those. Only now it had the added *whoa* of remembering what that mouth felt like on her skin, that skin under her fingertips, that…

*If you go much further down those memories, we're not going to make it past appetizers.*

"We've been downgraded," she told him, turning around and looking up at him. "Apparently, they only hold a table for two months, and then you're back to peon status."

"So long as we're not—"

"By the window. Taken care of."

He'd gotten a haircut. Damn. Although it wasn't as short as it had been before—she guestimated that she could still get a decent grip on it, which was all that mattered. And he had—

"Oh."

"I had no idea what you liked. Which is a terrible thing to have to admit. But I thought these were nice."

"They are. Oh, they are." Wren took the spray of freesia he handed her and sniffed at one delicate bloom to hide the sudden, embarrassing rush of water to her eyes. Nobody had ever given her flowers before.

"Table's ready." Callie saw the flowers in Wren's hand,

and blinked. "You want a vase for that? Won't last 'til you get home, otherwise."

"Yes, please, thank you," Wren said. Callie'd had a crush on Sergei from the first time Wren had brought him here. But she was dealing well with the whole flowers-for-someone-else, so Wren hoped the new situation wasn't going to affect service. She would really, really hate to have to stop coming here, and not just because it was so convenient to her apartment.

"Damn. If I'd thought of that I would have gotten you the rubber frog I saw, instead. Didn't smell as nice but it had a special reservoir that made it self-wetting."

Callie exchanged a long-suffering look with Wren, then pointedly turned her back on them and walked away, clearly expecting them to follow her like goslings to their table. So they did.

"So, you had a good meeting last night?"

"I think so, yes. The artist is an impossible brat, reportedly, but the agent seems reasonable, and I think we'll be able to work out a mutually acceptable deal that will make everyone a nice sum of money if the market responds."

"And if the market holds its collective nose?"

"Then we all take a moderate bath."

"I think I prefer my job to yours. At least when we stick to the rules."

"House rules, or lonjeack's rules, or...?"

"Yes."

House rules were their own guidelines: know the client's agenda. Know all the details of the situation before you go in. Get paid up front. Lonejack rules were even simpler. Get in. Get out. Don't get caught up in the Council's games.

They'd been criminally negligent of all the rules, lately.

Callie came back with a basket of fresh bread and two menus. "Do you need to look at these? It's been a while, you may not remember what's in them."

"Okay, how long is it going to take before you forgive us for eating in other places?"

"I'll let you know."

Sergei took the menus from her, and handed one across the table to Wren, who didn't bother to open it. She'd scanned the blackboard specials when she came in and made her decision already.

"I've remembered something, the past few weeks."

"Oh?" He had put on his reading glasses to look at the menu, and the sight sent a familiar surge of lust through her. God, she was so easy. He wasn't even *trying*.

"Yeah. I hate working through other people. I don't play well with others. Never did."

He took his glasses off, folded them, and put them away in his inner jacket pocket. "I warned you what this was going to be like." Working with the Silence, he meant.

"Yeah, I know you did. And I thought I could handle it." She extended her fingers, then flexed them, a pretty good sign of intense frustration. "I *can* handle it. I just have to be prepared. We weren't. We were distracted and off balance and ungrounded, and we got ourselves burned. That ends now."

Callie came back to take their order, standing in

classic waitress mode, hips cocked, pad and pencil ready. If this had been a less classy joint, she would have been cracking her gum.

"The scampi linguini, please," Sergei told her.

"The veal special," Wren said. "And a Diet Pepsi."

Callie gave them both a careful once-over, as though wanting to ask who they were and what they had done with the real Wren and Sergei, but finally decided against it. But Wren noticed that she was definitely shaking her head and muttering to herself as she went through the gated doors into the kitchen.

They had both ordered something different. Radically different, even. Poor Callie. She said as much to Sergei, who looked surprised, then thoughtful. "I'm sure there's some deep psychological reason for it all."

"Her surprise, or us shaking things up?"

"I meant the latter, but yes, the former, too. And speaking of shaking things up. You were saying—what? That you want to end the agreement with the Silence?" Sergei sounded—not dubious, Wren thought, but as though he were already plotting. Which he probably was. That was his specialty.

"No. We have a contract. We're going to honor the contract, at least until they give us a legal cause to break it."

"Good. I could get us out of it, yeah, but it would get sticky. And probably ugly in follow-up once word got out to other potential clients, which you know it would. So what, then?" He was listening. Good. She needed him to follow her, now.

"They caught us off balance once. Not again. Next time they try to yank chains, we dig our heels in and don't go anywhere until we're satisfied with the briefing. And if Andre doesn't like it, he can go sit and spin. But that's tomorrow. Today we're still screwed."

"Okay, a given that we went into this bass ackward. What's the status?"

Wren reached into her bag and pulled out a small notebook. She had bought it on the street that afternoon and spent a few hours putting her thoughts into order. Brainpower was for thinking, not storage. Let Sergei memorize statistics and details. She had paper and pen.

# Chapter Eighteen

The cafeteria had long, glossy wooden tables, comfortably padded chairs, and huge windows that nobody ever looked out of. Poul picked at his steak tartar, chasing the bits of meat around the plate.

"If you didn't want it, why did you order it?" Andre asked reasonably, finishing a bit of his own catfish filet.

"I was in the mood for raw meat."

The older man raised an eyebrow at that, but left it alone. Perhaps the weekend movie plans did not go as well as planned. "You need to eat some of it, or Christian—" the chef "—will be insulted."

"Christian will survive." Poul put down his fork and made as though to push back from the table. "If you don't mind, I think I will go back to the office. I'm not as hungry as I thought I was."

"Wait a moment and I will go with you." He was almost

finished, anyway. And the looks that they were getting from several members of Research & Dissemination across the room were making him lose any interest in dessert, no matter how good it had looked when they came in.

"All right."

It was closer to ten minutes by the time Andre felt comfortable leaving—he didn't want anyone to think that they had chased him out. And having Poul sitting there clearly waiting for him was a good reinforcement of his authority of his own people.

But halfway to the elevator, Andre stopped and waved Poul on. "Why don't you go on and get started on whatever it is you were working on. Duncan. A moment, if you please?"

Andre could almost hear the hearts stop beating around him, and let himself enjoy the shock wave for half a second before moving to intercept his quarry. You didn't go looking for Operations. He came looking for you. But Duncan had already done that, so what did Andre have to lose? That would certainly give them all something to really gossip about.

"Yes?" From Duncan's smooth expression, you would think they were being introduced for the first time at a cocktail party.

"Get Alessandro off my back."

Ops' expression didn't change, but his Adam's apple moved ever so slightly above the open neck of his shirt. "I beg your pardon?"

"You're watching us all too closely, and it's making him jumpy. Jumpy makes mistakes. We can't afford any mistakes now." Andre didn't say anything further—nothing about the unease he sensed in Sergei's reports, the tension building within the building, the fact that the FocAs Darcy had brought to him hadn't known anything about any of the questions put to him.

Andre didn't trust such complete ignorance. Information insisted on getting free, no matter what anyone did or said. So if it wasn't free yet, someone had buried it deep. And nobody buried anything that deep unless it was very, very bad.

His job was to make the bad stuff go away. Be damned if anyone within the Silence wanted it to stay buried. That wasn't what they did.

"I see."

And, since this was Duncan, he probably did.

"I'll see what I can do."

Andre watched Duncan collect his lunch companions and walk into the cafeteria, only now aware of the pain in his back where he had overtightened the muscles between his shoulders.

He nodded once, as though he had gotten exactly what he expected, then continued on to the elevator, sweeping his assistant along with him, and ignoring everyone along the way. As the doors closed in front of them, mercifully alone in the elevator car, Poul let out a low whistle that could have been relief or respect or both.

But where his assistant seemed to think things had gone well, Andre was not so certain. He had challenged Duncan. In public. And Duncan had backed down.

That worried Andre. A great deal.

They thought he knew something. Or had something. Something important to their plans, whatever those plans were.

And if they thought he had it, odds were that he did. Only he had no idea what it was.

That worried Andre most of all.

*"I never said you were stupid. I said you were an idiot!"* The crash of plates on the table.

Silverware rattled. *"If that's the way you feel, why are you still here?"*

*"Because you're a halfway decent lay."*

Lawrence winced. They'd been so angry at each other, trying to score the killing shot. The rest of the meal had been eaten in silence, each of them fuming, looking for that next perfect comeback. It was too hot, that's all. Too hot, and the apartment's air-conditioning shot to hell again, and the smallest thing started a fight that escalated because they literally couldn't cool down.

He'd escaped to work, but the renovations in the library meant the air-conditioning was off.

He shifted a pile of invoices to one side, wiping the back of his neck. It was hot even down here, even without the overhead lights on. You'd have thought that being underground would cool things off, but no, even the basement was disgusting.

If he'd a choice, all this could go hang until September. November, even. But they were supposed to open in three weeks, which meant that all the stuff they'd put away during the renovations had to be back out and in perfect audience-ready condition, and the storage areas were a cataloging disaster. It shouldn't have been his problem—he hadn't been the one to screw up the storage in the first place—but Stacy had quit last month, and they didn't have the funds to replace her yet.

"Yet. Hah." For that, translate "ever." They'd spent all their money on the renovations. Hiring anyone new on staff would require a major money transfusion, and there just weren't that many donors around. Not like in the roaring '80s, like the boss was always grousing about.

"Stupid, stupid, stupid."

*"I said you were an idiot!"*

Why did he keep remembering that? It had been a bad fight, yeah, but nothing worse than usual. Tonight he'd stop by the store and pick up some ice cream, and he'd be forgiven. After some groveling, anyway. And he'd forgive her for what she'd said. Probably.

Lawrence frowned, his hands stilling as he sorted through the next batch of invoices. Why had he thought that? Of course he would forgive her. He loved her. They were just both of them stubborn, that was all. And it was too damn hot.

*"God, just go, okay? Get the hell out of here!"*

That had been earlier this week…no, the week before, when it hadn't gone below eighty degrees even at night. That hadn't even been a fight, just her being grumpy. So why was he replaying all the uglier bits now? The fight itself had left him sick, shaking with anger and fear that she really would get out, go away and not come back this time. But now, thinking about it, it was almost like he…like he had *enjoyed* it. Enjoyed the look on her face, the snarling anger in his gut, even the pain when she'd slammed the door behind her.

Lawrence got up to walk around. Maybe working down here had been a mistake. But everywhere else, even now, was filled with dust and a stifling heat. The basement had seemed smarter—nothing was being done down here, and the fire doors were of a heavy enough metal to keep the dust out from all the work upstairs. And it was cooler, being a full story below ground level. But now the place was starting to freak him out.

"The boss swears this place was haunted. You there, Ghost? This is a library, so you behave, okay?"

"*Idiot. Idiot. Idiot.*"

He shook his head violently, trying to get the sound of his own voice out of his head. "Right. One more box, and then I'm out of here. I don't care how much the boss bitches."

Sitting back down at the makeshift desk, made of a folding table and an old leather chair that should have been thrown out years ago, Lawrence picked up the papers he had been going through and tried to focus on them again. But now the lamp, which he had chosen because it had a cooler, low-wattage bulb and positioned it in perfect reading distance, was starting to annoy him.

In fact, he was pretty much annoyed at everything. From his idiot girlfriend to this inane weather to his nutcase of a boss who had to have everything done exactly on schedule and God help you if you ran over. Because this place was going to have such an influx of visitors when it reopened, yeah. Boss had delusions of being the New York Historical Society, or something, Lawrence thought. And that just wasn't gonna happen. Nobody cared about a bunch of moldy old manuscripts and paintings that didn't get written up in the Arts section of the *Times*. That was just reality.

"Fuck this. I'm out of here."

He threw the papers back down on the table and pushed back the chair, coming up against a pile of boxes that were stacked behind him, waiting for the end of renovations so they could be replaced in their proper rooms.

In his hurry to get upstairs, into the heated but unspooky air, Lawrence didn't notice that, even after he turned off the light, one of the smaller boxes in that pile was emitting a faint, almost luminescent glow through a crack in the lining.

And humming, in what sounded almost like human satisfaction.

The flowers dipped slightly to the left, perfuming the table over the smell of their dessert. The restaurant had emptied and refilled while they were eating, the low murmur of conversation sounding almost like the backdrop of violins.

"Explain to me again about these old ones. We're not talking *Cthulhu* or anything, are we? Are we?"

Wren pushed the remains of her lemon tart around on her plate, sorry she had ever tried to explain any of this to her partner. "*Cthulhu* isn't real, it's just some really wacked-out guy dealing with his personal hallucinations. We've been over this." But he could almost hear the smile in her voice. "Okay. Fine. No, they're not of the Lovecraftian variety, not so's anyone's ever told me. But nobody tells you much about them, period."

"Lots of things you guys don't talk about. Old Ones, Upstairs Neighbors, dark spaces…"

The smile went away in an instant. "Names have power. That much of the old magic was true. Still is true." That was why she never minded people misusing her name. And why he didn't use her birth name except when he really, really needed her complete attention.

"And that's another thing I don't understand. What's the difference between current and old—" He stopped when he saw the expression on her face. "Okay, let's make it simple. What's the difference between magic and magic?"

She actually cracked a smile at that, shaking her head. "Depends on who you ask. And when you ask them. And who you are that's asking." Now it was his turn to make a face. "All right. Same as the difference between, oh, solar and tidal power. Same result, mostly, but different sources."

"But both better than oil?"

"Everyone can use oil. Got to have the right conditions, right abilities for the others."

"Don't get technical on me, woman."

"Excuse me?" The fork poked at him accusingly. "You're the one who started dissecting technicalities. Anyway. The truth is there's not a lot of difference in the energy. It's all about usage. And results. Current can be qualified, quantified. Sort of. You do A, you'll get B. Pretty much every time, if you can do it the first time."

"Skill sets."

She shrugged. "Yeah. Some things you're better at, some things, not. With old-style magic, the accuracy's not so good. You're calling it down but not directing it. And damn little real grounding."

"And Old Ones, which aren't Lovecraftian Old Ones?"

Wren didn't even bother to sigh. He was just yanking her chain, and she wouldn't give him the satisfaction of a response. "Old magic-based creatures who were— are—totally grounded. Not fond of humans. And really disgustingly powerful. As much rumor as anything else." No need to tell him everything. One of them should be able to sleep at night. "The Neighbors, now they're real. Dying out, for the most part, but real. "

"Any relation to the 'Good Neighbors' of lore and legend?"

Wren snorted at that. "Nothing 'good' about them. Humans, trying to placate the implacable."

"And you think this thing came from them?"

"It's a theory. A weak-ass, no reason to believe it theory, but all I've got, right now. Either that or a magic-user, pre-electrical age, who managed to summon up enough current to create this, without anyone ever noticing. And trust me, the *Cosa*? Generally notices that kind of current use. Especially back then."

Sergei finished off the wine in his glass. "Have we said yet that we hate this job?"

She made an expansive gesture. "Feel free."

"I hate this job."

"Yeah."

He had just handed his credit card to Callie when the sound of a bird chirping filled the silence. He took out the cell phone with an irritated grunt, looked at the number displayed, and tapped the answer button. "Didier."

Wren leaned back in her chair and watched him. From the reaction, he didn't know who was calling him, but it was something he knew about…work. But not something he was expecting. So odds were…

"He wants to talk to you."

Odds were it was someone she'd given his number to. Which meant…

"Sorry," she mouthed to him, taking the phone gingerly. "Yes?"

A torrent of speech exploded into her ear, and she winced. "Slow down. What?" Another torrent, and she made some sense of what he was saying.

"Right. No! Don't do anything. And don't touch anything. We'll be there. Don't look! Put it down and we'll be there as soon as we can."

She turned off the phone and closed it, handing it back to Sergei.

"That was Haven at the library. He's found something."

"Something being…" He was already rising out of his chair, signaling Callie to bring the receipt posthaste.

"Haven't a clue. But he sounded seriously wigged."

"I noticed that, yes." Callie brought over the black

folder, and Sergei scrawled his name, adding a tip and putting the receipt and credit card back into his wallet. "So we're just going to run over there and dash headlong into haven't-a-clue?"

"Pretty much, yeah."

"It's too dangerous. Damn it, Wren, you're a—" He realized that his voice had raised, and he moderated it, following her out of the restaurant. A woman stared at him, and he gave back his very best curt "what the hell are you looking at?" nod. She looked back at her dinner, not at all abashed, and he went out the door, catching up with Wren on the sidewalk. Night had fallen, and white lights and neon lit the street.

"You're a thief, not a goddamned hero."

"Always finish the job." His mantra, hammered into her from the very first day they'd worked together. Always follow through on the situation. Always seal the deal. Always finish the job.

"Damn it." Sergei stepped into the street and raised one arm, trying to hail a cab.

"We don't have time for that." She didn't know why, but the sense of urgency was rising in her. "If he found it, so easy, then something's going to happen. Something bad." Pieces started to fall not so much into place as into a pattern, random snippets of information coming together and trying to get her attention.

*The moot. The attacks. The Council. The manuscript. All coming here, happening here. I believe in coincidence. I also believe in fate. There's a hate in this city that would draw this thing.*

"We need to be there *now*." She grabbed his hand, and felt him wince. "Don't panic, I'm not going to Transloc. I don't need to." Her free hand raised to the skies, fingers outstretched, and then she clenched them tightly, suddenly.

And a cab turned the corner and stopped as though jerked on puppet strings in front of them. The "off duty" light mounted on the top of the roof sparked and went out.

"Get in."

The cabbie looked a little frazzled, but Wren was too focused on what was churning inside to worry about it.

*The vigilantes stepping up their attacks. The Council stepping up their attitude. Lonejacks getting aggressive. And this into the middle of it. Old magics. Talents powerful enough to bend old-time Popes into compliance. Stuff that's been stored so long it's been forgotten. My city. All in my damn city… I believe in coincidence, but sometimes it really is an enemy attack.*

As the cab pulled away and moved into traffic, a short, stocky figure stepped out of the thick grey shadows of the alley and stared after them, then moved in a determined pace down the street, slipping down the stairs into the subway station.

And a heartbeat later, another figure seemed to rise up from the sidewalk itself, its actions far more sinuous, seemingly boneless, and followed the second figure down into the subway.

A moment later the rumble of a train coming into the station underfoot could be heard, then the sound of it departing, heading uptown.

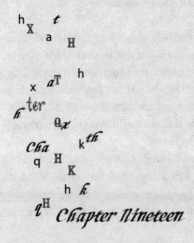

# Chapter Nineteen

The library looked even more beautiful in moonlight. The streetlights merely picked up the high points of the black wrought iron fence and the white marble steps, the narrow leaded glass windows and nineteenth-century architecture now restored to almost glistening cleanliness. It wouldn't last long—no matter how much better the air quality, exhaust and pigeons would have their due. But for the moment, Wren could almost pretend the building was brand-new, innocent, empty and waiting.

The only thing it actually was, was waiting. It certainly wasn't empty. And it wasn't innocent.

"You okay?"

She had shivered, even in the summer heat, the moment her soles had touched the steps. If she said yes, she was lying, and he would know she was lying. If she said no, he'd get all senior partner and protective and…

*Trust him, Jenny-Wren.* A familiar voice, soft and well spoken, and gone from her life if not her mind for all the years she had known Sergei. Her mentor, Neezer. The wisest man she had ever known. If her psyche was using his voice—she couldn't bear to think he was still aware enough to reach her in actuality and not call her physically—she was going to listen.

"Scared shitless. Something's in there. And awake."

Sergei stopped, as she'd known he would. "And it knows you're coming?"

"Maybe. I don't know how aware it actually is, or what it's aware of."

"We should—"

"We should go in. Now. Haven is in there waiting for us."

"Suckin sin."

"Okay, what was that last one?" She might not have been good at languages, but swearwords had their own poetry, especially in Russian.

"Something my mother would wash both our mouths out with soap if she heard me using. All right, *boi-baba*, let's go."

"Not we. Me." The words came out of her mouth before she had a chance to think about them. Or even be aware she was saying them. "You think it's dangerous? Damn straight. Even more so for you than me. You stay here." The current-core was stirring inside her, reacting to the presence of danger, and she could almost feel the tendrils reaching up to lick at her awareness of Sergei beside her. She'd taken him on jobs before. He'd been useful in dangerous spots before. But what she was feeling in that building was every nerve ending and bad juju feeling she'd ever experienced all wrapped up into a tight little ball of nerves and there wasn't a damn thing even an alert and aware Null like Sergei could do against that except get in the way.

"Anything else stupid you want to get out of your system now?"

"Sergei…"

"There may be civilians in there," he said reasonably, already walking up the stairs. She was forced to take the low steps two at a time to catch up with him before he put his hand to the door. "You'll need help getting them out."

It was a bullshit excuse, but it might also be true. And as much as she didn't want to take him in there, she didn't want to go in alone, either. Current hissed and seethed, and she reached down inwardly to cup it to her, bathing herself in the comforting sparks. If only she could share this with him, without burning him, inside *or* out….

The door was open. They stepped inside to the darkness, only intermittent security lights along the floor and walls cutting the dim visibility.

"Where to now?"

"Ms. Valere?"

They both jumped slightly, Sergei's right hand moving instinctively to where his holster would have been, if he'd had any foresight whatsoever. Wren hated that chunk of cold blue metal, but its presence here tonight might have been a comfort, despite the violence and death she could feel on it.

"Yeah, who—oh." It was Heather, the intern who had shown her around that first visit.

"Mr. Haven called me. He…he wanted me to stay here and get you."

The child was clearly terrified, her lovely eyes darting frantically back and forth, and Wren had a passing wonder if this place called Talented bloodlines to it, or it was something endemic to the profession of librarians as a whole, that they saw what others blithely passed on by. Either way, there was no reason to take this girl any closer to the source.

"Just tell us. And then go home."

Heather nodded enthusiastically, and led them down an unlit hallway, the flashlight in her hand jinking when she started at any unknown noise. She brought them to a metal door, and stood there, clearly uncertain.

"The basement, I presume?" Wren said.

The intern nodded. "Here," and she tried to hand Wren the flashlight. "I don't know if the lights are working down there or not."

"You keep it," she told the girl. "Now go!"

Smart girl, she didn't need to be told twice, disappearing back down the hall and leaving them standing in deep, red-tinged shadows.

"You know, every horror movie ever made says this is a bad idea."

"Jesus, Serg." She didn't want to go into the basement either. Not stupid her, no. But. "Finish the job. Finish the job. Finish the job."

She reached out and opened the door. It slid on its

hinges easily, with no ominous creaking or squeaking, and no jumping-out of bogeymen. With a subtle but almost identical squaring of their shoulders, they moved down the stairs—uncreepy, well-lit, really easy to walk on stairs, she noted with relief, envisioning a need to make a panicked flight back up those same stairs and breaking her neck when she fell. A turn on the landing, and they came out into a huge, high-ceilinged space filled with freestanding metal shelves that were in turn filled with boxes of varying sizes, shapes and stages of unpacking.

"Um. Hi."

Haven was seated at a rickety-looking folding table that had clearly been put to use as a temporary desk of sorts. There was one lamp behind him, and the white light cast on his face created an unhealthy pallor. Or maybe he really was that pale.

"Oh. God." The full force of it struck her, and Wren was pretty sure her face had gone as white as his. Maybe even more. With his tangential and untrained skills, it was probably like a stiff breeze off a charnel house. For her, it was like being dumped headfirst into the pit itself.

"What?" she managed to get out.

"One of the staff was working down here." His voice was calmer than it had been on the phone, but Wren didn't trust that calm. It sounded suspiciously like tightly restrained hysterics, all thin and reedy and not really trusting itself. "It was cooler down here. So he brought a bunch of materials to work on. Which he shouldn't have done. Not that it matters anymore, things have been so moved around anyway. But he was okay when he went down here and when he came up, I saw him as he was leaving and he looked like hell. Said nothing was wrong but obviously something was. So I thought maybe he'd screwed something up and I came down to look over what he'd been doing. And…" Haven looked at Wren, and even in the limited lighting she could see that his eyes were wide and white-rimmed. "It was laughing at me."

"Laughing?"

"That." A lift of his chin, just enough to indicate the box on the desk in front of him. It looked like one of those clear plastic shoe boxes Wren's mother used to keep old photographs in, except it was tinted green.

Except, as she watched, Wren realized it wasn't tinted. It was glowing.

"Green glows are never good things," Sergei said with a heavy dose of Russian fatalism in his voice that she would have laughed at any other time.

"It *felt* like what you described," Haven went on. "And I opened the lid and…well, that's when I called you."

"I love working with smart people," Wren said with heartfelt sincerity.

"It wants me to read it."

"I bet it does. You haven't, right?" Of course he hadn't. He was still here. A little shredded, but here.

"Looked, glanced at it, really, didn't read." He pushed back a little from the desk, and Wren saw that there was an old-fashioned vanity mirror behind him, mounted in a dark wood frame. "Mirror to mirror." And he picked up a silver-backed hand mirror off the table, his hand shaking enough so that the light from the lamp caught its surface and reflected directly into Wren's eyes. She flinched away, body and current anticipating an attack that didn't come.

*On edge, much? It's just light. It's just a manuscript. If you don't read it, you're okay.* But now that he had mentioned it, she did feel the faintest pull to pick the parchment out of the box and hold it, to look at it, to learn its secrets.

"Might be it. Might not." Sergei's voice next to her was reassuringly solid, and she grounded herself in it as best she could.

"What, you think we've got another nasty-ass piece of magic hanging around here?" They might, actually. This thing was sending off very nasty vibes, but they didn't know for certain if this was it, or just damnable coincidence. *God, if this isn't it, if it's some other disaster you've chosen to drop into my lap, and we still have no idea where the damned parchment is, I'm going to be really, really annoyed.*

"Only one way to know. Let me see it."

"What?" Haven, incredulous.

"Wren, are you insane?" Sergei, furious.

"Let me rephrase that. Let me *hold* it, okay? Sergei, as you damn well know I can't read Italian, so even if it forces me to look I won't be able to understand a word of it."

"And what makes you think understanding it has anything to do with it having any effect?"

"Haven's still with us."

The librarian swallowed hard, clearly not having thought of that when he set up the mirror relay.

"This is the stupidest idea you've come up with. Ever."

"You want me to wear a blindfold?"

"Excuse me?" Haven raised a hesitant hand like asking permission to go to the bathroom during a test. "But if you can't read it, how will you know if it's the right whateveritis?"

"Nobody knows what it says. Or if they do, they've never been able to pass word along before they vanished. So reading it's not going to prove anything."

"So then what good will touching it do?"

Wren stared at the box, letting down her defenses just a thread. The ooze of malevolence that had alerted her the first time pulsed even more strongly

Wren was talking directly to Sergei now, her words coming a little too quickly. "All I have to do is hold it. I touched the slate casing, I've got it, just a little, in my system." A lie, sort of. She had the echo of it. But she thought it would be enough. "I'll be able to recognize it that way, without actually looking at it, without getting trapped by it," She could feel the hiss and slither of its magic calling to her, enticing her, and blocked that part of her mind by focusing instead on Sergei's intent gaze.

"You're going to use current on it?" he said, his expression incredulous. "Is that—"

"Smart?" She shrugged, moving closer to the table. "Like you said, it's a stupid plan. Got anything better?"

"We burn this entire place to the ground."

Haven blanched even worse than he had looked at first, and Wren shot Sergei a dirty look. "Don't tease the librarian, partner."

"Who says I was joking?"

Haven clearly decided that Sergei was a madman but that he wasn't an actively dangerous one, and turned back to Wren. "What are you going to do?"

"It's called psychometry. I can touch something, and a little of its history passes on to me. I should be able to tell enough about it to know if it's what we're looking for."

"Stupid idea."

"Jesus wept, Sergei." She wanted to say something stronger, but her mother's training held. Instead, she moved around his bulk and reached into the box before she could talk herself out of it.

The moment she touched the parchment, the visions began.

*"Why can none of you leave me be?"*

*A man, not so old, not too young. His fingers were ink-stained and worn, the skin yellowed and age-spotted over ropey muscles of one who was not unaccustomed to physical labor.*

*"Brother Jacob, I wished only to help!" The servant, bowing, frightened in the face of the man's wrath, backing out of the cell, his hands held up as though to deflect a blow to the head.*

"They will not leave me be. They do not wish me to complete my work. None of them, none of them understand. They will not leave me be!" The quill in his hand snapped, and he threw it down onto the table.

*A jagged flash of current filled Wren's brain, shoving her into another memory.*

"He asks for materials we cannot supply." The clerk stood firm, although his expression was clearly that of one terrified to be speaking so. "Things he should have no need for. No God-fearing man should."

Father Adolfo did not bother to look at the scrap of parchment offered to him. "Brother Jacob is a very wise man. Give him the things he needs." And with that pronouncement, the precept of the monastery swept from the room with the regal bearing better suited to a king than a mortal servant of God.

"He is a fool." The monk standing with the clerk said, quietly.

"Who?" The clerk was still trembling, still afraid, although the stress of the moment was gone.

"Both of them. Adolfo for falling under that devil spawn's sway. And all of us, if we do not stop it now, before Rome burns us all for heretics."

The clerk turned to look at his brother, uncertainty replacing his fear. They had spoken before of their fellow monk's ways, his much-praised wisdom leading him down paths mortals were not meant to tread, to arrogance and near-blasphemy. But this…

"We must act now, or be forever damned by his actions under our roof."

*Another jagged flash of current.*

Screaming. Screaming and screaming and Jacob's hands not even shaking as the screams echoed in his head as he dipped his quill into the pot of red ink by his side and carefully etched the words onto the parchment.

"They who torment and hound me. They who doubt me. Unto them, a curse. Unto them, doubt. Unto them, the agony of incompletion. Unto them—"

It went on, every word carefully, lovingly placed, every swirl and stroke of the lettering perfect. When finished, it would keep those who doubted the worth of his work from disturbing him, would prevent them from interfering with his work.

The ink ran thin, and the monk added white powder to thicken it, making the natural reddish black of the blood turn a more readable tint. And all the while he hissed under his breath, an atonal counterpoint to the remembered screams of the original owner as the skin which made up the parchment was flayed from his body with painstaking care....

Footsteps outside on the stair. But the monk refused to hurry. The door was not barred, such was his confidence, and when they came to take him, clad in the scarlet and gold of the Papacy, he merely smiled and let them clasp irons on his hands and feet.

"Unto them, a curse. Until then, a curse."

"Take him from here. And let no man, no beast hear another word from his mouth until he is judged and sentenced."

As the guards took Jacob out, the clerk's friend stepped into the doorway. "You must burn it. Burn it all. Nothing of his work must be allowed to remain."

Jacob snarled, lunging despite the weight of his manacles, for the other man's jugular. A scuffle followed, elbows and robes flying, until the miscreant was subdued, facedown on the floor. The clerk's friend wiped his brow and stepped around the pile, moving further into the room. "Burn everything," he repeated.

"It shall be," the guard's leader assured him. "His Eminence has so decreed. Nothing of the heretic's words shall remain to taint or tempt others."

\*Another jagged flash of current.\*

Hands, shoveling through piles of parchments and papers. "Not here, not here. Where did the man hide it?"

"Are you sure it is here?"

"The fool bragged of it even as the rats consumed his flesh. Devil's spawn he might have been, but the secret of transmutation is here, assuredly."

Greed. Need. Anger. The emotions boiled into the room and fed the parchment where it had been stowed under a pile of other scribblings, hidden by magic from prying eyes. Fed the magics, and woke Talented energies from within the skin of the Talent it had been taken from, recharging the spells Brother Jacob had used, against all Church doctrine, to protect himself and his research.

*And, thus energized, the curse Jacob had etched with blood and pain grew, and changed, and evolved….*

*One last jagged flash of current.*

"*Que es?*" *An inquisitive voice. Acquisitive. The curse woke from a long, unhappy slumber. Emotions—greed-fueled curiosity, feelings of having been done wrong by—filled the air around it, and the entity which had once been parchment reached out, took its fill. None to profit. None to take what was not theirs to have. If its master was not allowed to finish his work, none should profit from it. Ever.*

The images came layered, heavy with the weight of centuries, as the curse fed and grew until it lost all memory of what it had been and gained a sort of malignant and malign sentience of its own. And then a cool blankness Wren dimly identified as the slate being placed around it, the current-spells wrapped around it, keeping it in stasis, if not killing it off completely. Another five or six decades, maybe, it might have done the trick. But it wasn't dead yet. And now…it had been feeding again.

*Read. Read the words and see in them your despair….*"
The voice was oily, silky, seductive in an unpleasant and unnerving fashion, like what you might think a pedophile might sound like, stripped of his everyday-person mask. She had never tried to read anything with an awareness before. Tendrils touched her and she recoiled, flinging her own current back in an attempt to keep it out. But they flowed

*through the current-walls, searching, seeking out the things inside her it could use, could feed on.*

*The envy. The fear. The petty jealousies and not-so-petty angers. Frustrations and bitterness. The thousand and one darker emotions every human hoards jealously, hugging to themselves in the cold of the night, intentionally or not. The things you think you've forgiven, forgotten, that remain just out of mindsight and fester in your soul.*

"God, why can't they just leave me alone?"

The oozing tendrils paused, then slid past her anguished cry, looking harder.

"You disappoint me, Jenny-Wren. I know you know how to do this." Neezer, her mentor, sitting on the stool in his classroom office. A textbook lay open in front of her, and she was trying, she really was, but none of the material made any sense to her. The scene slipped to another, same office, same man, later that same year. His eyes were red-rimmed, his face drawn with stress and strain, and her heart was tearing itself into shreds rather than hear what he was saying.

"Nooooo!"

A green pulse, tendrils tightening on her, drawing the memory into itself. Wren struggled, desperate to get away, and another emotion slipped between them.

"You don't really love me. It's all a game to you, something you're doing to see if you can, and when you're bored you're going to walk away."

A fear, more real than memory, more solid than flesh. The tendrils wrapped around that, pulsing green as it sucked the anguish like marrow, broke the bone in two and moved deeper.

"*I hate you!*"

An old memory. Her mother had done something— she had broken up with Joe. Again. Wren had liked him, had been thrilled when they started dating again. And now Joe was leaving town because he couldn't handle her mother's hot-and-cold moods.

"*You're impossible! No wonder my father didn't stick around long enough to—*"

Her mother's hand had been like a bullet, hot and fast on her cheek.

The tendril dug in deep, burrowing under her psychic skin, and Wren felt its teeth like poisoned metal sinking into her, preparing to consume her inner core, current and all.

*I know you,* she thought at it, straining against the invasion. And she did. Intent-given-force. Power allowed its own form. Not quite sentient, but self-directed. Whatever the monk she had seen had intended, his death powered something with its own agenda. All the hate, all the jealousy, all the paranoia, into an entity that wanted only to feed, only to consume and destroy.

*I know you, and I will not let you win.*

The tendrils dug in deeper, and she winced, feeling herself driven down to her knees on the cold floor.

*I will fight you. I will destroy you.*

The sound of its mocking laughter sank into her after the tendrils, and began to feed.

* * *

"What the hell is going on?"

"I don't know." Something was happening, for all that Wren was standing still. Too still. Her eyes were focused inward, the way she did while working current, and the manuscript lay on the surface of her palms, as though she could barely bring herself to touch it. Insane, but Sergei would have felt better if she were clutching it, crumpling it, giving some indication of stress or distress or anything other than that total damnably unnerving stillness. Sergei's skin felt like it was a size too small for his body, prickling and sparking tightly the way Wren claimed her thumbs did when something was wonky around her.

"Uh-oh."

Sergei did *not* like uh-ohs. Especially when they were accompanied by a finger pointing at his partner.

"Wren? Wren!" He took a step forward, then glanced at the parchment in her hand. He read Italian, if not fluently. Touching that would probably be the last thing he did before whatever happened to people who fell under its sway happened to him.

"Holy shit...."

A dark green line curled around Wren's waist, seemingly coming from under her clothing, snapping and hissing like a live wire. Sergei had only ever seen current through the loan of Wren's Mage-sight, but there was no doubt in his mind what that line was.

He also knew, somehow, that it wasn't Wren's own.

A second tendril snaked out from her side, this one

shimmering yellow, an ugly color that made Haven shade his eyes with one hand rather than look at it.

A third tendril, then a fourth, and a fifth, all the shades of an ugly rainbow twining and hissing and melding into a coiled rope of magic that shimmered while they watched, the free end thickening into a triangle of a snake's head that turned to look at them, a shining black tongue flicking out at them.

"No!" Sergei lunged, his hands outstretched to grab the snake. It was an impossible goal, and he knew it even as his body cut through the space between them. There was no physical entity to attack, really. He was a Null. He could do nothing against current, nothing except be sucked into the parchment and disappear, leaving his Wren alone against this thing, alone with a useless librarian who couldn't do more than stare with his mouth open like a rubber-necker at a five-car pileup.

*You're as much an idiot as she is, Didier,* he thought as his hands came into contact with Wren's body. She collapsed as though he'd hit her far harder than his speed or weight warranted, falling to her knees. Thrown off balance, Sergei slammed into her shoulder, jarring her arms and knocking the manuscript out of her hands and onto the floor. The dark red lettering seemed to glow on the parchment, and he found his eye drawn to it despite his best efforts to look away.

And he screamed.

*Chapter Twenty*

"No!"

Wren came to with Haven's yell in her ears. She knew, even before her eyes opened, that Sergei was in trouble: her heart was caught in an iron vise, squeezing it until she couldn't breathe, couldn't think. Sheer panic, a sense of loss overwhelming everything else.

Instinctive, then, to grab current. But there was nothing to ground on, no solid bedrock under her feet, no control inside her, all washed away by the attack of that…thing, that jealous hungry paranoid rage that was taking her partner, the dirty lines of current twisting around him, leeching the solidity, the substance out of him as she watched.

"No!" she cried, echoing Haven's dismay with anger, and took all that hate, that fear, that anguish the parchment had stirred inside of her, took it and braided it swiftly into the current, feeding it with the love, the need, the passion she had for Sergei. *Sergei Didier, son of Louisa, son of Kassian. Handler. Partner. Lover. Friend.* Everything he was, from the way he twitched in his sleep to the wrinkles around his eyes when he smiled, the intensity of his gaze and the unexpected music of his laugh. The love he had for her, given back full-fold, without reservation, without fear. The willingness to do anything for her. Anything. Even die.

And the current stretched out and found him, the essence of him, and sank into that essence, tying it to Wren. Tying it to this existence. Pulling it, slowly, back into reality.

"Stay, damn you!

Don't you dare leave me!

Return, now!"

She wasn't even aware that she had kept to her usual spell-pattern: the words simply came to her, as she intensified the current-rope and pulled it as hard as she could.

But the parchment did not want to let go. The green and yellow lines of current slapped back at her, sizzling when they came into contact with her skin, and she screamed with the pain, her throat sore and ragged. But she didn't let go.

"What can I do?"

*Nothing* she thought, then thrust the word away. No negativity. No doubt. Nothing but an awareness of him. Sergei. Love. No doubt about his love. He loved her. She loved him. That was the tie. No doubts at all that it was real. She couldn't afford to doubt it. Not now.

Her current-rope crackled with more energy than she had within her, somehow building despite her exhaustion.

"Stay, damn you!"

The spell focused the intent. The intent was power. Power was strength. And Sergei lifted his head and looked at her, and she saw awareness come back, depth and color and *solidity*.

And then something hit her from the side, knocking the air from her lungs and disrupting that needful connection.

And Sergei flickered out of sight for a heart-stopping half of an instant.

The figure—a bulky thing, showing white tusks and floppy, leathery ears under masses of shaggy black hair, rushed her again, and Wren barely had time to tug on the current-rope once more before she had her physical hands full with the fatae who had come out of nowhere.

"Die, interfering bitch!"

The minos slammed her against the wall, and Wren snarled back at him, risking a sliver of current away from Sergei in order to fight this new assailant.

"What. Is your fucking. *Problem*?" She needed this now? She did not.

"You stay out of our business, human."

Minos weren't great talkers—the tusks caused enunciation problems—but Wren got the gist of his words. If only they made any *sense*.

"What the hell are you talking about?" She risked a glance at Sergei, and her blood ran cold. She had to do something, *now!*

"Try make you stop. You not stop. Keep interfering fatae business. So now, stop forever."

And then, suddenly, things started to make sense. The hex on her doorway. The sense of being followed, earlier. The weird vibes she had gotten from the fatae leaders during that powwow in her apartment, when they argued among themselves rather than attacking Madame Howe....

Politics. She damn well hated politics. Especially when it got in the way of getting her partner's ass out of the fire.

"I don't have time for this now," she growled, trying to dodge past her attacker to get back to Sergei. But the minos caught her in one meaty paw, the tough chitin on his fingernails digging into her skin until it tore.

Then Haven was at her side, trying to drag the beast off her. He got knocked into the wall himself for his efforts, and, unlike Wren, landed badly and stayed down.

"You die, all die."

And the minos grinned, the yellowing canines more frightening than a double-row of shark teeth would have been in the same close-up, and fit one paw around her neck, thumb landing on her windpipe.

*Sergei!*

And then the thumb pressed down, and Wren could only see sparks of current in front of her eyes as things began to fade to grey.

*I'm sorry, love. So sorry....*

*Relax, girl. I've got ya.*

For a dizzy moment Wren thought it was the minos

speaking to her, and she resisted, then the familiar mental voice registered, and her body collapsed, as though every sinew had been cut.

Even as she did that, a whistling sound came through the air, following the arc of a shiny metal crescent.

A shiny metal crescent that came down hard on the minos's back. One of Lee's pieces, she identified hazily. He had done a series of blades as part of an installation, what, two years back? That was a...mezzaluna, she thought. Maybe.

The minos let out a bellow of rage, and turned to grab at the blade. In doing so, like the jealous dog with a bone, it had to drop Wren, and she collapsed to the floor, aching everywhere.

*Get to Sergei!* Lee told her. *We'll deal with this thing!*

She didn't stop to question, crawling forward on her hands and knees, over the remains of a broken table, not even giving Haven a second glance, following the still-connected current-rope to where Sergei was now almost entirely wrapped in malevolent current.

His form was fuzzy around the edges, like someone was erasing him from the outside in, or like something seen through a heat-haze. But he was still there. Still Sergei.

Wren tried to tug on the current-rope, but it slid through her mental hands, too drained to grab hold.

"No!" she howled impotently. "No!"

"Ground in me," another familiar voice said, a physical presence shoving up against her like an over-friendly dog.

She turned to stare at P.B., not quite able to process what she was hearing.

"Come on, do it!" he said, his red-pupiled eyes staring at her intently.

She had never tried to ground in anyone else before, only Sergei. It was too personal, too intimate. P.B. wasn't—

"It's what I was created for, Valere. *Do it!*"

Obeying the intensity of his voice, she grabbed his fur, digging her fingers into the thick ruff around his neck, burying her face into the musty pelt, and letting everything she was sink into him, diving down, burrowing into the solid flesh that felt so different from human flesh, and yet so disturbingly the same. Familiar, an old friend, and totally alien at the same time. In the middle of all that, Wren *felt* the place where she should be, and shifted herself there, like discovering handholds in a previously bare cliff.

With a strange click that twisted everything inside her, she grounded and centered perfectly.

And suddenly, she could do what she had to do.

"Stay, damn you!

Don't you dare leave me!

Return, now!"

Current surged through her, and if she hadn't been so firmly grounded she would have been carried through it, swirled out into an electrical sea. The sensation reminded her of riding a thunderstorm a hundred times enhanced, caught in the eye of a hurricane—no, *being* the eye of a hurricane. Current snapped and sparked and seethed around her, slipping in and out of her skin, burrowing deep into flesh and then out into the air, lashing itself to the existing rope and thickening it, strengthening it, pulsing down the line into Sergei's now-transparent form.

"Return, now," she whispered, and sent everything within her down that line, holding nothing of that glorious cacophony of power back for herself.

The next thing Wren knew, the current recoiled, surging back down the rope, and P.B. yelped and disappeared from her awareness. The entity snarled, the sound of metal scraping hard on metal, and retreated to the far side of the room, where it hovered balefully near the ceiling over the table where the parchment still rested, a serpent-shaped swirl of ugly current that was painful for her to look at. But, for the moment, it seemed to be quiescent. *Plotting its next move. Does it think that much? Or does it only react?*

"Wrenlet?" Faint, hoarse, but lovely to hear, and it drove every other concern out of her head.

"Serg?" She crawled over to where her partner was collapsed on the floor. He was pale, the ruddy tones to his skin gone completely, and she could see strands of grey curling in his dark hair, but he was there, solid to the touch, alive. Alive. Hurt, yeah, there was no way a Null could take that much current and not be hurt, but he was alive.

"Thank you, God," she said, wrapping her arms around him and luxuriating in the feel of skin to skin even as she realized that the rest of the room was too quiet. Blinking away tears of exhaustion, she looked around to see where the rest of the battle was.

"Gotta go, partner," she whispered into Sergei's hair, then forced her arms to let go of him.

If Wren had had to hand-pick someone from all her friends and acquaintances to help her fight an enraged fatae, Lee, for all his good intentions, would not have been at the top of that list. He was a good friend, an inspired prankster, but a lousy bar-brawler.

She had, obviously, seriously misjudged the artist. Because while she was trying to yank Sergei back into the land of the corporeal, he had taken on the minos and had managed to force what looked like a standoff: his current versus the minos's rather overpoweringly impressive brawn. They looked like one of Lee's own sculptures, in fact; Modern warrior meets the man-bull, frozen in combat. Only metal sculptures didn't bleed, and Lee had massive amounts of the red stuff flowing from his face and side, his arms raised into a chokehold around the minos's thick throat, the fatae's rough-callused hands gripping Lee's shoulders as though trying to rip him in two.

She came up along Lee's right, staying out of the minos's reach. The Talent's nearside eye was almost caked shut with blood, and his mouth was open in a way that made her suspect his jaw had been broken.

"Damn, Tree-taller."

*His bones. Metal. I think I've almost got his measure....*

*What can I do?* She asked along the same strand of current

*Nothing. Just—look out!*

She was already turning, warned, as he had been, by the rush of anger that filled the room. Thinking that the entity was recovering, Wren had done the one thing she should never have done—she'd ignored it. And that reignited all the hatred it carried from its creator, and all the venom built up by the years of being trapped inside the House of Holding.

*Stupid, stupid* stupid, *Valere!* And then she didn't have any more time to beat up on herself, because the entity was trying to do that itself. Having been there once already, Wren didn't want to get tangled in the current it was stretching at her, like some kind of midair squid-thing.

Emotions. No, hope. Hope was the answer to this thing. It tried to take her by playing on her insecurities, her fears. She fought it off Sergei by focusing on the things she *knew* without hesitation. It was born of pride, and of ego destroyed. She knew that now, knew the snarling desire to destroy in return, to tear down anything that was free. Anything that wasn't as subsumed with bitterness as it was, and nothing in this world could be that bitter.

But how did you make hope into a weapon?

A tendril of dirty-orange current snaked around one ankle and yanked. Wren fell on her back, hard, the air knocked out of her lungs. The tendril pulled her closer, tinglings of self-doubt and irritation like goose bumps racing on her skin. If it took her any closer, the bitterness would find a way in, this time; she was too weak, too battered to fight that anymore. *Control. Stay in control, Valere!*

Flailing over her head for something to hold on to, her fingers closed around something cold and hard and immobile. Marble, maybe—a table leg? Whatever it was, it was huge, and felt heavy, and should be enough. Maybe. She forced her shoulders to relax slightly, as though giving up, then pulled hard, dragging herself backward against the pull on her leg. *Love you, Serg. Love you love you love you…*

She could feel the entity scrabbling around in her head, and concentrated on the mantra, filling herself not with fear, but love.

*You're never going to make an athlete, are you? Scrawny chicken.*

"You're going to have to do a hell of a lot better than gym class," she taunted the entity, hoping that it would become more irrational. "I've got way worse memories than that."

The tendril yanked, as though she had irritated it by not sinking immediately into the hatred she used to feel for that sadist of an alleged teacher; she pulled, and the table shifted, giving way ever so slightly under her now-panicked grip.

When a Talent panics, bad things happen.

"Motherfu—" the rest of Lee's yell was mercifully cut off as current was pulled from the building, from the cables underneath the streets in front of the building, from everything Wren's core could sense, knocking him over, slamming her into the floor, and causing the weight she had been pulling on flying over her head and directly into the maw of the squid-shaped entity

Shaping as much of the stolen current into her as she dared, Wren got to her knees and blinked her eyes into focus in time to see the minos zap out of existence, the anger and violence that fueled its actions making it easy eating for the entity.

Without pausing to think, afraid that the moment of distraction—satiation?—would be gone, Wren reached out and pulled strands of current to her, sorting the cleanest, most un-tainted strands she could find, strands that had never been touched by Talented minds, and directing them into a specific shape.

"Let this be the gaol:
direct your power outward,
let no current through."

She only realized, as the cage settled in place around the entity, that she'd used a pun to direct the spell.

"You were right, Neezer. Doing the crossword puzzle all those weeks really did teach me vocabulary."

The entity screamed until Wren felt her eardrums pop and start to bleed, but it couldn't get through the cage. She had directed the current *outward*, rather than inward. It created a Null area, a dark space of her own devising, around the entity. It couldn't reach anything to consume to sustain it.

As good as she could do. For now.

"Sergei?"

"*Da*," a faint voice answered her, and the tightness around her heart eased just a bit.

"We all in one piece?"

"Think so, yeah."

She crawled over to Lee, who opened his one un-bloodied eye and looked at her.

"That's two, and I'm three—the powder-puff okay?"

Wren reached over and checked P.B.'s pulse, pulling down his eyelids to check his pupil response, and then nodded. "Yeah. Gonna have a headache, though."

"Well, that was…interesting." Lee grimaced, but didn't move. "Idiot minos. Bad guys all wrapped up? Whatcha gonna do with it now?"

Wren lowered herself, slowly, gingerly, back down on her side, watching the cage pulse with power. She intentionally only answered the last part of the question. "The Silence wanted it back? Let *them* deal with it. All I signed on for was to track down the manuscript. Manuscript's damn well tracked down."

She shifted on the hard floor, feeling pretty near everything protest, inside and out, and wondered briefly if she had internal bleeding. "We should drag ourselves off to St. Vincent's, scare the hell out of the E.R. staff again," she said. "Let me just call Andre and tell him he's got a pickup." She paused. "Assuming any phone in the vicinity still works, after the show we put on here. Tree-taller, you got a quarter on you, for a pay phone?"

There was no answer.

"Lee?"

She turned to look at her friend, and all thoughts of rest, relaxation and job-well-done fled.

"Lee, no!"

## Chapter Twenty-One

There were wooden folding chairs set up everywhere, but most of them were unoccupied. Instead, bodies stood in small groups, two or three or five per clump. The clothing was dark, the conversation somber. Wren circulated with a pitcher of iced tea, refilling glasses, looking the other way when something stronger was pulled from a pocket or bag and added to the tea.

She was stone-cold sober, herself. Control. She had to be in control.

"My dearest…"

Rori, her second visit to Wren's apartment, two in two weeks. Beyond unusual: a dryad left her tree only when there was no other choice.

"Yeah. I know." Wren fended off any more well-meaning platitudes by offering the dryad a refill on her iced tea. She modulated her voice, hearing how harsh it had sounded. "I know."

"Is the widow here?"

"No." Bitterness there, even if Wren understood Miriam's actions, totally. "No, she…they were having a family gathering, at Lee's studio."

A family gathering, where fatae would not be welcomed. Where lonejacks would not be welcomed. Not now, in the rawness. Maybe not ever. Wren had gotten her husband killed. She couldn't blame Miriam for shutting her out. Shutting the entire world out.

Wren only wished that she could do the same thing. Not wake up in the small hours, the memory of Lee's bloodied face, still and sightless. Not feel the guilt and anger that rode her like current, that not even Sergei's arms around her, his sleeping—living—breath warm on her neck, could hold at bay. But she was in control.

Lee did what he had to do. Because he had to. Because that was who he was. Miriam would remember that, some day, and be proud of him. Wren had to believe that. It was all that kept her standing, right now.

"I am not here merely as…a mourner," Rori was saying.

"No, I didn't think you were." A fatae had caused Lee's death. The fatae who were in Wren's apartment this afternoon had known Lee personally, had called him a friend. Rori wasn't one of those.

"We, the fatae, are like lonejacks. We convene only rarely, and those conveniences are filled with acrimony and doubt."

"I had noticed that, yeah." Wren didn't crack a smile. A smile might have cracked her, at this point. Tears, likewise.

"The minos…he did not act alone, no. There are those among us who want nothing to do with humans. Who did not respond to the demon's call to meet peacefully. Who see all your race as the same—a danger. A threat."

"Who want us to go to war with each other. Lonejack against Council. Talent against fatae," Wren observed.

Rorani bowed her graceful head, long green hair covering her face like a Japanese watercolor of grief and shame. "Yes."

"Lee died for that," Wren said.

"Yes. And for being our friend, P.B.'s and yours and mine, although we never met. He was a peacemaker." Rori raised her head so that her luminous green eyes stared directly into Wren's face. Just looking at the dryad stole some of Wren's exhaustion and anger away, and she fought it, struggled to keep her anger alive.

"We will remember," Rori said, making a vow. "We will always remember."

"Lee will still be dead," Wren said, and walked away.

She had gone into the kitchen to refill the pitcher when she saw, out of the corner of her eye, Sergei come ever-so-slightly to alert. It wasn't much; the way his head raised from the conversation he was in, the shift of his body, adjusted for the cane he was walking with until the swelling in his knee went down. Maybe even just the transfer of his attention from the lonejack he was talking to, over to the door, where someone had clearly just walked in.

Someone Sergei didn't think should be there.

"My dear."

Andre looked every inch the proper mourner, in his

tasteful charcoal-grey suit, subdued tie, spit-shined shoes. Among the rest of the mourners, lonejacks in summer-weight casuals, fatae in fur and scales and the occasional bare skin, he seemed a joke, a mockery of grief. And conversations were beginning to slow and stop as they realized he was there, staring with potentially unpleasant awareness at the outsider intruding among them.

"I'm not your dear," Wren said, hearing the echo of Rorani's words and feeling her hackles rise again. *Control…*

"Apologies. Miss Valere. I wanted to stop by in person and congratulate you on a situation well closed." He paused, as though gathering his thoughts. "And to offer my regrets—my sincere regrets—at the loss of your coworker. I know all too well what it is like to have someone—"

"Don't say it." Wren's voice was shot with ice, a perfect imitation of Sergei's The Deal is Off tone.

If the Silence operative took offense, he didn't show it, and Wren wondered, again, what else he wasn't showing. What intentions lurked behind his smooth and compassionate veneer? Had he known about the fatae faction working against them? Or were the Silence operating blind, too, and trying their damnedest to keep anyone from realizing it?

She didn't know which thought scared her more.

"Will you accept my congratulations, at the very least? There were those within the hierarchy—" and he seemed to be speaking over her head to Sergei, and probably was, and she really didn't care "—who doubted your ability to perform."

"But you never doubted us for a moment." Sergei's voice was as dry as a summer desert.

"Never for a moment." And he exuded such sincerity that Wren knew he was lying.

"Although your wrapping job was…" He made an open-and-closed hand gesture she thought was meant to indicate amusement. "Unorthodox."

"I hope you choke on it," Wren said pleasantly, and then made her own hand gesture. One of the fatae separated itself from the group, coming forward. From chin to toes it looked human enough, until you looked a little higher, past the square jaw and Roman nose to the impressive six-point antlers growing from his head.

"Throw him out," she said. "But don't muss his suit."

The fatae raised one peltlike eyebrow, but closed one narrow-fingered hand gently on Andre's shoulder and firmly escorted him back to the door and out onto the landing. The fatae didn't bother closing the door again: Andre had gotten the message.

"Fucker."

Sergei put his arm around her, and she turned to rest her face against his chest, just taking comfort in his nearness.

"I got him killed," she said, speaking out loud for the first time what she had been thinking nonstop for the past sixty-plus hours, since walking out of St. Vincent's emergency room, pushing Sergei in a hospital-mandated wheelchair.

He sighed, his arms tightening as though to protect her from his words. "What do you want me to say? That he knew the risks? He didn't. He rushed in out of friendship, and a desire to help." He paused, rubbed her back, and kissed the top of her head without caring who was watching them. "I can't think of a better reason to go into battle. Can you?"

"I need to get out of here," she said.

The hill had seemed larger, when she was a teenager. There had been fewer houses in the valley. But the huge trees lining the rocky cliff were the same, and the view, spread out over miles, was still magnificent.

You could see clear into Pennsylvania from here, rolling countryside under a flat blue summer evening sky.

"Enough, already," she said quietly, letting the rage and grief and fear and anger bubble through the restraints she had put on them. There was no entity here to feed on her, to consume her. And not even the best lonejack, the most Talented Mage, could stay in control all the time.

The emotions shimmered under her skin, oozed out of her pores, the sensations almost visible to Talented eyes until she was surrounded in a mist of bitterness and sorrow.

And joy. And love. And hope. Because those had always been Tree-taller's gift to the world. He poured it into every work he did, sending it out to every home his art came to. Every soul who looked at the fine lines and sleek curves of the metals he shaped.

His Talent was out in the world. Doing good.

Loving.

"Enough, already!" she cried, to what and about what she wasn't quite sure, and raised her arms over her head in supplication, in command. Against every precept Neezer ever taught her. Against every rule every Talent knew; you did not command Nature this way, not without the inevitable risk of wizzing, or the more preferable death.

She didn't care. Not anymore.

And the current that had reformed within her, in her core, surged up and out through her fingertips; purples and greens and blacks and scarlet, and a bright intense white at the core, lashing the darkening blue sky into a frenzy of particle-level activity.

Clouds formed overhead, seemingly from nothing, first sparse and white, then thicker, heavier, darkening underneath until they shadowed the landscape, sent the air from dusk to darkness. An anvil formed in the sky overhead, and Wren curled her fingers at it, baring her teeth up at it in pure mindless challenge. Virga formed underneath the clouds, a heavy dark fringe of precipitation, and the *cumulus congestus* shimmered in readiness.

"Enough!" she cried again, and wind rose to her words, lashing her hair into tangles and reddening her skin with its touch, heedless to her danger, or simply not believing in it. "Now!"

And the heavens opened with a crack of almighty thunder and the sharp white streak of blinding power running from the bottom of the cloud to the longest finger of Wren's outstretched hand.

And the rain came at her command.

* * *

Her hair drenched, clothing plastered to her body, Wren felt as though she had gone ten rounds with a heavyweight. But her skin snapped and her core purred and she could remember Lee as he had been, not those last horrible moments. Finally wearying of the feel of the downpour, she turned to return to the car.

Sergei stood there, leaning against the car, as soaked as she was. His pale brown eyes were worried, but the lines of stress that had formed between his brows had faded.

She opened her mouth to make a comment about Nulls who didn't know enough to get out of the rain, when the sound of a bird chirping halted her. He pulled an umbrella out of the car, and opened it for protection, then reached in and got out the phone, and answered it.

"Didier."

He got a look on his face that Wren recognized, even though it had been way too long.

"Job?" She looked hopeful. Sergei only smiled, and kept talking.

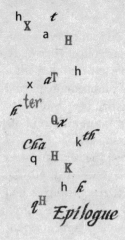

Epilogue

The suite wasn't as luxurious as she could have afforded. But it was lovely, and comfortable, and suited her.

"Pour me some more tea, would you please, darling?"

The gentleman in question lifted the silver teapot and refreshed her cup, adding a small lump of sugar to the brew, and bringing it over to where KimAnn Howe sat in a Queen Anne-styled chair. She smiled her thanks, then returned her attention to the ledger book opened flat on the writing desk in front of her.

"Would you like me to make dinner reservations for this evening, or would you prefer to dine in?" he asked.

"Dine in, I believe. Too much fuss and bother, going out."

"Very good. I'll arrange things, then." There was a discreet chime, indicating that someone was requesting admittance from outside the suite. The gentleman leaned over to place a soft kiss on her perfectly coifed white hair. "And that will be Sebastian, no doubt. I'll leave you two to your discussion, then."

"Thank you, darling. Enjoy the museum, and I'll expect you back before seven?"

Her husband let himself out of the suite via the side door, even as the front door was opened and a smartly uniformed doorman ushered in her guest.

"Madame Howe."

"Mister Bailey." She rose to greet him in European fashion, with a kiss to each cheek, then stepped back and took a long look at him.

"You're feeling better." It wasn't a question.

"A few weeks in the Alps does wonders for my system," he agreed. "I'm more than a match for anything you might have up your sleeve."

She merely smiled, generations of breeding and wealth in her poise, and gestured him to the arrangement of sofa and love seat across the room from where she had been working. She did not bother to close the ledger against prying eyes, and he did not even give it a first glance before walking away.

Sebastian Bailey was her counterpart from the San Diego-area Council. They were meeting here in New Orleans because the Big Easy had earned its reputation for neutrality the expensive way—by being bribed into it. No Council held sway here, no Mage called this town home. They left it to the old way practitioners, the fakes and the fakirs, the hedge-witches and the charlatans.

And the lonejacks, although not many of them seemed inclined to settle here, either.

KimAnn hated this town.

"Would you like some tea?"

"Hate the stuff. But thank you for offering." Bailey was unusual among the de facto Council heads, being neither old money nor old bloodline. San Diego was an upstart, relatively speaking, and their leader was likewise.

That was why she had contacted him first.

"All right. I'm here. What's going on, Madame Howe?" She had given him leave to use her first name, back when he had taken control of his Council. The fact that he deferred, showing respect to her age and seniority, amused her. Especially when he refused to play any other of the social games.

"I have a proposition for you."

He merely looked at her, and smiled.

"Have you ever thought about…becoming part of something greater?" she asked him, sitting back into the sofa as though they were discussing a matter of no greater import than the color of the wallpaper. "Something of great and terrible import?"

"Might this have something to do with your recent… difficulties in your sector?" he asked, his tone implying that she had somehow slipped, lost control of her people, when in fact she had settled that difficulty with a minimum of fuss or exertion on the Council's part.

She remained calm, despite his implication. Bailey was here, so he was interested. Or at least not disinclined to listen.

"We've always remained apart, independent, each Council for each area. And for good reason. But there are things stirring now, things that would lead me to believe that a coalition of sectors might be to our mutual benefit...."

* * * * *

*Don't miss any of Wren's adventures…*
STAYING DEAD
CURSE THE DARK
BRING IT ON
BURNING BRIDGES
FREE FALL

*And coming in May 2009:*
BLOOD FROM STONE
*Turn the page for a peek…*

# Chapter One

In the middle of a copse of trees, bordered on the side behind her by a dry creek bed and in front by a low stone wall covered with moss and bird shit, Wren Valere crouched, her backside an inch off the leaf-strewn ground, her palms resting on her knees, and her knees complaining about the whole situation. She was tired, sweaty and pissed off at the universe in general and one person in particular.

"Annoying, ignorant woman," she scolded that person, hidden inside the house on the other side of that wall. "You couldn't have taken the kid to Boston, or Philadelphia, or somewhere semicivilized? No, you had to go all bucolic and pastoral and…leafy." Wren reached up to pull another damned twig out of her braid, and wiped sweat off her forehead with the back of her hand. It was a lovely, autumn-crisp day, pale blue skies overhead, and she was sure that there were hundreds of people driving up and down the winding county road a few miles back for the sole purpose of enjoying the scarlet and orange display of the maples and oaks and whatever else those trees were. More power to them.

Wren Valere was not a nature girl. The leaves were pretty, and she was glad it was a nice day, but she wanted to be home, on concrete and steel, surrounded by the familiar and comforting hum of current running through the city. Home was Manhattan, where magic fed on and was fed by the torrents of electricity running in the city's veins. A Talent like her—a current-mage, a practitioner of modern magics—had no business being out here in the woods, miles from anything more powerful than a solar-powered bug-zapper.

*Genevieve, you're exaggerating,* she heard her mother's voice say, exasperated. All right, she admitted that she might be overstating things slightly. It still felt like middle-of-nowheresville to her: too quiet, too green and too still, electrically speaking.

The thought made her reach instinctively, a mental touch stroking the core of current nestled inside her, deep in a nonexistent-to-X-rays cavity somewhere in her gut, just to make sure it was still there. Like a bank, you could overdraw and forget to refill, and even though she *knew* she had enough in there, it was a nervous twitch, obsessive-compulsive, to make sure, and then make sure again.

Current was similar to but not quite identical to the electrical energy the modern world had harnessed to do its bidding. They were, so far as anyone could determine, generated off the same sources, and appeared in the same natural and man-made situations, but with a vastly different result when channeled by their natural conductors. Metal, in the case of electricity; Talent, in the case of current.

The more abstract and technical distinctions between current and electricity were lost on most of the *Cosa Nostradamus,* the worldwide magical community, except those very few who made an actual study of it.

Wren wasn't one of those few. She wasn't an academic; she was a Retriever. She came, she stole, she went home, with no interest in the whys, so long as it worked. Although she freely admitted that the feeling of it simmering inside was nice, too. Some Talent described their internal core of magic, the power they carried with them at all times, as a pool of potent liquid, or birds flocking together, their feathers rustling with power. For her, it was a pit of serpents, each thick-muscled neon beast sliding and slithering against each other. The touch filled her with a quiet satisfaction, a sense of power resting under her skin, ready if she needed it.

Reassured, she moved forward through the trees, only to be pulled up short by something tugging on her braid, before realizing that it wasn't an attack—or at least, not one she needed to worry about.

Reaching back, Wren removed her braid from the grasp of a branch and scowled at it, as though it alone were responsible for her bad mood. "I hate camping. I hate bugs. I hate trees."

She didn't really hate trees—Rorani, one of her oldest friends, was a dryad, in fact, which made her an actual, honest-to-god tree hugger. She had never needed to go camping to know how she felt about it. She preferred luxury hotels to sleeping on the ground.

She did hate bugs, though. Wren grimaced and reached a hand down the back of her outfit, scratching at something irritating her skin. She pulled her hand away and made a face, shaking the remains of the unidentifiable insect off her fingers. She especially hated bugs that kept trying to crawl under the fabric of her slicks to reach the bare skin underneath.

"Ugh." She wiped her fingers on the grass. "Next job? High-rise. Climate controlled. Coffee shop on the corner." She kept her voice low, more from habit than belief that there was anyone around to hear her. "God, I'd kill for a cup of halfway decent coffee…."

She really shouldn't be in a bad mood at all, even with bugs and twigs. Coffee and the rest of civilization would be waiting for her when she got home, same as always. This was just a job, and it would be over soon. And money in the bank made every job better in retrospect.

Tugging the hood of her formfitting black bodysuit back up over her ears, making sure that the braid was now tucked comfortably inside the fabric, Wren kept crawling forward until she reached a low hedge of some prickly-leaved bushes. Rising up to her knees, she scowled over the shrubbery at the perfectly lovely little cottage on the other side of nowhere.

All right, she told herself, enough with the griping and the moaning. Showtime.

She let herself reassess the scenario, just to get the brain in the right place. The area was on the grid. She could feel the quiet hum of electrical wires—man-made power—overhead, not far away. There wasn't a lot, but if she suddenly had a need it was there to draw down on. Comforting. And the house wasn't totally isolated—despite the screen of trees, a half-hour hike would bring her back to the highway, and it was probably only a few minutes' drive from the front door to the nearest coffee joint. If, of course, you had a car.

The job had specified no traces, though, which meant that renting a car, even using one of her many fake IDs, was out. Frustrating, but manageable. The client was paying large sums for this to be a spotless, trouble-free Retrieval, and that was what The Wren would deliver. No muss, no fuss, no anything the courts could use at a later date against the client. Everything had to be perfect.

It was more than just ego at stake, that perfection, although she was always about that. This particular job had come to Sergei, her partner/business manager, not through the usual route of the *Cosa Nostradamus* or his art-world contacts, but through a retired NYC cop now living upstate, a guy named McKierney who moonlighted as a bounty hunter. The client had gone to him originally, but this kind of grab wasn't McKierney's scene. He had heard about The Wren through his own contacts, and had given the client her name and Sergei's contact number as the go-to girl for this particular job. A totally nonmagical job.

She didn't get many jobs out of the urban areas, where most of the *Cosa* congregated. A satisfied client here, among human Nulls, could open up a whole new market for her, and there was no way she was going to give less than everything to it, even if it involved trees and bugs and crawling around in the dirt. Sergei had drummed that career advice into her head years ago: you never knew when the next client was going to be the million-dollar meal ticket.

Yeah, the job stank, on a bunch of levels. Money—and clients with money—got her into a lot of situations she didn't enjoy. But this job had something even better than money to offer: there was absolutely no stink of magic to the Retrieval. After spending a year of their lives immersed in a literal life-and-death struggle, when what seemed like half the city suddenly set out to wipe the streets clear of anything that looked like it might be magical, and then having to give over another nine months to the job of cleaning up the aftermath—and getting her own life back into some kind of order—Wren was more than ready for something distinctly unmagical. Even a be-damned custo-dial he-said she-said, with a four-year-old kid as the prize.

That was the job she was on, right now. Mommy had grabbed the kid and ran. Wren was here to Retrieve him for Daddy, who was the client.

Wren shifted on her haunches, still feeling the creepy-crawling sensation of bug legs on her skin. That was the real reason she was griping, not the green-leafy-buggy-nature thing. Live Retrievals were a bitch. She'd only done two before, and both of them had involved adults. One she'd been able to reason with, the other she'd had Sergei along to help conk the target over the head when the reasoning didn't work.

She steadfastly didn't think of the third live Retrieval she had done. That had been different. That…hadn't been her, entirely.

*Hadn't it?*

Nobody had judged. Nobody had said anything, after, except thank you. She had restored a dozen teenagers to their family, broken the spine of the anti-*Cosa* organization, the Silence. But Wren didn't list that Retrieval in her (nonexistent) CV. She didn't talk about it. She tried not to remember anything about it, the hours of cold rage and hot current spinning her out of control, making her—for the second time in her life—into a killer, however justified those deaths were, to save the lives of others. She hadn't been entirely sane at the time.

Inanimate things were easier to Retrieve, every way up and down. Adult live Retrievals were bad enough; it was seriously tough to stash a four-year-old in your knapsack. They tended to squirm.

And yet…the challenge was irresistible. The benefits for a job well done were deeply rewarding. So here she was.

Wren didn't let herself think about the morality of the Retrieval, either way. If possession was nine tenths of the law, The Wren was the other tenth. Not that she didn't have standards about what was just or fair, she just didn't let them get in the way of an accepted job. If something set off Sergei's well-honed antenna for fishy, she trusted him to say no before she ever knew the offer had been made. That was his job.

"And you need to be getting on with yours already," she muttered, annoyed at herself. Taking a deep breath, she felt her annoyance, acknowledged it, and then let it go, slipping away like water down a drain.

Dropping behind a hedge, Wren settled herself into a more comfortable crouch on the damp soil, and let herself sink into fugue state.

She pulled current from her core, shaping it with her will and intent until greedy tendrils of neon-colored power stretched outward, touching and tasting the air, searching for any hint of either current or electricity.

Nothing. A void stretched in front of her: no defenses, and no house, either. Nothing but trees. Impossible, if she believed what her eyes told her. Even if they had built a house without any electrical wiring whatsoever, she should have been able to sense the natural current within the wood, stone and metals, much less the flesh and blood entities moving within those walls.

Some Talent trusted their magical senses more than their physical ones. Wren wasn't that arrogant or that dumb. When the two senses disagreed, something was hinky. Either the house itself was an illusion, or something she couldn't sense was blocking it from being found by magic. Both options were…disturbing.

Giving her Talent one last try, she stretched a tendril of current out, not toward the building, but down, sinking it deep into the soil and stone, reaching for anything that might have been laid in the foundations, deep enough to be hidden to even a directed search. Wren felt a cramp starting, low in her belly, and ignored it, extending herself even as she remained firmly grounded in her body. Sink and stretch, just a little more, just to make sure…

*What the…?* She touched a warmth, a hard, sharp warmth, tucked underneath the crust, deep in the bedrock where there should only have been cold earth. It spread beyond the house, covering a wider range, suggesting that the house was only secondary, protected as an afterthought. Was that what was blocking her? She pushed a little more, trying to determine the cause. Wh—

At her second touch, something shoved back at her, hard. Unprepared, the magical blow almost knocked her over, physically.

*The hell?* she thought, pissed off as much at being caught by surprise as at the assault itself. She touched it again with a handful of current-tendrils, not quite a shove in response, but not gentle, either.

That something in the bedrock expanded, filled with thick, hot anger and a wild swirling sense of frustration that escaped containment, swamped her own current and shriveled the tendrils where they connected, like twigs in a wildfire. Angry, yes, and sullen, and a feeling of bile-ridden resentment that threatened to consume her, and something worse underneath, something darker and meaner and rising fast.

*Yeeeah, outta here,* she thought in near-panic. *Outta here* now.

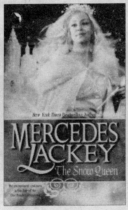